"A DELIGHTFUL AND ORIGINAL ROMP . . . BLOCK HAS A KNACK FOR CREATING ZANY CHARACTERS." —*Orlando Sentinel*

"Marvelous . . . A wicked satire that pleases with acerbic wit and a fascinating plot . . . Block does a marvelous job of skewering the egos of rich socialites, haughty accountants, oversexed cops, and just about everybody else who passes through her sights." —*Chicago Sun-Times*

"With her light, dancing rhythms and syncopated style, Block keeps us guessing as she leads us into lives that are neither perfect nor pathetic and reveals our deeply strange species to be, if anything, underrated." —*New York Newsday*

"[Block] has a comic streak that's ruthless yet weirdly compassionate, because it's truly character-driven. . . . With its cast of dozens, all fully realized, the novel is . . . always diverting." —*Publishers Weekly*

"Entertaining . . . Block has wisely chosen to tell this caper novel from the perspectives of both the police and the perps, a technique that allows her to humanize her characters by weaving in many details of their personal lives and histories. . . . Recommended." —*Library Journal*

"Block follows up her comic romance *Was It Something I Said?* with an unusual and hilarious take on the police procedural. . . . No one is immune to scrutiny in this sprawling, entertaining novel full of eccentric New Yorkers whose lives are not pro~~~~~ quite as they had planned." — ~

"Wickedly clever farce nny? A winner fro

NONE OF YOUR BUSINESS

Also by Valerie Block

Was It Something I Said?

NONE OF YOUR BUSINESS

VALERIE BLOCK

BALLANTINE BOOKS
NEW YORK

A Ballantine Book
Published by The Random House Publishing Group

www.ballantinebooks.com

Library of Congress Control Number: 2004090460

ISBN 0-345-46399-4

Text design by BTDNYC

Manufactured in the United States of America

First Edition: June 2003
First Trade Paperback Edition: June 2004

2 4 6 8 10 9 7 5 3 1

This book is dedicated to Alexis Romay.

NOTE

The Computer Crimes Squad described in this book is a fictional representation of the real Computer Investigations and Technology Unit of the Special Investigations Division of the New York City Police Department. The Frauds Department described in this book is a fictional representation of the Special Prosecutions Department of the Manhattan District Attorney's office. Although the detectives, prosecutors and cases depicted are products of the author's imagination, the command structure is real, as is the description of the police procedure. This is a work of fiction. With the exception of historical figures, any resemblance to persons living or dead is entirely coincidental.

NONE OF YOUR BUSINESS

PROLOGUE

When she arrived in New York in 1967, Patricia McCarey couldn't walk down the street without being asked which bus went where, would she give a pint of blood, push a stalled vehicle through an intersection, help with a physician's-assistant licensing exam or go to the airport to pick up a dog. Patricia decided she had a pink neon sign flashing on her forehead: JUST ASK ME: I'M UNBELIEVABLY HELPFUL.

And she was. People led to people, and Patricia McCarey, at twenty, was ravenous for people. Everything that had happened to her in New York was the result of meeting someone at a party she'd gone to with a roommate of someone else, whom she'd met on the street completely by chance, because she'd agreed to sit in a double-parked car during street-cleaning hours while the double-parker had an audition for a Breck commercial, for example. On the rare occasion when she did decline a request—to remove gum from the clenched jaws of a spiteful child, or sift through chum for GOOD chunks of fish—there was a moment of shock. The sign on her forehead must have said: WILL HELP FOR NOTHING AND WILL THANK YOU FOR IT! NO TASK TOO STRENUOUS OR DISGUSTING! RAISED IN VIRGINIA! DON'T HAVE A TV! THIS IS WHAT I DO FOR ENTERTAINMENT!

Now, dragging her ass through her days, never knowing what

ridiculous bomb was dropping on her next, Patricia Greiff wondered what she might do to the next stranger with the bad luck to ask her for the time.

"Smile," demanded a UPS man pushing a hand truck. This was the day she lost her New York apartment, the day she moved in with her son and his girlfriend, and discovered that he was still using cocaine, and selling it, too—mainly to teenagers. And this was the good son.

"Oh, come on, it won't hurt you. SMILE!"

"Who do you think you are, making emotional demands of passing strangers?" she shouted back at him fluidly.

The UPS man twisted, and the whole stack of packages collapsed around him on the street. He stared at her with a drained face.

"How do you know what happened to me today?"

"I'm sorry." The man in brown backed off with both hands.

Patricia stalked across the street, colliding into a young mother with a stroller, and almost lost it again. She was turning into a problem. She was generating as much shit as was raining down on her.

PATRICIA'S LIFE had become a relentless downward spiral on a Monday morning in late October of the previous year. She'd been in bed, on the phone with Cynthia Landau, discussing the active and inactive ingredients in decongestants, when the house phone rang. She considered ignoring it; she felt dreadful. The bell rang and rang, like a fire alarm. She dragged herself into the kitchen and picked up.

It was a Mr. Scopiletti, representing the insurance company, and Mr. Garvin, from the bailiff's office. She asked the doorman to put them on.

"We've come to assess your household," announced Mr. Scopiletti, with a thick slab of the Bronx in his voice.

She didn't understand.

"I am with Global Net Enterprises, Incorporated, a fully licensed collection agency," he shouted slowly. "As per the Maritime Atlantic Life and Casualty Company policy number 432H slash 69, which designates unit number 8A, 1167 Park Avenue, New York, New York,

10128, and the effects therein, as principal assets of Mitchell Alan Greiff, partner at the firm Friedman, Greiff and Slavin."

Patricia had a sinus headache, she had dental surgery scheduled for later that day and she was waiting to hear from her periodontist about whether the decongestant she'd just taken would mix well with the anesthetic. "This is really not a good time. Could we discuss this later this week?"

"Mrs. Greiff," he barked with the force of a slamming door. "At a time when $14 million are missing from your husband's firm, your husband, Mitchell Alan Greiff, is also missing. The Maritime Atlantic Life and Casualty Company has every right to make a full assessment of the premises, and Mr. Garvin, the bailiff of New York County, will attest to that. I also have every right to come and possess the contents of your aforementioned home. But for the moment, we are here for an assessment only. We're coming up NOW."

The men were upstairs before she had a chance to get dressed. She was in her closet, hopping into pants, and they rang the bell continuously, as if they were standing on it, grinding it into the ground. As she ran into the foyer, buttoning the first shirt she'd grabbed, she had a premonition that this sound, this incessant, aggrieved noise of alarm, was going to be the sound track of her life from that day on.

They had come up the front, not the back, and they burst through the door as she opened it like the Four Horsemen of the Apocalypse, enormous male officials in trench coats, with clipboards.

"HEY!" she shouted as they pushed by her, fanning out into the living room, dining room and kitchen like the secret police.

"We're in," the leader barked into a walkie-talkie.

"What is this? Who are you? How dare you?" she said, impressed with how calm she was. It must have been the decongestant.

The leader behaved as if she had not spoken and were not there; he propped open a fat briefcase on the beige silk–upholstered chair in the foyer. Out of this he pulled a cup of coffee and a corn muffin. He snatched a piece of the muffin and chewed with his mouth open. He took a sip of the coffee. He had thick features and a reddish-brown goatee. As an afterthought, he reached into his pocket and pulled out a card: *Alphonse Scopiletti, Certified Collector at Large, Global Net Enterprises, Inc.*

He strolled into the living room to look at the view. "How much you pay for this place?"

She wanted them out of her house. She wanted to get back into bed. Where the hell was Mitch?

One man was in the dining room, opening up the breakfront and peering at her dishes. Another trench coat opened the glass case where the African masks rested on thin iron armatures. A third guy was in the den, standing in front of her husband's ex-mistress: the 200-gallon reef aquarium, which at one time contained eels, yellow tangs and seven different kinds of live coral from the Solomon Islands. Now it was empty, except for murky, unchanged water and a shipwreck. She caught a look at herself in the mirror in the foyer: a woman about to turn forty-nine again, with a massive sinus headache and no information, accosted by strangers, afraid to speak in her own apartment.

"HEY! I'M TALKING TO YOU! WHAT ARE YOU DOING? PUT THAT DOWN! I DID NOT GIVE YOU PERMISSION TO GO THROUGH MY THINGS!"

The man in the dining room came over with a pair of sugar tongs to tell her that he was the bailiff, Garvin, and it would be best for her to stay out of the way of his associates, who were just doing their jobs.

Things were happening too fast to process. "What did he mean, $14 million are missing?"

"Where's your husband?" the bailiff said, flourishing the tongs.

"You tell me," she said.

The sinus headache was now in her teeth, mingling with the toothache that had kept her in bed all weekend, in too much pain to even locate her husband, delighted, in fact, that he wasn't around, with his moods, his needs, his goddamn fish.

His partner Glenn Friedman had called the previous Friday morning. Where was Mitch? He'd been out of the office for three weeks, ostensibly on vacation in Japan. Was he still in Japan?

"I have no idea where he went," she said without apology.

"So he didn't go to Japan?"

"He might have."

"He was due back a week and a half ago," Glenn said. "Should we be getting nervous, calling Missing Persons?"

"Well, I, for one, haven't missed him," she said, aware of how it sounded.

Within an hour, a Detective Andrew Herrick in the Missing Persons Squad of the NYPD called and asked to meet with her. He arrived shortly afterward with his partner, Detective John O'Hare. They smelled of cigarettes and coffee. They sat on the sofa in the living room, looking around, soberly asking her questions. When was the last time you saw him? Where was he going? Had he made reservations? What was his mood before he left? Was there anyone who might want to hurt him?

The kind of questions that would make a good wife fearful. And perhaps even recently, she might have been disturbed. But now she was just annoyed: even in his absence, everything had to revolve around Mitch.

"Has he ever disappeared like this before?"

"Not really, but we've been living separately in the same apartment for some time now."

The detectives took this in without a change of expression.

"Is there a girlfriend in the picture?" O'Hare said directly.

"Not unless she's a piece of live coral."

Detective O'Hare raised alert blue eyes from his pad.

"Well, if there is a specific girlfriend, I don't know her name."

The detectives closed their books in an unhurried way. They would do some preliminary investigating, they said, and would get back to her. They strolled out slowly, as if on a house tour.

Patricia debated making some phone calls—his sister, his mother, Cynthia—but she was embarrassed. She hadn't seen or heard from him in almost a month. Why look for him when she didn't want to find him?

The Missing Persons Squad had come on Friday. She slept past noon both Saturday and Sunday, ordering in soup, juice and Jell-O, which she had in bed watching cooking shows and baseball, letting the machine take all calls. There weren't many.

CONCHITA CAME into the dining room from the kitchen, still in her coat, holding her keys, looking pale and scared. "Mrs. Greiff?"

Patricia was never so glad to see anyone in her life. "Conchita!"

"I'm sorry I'm late. . . . What's happening?"

Patricia pulled her into the kitchen. "Something's going on, and I can't find Mitch."

"Did you try Long Island?"

Why would he be on Long Island? On the other hand, why would the police, the bailiff and the Maritime Atlantic Life and Casualty Company be looking for him? Patricia tried phoning their house in Amagansett. When the machine picked up, she pressed her code and listened to three fund-raising messages.

Scopiletti opened the mahogany chest and peered into her wedding silver, examining each butter knife at a glacial pace.

There was no way out of it now: she called Mitch's sister, who made life difficult from a town house in Westport, and left a brief, urgent message. She called Mitch's mother, who made life difficult from an apartment on East 72nd Street. No answer, and no machine. She ran hands through her unwashed hair and tried Mitch's secretary.

"Patricia!" Carol whispered. "There's a detective here who wants to talk to you."

Detective Dennis Sprague of the Computer Crimes Squad of the NYPD told her he was on his way right then. She shouldn't leave the premises.

"Leave the premises!" The laugh came out like a honk. "There are four gorillas going through every goddamn drawer in my house! Where am I going?"

Scopiletti turned his yellow eyes on her. She could tell that he enjoyed both his work and the discomfort that he caused.

CHAPTER ONE

The bus was packed. With her laptop between her feet, Erica King stood, along with passengers in various states of exhaustion, attached to briefcases, shopping bags or sticky children and their awkward accoutrements. A woman with a cell phone in one ear and a finger in the other enriched the experience with timely news reports. "I'm on the bus," she shouted. "We're on 53rd Street. We're on 52nd Street. We're on 51st Street. No, 2nd Avenue . . ."

Erica had had another dust-up at the firm: a new accountant had come into her office to introduce himself. After shaking her hand and looking her over, he asked: "Jewish?"

"No."

"You look Jewish."

"Excuse me?"

"I could swear you were Jewish."

"What does my religion, if I have one, have to do with anything?"

"So you're not practicing, but you were born Jewish, right?"

Erica stared at this intrusion.

"But you're something, right?"

It was not possible to raise her eyebrows any higher. "Something?"

"You're Italian, Armenian, Russian, something like that? Greek? I can usually guess it right away. I'm always right."

"You're right, I am something. I'm running late. If you don't mind."

"Oh, I get it. I'm supposed to leave now, like I offended you?"

Who hired these people? Who raised these people? What were these people thinking? People bothered Erica. People were overrated.

A thin woman in her mid-seventies, with straight white hair in a pageboy, boarded the bus and, seeing no empty seats, stood holding on to a pole. A seated woman called loud, "Ma'am, would you like to sit?"

The thin white pageboy didn't hear the offer.

"Ma'am!" She tugged on the jacket of the man standing above her. "Would you get that woman's attention, please?"

"Who? That old lady?"

"Yes, the old lady."

"Ma'am!" three people shouted at her.

The thin white pageboy turned around, startled, and acknowledged the gesture. Just then, a heavy, also elderly woman sitting in the first seat of the bus grabbed her wrist, and offered her seat. However, entering passengers blocked the way. In the meantime, the heavy lady was rapidly and elaborately shouting to the bus at large, in Italian.

The standing woman looked about her in studied bewilderment at the barrage. "What? What is she saying?"

What the woman was saying was this: "Look at me! I'm ninety years old, and I'm giving up my seat to that poor woman! I'm in good health, thank God! I didn't give my seat to you, with the baby and the stroller and the screaming toddler, because you're black, and you look so strong. But that woman there, she's old and pathetic. She's probably only in her seventies, but look at me, robust, and ninety years old! Giving up my seat!"

The parade of human beings making a spectacle of themselves on the M15 was revolting. Was it not possible for a human being to give something to another without insulting the recipient or praising herself?

The bus lurched, and Erica grabbed her laptop to prevent it from falling.

A seated man looked up past the visor of his Mets cap, and asked, "Are you pregnant?"

"Excuse me?" Erica said, with as much outrage as she could.

"I said, are you pregnant?"

"Do I know you?"

"What?"

"Even if I did, that is never an appropriate question," Erica said loudly.

"I mean, if you were pregnant, I'd offer you my seat."

"And if I'm not, you'll just insult me and let me stand? How gallant."

He turned to the woman next to him. "Doesn't she look pregnant?" The woman stared straight ahead, refusing to get involved in someone else's bad day. Erica pushed through people to exit out the front door. She walked the rest of the way home.

In fact, she wasn't Jewish, and she wasn't pregnant. She was something. And why was it up for public discussion? She went to Marjorie's apartment and ordered a chenille throw blanket in periwinkle for Marjorie from the Living Cove catalog. Erica was reveling lately in the proprietary interest.

Her first Christmas in the new job, Erica had arrived on the last day before the long holiday weekend and found a silver box from Bergdorf Goodman on her desk. Inside, a pair of tomato-red leather gloves with swanky gold buckles lay on a bed of smooth white tissue paper. The card, written in Mitch's secretary's left-leaning script, said, "Dear Erica, Happy Holidays, Mitch Greiff."

She wrapped the gloves back up and went about her business.

At the end of the day, Mitch said, "Did you get your present?"

"I did. . . . One moment." She darted back into her office to retrieve the gloves. "I appreciate the gesture, but I can't accept the gift." She handed him the box.

"Why not?"

"I'm here to do a job," she said evenly. "I expect to be paid for my time and effort. You don't need to give me presents. You already gave me the vase with the company logo."

"That was from the partners. The gloves are from me. I like to acknowledge the people who work for me. Don't you like them?"

"You're missing the point. Did you pick them out yourself?"

"No," he admitted.

"Now I have to write a thank-you note, and rush around in the Christmas crowds to get you a present, something you probably don't need, and, from the looks of your wardrobe, probably nothing you'd ever wear."

He smiled slightly. "I don't expect a present from you."

"Then can we just dispense with the seasonal niceties?"

He considered this. "Would you rather have cash?"

"What, in an envelope? Save it for your doorman. Pay me what I deserve, and let's eliminate the bullshit."

He sighed. "It's not that big a deal."

"I know I work for you; I like working for you. I don't need the feudal rituals; they make me uncomfortable and distract me from my work. If it bothers you, tack on whatever you'd pay in gifts to my annual salary."

He stood, head cocked. She was fascinated by his height, his authority, the thicknesses of his black-and-white curls, his heavy-lidded eyes. It was hard to tell what he was really thinking. This was also fascinating.

"Whatever you say," he said, sounding tired and annoyed.

"Good. And if it's okay with you," she added on her way out, "I'd rather skip the Christmas party. I have work to do."

She didn't want to offend him, but she was no longer able to even pretend to be neutral about social ceremonies.

ON JANUARY 3, Angie, the Office Manager, came by with her check.

"You're in the majors, kid," she said, handing Erica the envelope.

Mitch Greiff had given her a $5,000 raise.

Some gloves.

❖

Mitch Greiff wished that all his employees were as easy as Erica King. She perched there, with her clammy white face and coarse, nylon-looking hair, blinking, alert, no nonsense, no bullshit. She didn't ask about his wife, his kids, his fish. She had no patience for gossip—office or celebrity—or fools of any kind. If he asked, "How was the weekend?" she would respond, "Did you get my e-mail about the McPhain entertainment deductions?" and the day was off and running. Erica was the only one in the office who actually read all twenty-five pages of the *Daily Tax Report* every single day.

Erica bit her nails and ripped her cuticles to the point of blood, and beyond. The parched-mouth intensity of her was just too much for some people on an average Tuesday at eleven, and every six months Marty Slavin brought up "letting her go" at a partners' meeting.

"She does fine work," Mitch insisted. "She practically lives here."

"Exactly: she's slow. She's weird! She skulks through the halls."

"She's thorough, and deliberate, and this is not a personality contest."

"A good thing it's not a beauty contest, either."

"I notice your qualifications for accountants include beauty, and blond hair, and twenty-six years or less," Mitch turned to him. "Have any of your people stayed here for more than a year?" Marty's hires left because he grew tired of their after-hours company, and found them employment elsewhere. "Erica King works for me and my clients, and no one has a bad thing to say about her. She stays."

"Can we put a bag over her head?"

She was sharp; she could be dryly amusing. She enjoyed strategy, gamesmanship, outwitting the structure. Daily she came up with ways, small and large, clever and unusual, to gain advantage for the client, the department or the firm. Sometimes Mitch felt that Erica King was miscast, that she shouldn't be wasted on mere bookkeeping and tax planning, that she should be using her talents in the service of something larger—straightening out the Pentagon, for example. But she was invaluable to him. A nerd, he thought, in a nerdy profession. So what? All she asked was to be left alone to work, and her work was terrific.

On the other hand, for someone so work-oriented, she had a lot of office problems. She was having skirmishes at least once a week.

"She's so sensitive!" Glenn Friedman complained. "You can't even say 'Good morning'; she's down your throat lecturing you for making fun of her."

Marty Slavin pretended to be fascinated by her.

"What do you think she does on a Saturday night?" he asked Mitch at the urinal after they'd passed Erica in the hall, looking dour and humid. "I have it on authority that she's stripping in a Russian nightclub on Ocean Parkway."

The collective assumption was that the croaking voice, the dingy white tennis shoes and anklets and the dark, floor-sweeping skirts meant that she was a virgin and would die that way, just as they all assumed that she had thirty-seven cats and would end up ranting on a park bench, living on ketchup and sugar packets stolen from cafeterias. Although Mitch disliked the reductive thinking, he did assume that Erica King didn't have a personal life and had given up on romance. As a good accountant, she'd probably drawn up a cost-benefit analysis, and concluded that there was no future in it.

A meticulous person who trained herself to devote her full attention to details, Erica King nonetheless had a profound appreciation for the fresh air that sometimes flooded into her life when a slip on the keyboard opened up a whole new avenue she'd never even considered. Everyone makes mistakes, she thought. It's how you handle them that distinguishes you.

For example, by some fluke, she'd dialed into the internal e-mail of Sunshine, a corporate travel agency on lower Fifth Avenue. It was a sticky Sunday night in September, and the idea of going out for food made no sense. She was offended by every channel on the television. Ordering in for Chinese, she descended into the petty inter-office sniping among the Sunshine travel agents.

Heidi would be out for a week touring convention facilities in Marina del Rey. While she was gone, she wanted Cecile to authorize hiring a temp to switch her database over to the new software, as Cecile had promised her *eight months ago*. In a different e-mail, Erica learned that Cecile was going on vacation for a week starting on Monday. A general bulletin: since their recent move to the third floor, the Information Technology department was having a backlog on computer repairs. A quick note to Heidi: her laptop would be fixed and available on Tuesday morning. A nasty response from Heidi: a lot of good that would do her in Marina del Rey.

Tuesday morning at nine-thirty, Erica's first stop was the Sunshine IT Department, in their new offices on the third floor.

"I'm here to pick up Heidi's laptop," she announced.

She was ready for all kinds of objections, but all she had to do was sign on a clipboard. She waited at the elevator with Heidi's laptop.

A woman in her early twenties, bare-legged in a short skirt, turned to Erica and sang, "I feel soooo good. When I woke up this morning, I was feeling so cruddy and premenstrual. But I just went to the chiropractor, and now I feel fantastic! I am sooo relaxed!" She smiled at Erica in a beatified way.

"And you feel you need to tell me this because . . . ?"

A look of bovine density seeped into this woman's face. "Excuse me?"

"I am standing here, minding my own business, waiting for an elevator. Why are you talking to me about your menstruation?"

"I saw you, you're a woman, I thought you'd understand."

"You talk to every woman you see about your menstruation? How much understanding do you need? Is it very bad?"

"It's awful!" she agreed, holding her hand out to touch Erica. "Don't you hate it?"

Erica looked at the hand wrapped around her wrist and said firmly, "I will not bond with you."

"What?" The hand was removed.

"You want me to bond with you, and I am telling you, I will not bond. It is inappropriate to discuss menstruation with strangers, in public. It is inappropriate to touch people you do not know. I think you should go back to your chiropractor to be readjusted. You may be a little too relaxed."

"What a bitch!" the woman howled in surprise. "I was having a perfectly fine day," she backtracked self-righteously.

"So was I," Erica inserted.

"And here you are, totally shattering my peace of mind."

"Exactly my point."

"Well, fuck you!" shrieked the formerly relaxed woman, and stalked back down the hall to her chiropractor.

Erica took the elevator up to six with her new laptop, found Sunshine at the end of the hall and was intercepted by a middle-aged woman in navy blue.

"I'm a temp," Erica said blandly. "I'm supposed to be working for Heidi Somebody—am I in the wrong place?"

"Not at all, but Cecile is on vacation. I have to have you sign something. . . . Now, where would she keep it?" She rummaged around Cecile's cubicle and came up with a clipboard. "What agency?"

"Oh, I use several. When you're new, they don't necessarily give you enough work, never mind the jobs you want."

A look of pity passed across the woman's face as she presented the clipboard. Erica wrote the name of the agency that the previous temp had listed. She handed the clipboard back, and they went to Heidi's cubicle.

The woman sat her down at Heidi's desk, opened up the system for her and gave her Heidi's password, which was *Heidi*. As the office awakened, Erica spent an hour or so managing Marjorie's accounts, using Heidi's desktop. Then she booted up Heidi's laptop and reached a password screen. Any residual guilt Erica might have felt vanished in a wave of disdain when she typed *Heidi* in the password box, and the overture to Windows began to unfold.

When she'd finished with her own work, she wiped the keyboard and desk area down with a handkerchief she found in one of Heidi's drawers. She walked out with the lunchtime throngs, carrying Heidi's laptop in a shopping bag under a newspaper. This was not the first computer that Erica had acquired through a combination of chance and design.

❖

When she'd started work at Friedman, Greiff and Slavin, Erica was released into a rabbit warren of four-foot-high carpeted cubicles in the middle of the floor. Everybody could hear everybody else; there was nothing to prevent anyone from popping up behind the partition to look down on you, or looming up behind you at your desk.

During this time, she'd wasted a lot of energy dealing with Charlie Tierney, one of the accountants, who commented on her phone conversations while she was having them, and moved her things around the minute she left her desk. She'd complained to Angie, the Office Manager. How did she know that he'd done it? Because when she'd gone to the ladies' room, she told Angie, her banana was at twelve o'clock, and her yogurt was at three o'clock. When she returned, her banana was at nine o'clock, and her yogurt was at six o'clock. She saw the Look, and realized that Angie and Charlie would be laughing about her over a beer later that evening.

But Charlie was small change, time-wise, compared to the female office members, who saturated the air with incessant chatter, and frequently arrived in her small space to offer inappropriate glimpses into their personal lives and demand that she furnish intimate details in return.

One average Thursday, while minding her own business, Erica was nabbed by Heather on her way back from the ladies' room, and bombarded with a hard sell: what she really needed to do was to get rid of that old-fashioned hairstyle. A little eyeliner and a health club membership—well within her abilities. Suddenly there would be self-confidence in her aura, and a flood of suitors would wash over her shores.

"Heather, what gave you the impression that I wanted you to improve me?"

"I just thought, you know, you might want some advice."

"Advice on what?"

"Oh, what to wear, how to do your hair, that stuff. Makeup. Jewelry. Girl stuff. You know."

"So you're telling me that I don't know how to dress, how to do my hair, how to wear makeup."

"I'm just saying, maybe you want to update your style."

"Why would I want to update my style?"

"I mean, just for a change."

"A change that would make you feel better?"

"Look, forget it."

"You know, Heather, I think I will." And she went back to work.

"God," Heather honked two cubicles away. "I mean, you'd think she'd be grateful for a little advice."

"I'd be grateful for a little quiet," Erica said. "I can hear everything you say, Heather, and if you think insulting a coworker behind her back yet within her earshot is something she should be grateful for, why don't you come around here and say it to my face, so I can express my gratitude to you in person?"

Silence rose from the surrounding cubicles, followed by muffled, gleeful consternation.

"She has an integrity," Charlie said with a grudging irony, and was roundly shushed.

During the hellish cubicle period, Erica only got work done after hours.

ERICA HAD BEEN WORKING for the firm for ten years now, and she'd seen everybody age. She found herself enthralled by Mitch's tallness (it was all legs: when he sat down with her, they were on the same level), the way he folded himself into a chair or tossed aside a 1099. She considered joining the health club in order to see him. But she rejected this idea before it was even fully formed. He must never know. And what on earth could she even pretend to do in a health club?

When she left the office, she saw the black-and-white bus ad that stretched the length of the bus. It featured a young man lying on his stomach. Other than tight white underpants, the only thing he was wearing was an expression of desire and discomfort, as if to say: look what you're doing to me.

On Marjorie's new chaise longue, from the Living Cove, Erica considered Marjorie's life, in transit between one hotel and another, the forced chumminess of sales, the endless hours in her car. Did Marjorie eat alone at each stop along the way, or did she schedule dinner with business contacts?

Erica decided that even if Marjorie had a man in every port, none of them would be work-related. And, after an exhausting day selling and driving, room service and TV was probably all she was fit for. Marjorie must really love her car, Erica decided, and considered, for the sake of verisimilitude, whether she should be seen in the vicinity of Marjorie's apartment with a car.

Not that Erica could drive, a sore spot of long standing.

"Why? Where are you going?" Erica's mother had demanded when Erica begged again to take driver's education in twelfth grade. "When are you ever going to drive?" she teased, reducing Erica's horizons to the size of the five boroughs and the reach of the MTA.

Years later, the presumption still irritated her.

As the sky thickened from a clear sunset to the dense orange glow of urban night, Erica packed a few of Marjorie's accessories into her tote bag, and left the apartment wearing her own clothes and hair beneath a rain hat and poncho. On her way home she picked up the mail in Maria's mailbox, and a file in Maria's apartment. A twenty-three-year-old couple in the two-and-a-half-foot-square elevator in Maria's building were kissing and fondling as if Erica were not standing there, an inch away from their hot rushing blood.

"This is rude," she announced.

"Oh, really?" the boyfriend murmured, almost rhetorically, moving his hand up and down his girlfriend's ass.

Was it not possible to walk through a day without having your nose rubbed in somebody else's pleasure? Every time she came here, she was offended anew in this elevator; perhaps this was why she so rarely used Maria's apartment. Erica felt weary as she walked back home from Maria's, but consoled herself by remembering that few productive assets maintained themselves automatically.

CHAPTER TWO

"I am involved in a level of frustration that I never knew existed," Patricia growled to Cynthia Landau the morning the second collection agency swarmed through her apartment touching her things. "I want to kill him."

Patricia had every right to be angry, violent, anxiety-ridden and self-pitying. Still, Cynthia just didn't know how much more of this she could take, every morning at seven forty-five. "Nobody would blame you," she soothed, extirpating an errant hair from her temple.

Cynthia was in complete shock. She'd been sitting across the dinner table from these people for twenty-eight years. Mitch was her husband's best friend from college. She'd never liked him. Mitch was the kind who was always gazing off beyond your head to see who better had arrived. He'd always had some kind of all-consuming Hobby that he lectured about incessantly. Before fish, it was jazz. Before jazz, it was the Second World War. At thirty, with one short marriage behind him, Mitch had radiated a sleek, malevolent callowness.

Patricia had been one of the Vidal Sassoon girls in the early seventies; her short, flippy hair the color of tea was everywhere that year she started dating Mitch. Cynthia remembered meeting her on a double date to Asbury Park. Patricia made an immediate positive impression.

They'd driven down in Mitch's Buick, listening to him lecture about Rommel.

Patricia had waited until Mitch paused for breath—somewhere on the Garden State Parkway. Then she shouted, "Mitch! Stop the war! Now!"

As they left the highway, a billboard—featuring Patricia's giant head—had appeared. Jack and Cynthia congratulated her, Patricia made some modest comment and Mitch continued to lecture, oblivious. When Mitch pulled the car up in a second attempt to parallel park by the miniature golf, Patricia called impatiently from the backseat, "Get out of the car. You can't do it."

"Yes, I can," he said, not annoyed. Jack certainly would have been.

"Mitch. Get out of the car," she said. "We don't have all week."

And he did. They all did. They stood on the boardwalk and watched her park. She parked beautifully. He never had to park again.

What was Patricia doing with Mitch? It seemed less of a mystery back then: he was tall, good-looking, already successful, and before everyone knew her, Patricia was widely assumed to be one of those Christian girls from the heartland who didn't know how to hail a cab. They'd been snobbish back then.

By fifty-eight, Mitch wore an air of fatigued, melancholic superiority. He hadn't turned out to be a good husband or father. There were women in their circle who, with every advantage and all the good luck in the world, had succumbed to lethargy, gravity, despair. Even after her kids turned rotten, Patricia was always trying something. Of course, a lot of her energy petered out when she became a full-time caretaker to three (counting Mitch) disturbed children and a tankful of living coral. Strangely, with each passing year Patricia seemed to get more beautiful as her burdens became heavier.

The banks were insured, according to Cynthia's husband, Jack; they'd get their money back. Still, it was an outrage. Cynthia never knew what to say to Patricia. If she was sympathetic, Patricia got angry. If she was tough, Patricia got offended. If she tried to be a good listener and just let her vent, Patricia said, "Go ahead: say it!

Tell me: I profited in the good times, and now I'll have to suffer in the bad. Say it!"

Cynthia felt terrible. But Patricia should really see a therapist or a lawyer, someone who could help her, or at least someone who was paid to listen. Patricia was now shouting at someone in her apartment, and Cynthia heard the crash of something valuable. Cynthia got off the phone quickly and dialed Nancy. Talking *about* Patricia was easier than talking *to* her.

❖

The linebackers from the collection agency reeked of very bad news; the fattest one had pointed to one of the Greiffs' messy paintings and asked Conchita Santos, without saying hello, "When did she get this?"

When she didn't respond, he rolled his eyes and asked the question again, louder and slower.

"I . . . DON'T . . . KNOW," she shouted back.

He'd hissed at her, and she returned to the kitchen to avoid further contact. These people were animals.

Two detectives then barreled in through the swinging door. While the fat, older one talked to Patricia, the younger one peppered Conchita with questions. He wasn't bad-looking, in a scrappy, arrogant, Italian way. When had she last seen Mr. Greiff? She rarely saw him; he was usually gone by the time she arrived. Did Mr. Greiff ask her to pack for him last month? No. Did she notice what he took when he left? No. Where did he keep his clothes?

The young detective wasn't in uniform, just a trench coat with some kind of suit underneath. Early thirties and married, she could smell it: nice haircut, clean fingernails and spotless raincoat. Someone taking care of him. The other guy, the middle-aged slob, *he* was single. Not that either one of them was wearing a ring.

As if that had anything to do with it. As Hector pointed out, *he* wore a wedding ring, but Ignacio, his member, did not.

Had Mr. Greiff ever asked her to do something for him? Like what?

she asked as she led the detective down the hall to Mr. Greiff's closet. Like get him a phony ID card. Sometimes he asked her to press his pants, she said. He was the kind of man, she might have said, but didn't, who needed everything done for him, but wanted nothing to do with anybody—not her, not his wife, not his kids. When they arrived in the master bedroom, she told him that Mr. Greiff had been sleeping in the den for some time, and his bed in the den, a foldout couch, hadn't been slept in for over a month.

"This his closet?" he asked. She nodded. "This how it usually looks?"

Conchita peered inside the closet. A walk-in closet, like the smooth walls, the absence of extension cords and the invisible climate control in this apartment, was the kind of basic element, not even a luxury, that would always be beyond her means. The closet was even larger now that it was empty.

They had gone into the tiny room where the Greiffs kept the luggage. There was no luggage. Soon there would probably be no job.

When they returned to the kitchen, two thugs were sifting through dirty laundry in the hamper.

GRACIELA USED TO CHIRP HAPPILY on the way home. Now Conchita's child rattled off a list of needs. Tiffany had Rollerblades. Brittany had a portable CD player. The child wanted $135 sneakers. Tiffany had those sneakers; everyone had those sneakers; even the teacher had those sneakers. Conchita was in the hole on her credit cards to the tune of $13,765.79. She wanted to be able to think about something else.

A siren pierced the air. When she first moved to the city, Conchita would drag Grachy toward every misfortune. Fire truck? Firemen. Police car? Policemen. She loved a man in uniform. She'd met Hector, Graciela's father, at a three-car collision when she struck up a conversation with his partner. The Hector thing was an on-again/off-again proposition even at its peak. He was still on the force, still with the wife, three kids of their own. Conchita had taken Hector to court for child support, and got it. Which was fine, but it didn't pay for Rollerblades.

Hector's partner had been single. Single but not interested.

INSIDE, GRACHY WENT directly to their room and slammed the door. Nydia was lying on the sofa with a washcloth over her eyes. The phone rang, and Conchita picked it up.

"Men are the problem," Nydia called. "Not the solution."

Conchita made plans with Gustavo for Friday night, ignoring her. Gustavo wasn't married. He wore a FedEx delivery suit, and was getting his limousine license. Soon he'd be driving his own car, and renting another out to his cousin. If you listened to him, you could almost believe he'd have his own fleet by next year. Conchita wasn't holding her breath. Either way, she had to find another job. Patricia wouldn't be needing full-time help much longer.

A pity: the pay was low, but standard, and Patricia never objected to a child-related emergency. She never objected if Grachy came to work with her.

Of course, the child had been working her extortion act on Patricia.

"Nintendo! Well, I'd have to think about that," Patricia had said. Conchita wanted to crack the child on the head.

"You know, when I was growing up, it didn't even matter what the question was, the answer was always no," Patricia confided, leaning back onto one of the many uncluttered counters in the glamorous Greiff kitchen. "So with my own kids, I tried to be reasonable. But they wanted everything." Her voice trailed off. "And they got it, one way or another."

Conchita never asked about these kids.

Patricia sighed. "Stick to your guns on Nintendo. Anyway," she concluded brightly, "you can't spend money you don't have."

Which wasn't exactly true.

THE GREIFF BOYS were bad news. Brian had been jokey and overly familiar, asking Conchita to go dancing at the Latin Quarter. He must have weighed something like 400 pounds at that point. Now he was a soap opera star, and Nydia watched him at the salon every afternoon. Every night they had the same conversation: how was it possible that the gorgeous Trevor McBride was played by the formerly obese and pimply Brian Greiff? Every night, Nydia chimed, "You should have gone dancing when you had the chance."

It was clear that there was something very wrong with Randy Greiff, the older son. One warm early evening in June, Conchita saw him lurking in a big dirty coat around the stacks at the public library on 96th Street. He opened a window, sauntered backwards toward a shelf and, without looking behind him, grasped two books, wrapped them in a dirty blue baby blanket, shoved the roll into a plastic bag and put the bag on the windowsill. He took a drink from the fountain, drifted back to the window and, facing the room, swatted the bundle out the window and went slinking down the stairs.

She peered out the window. In a moment she saw him retrieving the bag from a bank of trash in the alley below.

Who, raised on Park Avenue, steals from the public library?

❖

Detectives Dennis Sprague and Anthony Ballestrino of the Computer Crimes Squad stood in the navy blue–upholstered waiting room at Daley Consulting. Conchita Santos was wrong about them: Ballestrino was single, and Sprague was married. In fact, Sprague was the marrying kind, on his third attempt. Sprague was a stout Caucasian male of English and German extraction, with thinning, colorless hair and a mouthful of troubled teeth. His mother had laughed out loud when he told her he wanted to be a cop.

Joseph Patrick Daley, founder of Daley Consulting, had been a Detective Sergeant with Special Frauds, back when the unit was called the Pickpocket and Confidence Squad. He'd set up his own shop in the early eighties, and every year he hired several cops off the force. Everyone on the Job continued to hurl themselves into private investigation or security, and why not? Some days it was all anyone talked about.

In the conference room, William Flynn greeted Sprague and Ballestrino with friendly pomp, subdued slightly out of respect for the clients. Flynn had been one of Sprague's first training partners. He was one of the ones who did his twenty and retired at half pay. Now he looked sharp in his pinstripes, like private practice and extra money agreed with him. He introduced his working-stiff former colleagues to his flush-looking corporate clients.

Flynn then introduced his three young associates who'd been swimming in bank statements for seventy-two hours. They looked considerably less rested. Everyone sat down at a glossy table in front of a dazzling view to the north, which included the sleek silver summit of the Chrysler Building.

There were no refreshments.

Flynn got to the point: "On Friday of Labor Day weekend, from eleven A.M. to three P.M., fifty-seven separate wire transfers were initiated from several laptops. Of these, forty-eight involved accounts held by Friedman, Greiff and Slavin clients, six involved accounts held by Friedman, Greiff and Slavin staff or partners and three involved accounts held by professional colleagues of Friedman, Greiff and Slavin."

"You should know that we three were seriously affected," said Glenn Friedman resentfully, indicating Marty Slavin the partner, and Jack Landau the lawyer, "and Marty and I were also hit collectively, as the partnership."

"On that day," Flynn continued, "a total of $96,564,217.78 was transferred, to a variety of offshore accounts in several countries."

A whistle escaped Sprague.

"Costa Rica, the Cayman Islands, St. Kitts-Nevis. In some cases, the entire contents of a client's account were transferred into a client's own offshore account, and then transferred elsewhere, also offshore."

Sprague put a hand on one of the boxes at the end of the table—bank records for all the clients. "Those are for you," Flynn said. "Spend as much time as you need going through them here. Joe, some history?"

One of the young suits spoke up. "There was a series of transfers that occurred in the six months prior to this big day of transfers. These transfers were smaller, and made from clients' checking accounts only."

"Testing, testing, one, two, three?" Sprague asked.

"Looks like," Joe said. "Then, beginning three months prior to the big day of transfers, larger and larger amounts were transferred, to the tune of $6.5 million. So we're talking $103 million all together."

"Were there false statements?" Ballestrino asked.

"You mean from the firm to the clients? We don't think so."

"Perhaps these people didn't look at their statements," Sprague said.

"If they had, what they would have found is new accounts in their own names in Costa Rica, the Cayman Islands and St. Kitts-Nevis. All the clients who were hit had opened up new offshore accounts in the last year. Whoever did this then sucked those monies out just before Labor Day weekend."

"Where'd it go?"

"Other offshore accounts," Joe said.

"Whose?"

"We've encountered resistance." Joe raised his hands. "Island bank security."

"We'll see what a little subpoena can do," Sprague said, knowing it was next to useless in Costa Rica, the Cayman Islands and St. Kitts-Nevis. "Meanwhile, we'll take the computer to the office. We'll give it an enema like it never had in its life."

"I'm afraid the laptops have vanished," Flynn explained. "We do know, however, that the lines originated in the Columbia Law School. When they last renovated the place, they put in an electrical outlet and a phone jack about every three feet. Whoever did this used several laptops simultaneously."

"Any surveillance cameras?" Ballestrino asked.

"In parts of the law school, but not on these particular jacks. Here's a breakdown of the damage," Flynn said, and passed them copies; the others already had theirs in front of them. "Read along with me."

"Sixteen million from Jerry Fabrikant," Marty Slavin said without affect.

"THIRTY-TWO *MILLION* DOLLARS?" Ballestrino said.

Sprague searched the sheet. "Who's that?"

"Celestina, the chantoosie," Flynn said. "She took the biggest hit."

"Yeah, and she can afford it," Slavin said.

Sprague said, "Laptop identification?"

"We traced one to a law firm about two blocks from here," Joe said. "The IT manager said it was stolen two years ago."

"Any reason we should believe him?"

"He plays second base for my cousin's team in Belport," Joe said without smiling. "Also, he reported it stolen two years ago."

"And the others?"

"Working on it," Flynn said.

"This is just absurd." Glenn Friedman paced. "How could this happen?"

"The firm has signatory privileges on clients' accounts?" Ballestrino asked. The partners nodded. "Hot Friday, Labor Day weekend, anybody still around has one foot out the door? I can see how it might happen."

"Do we have anything to trace this to Greiff," Sprague asked, "other than the fact that he's conveniently missing at the same time as this money?"

"No," Flynn said.

"He's such an incompetent," Friedman said. "He couldn't pull off a wire transfer if his life depended on it."

"No, I don't think that's fair," Slavin disagreed. "Mitch is the sort of guy who gets things done without seeming to put in much effort, like it was luck or connections or something, but he did work."

"Look, we need to get on the phone to everyone who was hit," said the lawyer, Jack Landau. "In the end, they can sue the partnership, but if it's *you* coming to them with the news, as a fellow victim, you'll look so much better. It's not the firm, just the one rogue partner."

"Why can't we sue the banks?" Friedman shouted, his round tortoiseshell glasses reflecting sunlight. "Multimillion-dollar transfers going to offshore accounts and they don't even *flag* it? If that's not worthy of a Suspicious-Activity Report, *what is?*"

A look passed between Joe and Flynn. "The banks did flag them, and they did call to confirm," Flynn said. "Apparently they were all confirmed."

"By whom?" Friedman shouted.

"That's what we need to find out," Flynn said, and smoothly broke the group up into two meetings: the partners and the lawyers, who needed to work the phones, and the investigators, who needed to slave over the paper. Because the partners were the clients, they stayed in the nice conference room with the view of the Chrysler Building. The cops and the geeks got a hot little room by the kitchen without a window.

No refreshments.

Ballestrino communed with the summary the consultants had prepared. Sprague found Celestina's statements in one of the boxes, neatly organized and flagged with bright sticky tags where Daley Consulting had noted activity.

Sprague hadn't become a cop to sift through cartons of bank statements. On the other hand, he enjoyed the luxury of being able to develop cases calmly and methodically in the Computer Crimes Squad. He didn't miss the hatred, the viscera, the emergency atmosphere on the streets. He had simmered for too long in the pool of rage and negativity. Everyone, it seemed, was dragging their children through the nail-studded tunnels of hell.

One night, while dreaming about a scumbag he kept having to arrest for raping underage family members, he discovered his hands around Sara's throat. He was choking his second wife.

Who wasn't in the picture anymore—and could you blame her?

Everyone looked up when the door opened.

Flynn sat down on the side of the table for a schmooze. "My man"—he clapped Sprague on the shoulder—"how are you?"

Sprague smiled. "Much better now that I'm talking to you."

Since Flynn had gone private, they saw each other even less frequently. Still, they'd bonded in the Four-Eight Precinct in Fort Green, a.k.a. "Gladiator School." They'd bought heroin undercover together in the Ingersoll Houses. They'd lost a colleague in a buy-and-bust that went wrong. They'd made Detective at the same time.

"You know you have an open door here," Flynn offered again.

"Tempting," Sprague said. He gestured to the celebrity bank statements in the box. "Talk to me about this. A hundred and three million!" He laughed. "You just can't drink that much."

"Well, you can try," said Flynn. They had tried, the two of them, on Atlantic Avenue, in Fort Greene.

"A hundred and three *million*?" Sprague looked at the huge bank of file boxes. "Is this guy supplying a liberation army?"

"The only reason Friedman and Slavin noticed as soon as they did"—Flynn sat down—"was that Jerry Fabrikant called last Wednesday with smoke coming out of his ears. You remember him?"

"*If I ever thought, ever thought, I'd fall again,*" Sprague sang, and Ballestrino put his hand over his eyes. "That song played in every elevator, in every city, for forty years. He must be rolling in it."

"He was closing on a crappy little tract house in Riverhead, and he was told he didn't have enough in his account to cover it. He was only buying the place because his ex-partner, the one who sued him, remember? The ex-partner was bidding on the house. Jerry wanted to prevent him from buying the place."

"Spiteful," said Sprague.

"The rich are different," said Ballestrino.

"Some of these people are so rich they still don't know they have money missing," Flynn said. "Sonny McPhain, the stadium rocker? He's been missing sixteen million since June. Hasn't even noticed."

"That's what I like, a victimless crime," said Sprague. "So Fabrikant calls Greiff, and they tell him that Greiff is gone."

Flynn nodded. "While Friedman's on with Missing Persons, Celestina's manager calls, looking for some of her dough. Then Friedman called us."

Sprague shifted. "So where's the girl? There's always a girl."

"Check out Heather Perkins, Junior Account Manager and Wire Transfer Compliance Officer," one of the geeks advised.

"Yeah?"

He nodded approvingly with a turned-down mouth. "Very nice."

SPRAGUE AND BALLESTRINO fought against the crowds streaming out of the offices at six P.M. Upstairs at Friedman, Greiff and Slavin they were ushered down long, carpeted corridors to the partners. Someone poked his head out of an office, then ducked back inside. The place seemed to hum with anxiety. Ballestrino took a left to see Slavin; Sprague took a right to see Friedman.

Glenn Friedman was a heart attack waiting to happen: his color was high fuchsia to begin with, and it deepened as he spoke and paced, stabbing his finger in the air in front of him.

"*What are you doing?* Don't waste your time talking to me, get out there and *find* the son of a bitch."

Sprague was aware of an urge to hit the guy in the face. He waited a moment, standing very still.

"We need to speak to you, and to everyone else in this office, to get some background on the missing man," Sprague said. "Will you cooperate?"

"What do you want to know?" Friedman gestured to a chair. Sprague sat. "He was a pretentious bastard, thought he was the living end. Hadn't been pulling his weight around here in years—years."

Nothing Sprague liked more than a colleague with an ax to grind.

"Go on. What part of the work did he do here?"

"He oversaw Tax Planning and Bookkeeping. Most of the high-net-worth individuals he's had for years. But they don't generate so much income for us anymore, and he wouldn't aggressively seek new clients."

Friedman settled into a groove, pacing. "He was also not aggressive about getting clients to *pay*. He'd do work for friends, and then kvetch and moan that they didn't pay."

Friedman was beginning to enjoy venting. This guy clearly wasn't going to offer him coffee or a drink.

"If they don't pay, then *you call them up and you say, PAY*! We don't rent office space in order to do you a favor! You want a partner to plan an estate, we charge $400 an hour! This is the going rate! We do not do pro bono tax planning for millionaires! He doesn't call. He'd rather take the loss than debase himself by calling."

Friedman was spitting with rage. Well, he had his own bills to pay: as Sprague had discovered from the Autotrack search they'd done that afternoon on every member of the office, the managing partner lived a very fancy life on the Upper East Side, with a mortgage, and was paying full tuition for a son in college and a daughter in law school. His wife was on the board of a blood bank, a volunteer position. His first boat, second home and second car were on a lake in the Adirondacks. Since he'd returned to his wife after an eighteen-month separation, he was making high-profile charitable donations, perhaps more than he could sustain.

The bile kept coming: "He doesn't collect, he doesn't bring in new business? Okay, that's one thing. But do you know he *actively* prevented *me* from generating new business?"

"How?"

"On more than one occasion, I'd worked out a terrific deduction for an important client, and the prince wouldn't sign off on it. Said he was *uncomfortable* with it. Said it was a *gray area*."

"He was being ethical?"

"He was being an asshole," Friedman concluded.

"You got insurance?"

"OF COURSE WE DO! WHAT DO YOU THINK I'M RUNNING HERE, A *GYPSY CAB SERVICE*?"

Sprague continued to sit and stare.

Friedman stood and stalked, a darker shade of violet. "But you think he was considerate enough to embezzle only up to what we're covered for?"

Friedman was now looking out over what would be, even in sunlight, an undistinguished view of a dirty concrete wall. "He seemed to enjoy his position in the world. I can't imagine how even this amount of money is going to make a difference to him if he has to hide. He's not the fugitive kind. He lives on Park Avenue with an ex-model. He's the kind of guy who needs to be seen."

"Family?"

"Patricia, the wife, although it sounds like they've been on the outs for a while. She's terrific, Patricia. The sons are bizarre. I mean, *bizarre*. A sister, one of his many unpaying clients. Mother, too. All his relatives."

"Who else should we talk to here?"

"Carol, the secretary. Heather Perkins, Wire Transfer Compliance Officer. Erica King, the troll at the end of the hall. He loved her."

"Loved?"

"*Euch!* Please, don't make me ill before dinner. No, she was his loophole rabbi. She's a Senior Account Manager and very good at what she does." He paused. "He might have had something going with Heather."

"And she's the one who approved these transfers?"

"She swears she didn't, but her signature is on every one."

"What kind of relationship do you have with Heather?"

He snorted, annoyed. "You'll find out anyway, so I'll tell you: we had a thing for a few months when I was separated. But it's over now."

Sprague took this in without expression. "Out of curiosity, why did it take you so long to call Missing Persons?"

"Because I thought he was just being a prick. He'd made a big deal about a vacation. He wanted to take three weeks, a month. We told him to go fuck himself. We compromised on two weeks."

"Where was he going?"

"Japan! Son of a bitch!"

THEY REENCOUNTERED EACH OTHER on the fluorescent-lit, carpeted space on the way out. "Well?" asked Ballestrino, once they were in the elevator.

"Kind of a guy you want to beat slowly with a jagged nightstick," Sprague said.

They compared notes on the trip downtown, said good-bye in front of the Building and drove home to their separate lives.

After dinner had been delivered and consumed, Sprague held up the video he'd chosen, *Cool Hand Luke*. "Want to fall asleep to this?"

"Why must we watch that movie all the time?" Cathy complained, trying to get the new cat to sit in her lap.

"It reminds me of my youth."

"Your youth on a chain gang?" asked the third Mrs. Dennis Sprague.

He watched it every year or so, to revisit the feeling of power he'd had when he saw it the first time. You got knocked down, you got up. You didn't stay down to avoid the pain: you kept getting up until they killed you. You had that basic choice, even if you had nothing else.

These days, Sprague didn't see the Paul Newman character as a nonconformist refusing to bend to the rules. This loser kept being dragged back to prison because he *wanted* to get caught. It was only within the narrowest area, with the strongest boundaries and the fewest options, that he could define his coolness.

❖

The following morning at eleven-thirty, as they drove uptown in Ballestrino's car, Sprague caught Ballestrino checking his image in the rearview mirror. "You look beautiful," he said. "Don't change one hair on your gorgeous head."

Ballestrino gave him a fish eye, and got busy adjusting the mirror.

Anthony Ballestrino wasn't Sprague's first Italian partner, nor the first so-called ladies' man whose aftershave he'd been privileged to enjoy day in and day out. In spite of all evidence to the contrary, Sprague had decided that his partner wasn't vain. He had a theory that these iron-pumping, aggressively well groomed, single Italian guys who lived with their mothers were actually paralyzed by insecurity and self-loathing. Real vanity was being forty pounds overweight and doing absolutely nothing about it.

Needless to say, the first Mrs. Sprague, and especially the second Mrs. Sprague, had a few things to say about this theory. The third Mrs. Sprague was doing precious little exercise herself, unless you counted squabbling over the remote-control device as an aerobic activity.

"You think Patricia Greiff had something going on the side?" Tony asked.

"*Of course* she had something going on the side," Sprague said, biting into an Almond Joy, pleased and irritated. "Did you see how she looked in that T-shirt? You think a woman like that stays home and takes care of the fish?"

The partnership between Sprague and Ballestrino was four months old. Ballestrino was a good Detective, and there had been no major problems. But it wasn't like the five-year union of Sprague and Drucker, where there had been understanding bordering on telepathy. Sprague retained the habit of believing that he knew what his partner was thinking, only to find, with irritation, that he was way off the mark where Ballestrino was concerned. They had some common ground, but ultimately Tony was opaque to him.

"Who are we eating lunch with?" Ballestrino asked as they pulled up just east of Friedman, Greiff and Slavin. "The looker who signed the transfers?"

"No, let's go out to lunch with the loophole rabbi," Sprague overrode him, flipping through his notes. "Ms. Erica King."

While they waited, they took a look at her picture, and Ballestrino read aloud from the Autotrack workup on Erica King, which painted a complete image of her, including her age (thirty-six), her education

(BA, JDA, CPA), her spending (thrifty), her property holdings (non-existent) and her known relationships (few). Then they filled each other in on what they'd learned independently that morning.

She appeared at twelve-fifteen and walked east with a purposeful stride. They sauntered behind her, keeping her navy blue coat in sight until she disappeared into the Citicorp building. From the top of the escalator, they saw her seating herself at a table in the public court-yard below. She pulled out a plastic bag.

"Too bad, I was looking forward to a real meal," Sprague said. It was his turn to do lunch. "The usual?" Tony nodded.

Ballestrino went downstairs to hold a table. Sprague waited on an absurdly long line for obscenely overpriced, sterile Midtown food. He was on his way to interview an accountant. An average day. An average day three years ago might have included a two-dollar chili burger eaten before a chase across rooftops, culminating with the capture and interrogation of a baby rapist.

He felt a weird nostalgia about those times. Sprague was never calmer than when interviewing someone he wanted to maim. He considered himself the conduit between the victim and the jail cell. He couldn't indulge himself by applying some punishment, because then the badguy would walk, not talk. So he had to take him down the path a little ways. Pull out the imaginary air pump, pump him up, make him feel comfortable, confident, well liked. Find some common ground, gain his confidence. Then the ghoul would spill his guts. It wasn't for nothing that Drucker used to say, "Sprague is so good, he could take off your socks without removing your shoes."

Things were more upscale in the CCS, but not by much. Sprague had worked a few cases with Anita Clemente, formerly of the Special Victims Liaison Unit, who now concentrated on sex crimes on the Internet. They'd pursued and broken up a steganography network run by a badguy who embedded child porn on his Web sites; if you didn't have the software, you saw close-ups of a big-eyed doe. If you did, you had a three-course meal of a four-year-old, with links to a dozen other encrypted sites. Sprague and Toby Crouch, a former hacker now in the squad, took turns visiting kiddie chat rooms, pretending to be a six-year-old named Samantha who liked bunnies. They waited for someone to try to lure her out for chocolate milk, and once in a while they hooked someone. Same scum, different medium. Every day there was a new way to commit an old crime.

By the time Sprague returned to the atrium, every table was taken. They ate quietly in the now-crowded space. Ms. King tossed her garbage in a can, then pulled out a paperback.

"Must be trash," Ballestrino commented. "She's got it covered in a plain brown wrapper."

"She talking to that guy?"

"He wants to share the table. She's making a face."

"Aw, come on, share the table. You might like the guy."

"He looks like a scumbag I sent upstate for second-degree assault," said Ballestrino, biting his sandwich with his perfect white teeth.

AFTER LUNCH, they showed their badges to a terrified receptionist and announced that they would be interviewing office personnel regarding an investigation. Ballestrino scanned a personnel list and said, as if randomly, "Why don't we start with . . . Ms. Erica King."

The accountant opened the door and looked them over with a sober directness. Her tiny office was overheated and covered in papers. Underneath a heavy fringe of wiry yet straight brown hair, she had deeply set colorless eyes and an unhealthy complexion. Sprague did the introductions, and she began carefully moving papers from the chair to the windowsill behind her.

"May I see some ID?" Sprague asked.

She took the lanyard from around her neck to show him an employee ID card. She wasn't wearing makeup or taking care of her skin.

"What about another ID?"

Her mouth puckered in annoyance, and she went to her pocketbook, hanging on a hook on the door. Sprague noted the frayed cuffs on her blazer, thick, reddish-brown supermarket panty hose and dingy white sneakers.

Erica King handed him a card. Ragged cuticles.

"Nondriver's ID. You don't drive?"

"No. Is that a crime?"

"Absolutely not," he laughed. "I wish more New Yorkers took that option. I commend you on your nondriving."

"It's unusual not to have a license," Ballestrino said.

"Not in this city," she said darkly.

"Oh, you grow up here?" Sprague asked conversationally. He tried always to convey the *all-the-time-in-the-world, nothing-I'd-like-better-to-do-than-talk-to-YOU* tone. He liked the schmoozing part of his job. He was good at it.

"What's this about?" Erica King cut the pleasantries.

"We're investigating the disappearance of a lot of money from the firm's clients' accounts," Sprague said, "as well as the disappearance of Mr. Greiff."

"Yes."

"He was going on vacation. Did he talk to you about it?"

"Why would he talk to me about it?" she said without affect.

"Why not?" Sprague smiled. "He was excited. Japan? First time in the exotic Far East, et cetera?"

"We rarely got into anything personal like that."

"Is that personal?"

"Well, it's not business," she said.

Ballestrino asked, "Do you think someone might want to harm him?"

"Why would anyone want to harm him?"

"That's what we're asking," Ballestrino said. "Do you think he might have had some kind of a habit?"

"You mean drugs? I doubt that. I seriously doubt that."

"What kind of a relationship did you have with Mr. Greiff?" Sprague asked with gentle neutrality.

"A good one."

"Father-daughter," he suggested.

"Boss-employee," she returned.

"Romance?" Tony tried.

She raised a long, raggedy eyebrow and gave him a stony look.

"Who helped him, do you think?" Sprague asked.

"I helped him," she enumerated. "Carol helped him, sometimes Heather, and Joshua and Charlie. Juan helped him when the computers broke down."

"No: who helped him pull this off?"

She swung slightly in her swivel chair. "You really think he did this?"

"Who else could it be?"

"Well, everyone here has access to clients' accounts."

"Everyone? There's no internal security?"

"Yes, but not enough."

In the old days, you would have called her *plain*. He could only imagine the number Tony would do on her when they got to the car.

"Must be exciting, working for all these celebrities," he tried.

"Not really," she said dryly. "Mitch sits in on some strategy sessions with clients, and once a year he might get a call from a client, but only if there's an emergency. Otherwise we deal with the money managers, the personal assistants. Bookkeeping, tax planning. Not exciting."

"Talk to us about Mitch Greiff," Sprague suggested. "He's not a detail kind of a guy, is he? More of a big-picture guy, right?"

"Actually, sometimes he's very detailed."

"Give an example."

"He once caught a mistake I made in a twenty-two-page report. I had combined two accounts into one entry. He caught it. I was stunned."

"Because he wasn't a detail kind of a guy," pressed Sprague.

"Perhaps for an accountant or a lawyer, he's not as detail-oriented as some. But his work as a tax *planner* makes the big picture more important."

"Were you aware of anything unusual happening in the accounts?"

"What do you mean?"

"Did you notice that most of the high-profile, high-net-worth clients suddenly opened up offshore accounts last spring?"

"Did they?"

Sprague said, "Would you look in the files?"

"You mean now?"

"Well, by tonight we'll have a subpoena and we'll be able to see for ourselves. But for now I'm just curious about the offshore accounts, and your managing partner has assured us that all employees will be cooperative."

She stared at them blankly.

"Try Celestina," Sprague prompted.

When she left the room, he scanned the spreadsheets on her desk, while Ballestrino darted forward to look at what was on her computer screen.

"Off," he mouthed.

Erica King returned with an armful of files. "You say she opened up an offshore account when?"

"During the late spring. May, June."

She leafed through the bank statements.

"Well, here's something, a wire transfer on June sixteenth." She pointed to the line. Her fingers sported hangnails in various stages of development, some bleeding new red blood, others with black crusts of dried blood.

"You shouldn't bite your nails," said Ballestrino.

"Why not?" she said.

"It's not attractive."

She paused to appraise him. "And?"

Sprague asked, "Where would the account-opening documents be?"

"We start a separate file for each new account." She flipped through the manila folders. "I don't seem to have that. Let me go look."

She walked out again. She was gone approximately four minutes, during which Ballestrino looked over the papers on the windowsill and Sprague poked in her purse. The book she'd been reading was *Polyunsaturated Mad*. He showed Tony, whose face widened in disbelief. Sprague sat back down as she returned.

"I don't see a file and I don't remember that bank being in her file."

"Where were you from eleven to three P.M., Friday of Labor Day weekend?" Sprague asked.

She pulled out a binder and flipped through some pages. "I was sick."

"Where were you?" he asked.

She looked annoyed. "In bed with a sinus infection."

"Anyone to vouch for you?" Tony asked.

"Lucille Ball and Desi Arnaz."

Ballestrino was annoyed now. "What?"

"Well, I was watching them." She lowered her voice to a whisper. "But I don't think they were watching me." She stared at them openly.

"What channel?" Ballestrino asked.

"Video."

"Yeah?" Ballestrino asked. "Where do you rent?"

"I own that one," she said.

Sprague changed the subject. "Would the file be somewhere else?"

"Not unless it's lost, or someone else is using it. Heather and I generally deal with Celestina," she offered, answering his next question.

"Perhaps we should speak with Heather." Tony stood.

"You go do that," Erica King said.

Sprague paused a moment. He didn't like being dismissed.

Heather Perkins wore a red suit with a skirt that fell just above the knee when she stood, creeping higher when she sat. She had streaky, long blond hair, a glossy, made-up face and perfectly manicured nails painted coral.

"Perhaps you could shed some light on this series of wire transfers of Friday, September second," Ballestrino said, with bland indifference.

Heather Perkins took a deep breath and smiled.

"I cannot understand how this happened," she said, and flipped through a black binder till she found what she was looking for. "That's his letterhead, that's his signature, on the request for the transfer. But I don't remember receiving the request or authorizing the transfer."

"Would you remember?"

"I don't recall them at all. This was months ago, don't forget."

"Tell us about that day," Sprague said.

She pulled out her date book. "That was my last day before vacation."

"What time did you leave?"

She assumed the air of a guilty soldier stepping up for punishment. "There's no getting around it, Detective, I confess. I did sneak out early."

"What time?"

"I think I took, like, a one-thirty jitney. So I must have left by one."

"Where'd you go?"

"To my sister's share house in East Hampton."

"Do you have the bus ticket?"

"I doubt it."

"Did you ask someone to cover for you?" Ballestrino continued.

"No. If I wasn't around, the transfers would just wait till Monday."

"Who was in charge of wire transfers when you were on vacation?"

"My buddy Charlie Tierney. He's right next door."

"Did you sign off on any transfers that morning before you left?"

"I don't remember any wire transfers on that day," she said, pushing away the binder. "I was trying to clear off my desk and get out of town."

"When did you become the Wire Transfer Compliance officer?"

"*Erica* used to do it." She leaned forward. "And then there was a thing."

"A thing."

"A heavy fight, between her and Glenn?" she said quietly, looking around theatrically to make sure she wasn't overheard. "She was doing the Office Manager's job, as well as her own, *plus* heading up the new software search. He felt it was too much for her. So he gave me the transfers. Last February."

"Tell us about your relationship with Mr. Friedman," Sprague asked.

"It's fine," she said.

"There are rumors," Ballestrino said.

"Indeed."

"So the rumors that you've had affairs with all three partners and one of the senior account managers are true," Ballestrino suggested.

"WHAT? I am *not* going to dignify that with a response. That *bitch*." She let out a shocked laugh.

"So did you have a thing with Mr. Friedman?"

"Well, yes. When he was separated. It ended a long time ago."

"Was his naming you Wire Transfer Officer an act of favoritism?"

"First of all, *he* didn't name me anything. *They,* the partners, voted. And don't you think Glenn would go out of his way *not* to show favoritism? Especially after it was over? And no, I didn't have affairs with the others."

Sprague looked in his file. "You and Charlie Tierney and Erica King all started at the same time, isn't that right?"

"Yes."

"And yet they're both Senior Managers, and you're still a Junior."

Her face became immobilized. Sprague readied himself for tears.

"You think this wire transfer job was a kind of a consolation prize?"

"That's one interpretation."

"Were you angry?"

"Angry? Yes, I would say so."

"Angry enough to look for work elsewhere?"

She gave a pat smile. "We'll see." She knocked on her desk furtively.

"Angry enough to steal money from the firm's clients?"

"You're accusing me?"

"Your signature is on every one of these transfers, Ms. Perkins."

"That *has* to be a forgery."

"That has yet to be determined," Sprague said.

"Who has access to the wire transfer logs, and the files of authorization letters?" Ballestrino pointed to the binder on her desk.

"Everyone in bookkeeping has the keys. I keep mine in here." She swiveled to kick the file cabinet behind her. "It's hardly Fort Knox."

"Tell us about your relationship with Mr. Greiff," Ballestrino prompted.

"It's fine."

"Fine?"

Ballestrino waited, looking at her directly.

"Well, okay, yes, there was a kiss. *One*," she said firmly. "After the Christmas party last year."

"Who started it?"

She trailed her hand over the arm of the chair as if she were in a rowboat, testing the water. "He did. Nothing came of it."

Ballestrino continued. "Was it a public rejection?" She shook her head. "Was he angry enough to set you up?" He pointed to her signature.

"Come on." She straightened up. "He's a *partner* here. Why would he steal from his clients? Because he was angry at *me*? That makes no sense."

ON AN AVERAGE TUESDAY night, having made little progress, they avoided the Gotham, the cop bar directly behind the Building, as it was always knee-deep with big bosses and people celebrating apprehensions, convictions or promotions. They went to Hanratty's, a low-key Irish place in the vicinity of the Building where everyone found themselves at some point during the week.

Sprague greeted all and sundry. "Oh, Nurse?" He called after the waitress. "Guinness for my partner, vodka cranberry for me."

Ballestrino took off his jacket and draped it carefully over the back of the banquette. "You think Perkins is lying, they're in on it together?"

"He vanishes, she stays on the ground, keeping tabs on everything? Could be. There's always a girl. This one seems consistently . . . girlish."

"This one couldn't tell a lie to save her life."

The waitress arrived with drinks and Sprague knocked back the cool, sweet liquid. "I'm thinking of the nail-biter." He wished he'd gotten his hands on her hard drive before they'd interviewed her.

"What?" Ballestrino was outraged. "He'd leave his wife, a former model, a class act with a great figure, for that big-assed spinster with a face that would drive you to despair? Why?"

"Maybe she's got a better trapeze act." Sprague crunched some ice, and waved to the owner of the bar, an ex-cop. "You never know what goes on between people, Tony."

He laughed. "How much you want to bet?"

"She had access."

"There's that old Italian suppository," Ballestrino smiled. "Innuendo."

They segued into a spell of fatigued silence while people in suits announced the news on the hanging television, and colleagues from Missing Persons got quiet and abstract over their vodkas at the bar.

"In fact," Tony said, "everyone had access."

"That's true," Sprague sighed.

Still: there was something about the way Erica King had opened up Celestina's manila folders—deliberately, self-consciously—as if she'd been waiting for them, and was aware that they were watching her.

CHAPTER THREE

A nthony Ballestrino had bad phone karma.

He'd interviewed a woman once on a case. Apparently he said he would call her back and he hadn't, because she'd been haunting him sporadically for years, calling his cell phone at all hours to yell at him. Whenever he was on phones in the squad room, something happened: a lawyer called to report a vandalized Web site, for example, and had a heart attack while talking to Ballestrino. Now and then, a woman he met somewhere became obsessed with him and started calling the squad repeatedly. There was always someone new, and the phone seemed to be the medium of the obsessed. Unwanted female attention was just one of those things he had to bear.

Sprague was wrong about Ballestrino: actually, he was quite vain.

DURING THE FIRST WEEK of November, Ballestrino and Sprague focused on the laptops used to make the wire transfers. One had been charged to Sonny McPhain's credit card over the phone in May, and picked up by his driver; another had been charged to Jerry Fabrikant's credit card over the phone in May, and picked up by *his* driver. Both musicians and their drivers denied having anything to do with these or any other laptops. The credit card numbers used were correct; the celebrities had paid their bills in June, or rather, the celebrities' *accountants* had paid the bills, without contesting the charges.

The third laptop had been stolen right out of the box from a law firm near Columbus Circle two years earlier. It had been registered to the IT director of the firm, who had originally told them he couldn't remember anything about the event. He'd since called to say that he remembered a strange temp, female, in his office around the time of the theft. He couldn't be more precise.

Ballestrino and Sprague interviewed current employees at the law firm, and employees from two years ago who had since retired or switched firms. No one else remembered a roving temp. They found addresses on two of the six female temps who worked at the law firm in the three months prior to the theft.

Of the other four, one had dropped out of the business, another had switched agencies, a third had moved to Georgia and the fourth had died in a freak scaffolding accident in Chelsea. The Detectives got one photo from a personnel department, and another from the Department of Motor Vehicles. They then spent three days locating the other two women and snapping their photos surreptitiously. Armed with photo arrays, they returned to the IT director.

Conrad Nunzio was an overgrown kid from Long Island with a bad complexion. He was eating a smelly hero loaded with terrible, greasy things. Ballestrino presented a photo lineup, including one of the temps.

"Please take a look at these photos very carefully," Ballestrino said.

"It was two years ago!" Conrad reasoned, and took a big bite of the hero.

"Please look at them one at a time, in any order you like, for as long as you like. Then look at me."

"Don't remember her. Don't remember her. Don't remember her," he said, pointing to each one. "And," he added, mouth full, "just because the woman *said* she was a temp doesn't necessarily mean she *was* a temp."

"It could have been anybody," agreed Ballestrino. He pulled out a second set of faces that included, among five female Caucasian felons with glasses and dark brown hair, a sullen picture from Ms. King's personnel file.

"Now, I'm going to show you another group of photos. Look at them very carefully, one at a time, any order you choose. Then look at me."

"Let's say the woman from two years ago *was* unattractive," Conrad Nunzio hypothesized. "So this one is unattractive too," he pointed to Erica King's photo. "But in the same way? I couldn't say."

"Look at the photographs," said Sprague. "Anyone you recognize?"

"No."

"How about this group?" Ballestrino showed him a third photo array, which included Heather Perkins's personnel photo, among five Caucasian female felons with long, streaky blond hair. They'd seen her the night before as she bounced from the office toward an assignation in TriBeCa. An hour and a half later she'd emerged from the restaurant with a ruddy, suited gent.

"Married bond trader from New Jersey," Sprague had said without hesitation. Lo and behold, a parking valet zipped around the corner opening the door of a red BMW with Jersey plates.

"Oh, you're good," Ballestrino laughed. They'd followed the car to the SoHo Grand, then packed it in for the night.

Now Mr. Nunzio pointed to the shot of Heather Perkins. "She's all right."

"Do you recognize Number Four?" Sprague asked.

"No. I would have noticed her. Not that she's such a knockout, but you know, she could be acceptable. Like a real person, around the office."

"Look at the photos, Conrad," Sprague said sternly. "Is there anyone here that you recognize for any reason at all?"

"Oh, no."

"If none of these women was the temp who came here around the time the laptop was stolen, how was the temp different?"

Conrad Nunzio took a swig of soda. "She must have been uglier, but I just can't say how."

So much for that week.

MONDAY AT NOON, Ballestrino walked into Hanratty's just as Sprague was sitting down at their booth in the back with the Captain.

Captain Schmidt was a good man. Not in your hair all the time, treating you like an idiot, micromanaging, like Ballestrino's previous two commanding officers. Like the Lieutenant. Although he had no experience with computers, Schmidt had been a Detective for a lot of years, unlike many of his peers in positions of authority within the Detective Bureau.

The Captain said, "You hear the Feds want in on Greiff?"

"Not the Federal Bureau of Incompetence," Sprague whispered.

"The Fucking Bunch of Idiots," the Captain verified.

"Forever Bothering Italians," Ballestrino added.

Like almost everyone else on his level, Schmidt had been a Marine and was carrying an extra twenty pounds around the middle, like a basketball. He leaned forward on top of his paunch and said slyly, "I'm told that the agent they have in mind is a good one. Cut from a different cloth all together."

"They said that about the last one," Sprague said. "From Idaho, remember him? That guy couldn't find a Chinaman on Mott Street."

"That guy couldn't find his ass with both hands on it," the Captain agreed.

"They take, but they don't give," Sprague groused. "They crapped all over my situation last time."

"We're fighting it," the Captain said, closing the subject. "So whaddya got I can tell the Chief? You got an informant?"

They looked at him.

"Okay, no informant. So where's the girl?"

"There is a blonde," Ballestrino stated. "Her signature is all over the transfers, although she says she wasn't there at the time. But my friend here thinks she's not The Girl."

"No?" The Captain turned to Sprague, who shook his head firmly. "*He* thinks The Girl is the Senior Account Manager."

"The Senior Account Manager has a master's degree in finding loopholes," Sprague insisted. "According to the Managing Partner, who doesn't like her."

"So can we connect *her* to the transfers?"

They looked at each other. "No," Ballestrino said.

"And where was *she* at the time of the transfers?"

Ballestrino said, "She *says* she was at home with a sinus infection."

"Humpty Dumpty was pushed," the Captain said with relish, knocking back some Scotch and exhaling loudly. "Nobody is on the level."

❖

Lieutenant Greeley had oily blue-black hair, and white-white skin with irregularly spaced blue smudges in the shaving zone; this skin turned dark red when he was upset or talking on the phone, which was what he was doing when Sprague and Ballestrino responded to his summons.

"We've done more than our fair share, as per our original agreement," Greeley shouted, and Sprague and Ballestrino turned to go. He snapped his fingers at them, and they perched on his visitors' chairs.

Sprague and Ballestrino had previously noted how angry the Lieutenant became on the phone, and how pleased he seemed when reading reports. The Captain, on the other hand, was happy on the phone, and angry doing reports.

"If you recall," he said, and his face froze. He stared at the receiver. "The prick hung up on me!"

Sprague silently blessed the day he'd failed the Sergeant's exam. It was a kick in the teeth at the time, and clearly he could have used the extra money. But in the long run, avoiding the boss track was a wise man's move. Who needed the headaches, the Florentine maneuvers?

Greeley inhaled, rolled his head from side to side, recovered his pallor and rubbed his hands together. "So where you at with Greiff?"

In fact, Sprague told him, the lab had confirmed that Heather Perkins's signatures on the wire transfers were genuinely hers. However, they weren't original to the documents: they had been scanned and reprinted. The details of each wire transfer had been printed directly onto paper that had the Wire Transfer Compliance Officer's signature on the correct line, in a blue ink used by all the printer cartridges in the firm. Whoever did this was either in the office to load the signed paper into the printer, or had doctored the log after the fact.

Not that this meant they were ruling out Heather as a suspect.

In the months prior to Labor Day Friday, "Sonny McPhain's" computer had been used to transact Sonny McPhain business only, "Jerry Fabrikant's" computer had been used to transact Fabrikant business only, and Conrad Nunzio's stolen computer had been used to transact Celestina business only. On Labor Day Friday, the perp had gotten lazy or reckless: he or she had made transactions for a variety of people with two of the machines. Nearly all of these transactions had been flagged by the banks, which had called account holders to confirm.

And all the account holders had confirmed the transfers, at the time. At *this* time, everyone hotly denied having approved anything.

"So who confirmed it?" asked the Lieutenant.

"The confirmation number on Jerry Fabrikant's now-empty bank account in Costa Rica is a voice-mail number for Jerry Fabrikant," Sprague said.

It was an 818 area code: Santa Barbara, California. The voice mail, however, was virtual. The account was started in June. When Sprague called the number, a male voice said, "This is Jerry Fabrikant. I'm not available right now, but if you leave a message, I'll get right back to you."

Jerry Fabrikant denied knowledge of this phone number and voice mail. The sound lab had confirmed that this was not his voice, but couldn't confirm that it was Mitch Greiff's voice without a recording of his voice.

The Lieutenant's eyes lit up. "Billed to?"

Ballestrino shook his head. "A year of service paid for up front, in cash."

"No name on the receipt?"

"Sure: Jerry Fabrikant."

A sour smile from the Lieutenant, who appreciated a clever move.

There was a similar phony message in a breathy female voice for Celestina's virtual voice mail, with a Miami area code, and for Sonny McPhain, with a Santa Fe area code. The voice-mail service was paid for in cash, a year in advance.

"Get moving." Greeley stood up. "I don't need to tell you about the parallel Federal investigation. And don't slack off on reports. Who are you seeing first? How long do you think it will take? You'll call in? And then where are you going?"

WIRES CRISSCROSSED the calm blue sky of Long Branch, New Jersey. Sprague rang the bell on a dirty white door with a torn screen. No answer. They looked in the windows, which were blocked by dark green shades that seemed to be pressed directly onto the glass, as if something behind were flattening them.

The door burst open. A thin, unwashed, unshaven Caucasian male in his mid-twenties with matted black curls pressed the screen door open and stood barefoot on the threshold in green army pants and a stained undershirt.

"You're looking for my father," Randy Greiff said.

"Yes." Sprague showed him his badge and introduced himself. "We'd like to ask you a few questions. Could we come in?"

Randy Greiff didn't answer, but pivoted into the house. The screen door slammed behind him. He stood inside, waiting for them to enter.

Inside, Sprague was hit with a smell like Off Track Betting on a wet day: urine, sweat, cigarettes, coffee, newspapers, mania and desperation. Every visible horizontal surface including the floor was covered with stacks of books, paper, assorted metal parts, lamps and electrical wires.

"May I see some ID?" Sprague asked.

"Why? This is my house, I am who I am. You show *me* ID."

"We did show you ID," Ballestrino said. "Do you *have* ID?"

"Of course I *have* ID," he said, incensed.

"So let's see it," Ballestrino said.

"No."

Sprague jumped in: "When was the last time you saw your father?"

A loud sigh. "A year and a half ago. Almost two years."

"So would you say you aren't close?"

"You could say that," Randy Greiff leaned against the splintering frame of a dark stairway, looking down at the dirty floor.

"You got a lot of books."

"Any other questions? I'm pretty busy."

"What do you do for a living?"

"I'm getting my Ph.D.," he said, eyes shifting left.

"Where?"

"University of Virginia."

"Tough commute."

"Yes, well, my course work is done. It's just my thesis."

"What's your thesis?"

"It's a history of air in America."

Sprague stifled a laugh.

Randy Greiff nipped a bleeding hangnail with his teeth.

Ballestrino said, "Air."

"Yeah."

Sprague said, "A History of Air."

"Mm-hmm."

Sprague said, "You a wise guy?"

Randy Greiff clearly had received this response before. "From the indigenous cultures prior to the arrival of Columbus, to the late twentieth century, the awareness of air as a substance," he lectured. He paused, then continued in irritated contempt: "The development, the ascendancy and the decline of the Environmental movement. The waning of interest in the idea of air."

Ballestrino said: "All these books about air?"

"No, I have all sorts of books."

Sprague picked one up.

"Hey! Be careful, that's valuable."

"*I'm* not bleeding, Mr. Greiff," he said.

Randy Greiff took the book out of his hands and put it back on the table. "You think you'll catch my father?"

"We'll certainly try," said Sprague. "Anyplace he might go?"

"He wasn't into places."

"Meaning?"

"He didn't like to *go* anywhere. He liked to sit in his record closet, with the door shut. Or stand over his fish tank. He's pretty stationary."

BALLESTRINO STRETCHED as he drove. "Remember that other guy with the books?"

"The one who stacked his family neatly in the yard, out in Ridgewood?"

"Yeah. Remind you of this one?"

"Only the book part." Sprague flipped through his pad, rattling off information. "Carol the whiny secretary has been working for him for three years. She says he didn't keep a date book until about six months ago, which may be why all those phone numbers in his date book led nowhere. Phony date book. Carol says he rarely got calls from his immediate family, but plenty of calls from extended family and friends in January and February, when they needed their taxes done. Says he started closing his door more often about six months or a year ago."

"Erica King is the butt of all office humor," Ballestrino said.

"Says who?"

"Heather Perkins, babe at large. When you talked to the secretary, I danced her around the table, nicey-nicey."

Sprague smiled. "You do have your way with the ladies."

"Look: the accountant doesn't strike me as the kind of woman you leave your wife for." Ballestrino glanced up at himself in the rearview. "Although she is younger, I'll give you that."

"She's sharp enough to pull it off," Sprague said.

"That has yet to be determined," Ballestrino said.

"Greiff, on the other hand, becomes more of a loser each time we talk to someone new. Now, if I were a gambling man, I'd put money on catching Mitch Greiff through Erica King."

"You're on," Ballestrino said. "I say we catch him through his fish."

"How much?"

"Dinner," said Tony.

Who bets dinner? "What kind?"

"If I win, or if you win?" Tony smiled.

They drove by massive, pulsating industrial decay.

"Why is the sky always white over the Turnpike?" Ballestrino asked.

"We should have asked the American air historian when we had a chance."

There were thousands of people in cars on this stretch of this particular highway alone. "He could be anywhere," Ballestrino said.

Sprague tore the wrapper off a Tootsie Pop. "Cheer up: even John Dillinger went to a movie."

❖

At the gym, Ballestrino saw the local talent in her black unitard, using free weights over by the mats. She must have been between twenty-eight and thirty-three. She was wearing gloves, but previously he hadn't seen any significant rings on her fingers.

"Hey, howaya," she returned his greeting. "What's your name again? I forgot."

"Tony." He smiled. "Looks like you've been doing some heavy lifting." He pointed out the dirty palms on her gloves.

"Better on the gloves than on the hands," she said, chewing, indifferent.

He really didn't allow gum chewing, and tried to ignore it. You're too good for this trash, his mother would say. He went to the bench press. If he were her trainer, he'd tell her to skip the free weights and get to work on her ass.

"Hey, Detective," said a bodybuilder Tony worked out with occasionally.

"You're a *Detective*?" shrieked the diva. She was suddenly beside him, standing up straight. "Which precinct?"

He finished all twelve reps before reporting, "One Police Plaza."

"Headquarters!" She was animated again, like the first time they'd spoken. She was wearing high-heeled sneakers: should he tell her she was risking injury?

"Homicide?"

"Computer Crimes Squad."

"Oh." She seemed disappointed. "Still: headquarters, that's neat."

Gum-chewing cop junkies were a dime a dozen. She had to be at least thirty. Who needed it? He had a good thing going with Janice, of late. Ballestrino nodded good-bye, leaving her to risk injury and develop the wrong body parts.

His cell phone rang. "What was the exact response from the account-opening agents in the Caymans, St. Kitts and Costa Rica?" Sprague asked.

" 'Fuck you' three times," Ballestrino told him. "Although they said it with more legal panache." They hung up.

It was getting better, but things had gotten off to a poor start with Sprague. Ballestrino had eleven solid years on the Job; it was insulting the way Sprague demanded he identify obscure songs from the sixties to prove himself. He also resented how Sprague began by asking him if he was a member of the Italian Benevolent Society, as if being Italian were his only vantagepoint.

On the way home he stopped at the cleaner's. The lovely Korean woman always had a smile for him, although she seemed to work there twenty hours a day, seven days a week. She should smile for him: his stains would be putting her children through college. On the other hand, there was a sincere flirtation going on each time she sorted through his clothes. "Detective! Tell your mother, got to stop with the red sauce," she chided him, laughing.

The apartment was immaculate, as always. Everything was dismantled, polished and reassembled daily. Roseanne Ballestrino kept her home battened down like a submarine. When he walked into the kitchen, her feet were up on the breakfast banquette, and the police scanner was chattering on the counter.

"Hey: you go out on that ten-thirteen on Myrtle Avenue?" she called by way of greeting. His mother's heart was in Patrol; she had no idea what he did in the Computer Crimes Squad.

The phone rang; she picked it up.

He peeked under the tinfoil. In spite of all their discussions about steaming and broiling, chicken and fish, there was a plate of fried breaded eggplant swimming in oil, and a basin of lasagna, made with beef and/or pork.

As they sat down to eat, the scanner reported a domestic disturbance in Boerum Hill.

"You're not meeting the right kind of girl," his mother began.

He dropped his fork onto his plate. "Every night!" he shouted.

She was undeterred. "Those cops you talk about? They're probably dykes. And the rest of them—the Nurses, the shop girls, the aerobics instructors—are either loose or psychotic, or they hate cops."

"Every fucking night!" he shouted again.

"You told me so yourself."

His cell phone rang. It was Sprague. "We asked everyone in the firm if they'd been to the Cayman Islands, Costa Rica or St. Kitts, right?"

"Yes, but nobody showed a passport."

Sprague grunted. "It's annoying me."

They hung up.

"Shirley Florimonte's niece Gloria," his mother continued. "Still young, in school to be a physical therapist, a good cook."

All the obvious, low-hanging fruit had been displayed before him already: now his mother and her network were beating the bushes. He took another slice of eggplant, although he certainly didn't need it. Roseanne was looking old and run-down. He decided to play nice.

"Why should I call her? I have the best food in town, the nicest company."

His mother pushed the serving plates at him coyly. He dug out another patch of lasagna, and watched her watching him eat. She pulled a scrap of brown butcher paper out of the pocket of her cardigan and passed it across the table. A phone number. He left it there in the center of the table.

She ran a hand through her short, wiry, black-and-white hair. "What about grandchildren?"

"Jason and Courtney are fine," he said as his cell phone rang. "You saw them yourself on Sunday in Jersey." He answered his phone: "Ballestrino."

"Guess what?" said Bobby Setzer, the first guy he'd met at the Academy.

"Your new roommate's getting married."

"Like clockwork! Move in with me, it's ridiculous."

Bobby and his cousin Ryan, also a cop, had been asking him to move in with them for ten years now. Initially his father was sick, and Tony couldn't find a reasonable argument to move out. Bobby and Ryan had taken in a series of roommates, all of them young cops; each had met the woman of his dreams in Bensonhurst, married her and moved in with her folks. When Ryan married a Bensonhurst girl and moved in with her folks, Bobby begged Tony to move in.

By then his father had died, and he really couldn't leave his mother alone. Roseanne had spent long days with Connie Falcone, whose husband had been a desk sergeant in the Six-Three in Red Hook, before he died of her cooking. Roseanne and Connie sat in the Falcone kitchen, playing Hearts, listening to the scanner, casting aspersions on neighbors and relatives. When Connie dropped dead of her own cooking two years later, Roseanne inherited the scanner. But she hadn't found another friend. If he mentioned moving out now, Roseanne would surely collapse.

"I'll get back to you," he told Bobby.

"No you won't," Bobby laughed.

Tony put the phone on the table. Roseanne cleaned her plate with a wedge of bread, pretending not to know what he was talking about.

"You're thirty-three already. When you gonna have kids?"

"When I get around to it."

"The gallbladder," she continued, "it could go anytime."

"So have the operation."

"You know how stupid I'd have to be to have elective surgery at my age?"

"You're young, Mom."

"My heart is another story. That could go tomorrow."

"And it will," he couldn't help saying, "if you keep eating like this."

She shot him a nasty look. His pager vibrated: the Major Case Squad. He returned the call. They were short-staffed: the Sergeant asked him to come in at midnight to assist with a kidnapping in Washington Heights. He agreed to work a double shift, and put the phone back on the table.

Roseanne Ballestrino said, as if wondering aloud, "What about that nice Christine? What ever happened to her?"

Things had reached a pretty pass if Roseanne Ballestrino was asking after that nice Christine, whom she'd called a German slut as recently as two years ago. It used to be that nobody was good enough for him. Now, if the girl had ovaries and walked by herself, she was *perfect*: what was he so picky for? Somebody, anybody: he should just get married and have kids.

It was disappointing. His own mother.

"That's Janice," she said, with disgust, as his phone rang again. "She always calls at dinnertime."

Tony walked into the kitchen with the phone. The scanner was reporting a burglary in progress on Flatbush Avenue. Janice wanted to see him, she said, but it would have to wait until Thursday night. They made plans.

His mother kicked open the swinging door, put a platter in the sink with one hand and handed him the phone number again with the other.

"Gloria Florimonte. Age twenty-eight. Physical therapist in training. Not married."

He put the piece of paper in his pocket. "What's for dessert?"

"Nothing if you don't call her."

"Fine." He swung out of the room. He changed into a fresh suit, then gathered all his communications devices and weapons.

"You're too old for this," she sang after him.

But why move to a filthy group house in Bensonhurst? If he was moving out, he wanted a nice, clean place of his own in Manhattan.

HE CIRCLED THE BLOCK, making sure there was no one hanging out or watching. He called her cell phone as he turned the corner.

"The kids are wide awake," Janice said, and he heard the shrieking.

"I'm right across the street. I have to kill some time before I go back in." He hoped she'd come to the window. "You may have a minute."

"Unlikely." At the window now, she looked very juicy with her hair down. She raised a hand, and was pulled back into the maelstrom of her life by one of the brats who now had complete control over her.

He pulled out the pack of cigarettes. He wasn't actually smoking again, but he lit one: he'd been looking forward to it all day. Kool had been her brand. He slipped The Cars' first album into the tape deck. Her windows on the second floor were framed with red Christmas lights that blinked on and off.

He hit his partner on speed dial. Sprague picked right up.

"I think we should be taking Greiff's picture around to aquarium stores in the Caymans, St. Kitts and Costa Rica," he said.

"Although Mrs. Greiff said he's got no patience for exotic places and food."

"So we focus on the cleaner, English-speaking islands. How many rare tropical fish stores could there be in the cleaner, English-speaking islands?"

"Although down there," Sprague said, "he could just drop a line in his backyard and pull up some rare tropical fish."

"Still, he needs the tank, the chemicals, that stuff."

"You're right. Think they'll send us down there?"

"In season? You're dreaming." Ballestrino took a drag.

"I'm looking into Ms. Erica King's banking history tomorrow," Sprague said.

"You going in on this thing for Major Case tonight?"

"See you there."

In a room full of cops, Ballestrino and Sprague were unusual: almost everyone had a wife, kids and pets in a house in Queens, Staten Island, Nassau or Rockland County, and an SUV that didn't fit in the detached garage because of the lawn mower, the snowblower, the gigantic red plastic toys and the grill. Sprague lived in a two-bedroom apartment in Riverdale; he didn't have kids, and it didn't seem to bother him. Ballestrino wondered whether it would bother him, or when.

A good woman, marriage: this was the next step. But how could a cop have kids in this city? How would he pay for them, where would he put them and when would he see them? Money, space and time. Also: children were exhausting. And if you weren't having kids, why get married, really?

Ballestrino lit another Kool. The previous day he'd partnered with Anita Clemente on a new case of Web-related sexual harassment on Staten Island. A guy impersonated his ex-girlfriend in at least six adult chat rooms, sending out very private pictures of her, along with her home, work and cell phone numbers, her e-mail and home addresses and her preferences. The woman was inundated.

Anyone in the CCS who pulled a sex case in the catching order partnered with Anita Clemente, unless she was too busy. Female, and, in all likelihood, black and Hispanic: a three-for-one. She looked like a decoy: skinny with wide shoulders, long legs, tiny waist. On very rare occasions, she laughed, displaying big, white, eccentric teeth that he found strangely compelling. Each time he worked with her, Tony wondered if something might happen. Nothing ever did.

That morning, while they waited for Anita's machine to boot up, Ballestrino asked her, "So come on, what are you?"

"What *am* I?" She stared at him with her big, round, green-flecked eyes.

"Yeah. You black? Hispanic? Irish? What's your heritage?"

Anita Clemente stood very tall by the filing cabinet and said, "No."

"You know I can find out anything I want from Personnel."

"You *do* that, Tony." She must have been about five-foot-ten, and then there were the platform shoes, on which she pivoted and glided away.

How dare she turn her back on him? He could feel the rest of the unit taking note. Anita Clemente was ambiguous. There were rumors of boyfriends, girlfriends, children. She never talked, which had to be part of the allure.

AT NINE O'CLOCK, the lights went off in the front room. Tony called Janice again, but she'd turned off her cell phone. He tossed the fourth cigarette out the window and let in some air. He called her home number.

She picked up right away.

"I need to see you," he said, liking the quiet urgency of his voice.

"You have the wrong number," Janice said, loud, as if to teach him. And hung up.

He drove back into Manhattan with a bad taste in his mouth.

❖

Erica King's mother had been the school Nurse at the Bradley School, grades six through twelve.

"Wadda, wadda, wadda," she greeted students who came into her clean white precincts. "Waddamaygonnadowidyou?" she would say, looking you straight in the eyes. If you were faking your stomachache or hiding anything, she would know. That amused look, peering directly into your eyes, with or without the flashlight, gave her daughter, Erica, the creeps.

Geri King was universally popular, applauded loudly in the end-of-school assembly, featured prominently in the yearbook, aging nicely, with her heavy makeup, fetching brown beauty mark above her upper lip, thick yellow hair in the dowdy updo. Geri had been born in Poland, and arrived in Chicago at the age of fifteen. She was completely fluent, but here and dere, a word or phrase would come out a little inflected. Let's extenuate de positive, she would say.

Over dinner, Erica's mother, the school Nurse, might say, "I saw you talking to Alison Chernik in the cafeteria. You know, she's not that interesting. Now that Melissa Berend, she's someone to hang out with, and not just because she's a looker." Melissa Berend had been the one to say to Erica, out of nowhere, while they washed their hands in the deep double sink of the ceramics studio, "You wouldn't be here if your mother wasn't the Nurse. You couldn't afford Bradley."

"What's it to you who I talk to," Erica responded to her mother.

"Did somebody get up on the wrong side of the bed?" Geri would sing gaily. "Tom Doolan came in for a bruise. I think something's going on in the home."

And Erica's mother, the school Nurse, would follow up on Tom Doolan in the home, and tell her daughter all about it: the father unavailable for discussion, the mother wearing sunglasses over what was clearly a black eye. The next day during Math, Tom would glance at Erica and away, and Erica didn't know what to do. She wanted to express something—I'm sorry about my prying mother; I'm sorry about your troubled home—but had no idea what was appropriate. It was one thing when she heard all about the kids at Bradley when Erica was attending school at IS 49. Now that she was a student at Bradley herself (yes, on scholarship), it was getting uncomfortable.

Erica's mother, the school Nurse, told her about Miss Kaiser, her current Social Studies teacher and former baby-sitter, who was getting married on a Tuesday afternoon at four-thirty, and had to bring her dress (which wasn't white) to school, and change in the third-floor bathroom, because she was pregnant. Erica didn't believe her. Geri also told Erica what you could do to avoid getting pregnant, which Lisa Kaiser had paid no attention to, like an idiot.

And Erica's mother, the school Nurse, told her about Miss Walsh, Erica's gym teacher, who was ostensibly out with the flu for two days, because she was having an abortion. Erica didn't believe her. "Honey, she came to me for a referral. Don't tell me you don't believe it." Geri paused to shovel more potatoes onto Erica's plate. "Why are you always fighting me?"

Erica avoided the Nurse's Office as if she might catch something there, but her English class was right next door, so she had to pass by every day. Her mother knew her schedule, frequently nabbed her in the hall and asked her to sit for a minute, because she had something to discuss.

"You know my daughter, don't you, Robbie?" Geri said as she taped the tennis star's finger into a splint, while Erica froze in the waiting chair. "Erica tells me you're in the same Biology class!"

"Of course." Rob Ehrenreich tossed his glossy black bangs, ignoring Erica, seeming to enjoy Geri's ministrations.

Erica throbbed with embarrassment. She didn't want Rob Ehrenreich to think she'd even noticed him, much less talked to her mother about him. And there was Geri, calling him "Robbie," talking about Biology. It was outrageous.

What Geri needed to discuss so urgently usually involved the Grief Center, a neighborhood place where she spent a lot of time and energy. It was run by a former divinity student turned psychotherapist named Sheldon. Out of his town house on East 30th Street, Sheldon offered individual and group therapy, classes in ethics, comparative religion and yoga, holiday celebrations, mixers and massage therapy. He also cut hair.

Most of the members of the Center were overweight middle-aged widows and divorcées who lived in rent-controlled apartments nearby. After a period of misery and drift, most of the women who found their way to the Grief Center gratefully transferred their attention from their absent husbands to the charismatic Sheldon. If you couldn't pay for a class or therapy, Sheldon kept you busy cooking his meals, keeping his books or vacuuming the rugs in his town house. You could organize a bake sale for the hurricane victims of Nicaragua, or drive him to Washington, where he planned to raise awareness in Congress about the plight of the Salvadoran peasants. Or you could clean out the incense bowls.

From the age of seven, Erica had been picking up mail and doing errands for the aging and increasingly decrepit Theresa Collecelli, one of her mother's friends from the Grief Center. Her duties soon included another widow, Maddie Olsen. These women didn't deal with Erica directly, but through her mother. So Geri would dart into the hall, a flash of pink cardigan and white uniform, and drag Erica into her office to announce, "You're picking up a prescription for Maddie, and then you're taking Theresa to the Center."

"Again?" Bringing Theresa to a lecture meant attending it herself, and bringing her home.

"Erica," Geri chided her, "the woman never gets out! Be compassionate."

As a younger child, Erica had taken off her shoes to sit on and run her fingers through the hairy white yak carpet in Sheldon's study during innumerable lectures, and if she hadn't paid attention, at least she didn't resist. But after Sheldon began having quasi-religious services on Sunday mornings, Erica began to resent everything about it. At thirteen, she looked at all the women jockeying for Sheldon's attention, and decided the Center was a personality cult. Erica had no patience for Sheldon, the personality. That someone named Sheldon could be a leader of anything was proof that America really was the land of opportunity.

Geri talked about Sheldon frequently. "Isn't he *charming*?"

"Oh, please!" Erica responded.

"Sheldon thinks that you don't want to come to meetings because you resent him for taking me away from you," Geri told Erica.

Erica put down her book to eat some more dumplings. "What exactly does Sheldon do for a living?" she asked her mother.

"Such a sourpuss!" Geri laughed.

❖

By the time she was in seventh grade, Erica's incidental chores included local errands, plant watering, light clerical work and electronics repairs for Theresa Collecelli, Maddie Olsen, Dorothy Findlay and her retarded son, Davey, and other needy, homebound members of the Grief Center. Her tasks involved no fewer than five sets of keys. Erica was paid in cookies, kisses and the occasional five-dollar bill. Her sense of injustice was building.

She chose her battles. One crisp day in late November, she announced that she wasn't going to services on Sundays, she wasn't going to lectures on Wednesdays and if she was old enough to be entrusted with five sets of keys, she was old enough to be by herself when Geri went to the Center.

Her mother countered: "We're going out with Sheldon tonight."

In fact, what Erica had planned to do was finish a lab report and devour *His Wife Is Not My Problem*. "I'd rather stay home."

"It's Saturday night! His nephew is coming too—he's a year older than you. Very handsome, I saw the picture."

"Why do I have to be with people I don't like?"

Anger passed over Geri's face. "What is the matter with you?"

"What I'd like to do is go away, go somewhere else for a change."

This stumped Geri. "Somewhere else?"

"California? Rome?"

"What's so great about *away*? Everything you need is here."

"That's not the point."

"And we have people that depend on us. On you."

"Theresa has arthritis, so I can never leave New York?"

"Well, I have never heard such selfishness."

THE FOLLOWING WEEK, her mother nabbed her outside the Nurse's Office. "I need you to pick up a prescription for Dorothy after school." She sat Erica in the waiting chair while she dealt with a good-looking eighth-grade jerk.

"Hey, Mr. Headache," Geri called cheerfully as she dispensed an aspirin to her patient's palm from a pleated white cup. "You remember my daughter, the one you didn't ask to dance last Friday night? Yeah? Got an excuse, wiseguy?"

Erica was on her feet, out the door.

"Oh, there she goes, leaving in a huff." And she called so loud that the History teacher popped his head out into the hall to see what all the fuss was about: "I'm on your team, Erica! Why do you never see it?"

❖

One Friday night after work, Erica lounged on Marjorie's couch with the remote control, flipping back and forth between a biography of Clare Booth Luce and yet another documentary about the Kennedys. JFK had so much sexual energy! CBL was always surrounded by powerful men! Joe Kennedy had an affair with Gloria Swanson, who had married a penniless French aristocrat and social climber! CBL was always looking ahead to her next man! Both Joe and Jack Kennedy had affairs with Marlene Dietrich at the same French resort!

Next: self-righteous women gesticulating wildly on the theme of "I want my man to stop having babies with other women!"

Next: angry women gesticulating wildly on the theme of "I want my thirteen-year-old daughter to stop having sex in the car after school!"

Next: furious women gesticulating wildly on the theme of "My man pays no attention to me in bed!"

Oh, enough. She switched off the TV and turned on Marjorie's laptop.

The detectives had been back four or five times to look through files and ask questions. The air was tense all day, every day. Glenn Friedman lashed out at everyone. Marty Slavin cried in his office with the door open. Erica kept her nose down and tried to stay in the present.

When she opened Marjorie's e-mail, there were six messages from Web sites proudly hawking pornography. There were several high-profile sex-in-the-workplace cases going on simultaneously. There was SEX SEX SEX on the covers of all the women's magazines. Women's fashions for all seasons involved visible bra straps and low-rise pants that bared the hipbones, if you had hipbones. Women of all ages and sizes were now displaying their naked stomachs on the streets and even in the office—sometimes just an inch, and sometimes four inches above and below the navel—as if offering a window onto their souls.

"I'm getting it," the bared abdominals seemed to shout.

Every six weeks, there was a different enormous billboard of a bare-chested eighteen-year-old with his hand down his own or someone else's underpants by the entrance to the Midtown Tunnel.

That afternoon, Heather had entered her office, closed the door dramatically and announced out of a clear blue sky that yes, she might *look* beautiful, but since her uncle molested her when she was twelve, she hadn't felt beautiful *inside.*

It was bad enough that Erica had to listen to this kind of conversation; why did people insist that she participate?

"And you're telling me this *because* . . . ?"

"Uh, I don't know. Because I thought you might be sympathetic."

"Why? Because I myself look like a victim of sexual abuse?"

"Oh, no . . ."

"Because I understand what it's like to feel ugly inside? Is that it?"

The intruder then burst into tears.

"Tears are not valid currency in this territory," Erica said. "You'll have to try something else."

"I'm sorry, I—"

"I accept your apology, Heather, and I hope that your childhood trauma doesn't interfere with our working together."

It used to be that no one talked about these things. Now no one shut up about them. That evening, Erica electronically transferred the interest from Maria's municipal bonds into Maria's second checking account. A little repression was a good thing, Erica believed. Talk was overrated, like everything else on television: sex, hair, confrontation, power. Well, maybe not power.

❖

Erica wore a striped knitted cap every day of eighth grade.

"I cannot stand it another minute," her mother said one day in March. "Take it off."

"What's it to you?"

"It's filthy. Give it to me to wash."

"So you can throw it out? I don't think so."

"So you wash it."

"I do wash it."

Her mother got up from the table. She came behind Erica, and took her plate and her hat. "There!" she sang in triumph. "I got it!"

Her mother stared at her head, and dropped the plate on the floor.

"What is going on with the hair, here?"

Erica picked up shards of plate bitterly.

Geri whisked her to two doctors the next day. There were tests. The tests were inconclusive, but both doctors mentioned a strong possibility of alopecia, a disease where some or all of the hair on the head and the body fell out, and never grew back. There was no explanation and no solution. They wanted to watch her.

"Watch, watch," Erica told the endocrinologist. "Everybody watch my hair fall out. That sounds like a fun thing to do."

"Erica," Geri hissed with disapproval and amusement.

Geri, meanwhile, was halfway through her first course of chemotherapy, and was losing hair herself. Up until that point, neither of them had mentioned it. On the way home, they bought a Yankees cap for Erica, and a red knit hat for Geri. Geri told Erica she was terrified of what might happen if anyone found out at Bradley. No one could know about her treatments. Nobody wanted a sick nurse.

When she sat down with her daughter the following night at dinner, Geri began, "Sheldon thinks a wig would be a good idea for you."

The rage that shot through Erica's veins almost short-circuited her system. Erica took her five sets of keys and walked.

At the drugstore, she bought a pack of Velamints and stole a book.

She arrived home after midnight, hungry and tired. Sheldon appeared in the foyer, ankh pendant swinging in his white chest hair. He gave her a disgusted look. "Next time, you might think about what your mother is going through before you pull something this stupid."

"And you are?" Erica looked at the leader of the sect, whom she'd known for nine years. She took in the sagging underpants, the hairy shoulders.

He stared at her. "I am concerned about your mother."

"Right," she said, and walked back to her room.

Erica wondered what her father, who had died in a five-car collision in Chicago when she was three, would have made of the Grief Center, and the various directions the members of the family were taking.

The following Tuesday, Geri wrote a note for Erica to be excused at noon, and arranged for a substitute for herself. She didn't want to be seen doing this locally, so they took the train to Philadelphia, where they were both fitted for hair and eyebrows.

CHAPTER FOUR

Sprague was home at eight-fifteen. The current dog, a jittery, barking schnauzer, greeted him like a conquering hero. Sometimes Cathy greeted him that way. Tonight she kissed him on the mouth when he approached, but continued to mist her ferns. She looked like a college sophomore in sweatpants and wet hair.

"You're early," she said.

He'd accepted a lift home from his Sergeant, Dave Sarkos, who lived in Rockland County. On the Henry Hudson Parkway, they'd caught up on the gossip, groused about the Job and the Lieutenant. Like clockwork, as Sarkos slowed down on the exit ramp, he asked, "So, when are you guys having kids?" as casually as if he were inquiring about summer travel plans.

"No kids," Sprague said. "Pets and plants."

"No kids! How come? You're not a man till you've changed a ripe, steaming diaper!"

This question came up at least once a month, and the parent asking always seemed to dwell on the shit. Because they lived in shit and chaos, *he* should live in shit and chaos? In fact, Sprague did live in shit and chaos, a goddamn three-ring circus. There was always something escaping, getting into the garbage, vomiting in the closet, expressing itself on the sofa.

"I have nothing to prove in the excrement department," he maintained.

Why did this question always come up? Both he and Cathy had been diagnosed infertile during previous marriages. Neither had been keen to adopt; both were grateful to escape the issue. Yet no one else would let it rest.

"I just want you to know," Sarkos dripped with pity, "I understand."

"Well, I'm glad you understand," he said, pointing out his apartment building. "And I'll forgive you."

"Forgive me? For what?"

"Well, if you have to ask, then perhaps you *don't* understand." Sprague thanked him for the lift and walked into his building. These people: you were either living their lives, or you aspired to their lives, and thus had failed.

He wondered how Erica King handled this kind of understanding.

He'd called her that morning for some documents, and she'd been, as always, perfectly correct. She'd given him what he'd asked for—no more, no less. She'd responded to his attempts to chat her up with a stony silence. She was colorless, disappearing into her spreadsheets. On the other hand, she was *willfully* colorless: he heard her blinking on the other end of the line.

With the dog frisking around his legs, he assembled the ingredients for a GLT: gin, lemon juice and tonic, in equal proportions. Cathy tossed him the envelope of take-out menus, and he pulled out the Chinese one. Unlike Sara, who had some kind of religious conviction that a family—even a cop's family—had to sit down for a three-course meal at the same time every night, Cathy never hassled him about his hours, his diet, his lack of health and fitness.

Sprague thought often about the three Mrs. Spragues:

-Scottish/Puerto Rican/German-Irish.

-Practicing Presbyterian/practicing Catholic/lapsed Catholic.

-Size 12/size 2/size 22.

-Math teacher/real-estate broker/animal-hospital manager.

-Read the horoscope first/read the obits first/did the crossword first.

-Medium-length straight brown hair counteracted with perm/short, frizzy black hair counteracted with relaxer/long, curly dark blond hair left to its own devices and often worn wet.

-Dog person/allergic person/protector of the entire animal kingdom.

You couldn't say that Sprague had a type.

He went into the second bedroom, which he'd set up for work at home. He turned on his laptop, inserted a disk containing a copy of Erica King's office hard drive and began poking around. The fact was, he wasn't good at living alone, but he wasn't particularly inter-active when living with someone. Numbers One and Two didn't get that. Cathy did, and had figured out how to get what she needed from him (frequent contact, rarely in-depth). They were very happy together.

They'd met when he was working Narcotics in Washington Heights. One of the nurses at her clinic was storing packets of heroin in the cages of the resident strays, and Cathy had reported it. He felt at home with her immediately. She was an upbeat, positive person.

On the other hand, everyone seemed unnaturally happy at the vet's. It was a culture of sympathy, petting and kindness: the polar opposite of Narcotics in Washington Heights. Sometimes he would come home after a bad day, and Cathy would look deeply into his eyes and stroke his head. He felt like a Labrador who'd found some-body who didn't know he'd been naughty on the rug.

Whoever hadn't been adopted she brought back and forth between work and home in the beaten-up and odorific vet van. Currently, there was the schnauzer rooting through shoes in their closets, two cock-atiels shitting on newspapers in a cage by the window and a black cat pissing all over the house. Until he'd put his foot down, Cathy had brought home wounded pigeons found by the bus stop.

LATER, HIS CELL PHONE RANG in the midst of Chinese takeout.

It was Ballestrino. "You think he's dead?"

They were working on sixteen active cases between them, but Mitch Greiff was all they talked about.

"He's dead, and someone else is rolling in celebrity dough in the Cayman Islands?" Sprague considered this. "It could happen." He had a flash of fear. "Did we send out a call to the morgues?"

"Missing Persons did, before we came on."

"Greiff's been gone eight weeks. He's not dead. He's probably in Costa Rica, enjoying his good fortune in an ecologically self-sustainable compound."

"So all his life he's been eating pistachio," Ballestrino said, "and now he's going for the cherry vanilla? It doesn't make sense."

"It happens," Sprague smiled. "One day, you look around your spacious, well-located co-op, gaze at your gorgeous, youthful, former-model wife and say, 'The hell with this shit! I want to live in fear!' "

Cathy took off her glasses and rubbed her eyes, smirking.

"We'll find him," Sprague said. "Hiding takes effort. He must be getting tired."

While Cathy spent the evening cleaning cages and chasing down escapees, Dennis browsed through Erica King's files; he found nothing more interesting than celebrity tax statements. She was organized, he'd say that for her.

❖

After the story exploded all over the TV and newspapers, there was a spurt of well-meaning people who wanted to help Patricia. There was also a flurry of vicious phone calls from friends, clients and total strangers who somehow got the number and called to express exactly what they thought of her husband.

There was a scene at Tessio's, where people she'd never met saw her eating with Cynthia and Jack Landau, and started ranting bitterly about the nerve of her, showing her face in public. They were friends of Jerry Fabrikant, they claimed, and they worked themselves up into a righteous rage that spilled over into confrontation just as the entrées arrived.

"If you took a minute to think about it," she shouted back at them, "you wouldn't attack me in public."

"I could *spit* on you *in public*," said the wife, but she didn't.

"And who are you, taking her out for Veal Milanese?" the husband accused Cynthia and Jack. True to form, Cynthia was less offended by their behavior than the fact that they'd never heard of her.

Thank God her mother was dead. At least Patricia didn't have to explain to Grace McCarey that her husband, the Jew, was a thief, yes; but there were other, nice Jewish people, who weren't thieves. In fact, many if not most of their friends and his clients were Jews, so they knew that Mitch had stolen from them not because he was a Jew, but because he'd lost his mind, or was just a selfish cad who'd left his clients and colleagues in trouble and his family in disgrace.

That is, if it actually had been him, which hadn't been proved.

One morning, avoiding bills, she flipped aimlessly through a dowdy sportswear catalog and recognized Laurie Charlotte, a model she'd hung out with in 1970—a different life. Laurie Charlotte was fifty-two if she was a day, and here she was, looking, yes, older, but terrific.

She found the Clave Agency in the phone book. Still on 57th Street. "Trafalgar-nine-five-thousand!" she sang the number as she dialed it, and left a message for Marcia Clave with someone who sounded fourteen years old.

Patricia ran out to the drugstore to get some new lipstick. There were catalogs that featured women of a certain age in comfortable velour ensembles enjoying an aromatherapy machine on one page, and incontinence panties, vitamin supplements and chin exercisers on the next. Patricia was in excellent shape. Everyone said she looked thirty-seven. She could activate her old contacts. Of course, almost all the photographers she'd known were dead.

As she picked up some shampoo (Vidal Sassoon: gratitude, nostalgia), she saw Judy Eisenfleiss, obliquely, in front of the Lancôme display. She hadn't heard from the Eisenfleisses, good or ill. There was stress in not knowing if they knew, and if they did know, where did she stand with them? She went to the register to avoid having to say hello. Judy might ask an awkward question, like "What's new?"

A woman behind the counter began to ring up Patricia's items. Judy Eisenfleiss sauntered over and cocked an eyebrow at the products on the counter. "Shouldn't you be shopping at Kmart now, Patricia?"

Innocent spouse! she seethed. She signed the credit card receipt with anger, pride and mortification mingling there above the breath mints. She stalked back home without the new lipstick that would change her life.

Judy Eisenfleiss had day care for her Yorkies. Why couldn't Patricia buy shampoo? Whatever else Mitch left behind, the worst was this aroma around her that she couldn't get rid of. She felt unclean. Everywhere she went someone reminded her that she was a thief by association.

Before Thanksgiving dinner at the Landaus', Cynthia sat on a needlepointed footstool next to Jack's armchair, looking up at him like a spaniel. Was this to show Jack that she was literally beside and beneath him? Was Patricia alone a threat to her? Patricia had no interest in Jack: Cynthia had to know that.

Cynthia's kids were there, looking bored and angry. Elliott was creating shelters made out of waterproof plastic for the homeless in San Francisco; Jack seemed nauseated by this announcement. Dominique still had a clerical job after three years at a local TV station; she complained about the waste of her education. Cynthia whispered to Patricia, "You think she'd get promoted if she combed her hair?"

Jobs, expectations, hair. This was the fabric of family life, in a normal family. The Greiffs had never been a normal family. The kids were too problematic. Mitch was too self-involved and obsessive. Her social activities were among her female friends, during the day. As her mother would say, Patricia hadn't been enrolled among the righteous for some time.

———

THE FOLLOWING MORNING she lay in a hot bath. This was the end of the bubble bath, but could she risk being seen buying more? The phone rang. She sprang from the bath when she heard Marcia Clave on the machine.

"I saw your picture in the paper the other day, Patricia. I'm so sorry."

"Marcia, I'm in an impossible situation, and I've done nothing wrong."

"Well, you look terrific, if that's any consolation. How can I help?"

Patricia shut her eyes. "I need work."

"Well, my secretary is leaving next week for Milan, and I haven't replaced her. Do you know the latest edition of Word Perfect?"

"Actually, I was wondering about catalog work."

"Patricia, the market for forty-plus models has grown exponentially, and you have the exact look a certain kind of company wants. But how can I tell them to put you in their catalog when your face is on the nightly news in reference to a criminal investigation? And I know it wasn't you. But think, Patricia."

"Of course. Thank you, Marcia."

"What about Word Perfect?"

"I'll call you when I learn how to turn the computer on by myself."

A THANKSGIVING DINNER of sorts happened at the home of the disgraced Greiff family on Saturday night. Patricia sat at the head of the table, her husband's place, and looked at her children, her major accomplishment in this life.

Brian was checking his hair in the mirror, and finding it highly satisfactory; she noticed that he really didn't attempt to remove the camera makeup anymore. *Torches of Desire* was on at the nail salon, the gym, the coffee shop and the bank. Since when was there television at the bank? He had called that morning as he did every day, and nattered on in voices and accents about the backstage dramas, his new loafers, the traffic, until she cut him off or his hairdresser arrived. She could tell he did this all day, going through his address book. Patricia found these phone calls profoundly disturbing. Brian was a gossip and an idler. But at least he was employed.

Randy was biting his bleeding hangnails, and stanching the blood with the white tablecloth. He'd arrived at dawn on Thanksgiving, holding a big brown box brimming over with a cut-glass chandelier coated with the dust of ages.

"Get that out of here NOW," she told him. "I don't intend to be charged with possession of stolen property in addition to all my other troubles."

"I have an appointment today," Randy said, irritated.

"On Thanksgiving? An appointment to loot the Americana section at the 42nd Street branch? Shall I call the police?"

He slid the carton down his dirty jeans in a huff. "What am I supposed to do with it?"

"I don't give a damn WHAT you do with it," she said. "You may not leave it anywhere in this apartment, or anywhere in the basement, or anywhere else in this building." She'd learned over the years to be legally precise with Randy.

Patricia had grown up in a hardware store: there was always something you could do to fix it, whatever it was. Nothing had ever worked with these two. She wanted to erase them both. ERASE. Start over with a blank tape.

Could she just walk away from her children? This was not a mature thing to do, but it was an option—an extreme one, to be sure, but reassuring to consider. It could be done: look at her husband.

A heroin addict dropped into an unfamiliar city will always find his drug. Every day Ballestrino went to Aquarium.net and browsed, making a list of everyone in the chat rooms, and taking note of new vendors offering equipment. He'd made contact with every top-of-the-line aquarium store in all fifty states, all ten Canadian provinces, as well as the United Kingdom, Ireland, Australia, New Zealand,

Switzerland and ten of the cleaner, English-speaking Caribbean islands; once a week he called them all again. Nothing. Sprague had done the same for jazz record stores. Together they'd made contact with Greiff's family and friends, his tailor, his shoe store, his doctors, his stereo consultant. Nothing.

That morning, Sprague stood over his desk, devouring a doughnut.

"Erica King," he said. "She's bothering me, but I can't tell you why."

"She's bothering me too," Ballestrino said, "and I know why."

"Not everybody is a looker."

"I've had many a successful romantic evening with women you wouldn't describe as lookers. There's such a thing as humor, as personality. There's an exchange, an interaction. It can be very sexy."

Sprague continued chewing.

"But this one! She's got no presentation skills, and no social skills," Ballestrino said. "When someone is this shut down, this incapable of giving back anything, it shuts *you* down. She makes *you* feel bad and awkward, and *you* stop trying. Erica King is just a black hole."

"Is she the black hole we're looking for?"

"Get ready to take me to dinner," Tony announced. "I think the friends and colleagues of Mitch Greiff—and now we—have radically underestimated his skills."

BALLESTRINO PULLED A NIGHT SHIFT and was sitting at the courthouse on Overtime, waiting to testify against a sixteen-year-old hacker. He'd been chatting with a Sergeant from Midtown South, who was stunned that Ballestrino was being called to the witness stand.

"You guys do investigations?" he asked incredulously. He thought the Computer Crimes Squad was the number to call if your hard drive crashed.

They solved case after case, but there was no press. Each time, the bosses put the kibosh on press coverage. For the first five years, the phone number of the CCS wasn't even listed in the internal directory. It angered him.

After testifying, Ballestrino plodded down Center Street, depressed anew by the narrow margins of current fashions. Every woman was dressed in black head-to-toe, with brown lipstick. Everyone wore the two-inch press-on nail extensions like fluorescent claws, and clopped along in clunky, chunky black rubber platforms—Frankenstein shoes.

AT FOUR THAT AFTERNOON, Ballestrino pulled pressed gray slacks and a gray silk shirt out of the nice dry-cleaning plastic. He unlocked his gun, strapped on his holster, phones and beeper. He pulled on a gray tweed jacket, and slipped the silly orange plastic miniflashlight key chain into his pocket. He bought a bottle of wine on Court, drove straight to Glendale, cased out the house and parked legally a block away. He never abused the perks of a Department car. He was early. He strolled down the sidewalk squeezing the miniflashlight key chain rhythmically.

This was one of his cousin Nick's properties; it had stucco, shingles, brick and clapboard on one house. The small, poorly lit apartment was ideal for Nick's storage and Tony's personal life. Tony returned the favor by giving Nick prime Mets tickets when he got them. He vacuumed, pulled clean sheets out of a shopping bag, made the bed, put on music, opened the wine and waited. Janice was ostensibly taking a class at Queens Community College on Thursdays. The kids stayed with her folks. Her husband had a poker game that didn't break up till eleven.

He had made a mistake with Janice. He could admit that now. At twenty-one, she was ready, and he was not. At the time, the idea of marriage was a thirty-foot-long jump. Who was married? He spent an entire summer bitching about it to his buddies: the *nerve* of her. They broke up. She found a husband within a year. At the time, he'd said, "She just wanted to get married. Anybody standing in front of her at that moment, she would have married them."

JANICE WAS LATE. "I have an hour, period." She tossed her coat on the kitchen counter, fluffing her dark brown hair.

"But you said your parents would take the kids."

"They're getting really rambunctious." She seemed taller than usual. "My mother says they terrorize them."

"You're taking a class, they should respect that."

"I'm not taking a class, Tony."

"Yeah, but they don't know that. One day, you *will* take a class, and is this the kind of support you can expect from your family?" He handed her a glass of wine. "Two and a half hours, once a week. It's not so much to ask."

"What do you want from me? There's very little time left over." She walked to the window and looked up at the street. "I *should* be taking that class. Pretty soon, everybody'll be in school full time. What am I going to do? I don't want to be a drone in front of a word processor."

She was wearing black platform Frankenstein shoes.

"Come on," she said, pulling off her sweater to reveal a big, ugly gray jogging bra. "I don't want to argue and I don't have much time."

SHE WAS GONE, as promised, within an hour. He stripped the bed. He'd bring the sheets to Kim, the friendly dry cleaner, with the rest of his laundry. He wondered what her story was. Was the wordless guy pressing pants in the window her husband? He should follow her one night after she closed, assuming that she did close.

He emerged into the gloom of nocturnal Queens. He slipped the key chain into his pocket, too disconsolate to squeeze it even once. He realized that he enjoyed preparing for these visits more than the visits themselves.

❖

In the middle of Erica's ninth-grade year, Geri broke up with Sheldon, whom she'd found humping Jane Childress next to the mimeograph machine on his pantry table, the day before Geri's surgery. Jane Childress, the one who had said, "You need to take some time off to rest, Geri. I'll organize Chinese New Year, St. Patrick's Day and Passover."

When Geri confronted Jane Childress as she zipped up her mauve velour jumpsuit, Jane said, "What do you mean, I had to go after him *now*? He and I have been *going after each other* for the last seven years! I'm sorry about your mastectomy, Geri, but open your eyes: you're not the only game in town!"

Sheldon was calm almost to the point of stillness; he was used to dealing with women in hysterics. He put an arm around both women and said, with such sincere heartbreak in his voice that you could tell he was being serious, "Sometimes, I just don't think there's enough of me to go around."

And then his next appointment arrived, a trembling blonde in her mid-thirties, new to the Center. Geri and Jane were stuck looking at each other among all the outdated lavender mimeographs in the pantry while Sheldon scurried off to the treatment room (in which they'd both been treated), to "do an intake."

"Don't believe what a man tells you," Geri told Erica that evening. "And don't listen to what other women say. Everyone has their own agenda."

And she burst into tears, briefly, which was upsetting to Erica.

GERI WAS TOO NATURALLY CHEERFUL to stay down for long. She bounced back into life after chemotherapy. She took up jogging. Her hair grew back. She resumed her Friday-night confessions with Lisa Kaiser and Frieda Walsh: Miss Kaiser still taught seventh-grade Social Studies; she had miscarried, and was single again. Miss Walsh was still Erica's gym teacher.

They discussed Erica the minute she left the room.

"She just *stands* there," Miss Walsh whispered. "She won't catch the ball."

"Oh, Frieda. Waddamaygonnado?"

"There are a couple of kids who are exempt from gym," Miss Walsh said. "On the other hand, she's gaining. She shouldn't give up exercise now. Maybe she could run around the track during her regular gym period. Yes! That's it. I'll make sure everyone in the department knows."

So Erica jogged slowly around the perimeter of the loud, shiny gym in hunter-green sweatpants while the rest of her classmates struggled after balls in the center, whispered about her between points and forgot about her in the fierce moments of the game. Once, three girls went after a ball and careened out of bounds, smashing into her from behind and knocking her down. All four of them sprawled on the hard waxed wood in a tumble of white thigh, thick green cotton and sweaty hair. She knew without reaching up that the wig had flipped forward.

The whistle blew.

In the process of getting up, she had dislodged the wig from its last remaining mooring. The hair was off, and she didn't rush to put it back on: it felt better with it off. The girls limped back to their game, politely glancing away from her, unlike the rest of the class, who stared openly at her baldness. There was nervous laughter.

The whistle blew.

"WHATCHOU LOOKIN AT?" Miss Walsh shouted, "Get back to your positions! Now! I mean NOW!"

Miss Walsh trotted by, squatted down and put her arm around Erica's shoulder in a coachlike fashion. "Ya okay?"

The heels of her hands were chafed and her knees were stinging. The wig was still on the insanely bright, shiny wood three feet away from her.

"You want to go, uh, get an ice pack from the Nurse?"

"No."

Miss Walsh had a light in her eyes; perhaps she thought that Erica was going to pick herself up, dust herself off, put the animal on her head and start running again. If this were a movie, she might toss the hair into the bleachers, and continue to trot triumphantly around the gymnasium, her bald head shining under the sodium lamps.

But this wasn't a movie; this was her life. She carried her hair off the court, affixed it in the locker room and walked out of the school unopposed. She walked around the corner, bought a pack of cigarettes and stole a pack of gum.

Two years earlier, when Angie, the Office Manager, took a medical leave to attend to a recurring hernia, Erica volunteered to take over the day-to-day office management for six weeks. In this way, she gained admittance to all the closets, the security codes, everybody's password and everybody's hard drive. Anyone stupid enough to leave something on an office hard drive deserved an invasion of privacy. And these people, her colleagues—constantly discussing their intimate details in a place of business, where one justifiably had the expectation of, if not *privacy*, per se, then at least neutral behavior, decorum, something more discreet than teenage sluts on the bus—deserved much worse than that.

As the temporary Office Manager, she had a closed-door policy: all requests came to her on e-mail. People were just as happy not to have to deal with her. She had never been so busy.

So it was not unusual to find her in her office on a Thursday night at eleven forty-five, working on the overflow from her own job that had to be put on hold when the air-conditioning broke. She could tell by the muffled roar that the cleaning staff had arrived. Someone knocked on her door.

It was a Filipino woman in a pink uniform, pushing a vacuum. Erica had changed the lock, and hadn't provided the cleaning staff with keys. She didn't like anybody in her business.

"That's all right, you don't have to clean here," she said, and walked out to pick up a file from the cabinet in the hall. The woman stood by the vacuum, peering at her. Erica pulled a file out of a drawer.

"Yes? You don't have to clean in here," she said, louder.

"I just looking to see you lose weight."

"Excuse me?"

"I think you lose a lotta weight. I see you before." The woman dropped her voice to signal drama, let her arms float out to signal girth and hissed with distaste, "You were *berry hebby*."

Everybody was a critic. She walked past the woman into her office.

"I give you compliment," the cleaning woman called after her, piqued. "Why you no say thank you?"

Erica shut her door, and began to peruse Marty Slavin's brokerage account.

❖

One late afternoon during the summer after ninth grade, a fat man in a powder-blue suit sat sweating on the sofa, calling Erica's mother "Mrs. Carlson."

He fiddled with a black briefcase on his lap and told Geri that the whole thing had been a mistake: a secretary in the office had confessed that she had made a clerical error. The President of the Union and the President of the Local wanted Mrs. Carlson and Maria Carlson to know that they had all their sympathy, what a tragedy, could there be any help for this additional grief, the Union was prepared to take care of Hugh Carlson's kin, after all these years.

During his speech, Geri flapped around the living room moving ashtrays and books. "We will be in touch with you through my lawyer, Sheldon Linzer," Geri said, and abruptly stood in front of him with her hand held out.

Erica had never seen her mother behaving this ungraciously. After he'd left, Erica peeled off her wig and threw it on the sofa. "What the hell was that?"

"All right, then, you're old enough," Geri said; she picked up the hair and ran her fingers through it. "Your father didn't die in a car crash."

"What?"

"He was caught embezzling from the Union. He threw himself out of a window the day before the trial. You had just started nursery school in a nice place on Clark Street. We had just bought a new Buick."

Erica took this in for a moment, wondering if it changed anything.

"Carlson?" she prompted.

"I changed my name when we moved. I changed yours, too, so

there wouldn't be questions." She draped the hair over the arm of the sofa. "You were Maria Carlson. But it never fit you. Even when you were a baby."

"Is this why we have no other family?"

"They wanted to stay in touch, the mother, the sister." She shook a Lark out of a pack and lit it fast. She exhaled. "I never liked them, they never liked me and I just wanted to get away from this whole scene," she said heatedly. "Everyone calling us, threatening us, the whole Union after us, shouting at me at the market, 'Elena, is that a new dress? Where'd you get the money?' "

"Elena?"

"Elena Krupalski Carlson. When I got to New York, I legally changed it to Geri King. The end of Elena Krupalski Carlson, wife of a thief, wife of a suicide."

"But he wasn't a thief, according to that guy."

Geri exhaled and shook her head in disgust. "He was a thief."

"But what about the secretary?"

"That's an interesting admission, don't you think?" She stubbed out the cigarette. "My take on it? They were in it together," she said, her eyes like slits. "Your father and this little clerical error. That was just his style."

"Why did you say that Sheldon was your lawyer?"

"Because I don't have a lawyer."

"That doesn't *make* him a lawyer; you should get a lawyer."

"I'm a single gal—why should I have a lawyer?"

SHELDON LINZER wasn't a lawyer, but he *was* an ethics specialist.

"Take the money," he said immediately.

"He was a thief."

"Did *you* profit from it?"

"No, he was caught before he could really spend it. Well, the Buick. But I gave that back right after the funeral."

"And you received no monies from his pension, his life insurance? No compensation after all these years? What are they offering?"

"I don't know—I wanted him out of my apartment."

"Shall I find out for you?"

"Yes. By the way, I said you were my lawyer."

Sheldon called back later that night.

"They want to offer you a onetime sum of $100,000 in restitution for the misunderstanding. I think we can get a hundred plus some."

"Plus some what?"

"Well, my fee."

"Your *fee*?"

"For legal services."

"But you're not a lawyer."

"They don't know that."

She exhaled sharply. "I know for a fact that my husband, that vermin, did steal from the Union."

"The Union itself is theft," Sheldon reasoned. "They're stealing from their members. The money he stole was probably earmarked for someone's Florida condo. That's why he was caught so soon. Why should *you* suffer?"

"How would they pay me?"

"In cash."

Geri considered this. "I don't like that."

"You don't like a hundred thousand in cash? What are you, nuts?"

So GERI ACCEPTED a onetime payment. It arrived with the same man from Chicago, neatly stacked, like drug money on TV, in a hard black suitcase. Sheldon wanted to be there, but a new widow was having a pancreatic crisis.

"You can't have all this cash here," Erica said. "It's not safe. On the other hand, if you put it in the bank, they'll want to know where you got it. Is it legal?"

"I don't know."

"Get a lawyer, Geri. Looks like you can afford one."

Geri called Sheldon, who told her that she could take a suitcase of

money to a bank in Switzerland, and no one would ask her where got it.

After a few weeks, Geri decided that they didn't have to go Geneva. It was easier to stay at home, taking money out of shoebox in the various closets.

❖

One night that same summer, Erica returned home to find Mr. Urbino, the Head of the Math Department, sweating on the sofa, holding one of her mother's delicate porcelain coffee cups in his enormous hand. He avoided looking at her.

After he'd gone, Geri calmly washed up cups and saucers in the kitchen.

"Mr. Urbino is married, Geri," Erica told her mother.

"I know." Geri sighed.

"His son was in my Italian class," she accused.

"I know."

"Is there no shame in this household?"

Geri laughed out loud. "I guess not!" She cackled delightedly for a moment, and then she got serious. "I want you to know that I would never get myself into this situation if I didn't feel strongly that he is *the one*."

Erica went into her room and slammed the door. She happened to know her mother's version of the ideal man did not wear white shirts with yellow stains in the armpits, or faded brown corduroys. Mr. Urbino was the one *what*?

CHAPTER FIVE

On an inky black day in late December, Sprague communed with the Friedman, Greiff and Slavin files while drinking thick, over-boiled, life-sustaining coffee at his desk. Mitch Greiff had lingered over their lives for months, without materializing. The investigation had gone off on tangents: Celestina's business manager, personal assistant and driver. Jerry Fabrikant's money manager, personal assistant, driver. Sonny McPhain's personal trainer, personal assistant, driver. The married bond trader keeping company with Heather Perkins.

Sprague and Ballestrino had been back to Friedman, Greiff and Slavin at least two dozen times. Collectively and independently, they'd pumped the staff and partners for details about their own lives, each other's lives and Mitch Greiff's life. They'd uncovered a snake pit of personal discontent and corporate dysfunction, but they were no closer to the fugitive. The stories about him were all from five or ten years earlier. It seemed people had stopped seeing Mitch Greiff long before he left.

Sprague took a powdered-sugar doughnut from a box. What made Mitch Greiff do what he'd done? He had all the money he needed to support his life—a nice life. Why now, and not earlier? The only thing that might explain the theft, and the magnitude of the theft, was an

expensive habit. But no one had mentioned anything particular, aside from arrogance, a lack of professional ambition and a tendency to drone on about his fish tank.

Why had it been Greiff, and not Friedman, or Slavin, for example? Respect? Fear of punishment? Would Greiff have stolen $103 as easily as he had apparently stolen $103 million? He didn't have a previous history of theft, although the son did, and Greiff's father had been accused of cheating at canasta at his beach club in the fifties, although nothing had been proved.

In fact, Mitch Greiff seemed to be indifferent to money. Had he done it as revenge? He hadn't shafted anyone who had owed him money. According to Friedman, Greiff had only taken from clients who had paid their bills, partners who owed him nothing and his best friend/lawyer, Landau, who'd apparently hooked him into the partnership in the first place.

Something didn't add up. People steal to rectify imbalances. People steal to get over on other people. Mitch Greiff was the last person you'd think would need to get over on anyone: he was the one who'd had all the breaks.

LATER THAT AFTERNOON, Sprague sat in front of Erica King. Ultimately, everyone wants to confess. Creating the appropriate atmosphere was the key. He went to her office, where she was comfortable and in control. He'd gone alone; Ms. King seemed to dislike Ballestrino as much as he disliked her.

He began to create a tone.

"You know, I'm impressed with how on top of everything you are."

"I do my job," she said, eyes on her monitor.

"It's been a pleasure working with you."

She looked up with slight amusement. "Whatever you need."

"You know, Ms. King, you're much too smart to be cutting checks for other people's phone bills," he tried.

She raised a thick eyebrow. "It's a living."

"You have a law degree: ever think of going into that?"

"I really don't think much about it."

"I have friends in the Manhattan DA's office," he said softly. "I could introduce you. . . ."

"That's kind of you, Detective." She sighed, fatigued. "I worked there one summer during law school. I decided that I wouldn't be very good at that."

"You'd be great at that—"

"What else can I help you with?" She cut him off.

So much for the schmooze. "When did you notice this new voice-mail account?" Sprague handed her a folder.

"I don't remember noticing that account."

"What do you mean, you didn't notice it?"

"I mean, for someone who really doesn't like telephones, Jerry Fabrikant has a lot of ways to stay in touch. May I?" she said, and walked into the hall.

She returned and spread the magnitude of Jerry Fabrikant's communications files over her desk. Jerry had four houses, with two phone lines in each house. He had several cell phones, some that worked in the East, and some that worked in the West. When he traveled abroad, he rented cell phones there. Plus he paid for cell phones for his driver, assistant, cook, maid, trainer-masseuse-nutritionist.

Sprague watched her carefully. "This firm is going belly-up, isn't it?"

She laced her fingers in a closed gesture and gave him her deadpan look.

"You looking for work?" he asked.

"Everyone is."

"Mind if I ask where you're looking?"

"Thank you for your concern, Detective; I'll keep you posted."

Life had dealt her a difficult hand: according to Angie, the Office Manager, her father was killed in a car crash when Erica was three, and her mother was dead of cancer when Erica was twenty-three. Plain-Jane looks, personality of a corpse. Unmarried, without many interests, he thought, and then he remembered *Polyunsaturated Mad*.

A difficult hand, but no hand is unplayable. He would catch her.

❖

Patricia stared into the magnification mirror, horrified by her skin. This mirror, the table it stood on and the chair in front of it were the only furniture left in her bedroom, besides the bed. Porcelain, silver, art—all gone. Each time she walked through the vacant, dusty rooms she felt run over.

The apartment was on the market. The house was on the market. She'd started street parking. She needed money, but if she couldn't find any, there was nothing more, really, that they could do to her.

The phone rang, interrupting her appraisal of pouches, blotches, shadows, snaking red lines and extra skin on her neck. It was Marcia Clave, calling to announce that a New York–based production company had expressed interest in buying Patricia's life story for a TV movie.

"Not interested."

"Don't turn your nose up. We could work out a nice deal."

"I couldn't possibly. But thank you."

"What if I got you the right to play yourself?" Marcia said, dealing. "As a mature adult, of course. Someone else would play you up to the age of thirty-five."

Patricia growled in frustration.

"Okay, thirty."

"You aren't getting it."

"No, I'm not. I'm trying to get you some money. I thought you needed it."

"Yes, but I won't strip on national television, not for any amount of money."

"They said nothing about nudity." They both hung up.

Where was her husband? Not that she cared: she just wanted to know. To put it to rest. If she'd divorced him, she could have avoided this bizarre third act. She'd been so close. Five, ten, even fifteen years ago. Even last year she'd been on the brink. But she lost her nerve: she couldn't make the first phone call.

The phone rang. "I found the greatest guy for you," Cynthia said.

"Guy?" The word was quaint. It hadn't applied in this context in thirty years.

"A guy! Cultured, elegant, intelligent, he knows everybody, he's a winner."

"And?"

"Specifics? He's a retired financier, but he's very busy with all sorts of things. He lives in Denver, but he's in town this week, and I thought I'd have him over for dinner—unless you'd find it awkward with me and Jack there."

"Age?"

"Seventy-six."

"He's seventy-six?"

"Yes, that's what I said; he's seventy-six."

"He's seventy-six and he lives in Denver? And this is terrific?"

"He's a fun guy."

"You met him?"

"I? No. But Lois said he's got a beautiful house in the mountains, and he's a lot of fun. Come on. What have you got to lose?"

"Seventy-six and he lives in Denver." There was no one available *under* the age of seventy-six, *even* in Denver. And forget about New York: there wasn't even *one* seventy-six-year-old male available in New York.

"I'm trying," Cynthia warned.

"So don't try, then, if you find it so trying to try."

She went back to the horror of the vertical lines that intersected her upper lip. The phone rang again immediately. It was Lenore.

"I think it would be a good idea for you to have more of a social life," said her mother-in-law. "A man in your life would be very good for everyone."

"Anyone in particular you had in mind?"

"Yes! That nice lawyer at the beach club who got divorced last year."

"You're right: I could use a lawyer. Shall I hire him to sue your son?"

"You could call him up and ask him out to lunch. For advice about your situation." Patricia's mother-in-law was of the generation that told you to go break your arm to meet a cute doctor.

"STOP. If you want legal advice, Lenore, I suggest you call a lawyer, and you meet him or her. It's about legal advice. It's not about lunch."

"You have lunch, you get advice, you go out to dinner, you get involved, he takes an interest in you, he meets your family over dinner."

Patricia had learned, over the years, to listen very carefully to Lenore. "Where would you like to go to dinner?" she asked.

"Oh!" There was a flutter of excitement. "I would love to try that new Italian place that was written up in the *Times*."

"I will take you out Thursday night at eight o'clock."

"I can't eat," Lenore said breathlessly, "so late at night. It just sits there." Patricia imagined her knocking her bony chest. "I need five small meals a day."

The marriage was over, but the in-laws remained.

Mitch had a regulation amount of Jewish guilt. What had happened to him, that he was able to completely forget about his mother? Furthermore: the man couldn't leave the house without his credit card, couldn't go to a restaurant without a reservation, even for lunch.

Forget where he was living: *where was he eating?*

❖

The Chief of Detectives was leaning on the Inspector, the Inspector was leaning on the Captain, the Captain was leaning on the Lieutenant and the Lieutenant was leaning on Sprague and Ballestrino. Everything came to a head on a snowy Tuesday in the midst of the Christmas craziness; the FBI demanded the establishment of a task force.

"This has to be a Federal case?" Greeley paced in front of the Captain's desk. "Fine. I'll dance with Secret Service, Treasury or even the Postal Inspectors. But I will not work with the FBI: they've screwed me over once too often." He looked ill, as usual.

"Treasury, Postal and Secret Service aren't calling me every five minutes to start up a task force," the Captain said.

"Last time, they took my informant, and denied me access to him." The Lieutenant paced as he vented. "They *deliberately* burned me."

All heads nodded in sympathy.

"You notice they don't make mistakes? Nothing they ever do is a mistake."

"How would anybody know?" Sprague agreed. "*They* don't hang their dirty laundry out to dry on the front page."

"They want a task force because they don't *have* anything," Greeley shouted.

"I hear you." The Captain picked up his ringing phone. He listened for a while. "The case should go to Interpol, if it goes anywhere," he said finally. "The Cayman Island banks don't respect the Feds any more than they respect us."

He listened some more, tried to speak, was interrupted and finally said, "Thank you" four times. He sent regards to somebody's wife and kids. He hung up and smiled. "Okay, boys, make it good. I just bought you one last chance."

Sprague leaned forward. "Remember Erica King?"

"You know I have CRS," the Captain announced. "Can't Remember Shit."

"I have that too," Sprague said.

"When'd you get it?"

"Can't remember." They both laughed. Greeley stiffened.

"We got the pinks on her, if you want them," Ballestrino said like an earnest recruit, showing the Captain the case folder bulging with pink DD-5s.

The Captain gave him a thin smile. He preferred oral briefings.

Sprague took over and refreshed the Captain's memory about Ms. King.

"Could we have a look at her again?" Sprague asked. "I have a feeling."

The Captain crossed his hands behind his head. "Okay, what do you want?"

"However much time you could spare. Two, three days?"

"Round the clock?"

"Well, she's an office slave. I doubt she's carousing in the wee hours, but let's keep a team on her overnight, to be safe. See what happens."

JOE FAUSTO AND CECILE BIALKIN of Surveillance followed Erica King for three days, and returned with the following report:

She left her apartment at seven-thirty in the morning, and took the Third Avenue bus to the office. She ate a bag lunch at the Citicorp Center at twelve-fifteen and returned to the office. At seven-thirty P.M., she went home. And stayed there. The next day was the same, except she'd either brought her lunch or ordered in, worked until seven and went home. And stayed there. The third day, she left home at seven-thirty, walked to Citicorp at twelve-ten, hit the drugstore on the way back to the office (soap) and stayed at work until eight. She picked up dinner at a bagel place around the corner from her apartment, went directly home and stayed there. She didn't have a cell phone. All her calls from the office were work-related; there was no chatting. During this time, she made one phone call from home: to the weather bureau.

"Now I'm remembering why I forgot about her," the Captain said, upon hearing this report. "You got anybody else to follow?"

Everyone in the firm had been tailed. Heather Perkins was still seeing the married bond trader once a week at the SoHo Grand. The married bond trader was also seeing other women at the SoHo Grand, but these he paid. Charlie Tierney was renting Scorsese movies, while his wife was studying for the GMAT. Juan Mendez was training a puppy and dating a male nurse. Glenn Friedman played squash four times a week and chewed out his wife every night in a different swanky restaurant on the Upper East Side. Marty Slavin bought the most expensive chopped liver in town and wouldn't let his wife eat it. Angela, the Office Manager, had found a new job and was about to quit. Patricia Greiff was holed up in an empty apartment. She had to let her housekeeper go, because she couldn't pay her. Conchita Santos, her housekeeper, was doing part-time cleaning and childcare, and dating a FedEx employee in the Bronx. Brian Greiff was dealing and probably using cocaine; he saw his psychiatrist twice a week. His live-in girlfriend, Ivy Pelt, was abusive to her clerical staff; she saw her psychiatrist three times a week. Randy Greiff had an impressive juvenile record of bibliokleptomania. On the day the wire transfers were made from the Columbia Law School library, he'd been caught loitering in the rare book stacks at the Huntington Library, in Pasadena.

"Nobody left," Sprague said glumly.

"I am not working in a goddamn task force with the Federal Bureau of Incompetence," the Lieutenant said. "If we can't keep them out, then let's just give them the case. They'd push us around and take credit for our work anyway."

"Okay, then," the Captain said. "Let's move on."

The case was closed, pending further developments; all their notes, disks and boxes of bank records were sent to storage. On the way back to his office, the Lieutenant tossed two new cases at them simultaneously, almost vindictively.

Geri King, the school Nurse, and Mr. Urbino, the Head of the Math Department, were caught kissing in the back of the auditorium during third period; Miss Walsh (of the second abortion that everyone had mysteriously come to know about) informed the Principal, and the entire school was buzzing about it by lunch.

Erica King and the shy, emaciated Danny Urbino were instant celebrities. Wherever she went, she felt examined. Erica could not forgive her mother.

Mr. Urbino immediately called Geri, crying, to say that he couldn't see her again, ever. He left the school, not voluntarily, after midterms. Geri also left then, replaced by a stern older woman with no bedside manners. Danny Urbino stayed through Christmas, then transferred out. As a favor to Geri, Erica was allowed to finish the year at Bradley. The six months were excruciating.

Geri waited a decent interval before calling her friends (at home, of course) to come over for vodka, cigarettes, lo mein and commiseration. Miss Walsh and Miss Kaiser turned her down; both said (Miss Kaiser with a little more embarrassment) that they didn't feel right associating with her anymore.

Geri burst into tears at the table and said that Erica was her only friend, and that friendship was bullshit, and so were men.

Geri was back with Sheldon a minute and a half later. He dropped a grieving widow like a hot potato when Geri showed up at the Center in acute distress. He found her a part-time job as an administrator at a senior citizens' center in the neighborhood. Although bitter not to be working as a Nurse, Geri didn't, for whatever reason, pursue leads on any nursing jobs.

PS 125 was a godsend for Erica. Nobody spoke to her, and that was fine. She did her work, answered questions correctly and reveled in anonymity. She could almost forget about the scorching she'd taken at the Bradley School.

❖

Although some of Erica's community service activities had been reduced by attrition (Delia Pleasance died), Theresa Collecelli and Dorothy Findlay were declining rapidly, and needed daily help. Davey Findlay had graduated from one assisted living facility, but hadn't yet qualified for another. Each time Erica went to help Dorothy, Davey grabbed his crotch and rubbed obscenely, screaming, "Charlie! Charlie likes Erica!"

Erica spent an afternoon avoiding him as he chased her around the house while his mother pretended not to notice. Unlike many of the teenagers at his facility, Dorothy told her, while Erica changed her sheets, Davey was functional in the day-to-day-living department, and very proud of brushing his teeth.

Davey was over six feet tall, and rather handsome, with curly dark brown hair and light blue eyes. Had he been all there, Davey would have been a catch. But he had a dense and dented look and spoke in an underwater singsong drone. Sometimes he stopped in the middle of a conversation to stand rigidly, with his head cocked, listening intently, as if receiving satellite transmissions.

One day after school, Davey cornered Erica in the kitchen, and rubbed himself up against her rear end. It was pleasant. After she fed Dorothy, gave her pills to swallow and pulled the shades down for her nap, she did the dishes while Davey fondled her breasts. She could stop this at any moment, but for some reason, perhaps curiosity, perhaps pure desire, she let things go on. He pulled her into his room, which was decorated with dinosaurs and toy trucks.

She smelled something odd. "When does Davey take a bath?"

"Never!" He grabbed her sweater, plucking at her breasts.

"Does Davey take a shower?"

"Davey takes a shower. Erica." He groaned, pulling her to the bed.

She smelled his hair while he buried his head in her chest. She pulled him into the bathroom. "Erica will give Davey a shower."

And she did. She dried him off, and followed him back into his room.

"Heavy Charlie." He moaned as she got on top of him.

She shushed him. "Quiet, Davey. Dorothy is sleeping."

She tried not to think about him, or his mother next door, or the SATs she should be studying for, the groceries and mail for Theresa, the medicine for Maddie. She tried not to imagine her mother doing this with Sheldon, or Mr. Urbino, or her father. She opened her eyes to look at him. Davey was blissful and unaware. Would she rot in hell for this?

❖

They didn't discuss anything, but Erica applied only to New York colleges. She wondered about the wisdom of this, but the financial aid was better, and she was so busy, the idea of adding on extra applications was not appealing.

She had a hard time getting Davey to enjoy himself discreetly. On the other hand, he was always screaming and singing and making obscene noises. Erica wanted to believe Dorothy didn't know, but couldn't be sure.

"Oh, Erica," Dorothy said, weak and flustered when she arrived to change her bed linen. "It's nice you're coming around so often, you're the only one Davey and I see lately. He just adores your visits."

"My pleasure, Dorothy," Erica said, feeling wretched and deceitful.

She was getting very relaxed with Davey. One afternoon, instead of wrapping her head in a towel, she took her wig off in the shower with him.

He was delighted. "No hair! No hair!"

Afterward, she took her pleasure on his bed with a flock of rubbed-raw stuffed animals watching from the windowsill.

"I love Erica," Davey droned afterward, playing with her fingers.

"I love Davey."

"Erica loves me," he said gleefully, wiggling in the bed.

Was this so wrong?

THE NEXT VISIT, he was on top of her before she'd even put down the groceries at the kitchen table. "Take off hair," he screamed, and plucked her wig off. Dorothy's face blanched in horror. She spilled coffee all over herself.

He danced around the living room with the hair, cackling. Erica ignored him, and focused on cleaning up with a sponge. "Charlie likes Erica."

"Bad Davey, put it back," Dorothy warned, not looking at Erica.

He wasn't too bright, but you couldn't have everything. Older, taller, charming in an offbeat way and he walked by himself. She could do the rest.

Still, she couldn't tell her mother. What would Geri say?

WHAT GERI DID was come running into Erica's bedroom with a paper-white face. "Why did you not tell me that Davey was bothering you?"

"He wasn't bothering me."

"Dorothy said that she thought he had molested you."

"He didn't molest me."

"I thought she was out of her mind," Geri said, relieved. "She said she saw you in bed with him."

Dorothy couldn't have *seen* anything, Erica thought. She might have heard something, or Davey might have told her something. Why deny it?

"Yes. I went to bed with him."

There was a moment of silence while this sank in.

Geri's face flushed purple. "Are you out of your mind?"

"Is it so strange? I like him."

"How long has this been going on?"

"Since last year."

Geri put her hand to her mouth and disappeared into her bedroom like a shot. Half an hour later, she opened Erica's door (no knock, in spite of all the signs) and insisted that Erica go to a therapist. She would understand if Erica didn't want to see Sheldon, although Sheldon was free.

"You get what you pay for," Erica said, glad it was out in the open.

"YOU KNOW THAT YOUR FRIEND is not capable of adult conversation," said the shrink, stroking his mustache. He was, at Erica's request, not even a friend of Sheldon's. He didn't look like a therapist. He looked like a cop. "He is not capable of using money, going out by himself, driving a car."

"Well, I can't drive a car either."

"Fair enough. So would you say it's mainly physical?"

"Yes. What's wrong with that? I've had mainly physical situations with other guys—normal, so-called—and I didn't even know or like them half as much."

"Yes? Other guys?" The shrink was interested now. "Tell me."

"You go watch a dirty movie," Erica said, hot and annoyed, "and stop prying into my life. I don't think what I did, what we did, was wrong."

"Would you take him home to meet your mom, or introduce him to friends?"

"Is that the test? Well, I don't have friends, and my mother is the reason I'm over there three times a week. If she thought it was such a horrible thing, why'd she send me there?"

"You were there to take care of Davey's mother."

"And I did. I do. You're missing the point. We're not getting married. We're just having fun. Who's getting hurt?"

The shrink was silent, his black glasses opaque with beige squares of light in the gloom of his room. "Don't you want more for yourself?"

"Who'd you have in mind? You think they're lining up around the block?"

In spite of Erica's request, her mother was waiting for her in the waiting room. In spite of Erica's request, Geri went to talk to the therapist afterward.

Erica stalked out. She bought a pack of Marlboros and stole a tin of cough drops at a deli around the corner from the shrink. She walked home down Fifth Avenue, smoking furiously, chewing on the numbing lozenges.

Of course, Geri was at home smoking in her bra when she got there. When was Geri not at home smoking in her bra? Geri immediately insisted that she come with her to get makeup at a department store.

"Is that what the psychotherapist told you? That I needed makeup? This was his *professional* opinion?"

She slammed out of the house and stalked over to the Findlays'. Dorothy was out of bed, standing bent but firm at the door to prevent her nineteen-year-old son from having twenty minutes of fun with a normal seventeen-year-old girl. "Hi, Dorothy."

"Erica bad!" Davey shouted.

"Your mother's going to be taking over from now on. We don't need you."

"I'm here to see Davey. Davey, would you like to go out for a walk?"

"Where? Where are you taking him, you pervert?"

"No fighting!" he shrieked.

"Don't you see he's fragile? Did you think for a minute beyond yourself?"

"Davey, you want to take a walk?"

"No, Davey. You stay here. Erica, get out and don't come back."

"Davey." She pushed through into the foyer.

Dorothy: "No, Davey."

Erica: "Yes, Davey!"

Davey: "Bad Erica!"

And on it went, pushing and pulling and struggling by the front door, the chain lock swinging as Dorothy pushed Erica out the door and Erica's head knocked into the doorjamb, and a hand got caught in the door that Dorothy slammed. Davey howled in pain. The door bounced open. Dorothy leaned against the door of the coat closet and dropped to the floor.

Leaving Dorothy there where she landed, Erica took Davey to the emergency room holding ice in a towel around his hand. On the plastic seats in the waiting room, he vocalized like a whale for the first half hour. People stared, people moved away. Then suddenly he was quiet.

"Mommy doesn't like Erica," he said.

"Does Davey like Erica?"

"No talking," he said tersely, and began rocking.

Her head was throbbing where she'd hit it. "Erica likes Davey," she said, as miserable as she'd ever been in her life. "Does Davey like Erica?"

"Charlie likes Erica." Davey patted her knee. "Davey doesn't know."

After the X ray and treatment, she took him home. He rushed into his mother's room to show her his splint. Erica left without saying good-bye.

❖

The fugitive woke at eight-fifteen—late for him, but then, he'd been too keyed-up to sleep the night before. He padded to the door and peeked out the front window. The day was dazzlingly bright. Should he wait for the street to empty of people on their way to work, to minimize his exposure? Or should he be coming and going during the rush hours, so as to be less noticeable? He looked like a caricature of guilt. He needed to lie low until he could grow some facial hair and approximate a normal face. A man in shorts tootled by on a bicycle. It looked like a Saturday.

It *was* Saturday, he remembered suddenly, sitting with his back up against the front door. It was Saturday of Labor Day weekend. He couldn't wait till people went to work: now he'd have to plunge into the weekend scene, who knew what it was, in this neighborhood.

He'd spent the night pacing around the dark, dingy house in a paranoid frenzy. He was starving. There was nothing in the kitchen, and he was afraid to go out or to call to have something delivered. And whom would he call? At about eleven-thirty, he scalded himself pouring boiling water over instant oatmeal.

From his many years as the creator of a tropical Ecosystem in a 200-gallon reef tank, Mitch Greiff understood that you could control many factors—heat, light, water, food—but there would always be something beyond your control, something disintegrating, something dying, something popping up out of nowhere to attack, take over, add nitrates. You could get a protein skimmer, but it might agitate the fish or send water gushing all over the floor. Even if you got it working properly, you might still have algae growing in sheets on your rocks, and slime covering the bottom of your tank. You could introduce less-powerful lights, to limit the photosynthesis of the algae invasion. But then your coral might get ill.

If there was one thing Mitch had learned from being a father—a father of two of the most impossible children that had ever walked, sucked a pacifier till the age of thirteen or begun a life of crime at the age of three—it was that you can't control other people.

And if there was one thing Mitch had learned in business, it was that you could give a simple order and you might just be ignored.

He'd told her to call it off. He'd told her that he wasn't ready, and she'd breezed right by him because she knew better, because *she* had been ready, because *her* momentum was carrying *her* along.

Mitch wasn't sure if his presence would be noticed in the house (another thing they should have talked about beforehand), so he turned out the lights and listened to the news in the bed with his ear on the radio, like a rhythm-starved teenager in an old rock-'n'-roll movie, petrified that the sound would give him away. He kept the lights off. He ran in and out of the bathroom all night, shuddering with diarrhea and cramps.

In the morning he used the mouthwash in the medicine cabinet, but couldn't bring himself to use someone else's toothbrush. Was it hers? He had no idea. All his clothes were at one of her apartments, the one he liked the least. He was supposed to have moved it all over by now, but he'd dragged his feet, and so he'd arrived with just the clothes he had on.

If there was one thing he'd learned as a human being and a tax accountant, it was that planning was vital. None of these issues would be problems now if he'd come here ahead of time, stocked up on food, for example. But he hadn't been ready to follow through. He had made lists of the things he needed to do, but he hadn't done any of them. Now he was starving. He was operating at a deficit now, trying to catch up.

IT WAS IRONIC THAT IN QUEENS, you could have a (tiny) lawn and a house, and a driveway right in front for your car, at probably one-tenth of what he'd paid for his apartment. He'd be living better in Jackson Heights than he ever did on the Upper East Side, he'd joked when he saw it the first time. Of course the house was a tacky redbrick box, with black iron railings over cracked concrete steps, and a chain-link fence. Neighbors in the exact replica of this house across the street had planted their lawn with plastic gnomes, which sneered at him as he contemplated leaving the house.

Inside there was an aura of intermittent attention: Someone had been thoughtful enough to exterminate, but hadn't been back to sweep the dead insects off the windowsills. Someone had chosen opulently styled cheap furniture in various shades of cream, and hadn't been back to do something about all the stains. Patricia, of course, would have been in and out of the place every day with new lamps and fabric swatches, even for a furnished rental in Queens. He'd assumed Erica would fix it up before he moved in.

She hadn't. Well, why should she? She had a full-time job and three apartments, after all. Had she assumed *he* would decorate? It was impossible to know what went through her mind, and asking her questions was trickier and trickier, now that she'd lost her temper with him.

The air conditioners worked, thank God.

At one-twenty that afternoon, he couldn't take it anymore. He beeped her.

She called right back.

"There's nothing to eat here!" he barked.

"Why not?"

"I didn't get food yesterday," he admitted.

"Why not?"

He was supposed to take the previous day to stock the refrigerator, move his things in, do everything on the final list. Instead, he'd spent the day at Tower Records; he had ten brand-new discs, and nothing to play them on. He hung up and ran to the bathroom again.

The next conversation, ten minutes later:

"I'm hungry!"

"Look," she said. "I can't run over there every time you want a sandwich. You're going to have to make your own arrangements."

He had to be careful, the way he spoke to her. She wasn't working for him anymore, not in the same way. He recalled several occasions when Erica had bitten someone's head off when she felt harassed or cornered.

"What should I do?"

"Get some food."

"You think that's safe?"

"Are you hungry or not? Wear the hat and glasses."

"What hat and glasses?"

"Look in the hall closet. I got you a hat and glasses."

"I'm really not comfortable with this. Could you come here?"

"I'll be done around seven-thirty."

He felt a shudder of fear and hunger. He had cramps. "What should I do until then?"

"Order Chinese."

"I have terrible diarrhea!"

"Order from that coffee shop on Roosevelt Avenue."

"You think it's safe?"

AT TWO O'CLOCK he rushed out of the house. It was sweltering; he had to slow down. A few people were out, washing their cars, tending their parched lawns and wilted plants in bathing suits or housedresses. He felt conspicuous in his business pants. He took off his shirt and tied it around his waist. In his undershirt, he headed toward the pizza place on the corner, two long, hot blocks away. The houses were identical boxes, built of the same red brick, and they went on and on. Each one strived for originality in window treatments, lawn ornaments and number display. Were streets longer in Queens?

Three people looked up as he entered the pizzeria, and a greasy garlic smell assaulted him. He backed out quickly and continued to the corner, where he'd seen a phone in front of the gas station on 35th Avenue.

"I'm really not comfortable being out," he whispered, while nearby a man covered in tattoos wiped an auto part on a blackened rag.

"So grab a pizza and eat it back at the house."

"It smells awful there. And it'll be cold by the time I get it home."

"What is the matter with you?" she asked, as if she really wanted to know. "If the temperature of the pizza is important to you—"

"I hate pizza," he interjected.

"So why didn't you get your sirloin and glamorous side dishes yesterday, when you were supposed to? Why are you bothering me with this nonsense?"

What was he doing? He was on the lam in an empty, tacky house in Queens, totally dependent on this high-strung, difficult woman. Had he lost his mind? He bought cookies, candy and soda at the gas station. He made it back to the house, receiving stares from the few pedestrians on his new street. Things couldn't get any worse.

But when he used the bathroom again, his heart nearly stopped: the toilet didn't flush. He flushed again, and the water rose dangerously near the rim of the bowl. His hands began to shake.

He was on the lam in an empty, dirty house with a broken toilet, totally dependent on a high-strung, difficult woman who probably didn't know how to use a plunger. The toilet began to overflow. He was staying in an unsanitary hovel like a refugee. He'd left a perfectly lovely Park Avenue apartment to live in Queens without the comforts of food and working plumbing. If he didn't already, he would soon have amoebic dysentery.

CHAPTER SIX

Erica wore Marjorie's black pantsuit with the gold buttons for the interview. She put on real shoes, tasteful jewelry, makeup and Marjorie's blond hair. It was a milestone.

Before Erica had a chance to deliver her practiced speech, the Director of Personnel sat down heavily, and delved into the details of her own fertility treatments for a good ten minutes. The woman's head nodded as she spoke, at first slightly, then in an exaggerated fashion. Erica restrained her head from automatically nodding along.

"The emotional impact . . ." continued the Director of Personnel, with a catch in her voice. "Nobody prepares you."

"How long have you worked here?" Erica tried to change the subject.

"Six years. It's a good company. Excellent benefits, maternity leave, once it happens," she said, and knocked on the desk three times.

"Come in," Erica called.

"What?"

"You knocked three times, and I said come in."

"I knocked on wood that I should get pregnant."

"Perhaps I'm in the wrong place." Erica smiled. "I'm here for an interview with the Director of Personnel. About working for this firm."

"I'm just so nervous. It's the third time and my husband says it has to be the last. You know that tone of voice husbands sometimes get?"

Erica put on a professional smile. "I'd like to talk to you about what I've been doing at Friedman, Greiff and Slavin for the last ten years."

"Of course. I don't see letters of reference here." She patted a folder.

"Let me confide in you." Erica chose her words with care. "You may have heard about my boss, Mitch Greiff."

"No!"

"Yes. Mitch Greiff would have been my main reference, as he was the partner I worked with most closely. I can certainly get a reference, but I didn't want to alert anyone at the firm that I was contemplating a move."

"Of course," the woman said. No doubt she would tell everyone she knew. "What was he like to work for?"

"Smart, fair, respectful of my time. A terrific boss."

"Unbelievable." The Director of Personnel now ushered her into a conference room, and sat her down in a lush leather chair. She brought in several partners, and introduced Erica as "a very talented accountant who has spent ten years at"—here she dropped her voice—"Friedman, Greiff and Slavin, working directly with *Mitch Greiff*, whom I'm sure you remember? Erica has asked that this visit be off the record."

The senior men shook her hand slowly. "Do you have any clients whom you think might be in need of a new firm?" asked the oldest partner.

"All of Mitch's clients are switching firms, and many of the firm's clients who worked with different partners are considering a change."

She could feel the room getting moist.

"I understand you have offices in Chicago." Erica stepped up.

"Does that interest you?" asked the youngest partner.

"Yes."

"Call Jerry in Chicago, make an appointment for Ms. King to fly out there and meet with them," the youngest partner said to the Director of Personnel, who went to a telephone and did just that.

ERICA CHANGED WIGS in the ladies' room of an Irish bar opposite Bloomingdale's, and walked back to her office.

"Nice suit," called Charlie.

"And look at the makeup!" said Heather.

"Who's that?" said Glenn, in all seriousness.

She cut right by them, and sat down at her desk with the door closed.

Someone pounded on her door.

She scanned her office for things out of place. She'd been interviewed on five separate occasions by Detective Dennis Sprague, sometimes alone, sometimes with the overconfident Italian sidekick. It had been two weeks since she'd seen him. The police might be following her or not. Presumably, they had access—legal or otherwise—to everything there was to know about her. They might be tapping her phone or not. They might be aware of her beeper or not. Not knowing what they knew, she would continue to be careful. She wiped off Marjorie's lipstick, readied herself for more questions and opened her door.

"It's a bad-hair day," Heather entered, fluffing up her natural, growing hair, and sitting down without being invited to do so. "Don't look at me."

Heather was there ostensibly to discuss some detail of what Glenn Friedman called "the Friedman/Slavin Recovery Plan," but what she really wanted to do was to bitch savagely for an indefinite amount of time about how Mitch Greiff had selfishly ruined everyone's life, particularly hers. She twirled her blondness while she crossed, uncrossed and recrossed her slim, bare legs self-righteously.

It wasn't enough for *her* to win. Heather had to lose.

"Heather," she interrupted, "I appreciate that you need to talk, but what makes you think that I need to hear you?"

She watched as Heather's face fell, and then recomposed itself.

"Bitch," Heather said, exiting in a flourish of hair.

The move to Chicago had not been part of the original plan, but neither had a recalcitrant partner. Mitch was not suited to life underground in Queens. She didn't want to hear about it anymore.

She called the first driver's-education company listed in the Yellow Pages.

❖

Patricia sat in front of bills, checkbooks, calculator, envelopes and stamps. Where could he go where they wouldn't be looking for him? Would he undergo plastic surgery and move to Argentina? She'd had to *beg* him to go to Paris. He hated transportation, foreign money, hotel rooms, unfamiliarity. He couldn't handle maps, peculiar toilets. At home, he couldn't go to the *dry cleaners* himself. He was like an *infant*; she'd taken care of everything. Who was doing that now?

The phone rang. Again. She was writing bad checks in an empty apartment. What the hell did they want from her? The machine said, "This is Eddie Fleisch. Marcia Clave gave me your number." The real-estate developer from the tabloids? Had Mitch stolen from him too? "Let me give you my *personal* number," he told the machine.

She called the personal number.

"I like a woman who doesn't play games. Come to dinner," he said without a pause. "I have a couple of functions tomorrow where I have to make an appearance. Come with me. We'll see and be seen, and dine afterward."

"Actually, I'm keeping a low profile lately. . . ."

"So clearly you need to get out," he said. "I'll pick you up at six-thirty. I just can't get out of these things. I'm in demand."

She thought about his five wives and assorted companions—models, cheerleaders, porn stars—and all the tall blond hair. "I can't be in the newspaper again, I just don't have the stomach for it," she said.

"No such thing as bad publicity," Eddie Fleisch sang, and hung up.

She called Marcia Clave.

"Oh, he's getting bored with the teenagers we've been sending him," Marcia explained. "I mentioned you as a wise old woman of the world, and he'd seen your picture in the paper, remembered the Sassoon ads. You'll be on Page Six tomorrow, with a very different slant—watch."

She wanted to throw up. "What kind of a man sees a woman in a scandal sheet and thinks, 'Hey, now there's a girl for me'?"

"Well, hey, a girl has to eat," said Marcia Clave. "And you haven't been intimate with a man in a long time, am I right?"

"Excuse me?"

Anyone could say anything to her, just anything.

"He could wipe out your debt with a single phone call," Marcia said fiercely. "He could make your life very easy."

"How is that different from prostitution?"

"Don't be naïve, Patricia."

She hung up the phone and looked at her unpayable bills on the floor. Who else would *want* to be seen with her?

The phone rang. What now?

"Ms. Greiff? This is Detective Ballestrino, of the Computer Crimes Squad, NYPD. How are you?"

"Detective," she said, exhausted. "I'm losing my mind in an empty apartment."

"May I invite you out for coffee?"

"You mean now?"

"No time like the present," he said. She tried to remember him. There had been so many law-enforcement people passing through.

She met him at the coffee shop on the corner. He was the dapper one with the aftershave. There was a ripple of recognition when she passed down the length of the counter. A few heads swiveled as she joined him in a small booth at the back.

"Is this about the case?"

"Yes and no." The Detective watched her carefully. "Shall we get this to go?"

They went to the counter. He ordered two regular coffees and asked for doughnuts. No more doughnuts, the Detective was told; he asked her to choose among the pastries, and paid. She thanked him. He held her elbow in his palm, directing her toward the exit in a courtly fashion.

Upstairs, in her empty living room, she slid down the wall to the floor, making an elaborate, hostesslike gesture to the floor beside her. He pinched the crisp pleats of his pants and sat down.

They both took exploratory sips of regular coffee.

"We're off the case—it's a Federal investigation now. It's been bugging me: your husband doesn't seem to have the kind of mastery of details to pull this off."

"Exactly!" she said, enjoying the sticky bun, a treat she hadn't allowed herself in perhaps thirty-five years. "He likes to think of himself as meticulous, but only so he can get somebody else to do the work and blame her. Look at the fish: *I* measured the strontium solution. *I* changed the water. Mitch is really lazy. If I were you, I'd be looking for a young, foolish woman"—here she thought of herself in 1971—"who is actually doing all the work here."

She noticed he wasn't eating his pastry. He sat up straight, and sipped in a delicate fashion; he probably didn't want to spill coffee all over his nice houndstooth jacket or his shirt and tie.

"Where is he?" The Detective crushed his coffee cup and tossed it into the carryout box. "It's driving us crazy!"

"Tell me about it!"

She finished her bun. She wondered if she might have his Danish, too. She was ravenous.

"Would someone want to harm him?" he asked.

"You mean, you think he's underground, literally?"

"It's a possibility."

"At any given moment, somebody was annoyed with Mitch. But annoyed enough to kill him? Unlikely," she decided. "But what do I know?"

Detective Ballestrino nodded. It was nice that he seemed to care about her case. He folded his napkin and tossed it in the carryout box. He still hadn't touched his Danish.

"What else is happening?"

She inhaled. "Regular calls from the bottom feeders of the press, and constant visits from collection agencies."

There was a pause.

"So what's the part that doesn't concern the case?" she asked.

He smoothed his tie down. "I was just wondering how you were doing," he said, and looked at her sweetly. He let this sink in, then leaned forward and handed her the Danish.

She tried not to, but she burst into tears.

❖

Sprague and Henry Chang had uncovered a scheme to defraud, in which the badguy, a Dutch national living in a metal container in a parking lot in Hell's Kitchen, had sold hundreds of thousands of gold Krugerrands over the Internet to thirty-six customers who had paid for them, and somehow never received them. He and Ballestrino had nailed a Colombian identity thief who created phony checks and passports out of a copy shop in Elmhurst. This twerp had completely lost his cool with Sprague, unleashing a foamy Spanish tirade into the dreary chill of the Tombs.

"*Tell* me how stupid I am," Sprague said calmly. "*You're* the one in the orange jumpsuit."

In his spare time, Sprague had begun visiting kid chat rooms as Evan, the nine-year-old *X-Men* fan. On a frigid afternoon in early February, he received an instant message from someone named Billy, whose AOL profile said he was ten years old. Billy nonetheless was the MC of this room, posing questions like, "Are genetically engineered clones sentient beings?" Billy spelled this correctly while simultaneously instant-messaging Evan to ask where he lived.

Sprague asked Ballestrino to join the room as Tim, ten-year-old *X-Men* fan, and lo and behold, Billy sent an instant message to Tim asking him where *he* lived.

"Is he local?" asked Anita Clemente, who had successfully caught more pedophiles over the Internet than anyone could count.

"I live on West 84th Street," Sprague typed. "Where do you live?"

"We are neighbors!" Billy typed. "You want to see my collection sometime?"

"Nail the bastard," the Lieutenant said in passing.

"I am cutting skool tomorrow," Sprague wrote.

"No, no, no!" Anita said. "That's too easy, he'll smell something."

"Too late, he already sent it," Ballestrino said.

"That's too teenage; nine-year-olds don't talk about cutting school," she said authoritatively.

"I did when I was nine," Sprague said.

Billy didn't return the instant message. In a moment, his name dropped off the list of the chat-room members.

"Ah, well," Sprague said, turning to Anita. "How's your steganographer?"

"Big breakthrough," she said, and returned to her desk. "One of my old colleagues in Vice got his e-mail—I have no idea how. Today's the day."

"How you gonna get him?" Tony asked.

"I'm sending him an e-mail with a key capture program," she said, passing him a piece of paper.

Sprague and Ballestrino looked over the code she'd written. This was a small program that would load into the pornographer's computer when he opened the attachment in her e-mail. "Nice," Sprague enthused.

"What are you sending to entice him?" Ballestrino asked.

"The prospect of photos of twelve-year-old boys without their pants."

If the pornographer opened the attachment, Anita's program would travel into his hard drive, and send a message back to her, saying, essentially, "I'm in," and reveal the pornographer's current location on the Internet. If she then directed her own machine to that Internet address, she'd be able to watch everything he did on his computer. She could catch every character he typed, including his passwords, and the codes he was using to encrypt the pornography he sent to his subscription members. Each time the steganographer connected to the Internet, his machine would be wide open to Anita; she could enter his hard drive and make copies of his files without his knowledge. They called this move the Trojan Horse; it required a search warrant, and had been successfully used only a few times. There were privacy issues, naturally. Hackers used the same technique to break into their targets.

"Now all I have to do is wait," Anita Clemente smiled.

SPRAGUE JUMPED when he saw the green eyes glowing in the dark of the closet: the current cat, in a new hiding spot. He shooed her out, and unsuccessfully ransacked his wardrobe for a pair of wearable pants.

"Nothing fits me either," Cathy said glumly.

Sprague didn't want to shop for new clothes. He didn't want to visit the tailor.

"Should we slim down for the summer?" Cathy asked.

"Not if it involves effort," he said.

"There's a diet that's been circulating around the clinic."

"A diet? Like specific things each meal? I don't think that's realistic."

"Well, you could give up doughnuts. I bet you'd drop twenty pounds in a month."

"Give up doughnuts," he said, hearing the prison door clanking shut.

"Or take up exercise."

He sighed. "Shopping is suddenly looking like a good alternative."

"There's that health class they give Tuesday nights at Cabrini," she said heavily. "They teach you how to make salad dressing without oil."

"I'll cut down on doughnuts. Only two a day now."

Dennis put on the pants he'd spilled duck sauce on the day before. He wondered if Erica King had her floor-sweeping skirts let out, or just went to buy new ones. Where did she find them?

———

SPRAGUE AND BALLESTRINO spent a whole day trying to figure out who had sponsored a hackfest the previous evening, when ten or twelve thousand hackers had invaded the Web site of one of the city's most important hospitals, where their host had provided free copies of a new software program before it was released to the general public. They were getting nowhere. Like most hackers, the host was too smart to use his own computer to commit the crime. They broke for an early lunch.

Sprague bit into the fried egg roll, and reluctantly asked Ballestrino what he thought was the best way to lose weight.

Ballestrino got a light in his face. He laid out the facts, speaking slowly, so as not to scare his catch. "But the most important thing is, are you going to stick with it? If not, you might as well forget it: you'll just gain more weight in the long run."

"Exactly what I told Cathy. Let's not do it."

"Or, you could make minor changes that could really add up in the long run."

"Like what?"

"Like mustard instead of mayo. Like water instead of soda. Like no Chinese, no Thai, no pizza. Like broiled instead of fried. Like no doughnuts."

Sprague spilled duck sauce down the other leg of the only pants that fit.

Back at the Building, Sprague considered Erica King. What did they know about her? She was left-handed. According to Angie, the Office Manager, her father had died in a car accident in Chicago when she was a toddler. Her mother died of cancer when Erica was in her early twenties. She graduated magna cum laude from Fordham University, and had worked on the *Fordham Law Review*. She started at Friedman, Greiff and Slavin two weeks after receiving her JD and CPA. College classmates didn't remember her. Law school classmates remembered her name, but little else.

The Lieutenant passed by. "Dennis: you don't get paid for staring into space and looking stupid."

"I'll keep that in mind, sir," he said, still focused on Erica. The case was closed, but it bothered him. She was senior accountant on many if not most of the accounts in which money had been stolen. She had no social life, and was the punch line of nasty office jokes. She had a checking account, a savings account and an IRA. She contributed heavily to her 401K plan. She had a credit card, but rarely used it. Her doormen and neighbors reported no noise, no friends and no activity. She sent her laundry and dry cleaning out, but cleaned her own apartment. She often ordered Chinese in. The delivery boy reported she gave him a one-dollar tip every time, even in the rain. She didn't have any subscriptions. She didn't have a personal e-mail address. She didn't make long-distance phone calls. She barely made local calls.

Was anyone this dull and unconnected? Dennis Sprague wondered if someone followed him, would his life look as pathetic as this?

No, he had a wife, and worked at an exciting job.

The fruit flies in his garbage can and the piles of other people's crooked paperwork scattered under dingy fluorescent lights on his broken desk mocked this idea. An exciting job, indeed. Ballestrino was right: Erica King was a black hole. She made you feel as bad as she looked.

WHEN HE ARRIVED HOME THAT NIGHT, Cathy was in a sweatsuit and actually sweating. The schnauzer was skittering around her anxiously. The kitchen was brimming with vegetables, vitamin bottles and xeroxed sheets of low-calorie recipes. A tape measure sat coiled by the toaster, ready to pounce.

"I'm afraid to ask," he said.

"Health. Fitness," she said breathlessly. "Exercise. Weight loss."

"What's for dinner?"

"I don't know," she panted. "I'm so exhausted from the shopping and the exercising that I'm too tired to deal with it."

He nodded. "Thai?"

"Fine." He dialed the number by heart, and she began putting away the healthy food. "Tomorrow," she told him, "we begin our new regimen."

"So let's get rid of the good stuff tonight. Any ice cream?"

THE FOLLOWING MORNING he arrived early and put his dietetic lunch in the departmental refrigerator. Anita was stalking the squad room looking like a wreck.

"It's a day and a half," she said. "He won't open the e-mail. What's he doing?"

"Nothing legal, probably. Go home," he told her. "Get some sleep. I'll watch your machine."

"You can't watch it all day," she said. "You have other things going on."

"Nothing interesting. If anything happens, I'll call you immediately."

She glanced back at her computer. "Wait! I'm in!"

As the squad arrived for work, everyone gathered around Anita's machine to watch as the pornographer went through his e-mail, poking into various letters, programming changes into his Web site and newsletter. Each page of his newsletter had a different photo of a naked boy under the age of fifteen, and Anita Clemente recorded it all. She browsed through his hard drive, making copies of his mailing list, his vendors and his date book. She had processed a warrant before lunch, and went out with Henry Chang in the afternoon to arrest the man.

At lunch, Sprague suffered through the dry tuna sandwich Cathy had made. The Lieutenant cruised by and caught sight of the baggie of cut carrots on his desk. "Going on a diet?"

"Considering it," Sprague said.

"Don't let your energy flag. It'll affect your work."

❖

Erica was accepted at Fordham, on a full scholarship, without housing. "What do you need a noisy dorm for, anyway?" Geri pointed out, and Erica felt a door closing on her face, violently. "The kids would drive you crazy. You stay here."

When could she escape this apartment?

Erica commuted to Fordham. Why hadn't she applied to out-of-state schools, or at least out-of-town schools? Still, she appreciated the dark Gothic campus, the enormous lecture halls with scarred old wooden seats, the intimate renovated seminar rooms with tubular metal furniture. Loved making her own schedule, loved her job in the library, loved reading on the long ride up on the 6 train.

That December, Geri discovered a new lump in the remaining breast, and went back into treatment. Erica took over all household issues, tended to the increasingly demented Theresa Collecelli, brought her mother to doctors for testing and to the hospital every three weeks for an intravenous infusion of poison. She scrambled up to the Bronx and back sometimes twice a day.

One day, when Erica arrived at Theresa's with groceries and cash from her pension check, Theresa's super pulled her aside.

"You're her niece. I seen you around here. I'm sorry."

"About what?"

"She died last night. Aw, you didn't know."

In fact, she didn't know. She wondered how Geri would handle it.

"You're the only relative, right?" Erica nodded. "That apartment. I have three people want it. But you have the right to it, under the law."

The idea of Theresa's apartment made her blood quicken. She wasn't sentimental about Theresa: Theresa was a stingy, small-minded bigot with horrifying breath. After all these years of unpaid service, here was finally compensation, of sorts. It felt right. "How much a month?"

"Three-ten. Still, these other people, they're offering key money."

This kind of a deal would never fall into her lap again. "Let me think about it," she said, fingering Theresa's pension money in her pocket. "When do you need to know?"

"By the first of the month—what's that, next week?"

WHEN ERICA GOT HOME, her mother was sitting in the dining room. Bills, insurance forms and pharmacy receipts were scattered over the table. Erica couldn't stop herself: the plan was out of her mouth before her coat was off.

Geri flew into a squall. "This is what I get?" she raged. A spot of red appeared on her cheek. "I feed you, I clothe you, I change your diapers and pay for your sleazy books, and then you leave me here to die?"

Erica burst into tears. "I am not leaving you here to die!"

Geri stalked into the kitchen and took some pills. Her hair, which had grown back finer and grayer after the first course of treatment, was falling out again. "You know, you're right," she said. "I don't want to live with you either."

Erica tried to get back into control. She wasn't deserting her mother.

They went to sleep without saying good night.

Geri woke Erica at two in the morning: she couldn't find a pen. She'd been looking and looking, she said. How was it possible that there were no pens in the entire house?

IN THE MORNING, Erica withdrew half the money in her savings account, and walked the three and a half blocks to Theresa's place.

"Here's the first month's rent, a safety deposit, and key money for you," she said, giving the super an envelope of cash, her savings plus Theresa's pension.

He looked her over. "I got other people give me more."

"Look, I'm her niece, and I have a legal right to the apartment," she said. "That I'm offering you money up front seems to me proof of good faith. You've seen me here over the years. You know I'm quiet and careful. I'd be a good tenant. I just don't have any more right now. I'm a student and my mother is sick. Okay?"

He looked her over and plucked the envelope out of her hand. "Okay."

It was interesting how the combination of truth and some lies made for an effective argument. He took her to the basement to fill out a form.

"Name."

"Maria Collecelli," she said, and signed the lease.

At a kiosk in Grand Central, she bought *House Beautiful* and *Newsweek*, and filled out subscription cards in Maria's name. When she got back that night, Geri was wandering around in a stained bathrobe. She acknowledged Erica with a disgusted nod; her face had blown up again from the medicine. Erica despised confrontations with her mother—she was outgunned, outmaneuvered, every time. Geri banged around the house, sifting through shopping bags full of outdated fliers from the Center, flinging open the kitchen cabinets, looking again for a pen.

Erica prepared dinner. She wanted to move out.

When she opened the dishwasher, she saw that the walls of the appliance were streaked a lavender blue: every ballpoint, felt tip, Magic Marker and pencil in the house was in the silverware basket or resting on the top rack.

It was time.

❖

The first time she opened Theresa's mailbox and saw a copy of *House Beautiful* addressed to Maria Collecelli, Erica felt a thrill rocket through her body. Then a comfortable stillness took over. She walked to the Epiphany branch of the New York Public Library (the Kips Bay librarians knew her) and asked for a library card in the name of Maria Collecelli, presenting her new lease.

"Any other ID with address?"

"Not *on* me," Erica said, and fished in her pocketbook. "What about this?" She flashed the *House Beautiful*, with the address label.

She walked out with a library card in Maria's name. She felt taller. She couldn't remember ever feeling so good.

All of the resentment that went into picking up Theresa Collecelli's mail turned into excitement when picking up Maria Collecelli's mail, from the very same mailbox. She was creating something. She was in the old apartment often enough: she still did the shopping, odd jobs and errands, and picked up the mail. Her mother had almost replaced Theresa in her schedule.

Geri got worse: she was in a state of constant frustration, continuously on the phone to the insurance company, the doctor's office, the hospital or Sheldon, not hearing what she wanted to hear from anybody.

Dorothy Findlay died, and Geri took over the funeral preparations. She approached the task with a grim resolve, and explained each detail of the arrangements carefully to Erica. Although she stopped short of telling Erica to take notes, Erica knew this was a dress rehearsal for Geri's own funeral. She paid for the event with some of the remaining Union cash.

"Davey will have to stay in the home permanently now," Geri said, and gave her the number of a social worker. "You're in charge of making arrangements."

"He needs to get a Social Security number," said the harried social worker. "Can you do that with him? I'm up to my neck, would you mind?"

Erica picked up Davey at Independence House, a place in the East Village where he and sixteen others were living and working. It had been four years since she'd seen him. He was unkempt and didn't interact with her. At the Social Security office, they waited on line and he moaned sporadically, asking for his mother every few minutes. She presented his birth certificate and ID card from Independence House, and they gave him a Social Security number immediately. She took him back to the home. A staff member asked if she wanted to take a tour of the facility, and she declined.

"Bad Erica!" Davey screamed.

❖

When her mother finally stopped taking care of herself, sitting and sleeping in a soiled orange terry-cloth sweat suit for weeks at a time, Erica took her to a new doctor. What was left of her hair was greasy, her unmade face was bloated, yellow and fatigued and her fingernails were ragged. Erica was applying to law school.

She rested her head on the wall for a moment.

"What kind of law would you practice?"

"Criminal defense."

"Stop it," Geri exploded. "You're scaring me."

A nurse peeked out from behind the sliding Plexiglas window.

"If it has to be crime, you go on the other side, the good guys. And second of all: public interaction, standing up in court? I don't think you'd be so great at that. I think you'd be better off behind the scenes."

Erica wanted to defend herself. But Geri had leaned her head back against the waiting room wall with her eyes closed, sealing herself off.

She pulled her head up again. "And what about a family?"

"What about it, Geri?"

"Family is the most important thing in this world."

"I can tell, by the way we spend so much time with our family."

Geri's name was called, ending this awkward line of inquiry.

❖

The experiments started, as these things do, by mistake. One day back in the cubicle period, despite rigorous attention to detail, Erica had realized she'd misplaced some municipal bond interest on a statement. She broke into a sweat. It had vanished completely. Could the rest of the office see how terrified she was?

She retraced her steps, number by number, line by line. An hour and a half later, she found the interest in a different account. She'd had two documents open on the computer at the same time. Her fingers must have slipped on the keyboard, and when she typed in the next number, she hadn't noticed the screen had changed. These things can happen: tiny errors can change the course of your life. Look at her father, an innocent man unjustly accused of embezzlement because of a clerical error. It was either that, or he was a methodical thief in an adulterous workplace affair that had gone sour. She preferred the clerical error.

Erica rectified her mistake, and resumed breathing normally. She took her lunch to the Citicorp atrium, to contemplate the meaning of this error. At the table in front of her, a woman in overalls sat breastfeeding an infant. Another woman pushed a stroller up to Erica's table and asked to join her while simultaneously sitting down. She pulled out a jar of baby food and began feeding her squirming child.

One mother nodded to the other, asking, "How old is he?"

"Ten months."

Erica tried to eat her yogurt and ruminate on the misplaced bond interest, which she felt held profound applications, but after this single exchange, the two mommies loudly compared their nipple swellings, deliveries and episiotomies. She looked up sharply from her lunch. They took no notice, so rapt were they in discussion of their gynecologists, their pediatricians, the color of their baby's stools.

"Hey!" Erica shouted.

These two stared, convinced she was insane.

"I'm eating here! Do you mind?"

"This is a public space," said the mommy at Erica's table. "We can talk about anything we want to."

"Exactly, this *is* a public space: is this *really* the place to discuss the color of your baby's excrement?"

"Why don't you sit *here*?" the other mommy said. "This is a child-friendly table."

"It's not the *children* who are bothering me," Erica announced.

The mommy at Erica's table got up in a huff. When she'd settled herself and her child, they loudly continued on to a sister's post-delivery hemorrhoids, a best friend's fibroids, a sister-in-law's myomectomy. It went back and forth, like an endless match of ovarian tennis.

"I feel sorry for her," the first mommy said loudly when Erica got up to leave. "She'll never have kids."

"Look at her," agreed the other mommy.

"*Cows,*" Erica said as she exited.

THAT NIGHT, filling in a crossword in Maria's apartment, she thought about her mistake. How long could funds go missing before someone noticed? It was a question worthy of an experiment.

Marjorie Slotweiner was one of the clients who had Friedman, Greiff and Slavin pay her bills as well as do her taxes. It was an interesting test case: if anyone was going to notice irregularities, it wouldn't be the dim and scattered Mrs. Slotweiner. On the other hand, if anyone had Friedman, Greiff and Slavin on speed dial, it was the needy, newly widowed Mrs. Slotweiner, whose husband took care of "all that money stuff" while he was alive. "In my whole life," she bragged to Erica, "I never even wrote a check!"

Erica opened a second checking account at Chase for Marjorie Slotweiner, and transferred some of her bond interest into it. Erica applied for a credit card in Marjorie's name, and had the monthly statements come care of her, at the firm, along with all of Marjorie's other bills. She practiced Mrs. Slotweiner's girlish, legible signature— not even a challenge. She bought a laptop for Marjorie using Marjorie's new Visa card, and set up an AOL account in her name. She began on-line trading to increase what she had to play with.

Monthly, she took care of Mrs. Slotweiner's affairs, including the bills for Marjorie's new Visa card, which she paid out of Marjorie's second Chase checking account, which she topped off quarterly with some of the interest from Mrs. Slotweiner's municipal bonds. She kept the second set of Marjorie Slotweiner files at Maria's apartment, which had become a storage area.

A few months later, Erica took a train to Boston one weekend to outfit Marjorie top to bottom. A blonde, she decided, with better taste than Erica or Maria. Marjorie would wear makeup and jewelry. Real shoes, not sneakers. She entered a department store with the new short blond wig, and felt taller, younger, freer. Men looked *at* her, not through or beyond her. People waited on her immediately. Nobody demanded that she check her bag; no saleswomen watched her trying on and dared to coo, "That's a *slimming* outfit for you."

Someone else might have concluded from this experience that she should move to Boston. What Erica retained from the weekend was the feeling that it would be better to be Marjorie.

CHAPTER SEVEN

Patricia vacated her apartment with one suitcase and a garment bag shortly after New Year's. Her cell phone rang while the cab was rocketing down Lexington Avenue with all her possessions. It was Detective Ballestrino. He'd called several times since the pastry, checking up on her.

"What are you doing today?" she asked.

"Oh, a little theft, a little fraud, some aggravated harassment."

"Sounds exciting."

"Not really. What are you doing today?"

"Vacating the apartment I've lived in for twenty-seven years."

The detective paused. He had to be fifteen to twenty years younger. "What would you say to dinner tonight?"

She made sure to wait a moment, as if thinking about it. "I'd say yes."

"Great. Shall I pick you up at eight?"

"That's fine," she said, trying not to look forward to it. She gave him Brian's address.

IVY PELT greeted her with an effortful smile.

"You'll be staying on the sofa bed in the office. I wanted to give you our bed, but Brian said you'd never dream of taking it, we shouldn't even ask you.

"You'll have the entire apartment to yourself all day while we're on the set. Enjoy. I don't know what you're intending to do, but let me know if I can help you. I'm quite connected in certain places in this town."

Patricia inhaled. Yet another situation in which she didn't think she'd ever find herself. "Thanks, Ivy. I'll be out of your hair in a day or two."

"Stay as long as you like!" Ivy pulled a ringing phone from a holster strapped to her waist. "Yeah." She took notes on a small pad. "Okay."

She holstered the phone and looked up with a false smile.

The phone rang again. "Yeah. Brian," she sang, handing Patricia the phone.

"Mom, how are you? Got everything you need?"

"Yes, I'm fine."

"I thought you should be staying in our bedroom, but Ivy was firm about it. She said you wouldn't dream of taking our bed, and we shouldn't even ask. Oh, there's my hairdresser. Gotta go, see you tonight."

Ivy bared her teeth again, and excused herself.

PATRICIA HUNG HER TWO PRESENTABLE SUITS in the "office" closet. It looked like a men's clothing store: she counted twenty-three jackets. Brian was a grown man; he could spend his money the way he liked. She supposed he was earning enough, and had been fat enough, for long enough, to justify the fascination. On the wall were three photos of bare-chested Brian reclining on a seamless background with a smoldering look. Even now, Patricia sometimes looked at other people's normal, healthy, well-adjusted kids and had to turn away in an excess of feeling.

The phone rang. She let the machine take it.

"Hey, it's Lucy, I'll be by around eight. I need three."

In the second bathroom, Patricia found compacts, tubes and brushes neatly organized on top of the sink: Brian's makeup. She wandered into the kitchen and opened a can of tuna that she hoped they wouldn't miss. She had $597 and a car to her name. Over the table was a big photo of Brian and Ivy in matching white sweaters on a seamless white backdrop holding white flowers and smiling.

She had forfeited her home, and it was possible that she now had a young man courting her. She felt the need to tell someone about how the story was changing.

Cynthia listened for ten seconds before cutting her off.

"Dominique is dating a starving songwriter from Seattle."

"That's nice."

"Don't be ridiculous! What can she be thinking? He's a waste product!"

"Has he been to jail?"

Cynthia laughed. "Of course not."

"Then I don't want to hear it," Patricia said.

"I'm sorry," Cynthia sighed. "What about that therapist I found?"

"I can't afford a therapist," Patricia said.

There was a pause.

"Is it true you're seeing Eddie Fleisch?"

"I went out with him once, because he wouldn't take no for an answer."

"And, interest?"

"Don't be ridiculous."

"Because, you know, *he* could afford to send you to a therapist."

Patricia looked around the unfamiliar kitchen.

"You know, Cynthia, I don't think either one of us is getting what we used to out of these conversations. I don't think I'm going to call you anymore."

"I'm sorry, Patricia." Cynthia sounded relieved. "I just have no idea what to say to you anymore."

IN THE LIVING ROOM there was a big photo of Brian and Ivy wearing matching red sweaters posed in front of a roaring fire. Piecing together the information she had, Patricia calculated that the Detective was between thirty-two and thirty-five years of age.

"Hi, it's Don. I'd like one and a half," said the machine.

Patricia resented happy couples. Not teenagers kissing in the street, but women her own age with men who were still functioning as husbands. Patricia used to envy some of her divorced friends their freedom, and the peace they must have in their own apartments. But around the advent of the second reef tank, she'd had dinner with Bibi Leyner, who'd been divorced six years. Bibi sat down and took off her jacket, exposing shoulders, cleavage and a shiny black bustier.

"Men," Bibi explained. "All they see is skin."

"Ah."

"The older you get, the more skin you have to show," she said, sitting up very straight. "And just when the skin isn't skin anymore."

"Skin is horrifying," Patricia agreed.

"Skin is *liquefying*! I'm sitting here in *lingerie* in *January*, on a *diet* in a terrific restaurant, and for what? Look around here: there's nobody. Nobody! And what's out there is looking for a twenty-four-year-old."

"No," Patricia said sympathetically.

"So they're looking for a thirty-four-year-old: does that make it better?"

Patricia scanned her memory for any single men, and dredged up several. Two out of three of them would be at the next fund-raiser she was organizing, and Bibi agreed to come, even though she was a Republican.

"That's the spirit."

"Any married ones I should meet?" Bibi asked, not facetiously. Patricia raised an eyebrow. "Well, I'm sorry, but I'm hungry and I'm tired and I'm lonely and I'm cold," Bibi said. Patricia went home depressed.

Her husband was in the bedroom. She delayed going to bed, because she didn't want to deal with him. On the other hand, the idea of being out there alone and undressed in the winter didn't have much allure either.

STARTING AT SEVEN, the bell rang every twenty minutes. Ivy jumped up to give the visitor a brown paper bag tied with a brown-and-white polka-dotted ribbon from a tray in the foyer. "What's this, trick or treat?" Patricia asked.

"We're giving Brian's fan club pictures and stuff," Ivy said.

"Pictures, in little brown paper bags?"

"Mm-hmm," said Ivy, shooting Brian a look of annoyance.

Patricia looked at Brian, and he followed her into the kitchen.

"I thought you were finished with drugs," she whispered.

"I'm clean!" Brian insisted, like a soap star wrongly accused.

"So you're just doing this for the sport jackets?"

"I don't follow you," he said, looking like a handsome daytime leading man not following her. The doorbell rang.

Now that Mitch had pulled off this stunt, the children's behavior made some sense. It wasn't like they'd come out of nowhere.

Patricia left to finish dressing. Stranger things had happened than a fourteen- to seventeen-year age difference. She wore the less dressy of the two pantsuits she had with her. She'd applied her makeup carefully, and then wiped much of it off, to counter the mutton-dressed-as-lamb look. But when the bell rang again—exactly on time—she quickly stroked on some of Brian's rouge.

"How do you do?" she heard Detective Ballestrino say. "I'm here to pick up Patricia."

Ivy was looking at him as if scanning a video in fast-forward.

"Anthony Ballestrino," he offered, and Ivy took his hand, open-mouthed. "We met during the investigation a few months ago. How are you, Ms. Pelt?"

Patricia greeted Detective Ballestrino as graciously as she could under the circumstances. When the doorbell rang again, she took his arm and led him down the hall to the office and shut the door.

Detective Ballestrino looked very handsome in a dark, pin-striped suit. He stood with his hands in his pockets, completely relaxed, gazing at her openly. Perhaps this really was a date. She dropped Brian's keys into her purse and paused at the door, listening for a cue to exit. The bell rang again.

He smiled at her. "They having a party?"

The situation—on an actual date with a serious prospect; in the presence of a cop while her son dealt drugs in the next room; standing between a bed and an attentive, attractive man while her son's beefcake photos gave her the come-hither look—was too much. How had her life become so absurd?

"Let's get out of here." She grabbed his hand and pulled him out of the apartment. She might have even enjoyed the waves of shock she left in her wake.

❖

It started with Brian's goldfish bowl. Soon there was a hundred-gallon tank with ugly tubing taking up valuable real estate in the living room, and Mitch had Patricia mashing peas to supplement the diet of the fishes. Mitch began going out to Long Island on Saturdays to get rare coral and better accessories. "The tang controls algae, so it's a biological solution," he droned, when once he might have discussed Ben Webster's phrasing, or Winston Churchill's calls for rearmament.

One afternoon, before the first reef tank was overtaken by bristle worms and had to be dismantled, she found a gray-brown blob in the center of the living room carpet, covered in lint. She wondered which member of her household to send to a new psychiatrist. She showed it to Mitch when he came home.

"The octopus escaped. The cover must have been off. How many times do I have to tell you to keep the cover on?"

Mitch seemed to be speaking to her through the tank: he needed the tank, and he needed her to take care of the tank, or he needed to blame her when something went wrong. So on some level, she was taking care of him, although this wasn't particularly what was on her mind when the tubing snapped, and she found herself bailing water off the bathroom floor.

When he got the second, larger reef tank, which featured voluptuous corals and live rock, there was twice as much work. Every day, as she fed the fish or cleaned the tank, she heard her husband's voice—always the expert, always exasperated by Patricia, the novice—prating endlessly about the Ecosystem.

"It's a living painting," he said one night when they had people over. The guests looked at the tank for a while; then the discussion naturally turned to the awful weather, a nasty new divorce and the benefits of omega-3. Mitch continued to lecture about marine life, unaware they'd moved on. After the party, he fumed about how rude everyone had been, how boring and unresourceful. He chided her for wasting his time with people so narrow in their interests.

Soon he told her he didn't want people over, and he moved the second reef tank into the bedroom, where it hissed all night and cast a fluorescent glow over their truncated, if infrequent, attempts at intimacy.

As his world contracted, she got out more. It wasn't anything she did on purpose, but she found herself living at the gym and avoiding the apartment on the weekends. There was an event or a meeting for something almost every night. She had a tryst with a married lobbyist she'd met at a fund-raiser. Patricia didn't want to get involved. This was a onetime thing, she told herself, just so she could breathe again.

THE FOLLOWING AFTERNOON, she called Mitch's therapist. "I've restrained myself from calling you thus far," she apologized, "but he won't talk, and it's been six months, and nothing is happening."

There was a scary pause on the other end of the line.

"Mrs. Greiff, I'm not allowed to discuss my patients with anyone, but I don't think I'm divulging any secret when I say that your husband is not my patient. He didn't return after the first session."

She got into her car and shot down the Northern State Parkway with her jaw clenched. She left a brief, controlled message on the machine telling him she was at the beach, he'd have to fend for himself. He called her once, the second night, to find out when she'd be back.

When she returned a week later, he immediately gave her a list of tank chores, and told her that the algae situation was getting out of hand.

"The algae is out of hand because you didn't take care of it," she said.

"And look at the bruise on the coral," he said.

"I've had it with the tank, and I've had it with you. Move the tank into another room; I really don't care which one."

"You know I can't sleep without the tank."

"Then you move with it. Oh, and by the way: I spoke to Dr. Carrol."

His mouth opened slightly.

"So what difference does it make where you sleep? I have no more patience for you or your goddamn fish."

The next day she had Conchita make up the sofa bed in the den, and together they set up a temporary holding tank for the fish while they moved the rock and coral, as per the aquarium store's instructions.

"I don't know if this is such a good idea," said Conchita, and Patricia smiled tightly. She really ought to fire Conchita for impertinence, if not insubordination. But she had no one to replace her, and no interest in looking.

That night, Mitch stalked around the fish-free bedroom in a rage.

"Well, that's just too bad about you," Patricia said, on her way out to a benefit for gun control.

AFTER THE INITIAL EXPLOSION, he didn't seem to mind sleeping in separate rooms. She saw the married lobbyist at the Dorchester again.

With the new arrangements, weird things began happening in the tank. Fish began disappearing. One every few days, gone. Every morning, Mitch said, "Are you taking them out and flushing them, to annoy me? These are *living beings*."

"The only thing that's different now is that *you're* taking care of them. Maybe you're not such an expert."

She avoided the den, but one morning, after he'd blown up about another missing fish, she went to look at the tank.

The aquarium now had an eerie stillness. It was just the rocks, the ailing coral and the shipwreck. She caught sight of a worm, about a foot long, lurking at the bottom of the tank in a cove of rock. This was what was left of the Ecosystem.

❖

Dinner was at a loud, boisterous family restaurant in Queens with a dozen long, multigenerational tables erupting into laughter. But the conversation was light and flirtatious, there was wine and it did indeed seem like a date was going on between Patricia Greiff and Anthony Ballestrino. When they came out into freezing air, he opened the car door for her in a gallant fashion. Patricia arranged herself in the passenger seat feeling flushed and amused.

"Detective Ballestrino," she said.

"Mrs. Greiff." He smiled, reaching for her gloved hand.

He drove well. He took a highway she'd never even heard of. When there was traffic, he went up onto the shoulder and sailed right by. At a clogged intersection, he turned on the siren: cars parted to let them through. She looked at him to see his profile, but caught his full face, looking at her. He took a turn at a dark, leafy park and suddenly everything got quiet and residential. They parked. He opened her door and helped her out. They walked to a house, and he opened a door to a large room that was half storage, half bedroom.

They could have been anywhere. She really didn't care.

"Is this home?" She hoped not, for his sake.

"Sometimes." He took her coat. "Something to drink? Wine?"

"Nothing, thank you."

"Good." He pulled her toward him, kissing her on her mouth with urgency. Everything was unfamiliar. She liked not knowing what would happen next.

"I've been wanting to do that for a while," he said.

"Since when?"

"Since I first met you." He pushed her hair out of her eyes. "You were looking so harassed and helpless."

She exhaled slowly. She didn't need to be reminded. She sat down on the bed, pulling him toward her.

He sat down next to her. "It's kind of dusty."

"Stop talking," she said, and kissed him.

"WHEN CAN I SEE YOU AGAIN?" he asked at five the following morning, as they approached a bridge.

She sighed. "You're not concerned about the age thing?"

"What age thing?" he said tonelessly. "I'm ageless, you're ageless."

"Not everyone thinks that way."

He laughed. "What do you, of all people, care about what everyone thinks?"

He drove slowly over the grooves of the bridge.

"I have to tell you something," she blurted. "My son is involved with drugs."

"I know," he smiled slightly.

"You know?"

"Certainly."

"From last night?"

"No. It came up during the investigation."

"If you knew then why didn't you arrest him?"

"Because we figured we could catch someone bigger by letting him operate. Either his supplier or his father." He looked at her. "When can I see you again?"

"Let me think about it," she said.

Tony began to question her: How long did she plan to stay with her son? What was she doing that night? Where was she going that day? With whom? Would she take her cell phone? Why was she not answering his questions?

He was scaring her slightly.

"Back up." She laughed. "There's chronological age, and there's stage of life. Wouldn't you say that you and I are in different stages of life?"

"Yeah. So what?"

"I'm bringing this up because I want to be clear about things."

"It's clear that I want to see you again," he said, picking up her hand to kiss it as he drove. "When could that happen?"

Detective Anthony Ballestrino was the un-Mitch.

THERE WAS SOMETHING DELICIOUSLY PERVERSE about the way she tiptoed into her son's apartment at five-thirty in the morning, exhausted and alive.

Ivy was making coffee in the kitchen in a short pink bathrobe and matching fluffy slippers. "This was hardly what we expected, Patricia," she announced with a pinched expression.

Too much was happening, all of it unprecedented.

"When you didn't come home last night, Brian burst into tears."

A laugh escaped Patricia. "Oh, that's a good one."

Ivy snapped to attention, infuriated. "Forget about what I think: you might have considered your son's feelings."

"Interesting. Did my son consider *my* feelings? EVER?"

Ivy had no response, but she stood with her hand on her hip, fuming.

"I'll be out of here as soon as I can, Ivy," Patricia said sweetly. "In the meantime, I'd stay on my good side, if I were you. My friend the Detective has buddies in Narcotics."

By the time she turned on her cell phone at noon, he'd left her a message.

"Patricia. You said you had plans tonight, because you want me to slow down. But we both know that you don't have plans until tomorrow night. So why don't I pick you up at eight? We can go to that movie you wanted to see. Perhaps we should meet in the lobby of your son's building, instead of upstairs. See you then."

In fact, he was right: she didn't have plans until the following evening. How did he know that? Well, he was a Detective. She began to feel thoroughly pursued and attended to. It was a strange feeling. She wanted to like it, she supposed.

❖

Shortly after his second reef tank was operating smoothly—about a year before he'd disappeared—Mitch had begun feeling confident about the technology and procedures. But at night he had a recurring nightmare: his fish were healthy, his coral was flourishing, his filters were working perfectly but for some reason he had to add a new element to the tank (it was never clear what it was) and this element operated only in DOS. DOS, the symbol of everything he didn't understand and everything that could fuck him over. Each time he had this dream, the fish and coral died a violent death because of his inability to work in DOS. He woke up in a sweat.

One morning he told Patricia about the dream.

"Who is Dos?" she asked, fluffing her orange hair at her dressing table. He went to the office angry and confused.

Breaking with their strictly business tradition, he told Erica about the dream, because if anyone knew about DOS, she did.

Erica emitted two derisive hoots. "Don't lose sleep over DOS. A year from now, DOS will be like cuneiform."

That night, the dream began as it had previously, until he remembered that DOS had been overcome, and he needn't be frightened. But the dream continued, because the new thing that replaced it was even more terrifying—he didn't have a name for it, or any idea of how it worked. He was so handicapped, he didn't even know the name of his new adversary.

He came in the next day, and asked Erica to switch his computer over to the new technology. She immediately hooked him up with something very easy and colorful, telling him he would never look back, and that she was pleased that he'd gotten over his phobia. It would make it much easier to pass documents back and forth.

That night, he told Patricia that he now had the newest, fastest, most sophisticated technology on his office computer. She shot him a look of long-suffering disgust, and went back to her fashion magazine.

This was the first time that he'd thought about Erica outside the office.

❖

Mitch's first wife had been the daughter of his parents' friends. Nice girl, Candace, perfectly correct. Nineteen years old, he thought now: too young to be married. She was constantly looking at him, waiting for him to tell her what to do. It made him anxious. He divorced, the first member on either side of his extended family to do so, ever.

Patricia treated him in a light, offhanded way that he thought was more his style. He didn't have to entertain her, or tell her what to do. But about a year after the wedding, he'd wanted out of that marriage too.

"Once is a mistake," his mother told him as she flipped his eggs. It was a Sunday, and he'd come without Patricia, ostensibly to get their signatures on some tax forms. "But *twice* would look like you have some kind of a problem. God knows, I wouldn't have picked this one for you," said Lenore, never one to hide her dislike of Patricia. "You need to get in there and make it work with her. Marriage isn't a walk in the park, you know. Ask your father."

He'd found his father looking for a lightbulb in the closet.

"If I was lucky enough to marry a gorgeous, lovely girl like your wife," Herb said resentfully, "I think marriage *would* have been a walk in the park."

And then there were the children, like two separate horror movies playing simultaneously. Patricia would greet him at the door by throwing at him whatever terrifying incident had happened that day. Some nights she was stewing with anger at the offending child, who was lurking in his room, and she needed Mitch to throw his weight around. Some nights she was lying on the bed exhausted. Often she was brimming with a fresh solution to the problem, whatever she'd discovered by spilling her guts to everyone they knew, plus strangers she'd met at the hairdresser's, the supermarket and the street. She spent entire days on the phone with Cynthia Landau's mafia, a many-headed Hydra with ties to every imaginable specialist, hospital, movement and disease. Before dinner, Patricia would tell him how the first call led to the second, and trace the evolution of the referral through the entire known Jewish world.

"And how was your day?" she would ask.

He would excuse himself, go into the storage room where he'd set up his turntable, listen to something bracing or soothing and emerge when he was ready to handle the horrifying spectacle of his possibly psychotic children misbehaving at the dinner table. The repetitive nature of family life left him gasping for air. Did these children have an upside? Mitch began buying the Verve catalog recording by recording. The storage room became the Record Closet. The marriage continued. There were no options.

Brian brought home a goldfish one day, and Randy cut it up that night, leaving the ragged tail floating on the surface and the severed head under Brian's pillow. As a consolation, Mitch helped Brian put together a real tank. Randy's then-psychiatrist decided that his expulsion from the Maddox School was a blessing in disguise: clearly the thirteen-year-old needed more structure. So Randy was enrolled in an old-fashioned boys' academy with uniforms. Brian's then-psychiatrist decided that the twelve-year-old's bed-wetting might be traced to the sibilant sounds of the fish tank, so they moved the tank into the living room. When he was expelled for stealing, Randy was sent to a military-style boarding school in Connecticut. When Brian stopped feeding the fish, in order to have more time to feed himself, Mitch became the tank commander.

For years, Mitch had yearned for someone other than his wife, but he was humiliated in advance. And whom would he fling with? Most of his business was done over the phone. He met the occasional attractive woman at Patricia's various social functions, but it couldn't be any-one who knew Patricia, or fit into any of their circles—it would be awful if anything got around.

At the office Christmas party the previous year, Mitch had found himself alone with Heather Perkins in the Xerox room. For whatever insane reason, he kissed her. She responded in an unambiguous way. He was aroused, and pressed her up against the copy machine. She reached behind her to turn the copier on. His forehead broke out in sweat. She flicked the lights off and kicked at the door, but left it par-tially open. He had noticed in the course of working with her that Heather had a knack for making everything more complicated than it needed to be. Did he really want to get involved with her?

He disengaged from her mouth. "This is not a good idea," he said, feeling flooded with relief as he said it.

"Fine," she said, pulling away. "Let's just remember who started it."

"You're completely right. I had no right to do that."

She registered her impatience, flicked the lights back on and left him standing there as the slumbering gray machinery made noises of awakening.

It was around this time that Erica King began saying things just as he was thinking them. At least once a day, they would be in the same room, looking at something, Sonny McPhain's business expenses, for example. They arrived at $769,954 on the food line.

"That's a lot of chicken," they said at the same time.

Or he'd give her the file of a complaining client and she'd say, "An-other satisfied customer," just as he said it.

She inhaled sharply, and raised her strange, heavy eyebrows on these occasions, but she never smiled. At least once a week, Erica came up with an astonishing end run around the Federal tax code. She presented these maneuvers with dry precision. When he compli-mented her, she cocked her head slightly, like a courtier, and he found himself wondering what else he could give her to do. She made him look very good.

Erica woke up every morning, made herself coffee, dragged on her clothes and went to work. Her needs were minimal. She took the bus, ordered in Chinese from the joint on the corner, rarely shopped.

Marjorie was another story. Marjorie involved makeup, jewelry, special shoes and hose, matching outfits: she wasn't built for speed. Maria was something in between. With Erica's wig, she wore some makeup and some jewelry, but Erica soon got bored with her: Maria was too much like Erica herself to offer Erica much of a respite. When Erica ordered a snappy red canvas bag for Marjorie, it was better, sweeter, more exciting than when she ordered one for herself. Not that she ordered one for herself—*she* didn't need one. She'd never order one for herself. And perhaps that was the point.

Once Marjorie was up and running, Erica decided to color-code for simplicity. Erica was navy blue, Maria was green and Marjorie was red. She kept each woman's color-coded wallet and keys in a different pocket of her own black carryall. Each woman had her own account at a different local bank, a credit card, a nondriver's ID, an apartment. They all paid their bills on time. The only reason it was possible to keep up with everything was that all the apartments were within a five-block radius of each other, and all were a fifteen-minute bus ride or a twenty-minute walk from her office.

Marjorie continued to be the source of discoveries. Men spoke to her. She was surprisingly able to talk back, and with a genuine sweetness that Erica was incapable of pulling off. Naturally, there were moments of confusion. Once she was caught by an old acquaintance who, against all odds, recognized her in Marjorie's short blond wig and snazzy red pantsuit, and screamed down the dairy aisle at D'Agostino's: "Erica! You look so fabulous, I never would have recognized you!"

Erica found herself between several apartments one night, closer to her own than the others, and was tempted to go home. Uch, she thought, Erica's such a drag, and had to laugh. Marjorie had started out like a colonial outpost, but now Erica found it more relaxing, more natural, to be in Marjorie's apartment. She felt more herself there. She considered consolidating her holdings.

One evening, on her way to Marjorie's, she saw the new neighbor from Maria's building, the last man Marjorie had had sex with, a kid (now thirty-six) who had gone to PS 125 with Erica, and the nurse from Geri's oncologist's office. She walked on, staring straight ahead behind Marjorie's big dark glasses, greeting no one.

Was it possible to disappear in a thick matrix of ties like New York City? The East 20s and 30s, unlike much of Manhattan, were still something of a provincial backwater. When she considered this, an old feeling of confinement, of thwarted expectations, welled up in her throat. On the other hand, the neighborhood was *so* provincial, that one block east, on First Avenue, she was essentially in a different village, with a separate supermarket, newsstand, dry cleaner and video store, and a whole different set of people going about their daily rounds separately. A certain amount of big-city anonymity was possible even within small-town Manhattan.

Did she honestly believe she was another person? Of course not. Why didn't Erica just put on the short blond wig and the snazzy red pantsuit in the morning and be Erica, the sweet, snazzy, put-together blonde? She could just imagine how Marty Slavin would ridicule her transformation to Mitch behind her back. She could hear Charlie and Heather gossiping in the pantry. What she did in her spare time for entertainment was just that: entertainment. Marjorie was a diversion, but that wasn't her life.

Why didn't Erica pool the money she was spending on three rents and get one good apartment, in a neighborhood that didn't have a bad memory on every corner? A good idea, but one that somehow didn't stick. Again: it wasn't her life. For whatever reason, the impulse to upgrade was manifested laterally: more options, not better ones.

And it wasn't as if Marjorie Slotweiner of Park Avenue was missing her municipal bond interest. Marjorie Slotweiner wouldn't notice an earthquake if it happened in the midst of her bridge game.

❖

One early afternoon in late March, something happened, but it wasn't clear what or why. Erica and Mitch had decided to take a break, and they walked down the hall to get sodas from the pantry. A radio was blaring as the top half of a deliveryman replaced cans in the soda machine, while his bottom half remained in the center of the room, exhibiting an unseemly amount of rear-end cleavage.

"Any chance I could get a Pepsi from you?" Mitch shouted over the noise.

"Me too," she said.

They were ignored. A portable radio on the counter said, *"Men: are you tired, listless, ashamed of your waning sex drive? Great Expectations will give you the vigorous sex life you've only dreamed of!"*

"Oh, please," Erica said.

"Men with lagging sex drive: you have nothing to be ashamed of."

"Do you think he heard us?" Mitch asked.

"I heard you fine!" The deliveryman straightened up to a squat, and swung his head out of the soda machine to fix a look of venom at them. He looked unstable. "You can wait."

"Listen to Mark Vacarro, a regular person, who sometimes has trouble maintaining erections."

"This is Mark Vacarro. I was feeling so low, my self-esteem was in the basement. But Great Expectations gave me the stamina, the vigor and the self-assurance to have the sex life of my dreams."

"Do you sometimes feel that the mainstream culture is assaulting you?" she shouted to Mitch over the din. He didn't respond.

The radio said, *"My wife is so grateful."*

"Euauggghh!" Erica lunged at the radio and shut it off.

The soda guy brushed by her and turned the radio back on, louder. *"This is Judy Vacarro. Thank you, Great Expectations!"*

"Oh, ENOUGH!" Erica said, and switched the radio off again.

The soda guy shot up out of the machine again, picked up the radio and turned it on again, even louder.

"This is a place of business," she insisted, turning it off again.

"Bullshit!" he shouted. "This is a kitchen, and you're in here because you're procrastinating." He turned up the volume.

"This is our office. We make the rules here," Mitch said. "No radio."

"I don't work for you," said the deliveryman, sweating and furious.

"Oh, really?" Erica said, reading the monogram on his uniform. "What's your last name, Bob?"

"None of your fucking business."

"I am the Office Manager. I am calling the people who hired you and telling them you are rude, unprofessional and aggressive. I am also telling them that if they send you here again, we'll find another soda service."

She pulled Mitch down the hall to her office. He sat in her visitor's chair, staring at his hands, while she reported the incident to the vending machine company. On their way back to Mitch's office, they peeked in the kitchen. The man was gone, but a bright yellow puddle lay in front of the machine.

"Oh, my God," Erica said.

"He peed in our pantry?"

They went downstairs to the vendor on the corner. She surprised herself by following his lead, and getting a hot dog as well as a soda. Without discussing it, they walked to the empty waterfall patio three doors down from the office, sat on some frigid wire chairs and quickly ate and drank the too-hot hot dogs and the too-cold soda in the icy March afternoon.

They returned to the office, windblown and excited. Mitch put his feet up on the desk, tilted his head back and took a swig of soda.

"To answer an earlier question. Yes: sometimes I do feel assaulted by the mainstream. All day long."

She was quiet. They sat for a few moments in silence.

There was a fast knock on the door. "Is it true that somebody just defecated in the pantry?" Marty Slavin popped his head in. "Oh, sorry, Erica."

"Now that's inflation," Mitch said.

"The soda delivery guy got angry that we turned off his radio, so he pissed on the machine," Erica informed him.

"In front of you?"

"No, after we'd gone."

"Who will clean it up? I want to make popcorn."

"I'll leave a note for the cleaning woman who comes tonight," Erica said, enjoying the idea of unloading the task on the woman who had insulted her, and thwarting Marty's daily popcorn festival, which stank up the entire office.

Mitch and Erica worked together and separately until eight; then he casually asked her if she would like to go for dinner, another first. She agreed, and they walked in fierce wind to a nearby Japanese place with an indoor waterfall, a numbing sound in a huge open space of granite and glass.

"This is the second waterfall of the day," she shouted.

"That's right." He smiled. "I liked the first one, too."

There was something intimate about the way they spent the rest of the dinner in silence.

When they parted, on a windy corner, there was a strange moment when Erica thought her boss might just kiss her. But he gave her upper arm a brief pat and hailed a cab. She walked home in a windblown trance, elated by the strange change of mood.

The day after the two waterfalls, Mitch looked at Erica in a new way, and was simultaneously aware that he didn't have to act on it. Erica could be the perfect partner: no one could ever suspect him of having an affair with her, and outside of the office, he doubted they knew anyone in common. He liked the idea that a door had opened up in his life, and he could walk through if he chose.

She arrived as usual, in a dark schlumpy outfit with a typed-up list of daily business, and started right in. This itself was sexy, that they were going through the whole meeting as if nothing had happened the previous day. Not that anything had happened the previous day. Would she mention anything? He could feel himself getting aroused by the idea of her, Erica the dowdy, Erica the nasty. He could feel her big body underneath him; *was* she a virgin? This he highly doubted. But clearly she was frustrated. This was itself an invitation. He imagined her sitting across from him minus the skirt and sneakers, in heavily buttressed, nurse-white underclothes, going through the list of daily business as usual.

He wouldn't decide, he decided. He would let things develop if they did, or not, if they didn't. How did anything get started? The last time he'd faced this, in 1971, it was enough just to pick a girl up at her apartment. The rest somehow took care of itself.

"So that's it," she said finally, and got up to go.

Don't go, he thought.

She stood without leaving. His heart rose.

"I'd like to tell you," she said formally, "that I had a nice time last night. Thank you for an enjoyable and unexpected dinner."

Possibility. Of course, there was always the sickening khaki cloud he lived under.

"Perhaps you'd like to have dinner again sometime."

She stood still, her hair shining copper in the fluorescent lights.

"Anytime," she said with a slight smile. She opened the door, gave him another glance under her strange eyebrows and walked out.

MITCH SPENT A LOT OF TIME PLANNING where they would go, and wondering what they would talk about. But why was he doing that? The whole point of Erica was that she was completely unpredictable, and unexpectedly attractive. The empty Japanese restaurant in the cavernous atrium—why would that be romantic? And yet somehow it was. He should just take her to any old place and see what happened. He shouldn't take her somewhere he'd been with Patricia. He didn't want to bump into anyone he knew.

He took her to a steak place in the neighborhood, no reservation. They had to wait at the bar. She put on glasses (had she always worn them?) and ordered straight vodka: again, completely unpredictable. Every weird thing she did seemed to beckon to him: she was completely unknown, and he hadn't realized how unbelievably compelling he would find this. Something was wrong with him: he was smiling, his face felt hot. He was babbling on about his tank; she was listening with a cool expression. It was impossible to know what she was thinking. He was trying to impress her. He was trying to get her into bed.

This thought sent a wave of fear rolling over him. He hadn't tried this in many, *many* years; it was ridiculous. Nothing had happened the previous night and nothing was going to happen that night.

When they walked out of the restaurant, she immediately turned to the right, and he followed her.

They arrived at a decaying brownstone with dead plants in the window boxes. She took out keys and opened a door. No discussion in the tiny elevator.

Soon she was unlocking another door, and they were in a narrow, fluorescent-lit room painted a livid, ill-considered lavender blue. They took their coats off, and she hung them on a stand near the door. She gestured to a run-down blue sofa, and he sat down, noting the tiny kitchenette near the door. A bright blue place, cold and depressing. She sat down next to him, fairly close.

When she took off the sweater, he saw that she had a short-sleeved T-shirt on underneath. She'd been working for him for ten years, and he hadn't noticed (perhaps she'd been hiding it) an ample chest and fleshy upper arms. He hadn't thought about Patricia all night. In two days, in fact.

———

MITCH GREIFF SEEMED PETRIFIED. It was clear what he wanted, but he was having some trouble acting on it. Perhaps he was waiting for some kind of sign.

She took off her cardigan.

He was watching her steadily, and moving with deliberate slowness, as if she were a wild animal and he didn't want to startle her with any sudden movement. He began scratching at the sofa cushion in the space between them. She picked up one of his hands and began looking at it, touching it.

He ran his hands over her forearms. "You have no hair on your arms," he said, surprised.

"You're observant."

"Why?"

"When I was thirteen, I started losing hair. On my head, on my body."

"Why?"

"I never received an adequate answer. By the next year, it was all gone."

"So this," he asked, looking at her head.

"Is a wig."

He breathed in. "What's underneath?"

"Just me."

"Let's see," he said.

"Are you sure?"

"Unless you'd feel awkward."

"When I'm alone, it's the first thing I take off. But in company—especially male company—it's usually the last thing I take off. And sometimes"—she paused—"I don't take it off."

She noticed his smile at the mention of "male company." Perhaps like all the other morons at the office, he thought she was saving herself for Jesus.

But here he was on Maria's sofa, the tall, gorgeous, dryly amusing Mitch Greiff, the first man since Davey to request that she *take off* the wig. Why ruin a lovely moment with office resentment?

In fact, she was ready to take it off. She had a beautiful head, which she was quite proud of. "Why don't *you* take something off?" she suggested.

He took off his tie, and raised an eyebrow.

"Something else."

He took off his jacket, and began working on his cuff links.

She unbuttoned his shirt. Kissing started here, and he was careful not to touch the hair, it seemed, but just her face. In short order they were naked on the bed, and she reached up and pulled off the hair. "Ta-daa," she sang softly, and tossed it onto the armchair. She watched his reaction. Once a guy in college had flown out of her room screaming when the wig came off.

HOW HAD HE NOT KNOWN it was a wig? It was almost preposterous that he hadn't noticed all these years: the thing was so clearly false, sitting on top of her like a dark brown nylon mop head. Had everyone else known?

Now she was completely open. He'd never seen anything like this, so naked, so white. He reached up to touch her scalp, which was hard and smooth. Things moved on rapidly from there. Whenever a negative thought flashed through him, he looked up at her white head, and all was right again. There was something unbelievably transgressive about it.

He returned home exhausted, exultant and amazed.

The following morning, when Erica arrived in his office, Mitch closed the door, sat down at his desk and looked her over top to bottom. Erica King wasn't universally gorgeous, like Patricia. Strangers wouldn't stop her on the street, for example, to rave about her skin. But underneath the wig and the clothes, Erica was actually attractive. Yes, this was what he wanted to confirm this morning: he wasn't revolted by her.

What on earth would Marty Slavin say? But Marty Slavin would never find out. Mitch wanted to continue the conversation that had begun the previous evening in her apartment, to solidify this feeling of success.

He rose, sat next to her and held her hand.

She looked at him coldly, freeing her hand. "Office behavior."

He went back behind his desk, ashamed and somewhat stunned. Well, of course she would be difficult. Who had he thought he was dealing with here?

"I enjoyed last night," she said, with some warmth, and he relaxed.

He was imagining her with her wig off. "When can I see you again?"

"Come over after work, around eight." She wrote an address on a piece of paper. "I think we should go there separately."

"Good thinking." He looked at the paper. "Different address."

"Indeed. I'm counting on your discretion," she warned. She had a charming smile, with a pointy canine overlapping its neighbor. Had he never noticed or had she just never smiled?

"You get more and more interesting," he said, stunned at the idea of it.

HE ARRIVED AT THE SECOND APARTMENT BUILDING: a big, new doorman building on First Avenue. She was waiting for him in the lobby, wearing a red kerchief, with short blond hair sticking out of it. She looked younger, more modern, artistic even. She led him upstairs into a chic, elegant apartment full of pastel colors and large furniture. Whose place was this? She marched him directly to the bedroom, where she began removing his clothing.

"I thought about you all day," she pushed him onto a large, tall bed with pea-green sheets.

He pushed the scarf and the wig up and off, running his fingers over her smooth scalp, impressed with and frightened by how excited it made him. What did this say about him? He had a former model with a full head of gorgeous red hair sitting at home, but it was a freakish bald accountant who aroused him. Was this deviant, perverse, *gay* somehow?

He tried not to think about it.

If things didn't work out, Erica was a professional. She wouldn't jeopardize the office relationship. She would continue to do terrific work, or she would leave if it proved too awkward. If she left, he had nothing but the highest praise for her. She'd worked for him for ten years, and couldn't imagine a more precise, thorough or inventive accountant. He stopped himself. He was writing her a recommendation letter while she was running her face over his inner thigh. He really ought to enjoy this while it was happening. God only knew what might happen next.

CHAPTER EIGHT

A clandestine situation with a much older married man felt like coming home to Erica. Mitch had an aura of sadness and frustration, although he was a partner, had celebrity clients, a glamorous wife, two grown children and a second home. On the other hand, she knew that he rarely used the second home and his children were problematic.

Even three months earlier, she wouldn't have believed this scene, herself naked in bed with Mitch Greiff, without hair, eating lo mein, watching *Double Indemnity*. I am the luckiest woman alive, she told herself, as he released an overfed sigh and turned away from the movie to watch her.

AT INDEPENDENCE HOUSE, Erica signed out Davey Findlay for the afternoon. She took him to the Social Security office. She'd gone through the same motions with him ten years earlier when his mother died. She took him to a different branch, just in case, but he didn't remember. Erica was, as she had been before, a friend of the family.

"Up until now, his mom was taking care of him, but both his parents are dead now and he has to go on public assistance." Erica handed the clerk Donald Spivak's nicely crushed and stained birth certificate, which she'd obtained from the Department of Records after having read the promising obituary in the *Times* a few days before. The clerk asked for a death certificate, and Erica told her that she didn't have one; she passed the newspaper with the obituary of Muriel Spivak, survived by a son, Donald, donations in lieu of flowers to the Crestwood Autism Research Center.

"Dead mom, dead mom!" Davey shouted, displaying his now rotted teeth. The clerk looked him over and moved some papers around on the desktop.

Donald Spivak was forty-six, Davey Findlay was thirty-eight and Mitch Greiff was fifty-eight. Comparing Mitch to Davey in the dingy Federal office building among snaking lines of miserable people made her somber. She could see none of the attraction now. She grieved over her lack of options when she was seventeen.

Donald Spivak's new Social Security number, plus his name on Maria's Con Ed bill, plus the magazine subscriptions, would lead to the library card, the voter registration card, the checking account and the credit card. It was never too early to start the process. Davey sang as she maneuvered him through Chinatown. I spend my life doing bills, she realized, my own and other people's. For fun, I create new people, who have more bills. What kind of life is this?

On the other hand, why was she automatically seething? She was seeing a man who liked her with her hair off. Things were looking up.

❖

Mitch walked around in an erotic haze. In the halls, he wondered if his colleagues noticed something different. Even four days ago, he might have thought, Who could ever imagine that I was in bed with Erica King? Now he wasn't so sure. Why had they all thought her pathetic? The wig was hot, so she was often in a sweat. Poor thing, he thought. Her naked head was strangely beautiful, but they would never know. This excited him.

Erica seemed to exist on bananas, instant oatmeal and greasy

Chinese takeout. She didn't work at her body, like Patricia, of sculpted biceps and back definition. Erica had milk-white, hairless skin, large breasts, a potbelly and a doughy derriere. Cellulite! He was having an affair. This in itself was remarkable. But he was getting more and more attracted to her, even though each time he saw her, he found more things about her that should have been problems. This he found transfixing.

Patricia, meanwhile, had not verbally registered the fact that he'd been coming home at two-thirty and three in the morning. Part of him wanted to have it out with her. To tell her everything, down to the last steamy detail, so she would know.

Marty gave an exaggerated sigh when Erica passed him in the hall, for Mitch's benefit. Mitch, who was walking behind her at a distance, imagining the smooth, strong, hairless legs moving unnoticed under the shapeless suit, thought that there was something confident in her decision to just be who she was and not bother with the trimmings. Marty had a new one: twenty-nine, blond, petite, perfectly dressed and made-up, always with a matching silk scarf.

Erica had taken off her eyebrows for him the night before. She said it was the first time anyone other than her mother or the woman who'd sold them to her had seen her without them. The combination of the sleek, uninterrupted forehead sloping upward and the idea that he was the first to see it left him reeling.

She came into his office after lunch and closed the door.

He held her hand. Her fingers were rounded, short and swollen, like a child's drawing of a hand. "You want to go away somewhere?" he whispered. "Something private, with a beach? I was thinking about Grand Cayman."

A slight smile. "Fine."

"I'll make the arrangements."

"I don't think it's a good idea to travel together."

"You're probably right."

"When you reserve the flight, why don't you use this card, in this name." She reached into her wallet and handed him a credit card.

The card said Maria Collecelli. "Who is this?"

"Me," she said.

He felt cold. "Erica?"

"It's a long story. My mother changed my name when I was a child, and I have documents in both names."

"Whose apartment did we go to the first night?"

"Mine."

"Whose apartment did we go to the second night?"

"Mine," she admitted, with a delighted smile.

His mind wasn't working fast enough. "You have two names?"

"It really is a long story, but it'll work in our favor. For the sake of subterfuge, use that card, and book the trip for Maria."

Whoever she was, she had saved his life. He asked, "How did I know you would be a shrewd co-conspirator?"

Seven Mile Beach on Grand Cayman Island was fairly empty. Although Mitch doubted that he would bump into someone he knew, he was busy coming up with reasons for being there in a bathing suit with a woman not his wife. They sat in an outdoor café near the beach, and Erica read the newspaper. In a million years, could he ever imagine a woman who not only wouldn't mind that he read the newspaper, but would actually initiate newspaper reading in a restaurant herself?

He was getting to know her, but she was still unpredictable. The night before, he'd made a wisecrack about Marty Slavin. She let him laugh at his joke, then said, "That's the last unnecessary mention of an office member in this space."

"You're right," he said. "It's a sanctuary."

This angered her. "It's not a religious thing. Why does everybody bring religion into everything?"

Erica was impatient, not unlike Patricia, but from a completely different direction. Where Patricia might be angry that he'd forgotten about plans that she'd made, Erica was angry that *he* made plans. Where Patricia might get angry that he wasn't listening to her, Erica was out of sorts when he wanted to chat. Erica was like him, only more so. She liked to do her own thing and stay at home, in whichever apartment.

His father would have done quite a number on Erica. Whenever a woman appeared, in an elevator, on TV, to give him a menu, Herb Greiff would size her up and announce, "Ugly," "Eh" or "Va-va-voom."

Mitch looked up from his book. Erica sat next to him in the shade, doing a crossword puzzle, wrapped up in a white linen shroud. Patricia would be in a bikini, running up and down the beach, scuba diving, parasailing, chatting up everyone within earshot, stalking him with sunscreen, introducing him to people who had to be their new best friends.

Erica tucked the tail of her scarf into her straw hat with one of her stubby fingers. Was Mitch selling himself short here? There had to be something between Patricia and Erica. Of course he was too tired to seek it out.

But who was he to be so picky? Erica King had brought him back from the dead.

AFTER THEIR RETURN FROM THE CAYMANS, she'd brought him to yet another apartment, the largest so far. He spent that night there, which was a Sunday. She told him, after a long hot shower, that she could afford three apartments because two were rent-controlled, and the other was rent-stabilized. This raised so many questions that he didn't even pursue the topic. He decided the less he knew the better. Sooner or later he was going to get sick of chicken lo mein and spareribs, but it hadn't happened yet. Her mysteries kept deepening.

They went to work separately on Monday. By the time he'd caught up on his paperwork, it was late. He took a cab home and, as an experiment, he slipped into his old bed. Patricia was sleeping heavily on her side. He began running his hand over her lean haunch. She turned over. He kneaded her muscled thighs, remembering her body.

She sat bolt upright, grabbed the blankets and screamed.

"What the hell are you doing?"

He rolled onto his back.

"You scared the SHIT out of me, Mitch!"

He retreated to the den, where his murky tank mocked him. He heard her slamming around in the kitchen.

He took a cab to the second apartment, where he knew he'd find her. Erica was up, doing bills at the dining room table. He sat on her bed and began unbuttoning her shiny red pajamas.

"This is more fun than I've had in a long time," Erica said, sounding amazed and grateful. He spent the night again with her. The following morning, they left separately. He walked to work up First Avenue, the first time he'd ever walked up First Avenue in the morning.

It felt new.

❖

It was around this same time that Patricia arrived home one morning after another night with the married lobbyist at the Dorchester. She wandered into the kitchen out of habit, and saw a half grapefruit facedown on the floor near the sink. Everything else in her stainless-steel-and-white kitchen was in place. There was no garbage in the can, no cutting board and knife on the counter, nothing in the dishwasher and the juicer was clean.

Just a single half grapefruit facedown on the floor. What did it mean? Where was the other half? It had to be Mitch: Conchita was in Santo Domingo that week. The kids were never there.

Was he insane? Was she? She left it there, as evidence.

They couldn't go on like this. Where was he spending his time?

When he came home that night, she asked him.

He put a garment bag on the chair in the foyer. "What do you care?"

"What's the story with the grapefruit?"

"What grapefruit?"

She pulled him to the kitchen and pointed at it. "That grapefruit."

"How should I know? I don't eat grapefruit. I wasn't here last night."

Patricia looked at him. She'd been out last night also. When you don't pay attention to things, it shows: strange grapefruit on your floor, husband out all night. If it hadn't been Mitch, then *who*? Who had broken into her kitchen to toss around grapefruit? It was weird, inexplicable and troubling.

"Why don't we stay out of each other's way for a while," she said.

"You took the words right out of my mouth," he said, and took his garments back to the den.

She threw the grapefruit into the garbage, still disturbed. Later in the day, when she spoke to Brian, she asked him about it.

"Yeah, Ivy and I were in the neighborhood, and we stopped by to say hello. But nobody was around. Did we make a mess? Sorry."

"So you made juice," she said, relieved that there was a rational explanation.

But the question remained: where *had* Mitch been the night before? And the night before that? Did she care?

❖

Mitch and Erica were curled up on the big dark sofa under a comforter in Erica's second apartment, the one he liked best, on First Avenue. The rain had stopped, and the light was waning outside. The feeling of possibility continued to grow; each day, Mitch felt he'd been introduced to something he'd never even considered before.

"Where have you never been that you always wanted to go?" he asked, stroking her shoulder while she opened up somebody's mail.

"Where *have* I been: the list is shorter."

"You've never been anywhere?"

"Hardly out of Midtown. My mother was afraid to travel."

"Where would you like to go?"

"California," she said immediately.

"Okay! Let's go next weekend: San Francisco or LA?"

"LA!" She hopped off to the bedroom. "Oh, I'm so excited."

It was a shock, after all these years, to see Erica King get excited. It pleased him that he was the cause of it.

"I want to go with Donald Spivak," she said, handing him a credit card.

The card belonged to Donald Spivak. "Whose card is this?"

She handed him a Friedman, Greiff and Slavin ID card bearing his picture and the name Donald Spivak. "It's yours."

"How did you do this?"

She waved the question aside. She gave him a Social Security card. Mitch fingered the cards. "Why Donald Spivak?"

"You don't like the name? Well, that's tough."

"No, no! I was just wondering how you came up with it."

"I didn't come up with it."

She was frightening. "A forger?"

"No, Mr. Spivak, these are real. You have a credit line of $1,000 with that card. You have a Social Security number, and it all checks out."

There was almost nothing that she could tell him anymore that could surprise him. Almost everything about Erica was a shock, though he supposed he was growing accustomed to it. Every time he went home to Park Avenue, there was a pink note from Patricia accusing him of some kind of dereliction of duty. He was accustomed to everything about his wife, including her notes, and yet each time he found a pink missive stuck to his mirror he was shocked and enraged anew.

Erica continued: "Once you begin using these, you'll start establishing the identity. Donald Spivak has been using Maria's address, but I was thinking that you might want to rent your own place, and start being seen there."

His own place: the idea carried with it a nice open feeling. How many people had more than one apartment? They agreed to go to dinner at a French place on First Avenue as an exploratory mission for the card.

"So we go to LA as Donald Spivak and Marjorie Slotweiner," she said.

He felt a strange elation. "Who's Marjorie Slotweiner?"

"Another alias," she said, nosing around the back of his neck.

"That name sounds familiar," he said.

She pushed him back into bed.

HE LAY IN BED for a long time and watched her as the rain pelted the window. She stood in front of a dresser in an elegant red bathrobe, brushing on makeup, wigless. He had nothing but questions.

"Do you wear the blond wig in and out of the house here, and then change into the brunette one on the street? How does this work?"

"I have a revolving door that I change in, when the phone booth is unavailable." She said this without smiling.

THE MEAL WAS QUIET AND UNEVENTFUL, although his entire body was on full alert. Meanwhile, his accomplice sipped her water, cool and natural. He tried not to think about what he was going to do.

He asked for the check, and put his new credit card down to pay.

The restaurant grew quieter with each passing minute; if there was a problem with the credit card, every last diner would hear and see it. Did it normally take so long? He didn't have enough cash on him to cover the dinner. What if Donald's card was rejected? He couldn't give them one of his own cards, with a different name. But of course, she could use one of her many cards in an emergency. He assumed she had them with her. She was carrying a small purse: did she?

She was applying dark red lipstick, looking into a small compact mirror while the waiter poured more water into her glass. In a million years, would Marty Slavin believe this was Erica?

He realized that even when he sent *Mitch Greiff*'s credit card off with a waiter—Mitch Greiff: JDL, CPA, legitimate citizen professionally entrusted with millions of dollars—there was always a small fear that he might be refused.

For a moment, his heart stopped: was that Jack Landau at the bar?

But of course it wasn't. Cynthia wouldn't be caught dead in that place.

The waiter brought back the black padded folder, and he signed his new name, Donald Spivak, with a flourish. He looked up at her. She raised a false eyebrow and gave him a smile of complicity.

Outside on the street, they were hit with a wall of humidity, portending a long, grisly New York summer. And yet he felt light, graceful, young; he felt like walking for miles! They strolled up First Avenue side by side.

"Where does the bill go?" he asked.

"Maria's. You'll pay with checks from the account I opened for Donald."

"What's in the account?"

"Oh, some money."

He was struggling to catch up with her, ashamed that his mind didn't work that fast.

"You'll need a driver's license to rent a car in LA, so get yourself down to the DMV first thing tomorrow, with all your papers."

They kissed on First Avenue, the first public kiss of this partnership.

"Erica, Maria, Marjorie," he said, feeling intrigued, wilted, energized.

Erica planned to have a quiet dinner and do bills at Marjorie's. But Mitch arrived unexpectedly at nine, looking pale and sick.

"Marty Slavin had a heart attack on the way home on Metro North."

"Oh, goody," she said.

"Don't say that."

"Why not? I never liked him."

"Well, he's not my best friend, but it's shocking. It makes you real-ize: what are we doing? How much time do you spend with people you can't stand?"

"Well, less, once Marty's gone."

"He's in the hospital." He shot her a look. "Patricia burst into tears, you know."

"Don't tell me to weep. Marty Slavin is a nasty schmuck who makes jokes at my expense." She resented the mention of his wife.

"What if I died tomorrow?" Mitch whined.

"What if you did?"

"Uch, sometimes I just wish I could walk out of this life and never come back. Nobody would miss me."

"I'd miss you." She sat in his lap, and he kneaded her scalp.

"Would you come with me?"

"Where?"

"When I walked out of my life."

"Certainly." She slid down, so her feet were over the arm of the sofa and her head was in his lap. "Where would you go?"

"Someplace they'd never find me. Morocco."

"Why wouldn't they find you there?"

He had no response.

"Do you speak Arabic or French?"

He shook his head. She reached up to run a hand through his gor-geous, thick, black-and-white hair. "So you wouldn't stand out there, or anything."

ERICA ESCORTED MITCH TO the Department of Motor Vehicles the following morning. He set the bureaucratic wheels in motion for Donald Spivak's driver's license. He kissed her on Center Street as if she had saved his life. She had been right about Mitch: he understood completely.

Back at the office, Erica caught herself smelling a jacket he'd left on her chair. A good thing she wasn't in a cubicle anymore.

She'd never been so happy, either. She kept bumping into moments of delight, and thinking, yes, but how long can it last?

❖

Donald Spivak and Marjorie Slotweiner sat in an outdoor café in Santa Monica, soaking up the June sunshine, the shore breeze and the parade of the young and the nearly young passing by. How easy it was to travel as somebody else! He was petrified that he might bump into someone he knew with his fresh new documents shrieking in his hands.

And, in fact, at the airport, there was Dominique Landau, Cynthia and Jack's daughter, sitting in one of the lounges, looking up from a magazine just as he passed by. She'd waved to him. Erica, thank God, was walking separately, and their gate was at least half a mile farther on. He'd waved, pointed to his watch and smiled apologetically as he walked on rapidly. She might tell her mother, she might not. At this point, he didn't give a damn if he was caught with a woman not his wife; it was the false documents that made him anxious.

Interesting, how the bar kept being raised a notch.

At the café in Santa Monica, they continued to explore the idea that he'd voiced on Maria's sofa.

"Where is the last place anyone would look for you if you disappeared?"

"Istanbul."

"Wrong." Erica dumped out a bowl of paper-covered sugar cubes on the table, and began to build a wall with them.

"The Bahamas?"

"Closer. Think of the Mets, think of the airports."

"*Queens?*"

"Exactly." She crowned the top of the wall with the last sugar cube, then knocked it down. "You leave a matchbook from, oh, Los Angeles in the pocket of a jacket, with a phone number scribbled on it. With a question mark after one of the digits—a two or a five?"

She began building a new wall. "A bunch of names and phone numbers in London and, say, Antwerp, in your date book. Seeded all through the months. Maybe you leave behind a separate address book. This could keep them busy for weeks. By then you're gone. Far away. Just across the East River. They'd *never* look for you there."

"What would I be doing there?"

"What have you always wanted to do?"

"Start a serious tank," he said, and she nodded.

A brigade of skateboarders rolled by, showing off for one another.

"Learn German."

"Exactly."

"Read the Churchill memoirs—you know it's at least ten enormous books, plus all the speeches. Never mind the biographies."

"Interesting."

And then he began strategizing out loud.

"I know that it worked for you and your mother, but cash under the bed isn't particularly safe. Something is always burning down in Queens. I say, we spread it out among Bermuda, Switzerland, the Caymans. I'd have to have some local bank account, with an ATM card."

She shook her head. "Cameras."

He thought for a minute, and chewed his straw. "So a certain amount of cash under the bed is necessary. Credit cards whenever possible."

"Until they figure out your alias."

Unusually dressed people of all ages strolled by, casually exposing tattoos and jewelry piercing unthinkable body parts.

"Then I'd have to have another alias ready. Perhaps I could use more than one simultaneously."

"Risky, although I suppose I'm doing it."

"No. Cash is the answer, but not all in one place. Business trips to the various banks once a year to replenish the supply."

"On the other hand, why not simply do it legally? Set up a local account at Chase, and pay taxes, as Donald Spivak."

"And use the ATM? But what about cameras? What if I'm audited?"

A squad car parked in front of the restaurant, and two members of the Los Angeles Police Department sat in it, not moving.

She lowered her voice and leaned in toward him. "What if you gave *me* the ATM card? I could supply you with cash."

He held her stubby hands. "I can't believe we're discussing this."

"This is the most exciting thing I've ever discussed," she whispered.

Mitch sighed. He'd given a good deal of thought to the idea of escape; he'd called a divorce lawyer once. The lawyer had asked a series of questions, and sent him some preliminary paperwork to set a separation in motion. The paperwork sat at the bottom of his in-box for months, while Mitch ducked the lawyer's follow-up phone calls. He didn't have the courage to openly announce that his marriage was over. Nor did he have the energy to start all over in a new firm, or in a new career. So the idea that he would become a criminal at this late stage in life was just as preposterous. This discussion was just that: discussion.

"It would never work," he said.

"Why not?"

"Do you think you have the heart of a fugitive?"

"But I wouldn't be a fugitive. I'd be the operative on the ground. I'd stay at the office. Keep track of everything."

"And when the police come after me?"

"I'd find out what they know and warn you." She thought a moment. "Cash in safe-deposit boxes around the city. Offshore accounts. Pay by check and credit cards, skip the ATM all together."

"But you have to sign in, and deal with people at the vault. Guards."

"I'd be the one to go. You'd be underground."

An elderly woman in a canary yellow T-shirt and leggings gracefully rolled by on skates.

"Interesting," he said. He'd never do it.

Two nights after they'd returned from California, Mitch arrived at Erica's apartment, red in the face. She closed down her laptop.

"Tell me again how it would work," he demanded.

"You could disappear, simply, or you could disappear with money."

He paced the living room. "How much?"

"Well, you would need a *lot* of money. It wouldn't make sense to walk off with just a little. You'd need money for every eventuality, so that you wouldn't ever have to worry about surfacing. You have a lot of years ahead of you."

"At least fifty million," he said.

"At least. You have access to a lot more, as you know."

"And I'd never have to see anyone again."

"No, you wouldn't *be able* to see your family or friends again."

"No loss there."

Something had happened, and it wasn't clear what.

She wasn't going to pry. "Anything you want to discuss?"

"Not particularly."

He went to take a shower. She put her foot in his shoe, and felt the roominess. She walked around the room in his big shoes. When he emerged, he stood in front of her, drying himself, watching her. She loved the proximity, the strangeness of company, the festive quality his presence gave her rooms.

❖

Geri had died Erica's first week of law school. Erica gave her Dorothy Findlay's funeral. Sheldon was there, comforting the bereaved one at a time.

For months afterward, Erica lived entirely at Maria's, not even stopping by the old apartment, too busy with work. The beginning of Christmas break she went home, ready to deal. She was unprepared for how normal everything was. Everything was exactly the same, although her mother was gone.

But when she opened the closet, she was hit by her mother's perfume and had to sit down. The strength of her feelings surprised her. She found she didn't want to leave.

She didn't need the apartment, but it was bigger than Maria's. It had furniture, and it was closer to the stores, the subway and the bus stop. She wanted to keep both places.

But she needed to make room for herself here. The books—all New Age tracts, all approved by Sheldon—these had to go. The notebooks: endless notes from Sheldon's lectures, perfectly legible, meaning unclear. Could she throw out her mother's handwriting? She threw them out. The hats, coats and scarves didn't suit her. The gloves, dresses and shoes didn't fit her. She gave them all away. She spent time in both apartments, supplementing her job in the Law School library with cash from the Union settlement.

She got rid of all Geri's dark, claw-footed furniture and chipped porcelain coffee cups. She ordered an entire home over the phone from the Living Cove, and painted the walls bright yellow with sky-blue trim, as she'd seen in the catalog.

Without thinking about it, she paid for Erica's new furniture with Maria's credit card, realizing the mistake only as she gave the card number. She would keep her lives and bills separate from then on.

The Grief Center had been spiffed up and renovated. It was now called the Institute for Well-Being. On a heavy, overcast day in July, she dropped by during her lunch hour and asked to see Sheldon. A woman her own age behind the reception desk looked at her with a face full of tragedy and hope. Sheldon was still at it, clearly.

He was tickled to see her. "Erica! What's new?"

"I'm a tax accountant."

"Good! Would you like to attend a lecture in five minutes? Some of the old guard are still here, but I've got new ones, too. Young."

"I bet you do," she murmured. "Will it be in your study?"

"No, my dear! You haven't seen the glamorous renovation that we did. When was that? Eight years ago! Come see."

He led her on a tour, and she complimented all the fine woodwork, the intelligent use of space. "So where do you hang out these days, the lecture hall, the kitchen and the office?"

"Basically. We have so much space. I want to rent some of it out, but it's in no condition. I have so much stuff up there. And, oh, I don't know: it's not like I need the money, or want more company. So there's no motivation."

"Maybe I can help."

"What a turnaround, Erica! You've never been interested in our work."

"My interest is in the space, actually," she said. "I'm thinking of starting up my own shop. You have no idea how expensive office space can be. If I clean up the space, would you give me a break on the rent?"

Sheldon stroked his beard and smirked. "You know, I always told your mother that you would be an ideal person to do business with."

"Show me the fourth floor."

It was, as advertised, a mess. "Wow," she said, as if dispirited.

"I know," he said.

They lingered on the landing. "Well," she said vaguely, "it's going to take a while. But that's okay, because I'm not starting this thing up tomorrow. I'll need some time to get my plan together."

"Take as long as you need, and don't be a stranger, or all business, either. We still do classes and dinners. I still cut hair, you know; I'd love to get my hands on your gorgeous tresses."

"Ah," she said, backing up before he tried. Had he forgotten?

On her way downstairs, she noticed a closet bursting open, an alcove stuffed with junk and an out-of-order bathroom. As Sheldon lumbered nimbly down the stairs toward a female call for help, Erica wrapped the pouch of cash in a second plastic bag, and stuck the package between a dusty framed picture and what looked like the white yak carpet from Sheldon's old office, now rolled up and covered with twenty years of soot.

❖

Mitch had been approaching his confinement with excitement, although everyone got on his nerves: Marty Slavin, and his mean, vulgar cracks about Erica; Friedman and his self-righteous badgering;

his sons, and their incessant need to disappoint him; his wife, and her incessant need to be right; his mother, and her incessant need for contact; his sister, and her incessant need for everything. He made a list of chores he detested that he'd soon be free of.

Erica had found a house in Queens, ostensibly for someone relocating from Phoenix. It was near one of her mother's old friends, she told him, in case she needed an excuse for being seen there. Mitch hadn't looked at the place, but approved it from her description. He paid the first month's rent and a security deposit with checks drawn on the new account for Donald Spivak that she'd started at Chase.

He had a sense with Erica of small actions adding up over time, like a good chess game. She was slowly developing physical evidence of the existence of George Matarano, Mitch's alternative identity, against a time of future need. Every day she asked him to make entries in a date book. Over the course of five months, in his own hand, in different pens, with some truth, fiction and inspiration, he would create a dense pattern of valuable leads, going nowhere.

Every day Patricia outraged him in ways large and small. But he looked at Erica, patiently accumulating documentation, and decided to take the high road. This was a liminal period. The annoyance and humiliation would soon be over, and then he'd never have to deal with these ingrates again.

❖

On Friday morning of Labor Day weekend, Erica swiped her student ID through the Columbia Law School library turnstile. She'd signed up for a General Studies class in the name of Emily Knorr—a onetime name, with a made-up Social Security number. She'd paid in cash. School had just started, and the lounge was brimming with high spirits and student traffic. She wore Marjorie's wig and a new beige cotton pantsuit with red sandals.

In the stacks, near the Federal Court Reporters that she'd identified in previous visits as an underused area, Erica set up Sonny McPhain's Toshiba, clicked on AOL, went to the Barclays homepage and calmly typed in his account number and password. He'd be first, as his people were the slowest. She transferred $3,760,000 to an account in Costa Rica that she'd set up a month ago from the office.

Erica took $2,750,000 of municipal bond interest that she'd moved to Celestina's account in the Cayman Islands the previous week, and transferred it to an account in St. Kitts. She took $29,150,000 from Celestina's Swiss account that was earmarked for taxes and transferred that to a different Cayman Islands account. Plugging in Jerry Fabrikant's iMac, she dialed into his private investment bank. Several screens and passwords later, she cashed in $4.2 million from his stock portfolio, and transferred it to an account in St. Kitts. Still using Jerry's laptop, she rapidly made twenty-three more wire transfers, raiding the funds of some other clients. She finished with a dip into Glenn Friedman's brokerage account, and a heavy swipe at Marty Slavin's trust.

Erica got up and stretched when she received e-mail confirmations of the transfers. She walked to a glassed-in book-sorting area near an internal elevator. She beeped Mitch. He called back on Maria's cell phone.

"Under way," she said.

"I don't know if I can do this," he said.

"What?"

"I said, I don't think I can do it. This is not a good idea."

"That's not what you said as recently as last night."

"I know, but now that it's almost happening—"

"It *is* happening," she interrupted. "It *has* happened."

She looked around to see if this highly incriminating conversation had been overheard. No one there.

"I can't do this." He sounded weak and sick.

She had to keep her temper. A student walked in to grab books to reshelve—a job she'd once had, in a different life. She went to the ladies' room and made sure she was alone. "What's the problem?"

"What if they follow *you*?"

"We've been through this: *I* am staying in place."

He had no response. She looked at herself in the mirror. Marjorie, sleek and competent, hadn't counted on anything other than complete cooperation and professionalism from her partner.

"Donald," she tried, "where are you?"

"Somewhere near Rockefeller Center."

The lost and aimless tone frightened her. "Listen to me. Walk east to Grand Central, and take the 7 train to Queens."

"I just don't think I can do it."

"It's done. Now I'm counting on you to pull yourself together and go."

She smoothed a chunk of Marjorie's springy blond hair to the side.

"Think about the tank," she said. It came out somewhat patronizing. "Please go to the house," she pleaded. "The way we discussed."

She hung up, left the bathroom and looked around at the looming stacks of fraying books. There wasn't a window in sight. She had a head full of numbers and she was in complete uncertainty.

CHAPTER NINE

Mitch woke up in Queens. Every morning he had to remind himself: I am free. It's a gorgeous day, and I don't have to go to the office. I don't have to please my wife, I don't have to bail my sons out of jail and I live in Jackson Heights.

This elation fell between moments of panic when he burst into a sweat remembering the irrevocable nature of what had been done. Not only did he not have to call his mother, he *couldn't* call his mother, ever. Then there were moments of despair when he realized that after a career spent thinking ahead, he found himself in a bleak, uncharted environment where he couldn't plan the following day. He oscillated between self-congratulation and self-pity. He did nothing all day and was exhausted.

The third night of his exile, he'd put on a hat and beard that Erica had left in the closet, and drove into the city at three A.M. in the Toyota, looking like a Hassid. He and Erica had paid cash—literally cash—for this car, at a car lot somewhere in Nassau County two weeks before. Never in his life had he bought a used car, and it troubled him: anything could go wrong with it.

In Manhattan he sweated at every red light, a throbbing mass of guilt ready to be picked up, interrogated and incarcerated.

Erica waited in Maria's vestibule with his luggage and five bags of groceries. She got into the passenger seat, still furious, and didn't help load the car. He held his breath as the car dipped down into the deserted Midtown Tunnel. He took the Queens side streets carefully, petrified of an encounter with a real Hassid. When he arrived in his new driveway without incident, he wondered if he'd ever be able to relax again. She was too mad to speak, apparently; they went to bed without a single word.

After the pizza fiasco, he didn't go out unless absolutely necessary. There was a tiny concrete patio in the back of the house, but it was exposed to the surrounding houses. A woman, possibly South American, or Southeast Asian, frequently appeared at the back door of the house opposite, sweeping the driveway. She had squinted toward his back door on more than six separate occasions. They should have had some kind of porch or awning built beforehand. Now it was too late. He propped open the door, dragged the armchair to the threshold and took the air. He began reading volume one of Churchill's history of the Second World War.

TAX PLANNING was hardly an addiction: he didn't mind not working. And although he had a certain facility with people, he didn't need much social interaction. Glenn Friedman was wrong about Mitch Greiff: he didn't need to be seen. Rather, he needed to make an entrance, but afterward, he was happier out of the spotlight. Two weeks passed. He was barely aware of the time.

As soon as she felt comfortable, Erica started coming to Queens for dinner, then returning home, to whichever home, at about eleven. Although she'd insisted that he do all of his business in the far reaches of Brooklyn, Queens and Long Island, Mitch decided he couldn't effectively hide in an environment that he didn't know. He began to venture out into the neighborhood.

He had a new buzz cut (Erica had done this in the bathroom, and the hair was still there on the floor), and his face was almost camouflaged. He'd never in his life had a beard, and he observed the growth of the slanted black lines with fascination. He took the opportunity to have an ear pierced at a tacky jewelry store on 82nd Street. Now even his own mother wouldn't recognize him. He hovered around the racks as two neighborhood types tried on clothes in the adjacent menswear store, things he'd never look at. He tried on what they tried on. He looked like an aging gay Latin clubgoer. He had them cut the tags off and he wore the clothes out. On his way home, he noticed men all over the neighborhood wearing jackets in the same style.

The neighborhood seemed to be working-class, or ethnic middle-class, or something. Not wealthy, but not dangerous. As he exited the drugstore and turned the corner, he realized that *he* was the criminal element walking down 35th Avenue. He burst into laughter.

This caught the eye of an elderly woman with jet-black hair doing laps with her chrome walker on the second-floor balcony of a high-rise. Moving to Queens was like introducing live rock into your tank: you had no idea what was living in all the cracks and hollows. The elderly woman turned her walker to stare at him directly, if thickly, through enormous black glasses.

"What's so funny?" she called from the balcony as he got nearer.

"I am!" he called up to her.

"You don't look so funny."

A cop standing at the entrance to her complex looked over at him. He nodded back to avoid looking guilty.

"You're probably right." He waved cheerfully, pleased with himself for adding outer-borough intonations and a cocky walk he'd seen practiced around the neighborhood. He probably should have been more attuned to the police, but he figured inattention was his best strategy. Those who felt hunted did stupid things and always got caught.

He was glad to get out of the house, but annoyed to be on his way to the Jungle Food. He didn't like having to shop and cook and clean the apartment. He had millions of dollars in various locations: why was he vacuuming carpets and schlepping to the supermarket? Surely in *Queens*, of all places, they could find someone to shop and clean. He brought it up that night.

"You are such a prince," said his mistress/accountant/accomplice.
"I like a clean apartment."

"You're missing the point. Someone comes in here, sees you and goes directly to the police."

"Why would she have to see me?"

"Oh, so this is one more thing that *I* have to do for you?"

"She wouldn't have to see *you* again," he insisted. "Not after the first time. You tell her what to do, show her where everything is and, after that, she just does it."

"How does she get in?"

"You give her the key."

"Why don't we give her the passwords to the bank accounts, too, while we're at it?"

Erica had also talked him out of the tank; she claimed that a tank would mean regular visits to fish stores, where he was known. He maintained that he could do it over the phone and the Internet. He didn't need her permission. He did need her to set up his computer, so he could start the research. He had to work on her. She was edgy, waiting for the other shoe to drop. It was late September. No one had missed him at the office. In three weeks, no one had noticed anything missing.

As he turned onto his block, a middle-aged black woman nodded at him and smiled. "Happy New Year," she said, and he tripped.

"You're Jewish," she was saying, essentially, "and I know it." How would she know he was Jewish? Was he wearing a yellow star on his new Latin leather jacket? On the other hand, she was black, and he knew it. Why did it bother him? Was it some ancestral memory of persecution? Was it that he was failing in his attempt to blend into the neighborhood? Was it the need—here not respected—to be a private person without unnecessary interaction, affiliation, identification? Whose business was it if he was Jewish?

The streets of Queens were lined with identical houses striving for originality. *What* was Donald Spivak? Shouldn't he work up a personal history for him, in case he was called upon to answer questions?

When he got home, he beeped Erica. Enough with irrelevant distractions: he needed to plan his tank.

❖

Lately everything was an outrage, although Erica was theoretically a happy woman. The only empty seat in the Jefferson Market branch of the public library was surrounded by a display of books on the theme of love: *The Lesbian and Gay Book of Love and Marriage, Giving the Love That Heals, Dumped!* and *The Complete Kama Sutra*. At the public library. Granted, not in the children's section, but really. Even now that she was getting it regularly, this incessant communal appetite for sex in the public sphere offended her. What ever happened to fall foliage, Halloween?

She turned her back to the exhibit and opened her budget files. The man across the aisle was trimming his nails. The sound of the clipping echoed in the space. She had been trying to set aside money for every contingency. She wanted to get her own car. How many nails did this man have? She glared at the nail clipper. This would mean lease payments, insurance and garage. Or should she just buy the car outright? First, of course, she had to learn how to drive. Then she needed driver's licenses. The nail fragments must be ricocheting around the library. This was surely a private act: why was it happening in the nonfiction section?

Erica bought groceries in Midtown and dragged them to Queens on the subway, although nothing had even been noticed yet. She understood that Mitch didn't want to go out for food and had agreed that he ought to lie low. But she was outraged that not only did he expect her to bring the food, but also to *make* him dinner once she'd arrived. A confrontation was brewing.

She trudged up Maddie Olsen's steps, wondering how the woman would offend her this time.

"Erica!" Maddie greeted her. "Come in."

"How are you feeling?" Erica put the bag on the kitchen table.

"Not so great, dear. What's new?"

"Not much."

"I didn't think so," Maddie said, sounding pleased to radiate pity. "Maybe you'd find a boyfriend if you dressed a little nicer."

Erica put the milk in the fridge. "Maybe you'd smell better if you bathed more often," she replied, smiling sweetly as she went out the back way.

But she was happy, she reminded herself, as she crossed the neighbor's driveway and emerged on the next block. They'd been an item for almost seven months now. And he wasn't going anywhere.

The car was unlocked, and Mitch had left the garbage outside on the wrong day. He was incompetent. The Toyota was sitting in the driveway, unused, unappreciated, coyly beckoning her to join the club. Mitch could teach her how to drive. It was the least he could do.

He hurled himself at her as she opened the door, as if he'd been coiled in a state of tension all day, attached to the hinge. "Let's go out to dinner!" he sang, between furious kisses. "What's the best restaurant in Queens?"

She put the groceries on the table. "The Pastrami King." She fended off another kiss so she could breathe. He was behaving like a puppy.

"Be serious. Something swanky."

"You be serious. The more high-profile the place, the better the chances of being recognized."

He made sure she saw him pouting. Perhaps he was just playing, forcing her to play the prudent, restrictive authority. She didn't like it.

He saw her noticing the sinkful of dishes and said, "Where do you suppose they'd keep the dishwashing stuff? I don't see any."

"Did you look under the sink?"

"Oh, do you think they'd keep it there?"

She looked at him. "*They* are *you*, you know. This is *your* place. Where do *you* keep the dishwashing stuff?"

He looked at her. He expected her to wash his dishes.

"Patricia was a saint." She walked upstairs.

———

AFTER DINNER, even though she was full, and in company, Erica suddenly felt like eating oatmeal and shopping on-line for Marjorie while listening to the news and doing a crossword puzzle. She turned on the computer. Mitch came and sat next to her, begging her to set up his e-mail. The haircut made him look much older, oddly. The way he was fondling his newly pierced earlobe was irritating. She couldn't get used to the beard.

She turned on the news.

He talked through it.

There was the drinking-water controversy ("You have to have a water cooler? That's another deliveryman to recognize you. Think, Mitch."), the sleeping arrangement controversy (he sulked when she didn't spend the night, and used his pique as leverage to beg for a trip into Manhattan, the forbidden city), and then the sugar bowl controversy, when he put spoonful after spoonful of salt in his tea, wondering why it wasn't getting sweeter.

"What the hell is the salt doing in the sugar bowl?" he exploded.

"That's the salt bowl."

"Salt goes in a shaker."

"In my house, the salt goes in that bowl, and the Equal packets go in a bowl just like it."

"Well, I'm not on a diet."

"So put the sugar out."

And on and on.

Perhaps these were just the usual disagreements in starting up a joint home. She wouldn't know: she'd never done it. And now, on the shady side of thirty-five, set in her ways three times over (three apartments, three bowls of salt, three bowls of Equal), she was unaccustomed to compromise. If she was the one renting the apartment, paying the bills, making the tea and buying the bowl, why shouldn't she put salt in it?

The irony was that there was no real money yet; he was living on some cash that he'd taken from his own account the week prior to Labor Day. She might actually have to lend this whining, passive embezzler some money, until it was prudent for her to leave the country.

She left the house after the ten-o'clock news. He pouted. He wanted to be with her. Which, she supposed, was a good thing. She was happy. She was.

AFTER WORK ONE NIGHT, Erica took the 6 train down to the Rainbow, an assisted-living center that she'd identified in her research, once she'd decided that it was best to spread her volunteering around. She was given charge of a woman around her own age named Debbie Goldman, who greeted her with a seal bark and a hug. With other volunteers and members of the Rainbow, she went to a puppet show at a church.

She took the 6 train back to Grand Central, and the 7 train to Jackson Heights, weary from all the back and forth. She was rushing around, accomplishing nothing. She had to give up an apartment. It wasn't a question of money, obviously. But Erica couldn't spend enough time in all three places, plus the residence in Jackson Heights, to justify keeping them all.

The question was, which to give up? This raised all sorts of existential dilemmas. She decided to talk to Mitch about it. She now had someone whose opinion she respected whom she could talk to about this.

"I don't see the problem. Live here, for God's sake."

"You know that's not possible, as much as I'd like to."

"Live at Marjorie's, work at Maria's and get rid of Erica's."

"Erica needs an address."

"Use Maria's address for Erica."

"The new super is nosy."

"So get rid of Erica's and move into Marjorie's as Erica."

"You mean, brown-wig, dowdy Erica?"

"Why does Erica have to be dowdy?" He poured himself a cup of coffee, not asking if she wanted one. "Marjorie isn't dowdy, Maria isn't dowdy. I don't like how you talk yourself down."

"I suppose I could give up Maria's, but it's a good place to work."

He signaled exasperation with her. Her time was up.

She respected him. She listened to his endless and recurrent lectures about the isolation of Churchill in between the wars, the value of sifting gobies and the freedom he felt, not having to be charming at cocktail parties.

But he didn't have patience to listen for *five minutes* while she discussed this critical issue, which needed immediate attention. This clearly had roots in their previous power dynamic, when he'd stood up to indicate that it was time for her to leave his office. But the power had shifted.

Erica left the house with her four sets of keys, out of sorts. She climbed the stairs to the 7 train, which took forever to come, and forever to get into Manhattan. She resented his complaints about the décor of the house, the tackiness of the neighbor's lawn ornaments, the lack of inspiration in the scenery of Queens. What the hell was he talking about? She had planned, financed and orchestrated his escape. What else did he expect her to do: plant roses and reupholster?

ALTHOUGH SHE APPRECIATED MARJORIE most of all, Erica decided that keeping up Marjorie would be too much of a risk. Once the story broke, and the firm came under scrutiny, Marjorie Slotweiner would be part of the investigation as one of the firm's clients.

She brought Marjorie's computer and clothes to Maria's. She couldn't send Marjorie's furniture to Maria's without leaving a trail. So she had all the big, lovely furniture picked up by a thrift shop. She popped by the rental agent in Marjorie's building to say that she was taking a sales job in Raleigh and would pay the last month of her lease right then. The apartment would be vacant October 1. She paid Marjorie's last bills, canceled all of Marjorie's accounts and carefully put Marjorie's files, credit cards and driver's license in a file cabinet at Maria's.

❖

Mitch was calm when Erica got behind the wheel of the Toyota.

Immediately, however, she shot out into traffic, nearly hitting a car traveling in the far lane.

"OH, GOD! Erica! What if we get in an accident?"

"It's okay, you'll just say you're teaching me how to drive."

He gripped the armrest. "Watch the oncoming traffic!"

"I'm watching!"

"Pull over," he said firmly. "I think we need to go somewhere quiet, a parking lot somewhere."

"What's that?" she said, excited.

"Don't look over there. Look at the road, the traffic lights, in the rearview mirror, the oncoming traffic."

"This is fun! I can't believe I'm doing this!"

"Me neither," he said.

One week had led to two weeks had led to two months. Before his name exploded over the TV and the newspapers, he'd spent long days traversing the dreary redbrick precincts of Queens, exhilarated and depressed.

Now there was something in the paper or on the TV every day, and he was lying low. He organized his schedule around the news, taping the five-, six- and eleven-o'clock local shows, and the six-thirty national shows. He checked the three all-news cable channels every hour. He felt an odd hysteria hearing his name, seeing his photograph. They all used a picture of him in a tuxedo, with his arm around a smiling Jerry Fabrikant. Every media outlet used all three of his names, Mitchell Alan Greiff, as if he were a serial killer. Never in his life had he paid attention to the tabloids; now he was buying the *News* and the *Post* every day.

They were calling him the "celebrity accountant mastermind." At night he replayed the tapes, fast-forwarding through wars and local violence to get to the parts about him. There were some beautiful shots of Patricia getting out of a squad car looking haggard and grim. Previously, he'd been dreading the break of the story. Now that it was out in the open, he realized what he'd been missing all this time. He had to drag himself to bed each night; there were chat rooms on AOL devoted entirely to discussion of *him*.

Erica had been interviewed several times by the cops. She'd stopped visiting for a few weeks, to be prudent. Which was fine: he was inundated with all the magazines, newspapers, TV and Internet coverage. He had so much to do.

The Christmas season was in full swing already, and he was neither sentimental nor depressed. It didn't specifically apply to him. But he was getting antsy.

"You can go out." She hit the brake hard for no reason. "You *do* go out. All the time."

"I'm bored already with Jackson Heights. And don't tell me to go to *Corona*," he said, disgustedly. "Don't tell me to go to *Flushing*."

"You want to go back to your old life?"

He sighed. "No. Get in the left lane."

"I don't know how," she whimpered.

He checked all sides. "Go now. You're fine."

She switched lanes, slamming on the brake when she saw a car ten feet ahead. He smelled her terror. It was odd to see her as a beginner; she was the complete authority in his life now, providing money, rules and information, telling him no. She had exhausted him earlier with a long romp in bed. What would happen when her desire outstripped his ability?

She had calmed down now, and was doing long loops around the neighborhood, always coming back to Roosevelt Avenue under the slatted shadow of the El, which was decked out in tacky Christmas bunting and teeming below with shivering people in dark parkas and jeans.

She slammed on the brakes once too often.

"This lesson is over," he said.

"But what about parking?"

"Park in the driveway."

She drove home, chastened. He got out of the car, stiff, heavy, shaky, nauseated. Had it only been half an hour in the car? He hadn't been this frightened since he'd taught his sons to drive some ten years ago. This was no thing for an old man to do.

An old man! Well, he supposed he was.

"I need time to settle my stomach." He fell onto the couch. He saw a squad of dustballs lurking under the chair.

"When can we do that again?"

"After I'm dead."

"Oh, come on!"

He wanted to have a good meal that night. He didn't want to look at this dingy rug getting dingier. Whatever else you could say about Patricia, the food was excellent, the setting was elegant and there were no dustballs. She'd approached her role of household manager as a challenge: everything was the best, the most delicious, the most stylish. Was he really going to pack it all in for a life with a woman whose idea of a good meal was greasy Chinese noodles? Couldn't she take a course or something?

Erica strapped herself into the driver's seat. The instructor was a portly man in his sixties stinking of tobacco, old sweat and aftershave.

He eyed her brazenly. "Now, step on the exhilarator," he said smoothly, with no hint of irony. "That's the right pedal. This one, dear," he said, placing a thick white hand on her right thigh.

"If you touch me again," she said, eyes on the street, "I will get out of this car and report you to your superiors."

"So sorry, so sorry, please don't be alarmed," the fragrant instructor said, not watching the road. She could feel him lapping up Marjorie's wig and makeup with his eyes. "*You* knew right away, but you'd be shocked how many blondes forget which leg is which."

She should take off her blondness and give *him* a shock.

Erica gripped the wheel. In spite of the chaos on Second Avenue, she drove straight with relative calm. Turns were another story.

Detective Sprague's calls and impromptu visits had tapered off, but she was careful not to get too comfortable. She was glad she'd closed down Marjorie's place, although she missed it.

The instructor requested that she switch into the right lane. Erica looked in the rearview, and turned around to double-check, because of the blind spot. As she hit the turn signal, she caught a glimpse of a guy she'd spent the night with some ten years earlier. She almost jumped over the curb.

"Smoothly, smoothly, never get flustered." The driving instructor overrode her with his wheel and his brake.

She went home, unnerved and infuriated. She needed to start all over in a new place, where there wasn't an embarrassing memory on every corner. Of course, anywhere else in America, she needed a car.

Her father had *not* been killed in a car accident. Geri had been wrong: Erica *was* entitled to learn to drive, whether or not she had a car, or even a destination. There was no impediment to driving: it was now an imperative.

❖

One blustery Saturday afternoon on Roosevelt Avenue, beneath the riot of shiny red garlands under the El, Mitch saw Conchita Santos, and instinctively looked away and walked on. But he knew that she'd recognized him, so he wheeled around and called, "Conchita? Is that you?"

"Mr. Greiff, what you doing here?"

He smiled. "What's new?"

"You're the one! Where you living? People looking for you. . . ." She ended on a high note and let the idea trail in the air. He could see her awareness of her position grow.

"Are you still working for my wife?"

"She had to let me go."

"Are you looking for other work?"

"I have some other jobs, but sure."

"Why don't we discuss it? I'd pay very well."

"Where you living?"

"Why don't we discuss it first, and then I'll show you." He leaned in confidentially. "I don't need to tell you that you can't talk about it, right?"

"Right, right."

"I mean, you know that I'm underground, right?"

"Right, right, right."

"But even underground, I need some help: vacuuming, laundry, shopping."

"When you're a fugitive, you have to pay more for the basic services."

"That's right," he said, smiling. He was so sick of the smell of antibacterial kitchen Lysol that he'd been letting the dirt just accumulate.

"How much more?" she wanted to know. She, too, was smiling, flush with power, enjoying this banter in the lively wind under the El.

"Let's discuss it!"

"Now?"

"If it's good for you."

They slid into a booth in the back of the Galaxy Coffee Shop. Perhaps he'd been spending too much time on Roosevelt Avenue: Conchita looked attractive. But he wanted to keep this pure business: hush money and housekeeping. He needed help.

"So what have you been up to since I saw you last?" he asked.

"Well, my daughter, Graciela, is ten now. She's in school here, PS 87."

"The one on 35th Avenue?"

"That's right. We live with my aunt Nydia over there on 86th Street. We don't have any space. I'd like to move."

"Would you stay in the neighborhood?"

"Depends. If I could find something nice around here, I would stay. I'd like to have my own place."

"So there's rent for you, and rent for Aunt Nydia," he said, and wrote it down on a napkin. "We'll do numbers later. Tell me what else is going on."

She looked at him shrewdly.

"There's a big reward for information about you, Mr. Greiff."

"Call me Mitch. How much?"

"I think $25,000."

"So then there's the reward money." He wrote this on the napkin.

"You know, I don't know whether we ever discussed it," she said smoothly, "but I got a serious problem with my credit cards."

"No!" he whispered.

"Yes!" She laughed.

"How much?"

"Well, if you add it all up—"

"Please! Add it all up," he said festively.

"Over twenty thousand," she said.

He could tell she'd padded a little. "Conchita, that's terrible," he said, turning to his sandwich. "How do you sleep at night?"

"I know, I can't stand it."

THEY SETTLED ON A PRELIMINARY FIGURE of $60,000, to be paid in twelve installments. She couldn't move into her own apartment—Nydia would be suspicious, and couldn't make the rent on her own. Moreover, she couldn't pay her credit cards off right away—this might alert the authorities. He'd give her some additional cash each week. This she would use for food, toys, transportation: her life. She would pay off her credit cards with money she earned from her jobs, over the course of two years.

As for the living situation, she would find a nicer apartment with a real kitchen and three separate bedrooms; she could tell Aunt Nydia that the rent was the same. He would pay for whatever the difference was. In cash.

"How do I know you'll do it?"

"How do I know that you won't call the police?"

"I don't want to be stuck paying big rent if you disappear on me."

This was fair. "So maybe I should give you some cash up front that you would only use toward rent. What do you say, a year of the difference between the old apartment and the new one?"

"Two years."

"A year and a half, okay?"

She smiled and sat back on the banquette, assessing her new position.

"How am I going to work this with Nydia?"

"Find the place. Then make sure the rent bill is addressed to you."

"What rent bill?"

"No rent bill?"

She looked at him gravely, and then burst into peals of laughter. "You got a lot to learn about Queens, Mitch."

THE LATE LUNCH with Conchita made him feel back on top, in charge, capable of handling complex arrangements with flair. He saluted the cop at the 23-76 80th Avenue apartments on his way home.

"You WHAT?" shrieked Erica when he told her. "Are you INSANE?"

He refused to get sucked into the violence of her tone. "I handled it brilliantly. She recognized me on the street—she would have gone directly to the police for the reward. This way, we get a clean apartment. And she's cheap."

"*Now* she's cheap," Erica said, sounding like a tough old barkeep.

"All she wants is to get rid of her debt and move into a nicer place."

"Now. In a year, she'll want half of what you have, in cash."

"We'll see. I think she liked the subterfuge. I think she never liked Patricia, and she's enjoying the power."

"I think you just don't want to pick up after yourself."

"We may need her for something. And she's untraceable."

"Nobody is untraceable."

"I mean, she's not here legally, and she's not working for Patricia anymore."

"But she was at the time, and I'm sure the cops interviewed her."

That hadn't occurred to him. "Whatever. She's in our corner now."

"And how are you going to pay her?"

He hadn't thought about this.

"I guess you'll have to take that vacation sooner than we thought." He buried his nose in her neck. She disengaged without apology.

❖

January sunshine was flat and relentless on Grand Cayman Island. Erica lay naked beneath the ceiling fan. She'd arrived the previous evening, a Thursday, and would be leaving the island on Sunday morning. Detective Sprague and the arrogant Italian partner had backed off; she knew from monitoring Friedman's e-mail that there was a Federal investigation going on. The money was under the bed, in two medium-sized suitcases with false bottoms. She wondered how much money the NYPD paid its Detectives. It was likely that their investigations were fueled by resentment.

The previous afternoon, she'd changed wigs in a ladies' room at a Barnes & Noble, packed at Maria's, dropped her suitcases at the Institute for Well-Being, changed wigs again in a busy Third Avenue steakhouse, swung by the Institute in a cab, picked up Maria's suitcase and went to JFK.

It was a relief to be away from Mitch. After all the years she'd been yearning for him, it was ironic that now that they were involved, all she could think about was planning her next driving lesson, reorganizing Maria's files and adding to the Debbie Goldman paper trail. Her mind was on him only in the abstract: how to work with his moods, how to manage him.

The night before she left, she arrived at the house and called, "Okay if I take the car out to practice?"

"Don't get yourself killed," Mitch shouted down the stairs.

They hadn't even said hello.

This had been her first time alone in a car. Where was the emergency brake? There it was. She backed out of the driveway and drove around the block slowly, making right turns. In spite of four classes with different instructors, she still couldn't switch lanes or turn left without anxiety. Driving was practically aerobic at this stage.

THE PHONE RANG in her hotel room. Who knew she was here?

It was Mitch, calling to chat about a new fish he'd seen on the Internet. She had to control herself; she wanted to crush him. She said, "This is unwise, and you know it. I'll talk to you when I get back. Good-bye." She hung up with exaggerated patience.

Mitch was getting cavalier. She knew he'd been to Westchester several times—towns where he knew people. The night before she left, she'd found him lurking on-line in a Mitch Greiff chat room.

"What are you doing?"

"Just enjoying the debate here," he said without looking up.

She didn't bother shutting down AOL: she just pulled the plug.

"How dare you?" he roared over his blackened screen.

She spoke with deliberate calm, softly so he would have to lean in to hear. "When you connect to your server, your computer is assigned an individual electronic number. When you enter a chat room, you emit that number. That number can be traced directly to your computer, and the phone number you are calling in from can be traced as well. Did you know that?"

He stood with his arms crossed, like an angry teenager. "So?"

"So, if I were a cop on this case, I'd probably go directly to a Mitch Greiff chat room, and take down all the names of the people in it. I'd trace them back to their computers, and trace their phone numbers back to them."

He turned away from her, standing in front of the closed shade at the window. "No, I didn't know that."

"Well, the cops on this case are in the Computer Crimes Squad. They do know that. In fact, if I were a cop on this case, I'd probably start up a Mitch Greiff chat room, and see who showed up."

Mitch faced her. "Well, I know for a fact that this Mitch Greiff chat room wasn't started by the cops," he said with some arrogance.

"You know that for a fact," she said, controlling her anger. "How?"

"Because I know the guy who started this chat room," Mitch said.

She looked at him, this big, misguided, middle-aged problem. "Oh, yes? And who would that be?"

"A guy I've been instant-messaging with. He's obsessed with Mitch

Greiff, and has a theory that Mitch is hiding on a barrier island in Georgia. He e-mailed me an invitation to join the room this afternoon."

ERICA SAT UP in the tropical bedroom, annoyed. Why did he put her in these positions? Why could he not see his own stupidity? He would draw a fluorescent green line between himself and the money; she had to be ready for it. She couldn't control everything he did.

She took a swig of mineral water. Some of it spilled down her neck and fizzed on her pillow. She didn't want to sit in that room, replaying his stupidity. She didn't like to think of him that way.

The landscape was filled with green golf course, blue sky and pink hotel. Her business was done; she might as well do something. She flipped through the hotel directory, settling on the spa page. She made an appointment for a manicure. She pulled on a caftan; in deference to the heat, she left her wig behind, wearing a scarf and a hat only.

As soon as she was seated in the salon, the beautician began digging: "Are you on your honeymoon? No? Are you married? No? Are you here with a boyfriend?"

Erica just stared at the woman.

"Are you American? No? The reason I ask, there was another woman in here last week, and she had shaved her head, too. She was an American."

"Tell me," Erica said, "are you not sufficiently amused by the television you have on?"

"I was just being polite."

"Is it polite to pry into people's personal lives?"

The woman used the cuticle scissors tensely, and cut Erica's thumb. She rose, bleeding. "What is your problem?"

The manager arrived, a middle-aged woman swallowing quickly, as if she'd been watching behind a one-way mirror while eating her lunch. "I am so sorry, madam. Would you like a cup of tea?"

"No, I do not want *a cup of tea*! I want to get out of here."

"You must let us use the disinfectant."

"I'll do that myself."

"Leaving without the disinfectant is against the rules."

"But drawing blood from the guests isn't?"

"I'm terribly sorry, madam."

She slammed out, bleeding and furious, with the manicurist chasing after her, brandishing a cotton ball and an evil-looking brown bottle.

Down the lush path, strewn with gorgeous fuchsia flowers, Erica seethed with irritation. If she hadn't wanted to please Mitch—meanwhile ignoring her own intense dislike for the much-too-personal contact with beauticians—she would never have put herself in such a position. But the minute you needed something—a product, a service, a look of approval—it set up a series of interactions with other people, and expectations on their part. The minute you needed something, you yielded your power to other people. She cursed Mitch and her need to please him.

Even if she *wanted* to be an evil person, Erica realized, she couldn't pull it off. She was foiled by the exigencies of the everyday world. And by people, especially people: intruding, prying, flaunting their tiny waistlines, performing intimate acts two inches from her face, presenting their expectations and needs, retaliating nastily if she didn't meet their expectations and needs.

And what about *her* expectations and *her* needs?

She had a need, lately, to be completely removed from the abrasion of human contact. But even if she had everything delivered, she'd still have to deal with the deliveryman. And if ever she needed air and ventured outside, there were always people on the street to peer beneath her hat, to call attention to the circumference of her belly, to invade her space while confessing something, for no other reason than that they were spilling over and needed to spread the extra around. This wouldn't change in Chicago.

How did the rich and famous deal with the world? Presumably they didn't use rent-controlled apartments in the East 20s as a base of operations. They were protected within a sealed compound. They hired people to screen the people who entered to perform services or deliver goods. But then they had to deal with the primary screen of people. So what was the difference?

The difference was that they paid the primary screen.

On the other hand, that didn't always ensure respectful behavior. People who did things for other people usually held them in some contempt. Look at these bored, bitchy beauticians so starved for intimate facts about random strangers.

Why was privacy so impossible?

ERICA TRAVELED HOME without event. She unpacked the cash, putting a quarter of it in Maria's coat closet. The rest she wrapped in tinfoil and stuffed into Marjorie's red canvas tote. At the Institute for Well-Being, Sheldon waved to her across the lobby, on his way to a session. She was in and out in three minutes. If only every interaction could be so easy.

She didn't call Mitch. She sat on Maria's couch, thinking ahead about alternative plans.

CHAPTER TEN

Patricia swatted Tony's hand off her butt as they walked into the restaurant. As delighted as she was with him, he was constantly climbing all over her, in public as well as in private; she felt exposed enough. Much of their time was spent at his cousin's apartment, but eventually they had to eat.

Leaving the pod was a problem.

The twenty-three-year-old hostess checked them out, eyes passing back and forth between them, doing the math. Everyone watched as they were led to a table.

If Patricia's life had, since Mitch's exit, become a bad movie, since Tony's entrance the previous month it had taken on the surreal tones of a Western. They walked into the saloon. The music and the merriment stopped. Everyone stared. Silence. Would there be a fight? Lately Patricia had found herself fascinated by mismatched couples she saw in the street—tall and short, fat and thin, black and white, pretty and ugly—people choosing each other and being together in spite of the commandment to form a matched set.

"Patricia!" she heard someone squeal, and she paused.

It was Denise Levine, someone she'd worked with on a famine relief benefit some five years earlier. "How are you, sweetheart?" Patricia could see her trying to avoid the topic of Mitch. "Um, is this your son, the actor?"

"Anthony Ballestrino, how do you do?" He stuck out his hand.

Denise shook it, confused.

Tony draped his arm around Patricia's shoulder and said, "Is this your father?"

Denise blanched. "No, this is my husband. Patricia, you remember Sol?"

"Yes, Sol, good to see you. Good to see you both." She grabbed Tony's hand, which was dangling down and grazing her breast. He was infantile.

As she pulled him to the back of the restaurant, she felt a hand on her butt again. She was furious. This need to establish ownership: was this a product of his age? Sometimes when he was driving, he didn't watch the road, he watched her. And he would look at her, she noticed, until she looked at him. Only then would he put his eyes back on the road. She had expected to feel safer with a cop.

Seated in the back of the restaurant, Patricia saw Denise and Sol doing the math like everyone else, and coming up with the lowest common denominator. She shot Tony a look.

"Well, why shouldn't I?" he said like a teenager.

"You'd better watch it," she said, like a mad mom. "If you want to be with me in public, you'd better watch how you behave."

"You wouldn't be out in public if it weren't for me," he said.

"What do you mean by that?"

"I mean, you'd be hiding in your son's apartment, sneaking cans of tuna fish and hoping they wouldn't notice. Don't think I don't know you, Patricia," he said. He stroked her knee.

Once again, Patricia had to ask herself: what was she doing with him?

Tony was seeing Patricia three times a week; they were leaving clothes and toiletries at his cousin's apartment now. He wanted to love being with her, having breakfast with her at five in the morning at various Glendale locals. He wanted to parade around with her on his arm. But she'd become paranoid about being seen in public and sensitive to every passing glance. Instead of just being together, she seemed to talk about whether they *should* be together. Sometimes she shut down completely, refusing to speak. The more he saw her, the more inaccessible she became. He grew tired of chasing her.

Promotions were announced. Once again Ballestrino was passed over. So was anybody with an ounce of intelligence. Three guys from Aviation were made Detectives, Second Grade. A mouth-breather *in the Equestrian Unit* made Detective, Second Grade. All the cops who were really just glorified secretaries for the PC or the Chief of Detectives were Detectives, Second Grade.

"It's all who you drive," Sprague sighed.

Some guys enjoyed the prestige of driving someone important. Ballestrino hadn't become a cop to be a chauffeur. He resented this compliance in his partner. The Lieutenant seemed watchfully idle that morning, as if he were surveying his troops for signs of humiliation. Why wasn't Sprague angry?

Although Anita Clemente's Trojan Horse had netted over 250 names, including prominent congressmen, doctors, NYC schoolteachers and Catholic priests, even she wasn't promoted. When the Mayor had held a press conference at City Hall with the Police Commissioner and the Chief of Detectives to announce the breakup of a major child pornography network, Anita Clemente wasn't even invited to attend. There was perverse satisfaction when someone else did well and wasn't rewarded for it either.

TONY BEGAN TAKING PATRICIA to the gym as his guest. She thanked him profusely. She'd had to give up her gym membership, and she missed the weights. He felt good whenever he could give her a moment away from her life. He enjoyed the sight of her thick red hair piled on top of her head in clips, her pale, graceful limbs bending in spandex and the ripple of interest she aroused among the regulars.

She was a gorgeous woman: perhaps not forever, but for now, she really was ageless.

One morning, after the gym, he'd made the mistake of stopping home with Patricia on their way into Manhattan. He'd forgotten to bring Sprague's birthday present, and the Unit was taking him out to the Gotham after work. He thought he might just pop by the house and pick it up. But his mother was out in front with her shopping cart. He could see her spotting his car from afar, so he couldn't just drive by. He double-parked.

Roseanne bustled up to the car window. "Let me see the reason why I don't have to cook for two anymore." She peered in.

"Patricia Greiff," said his girlfriend, holding her hand out.

"Hey, I remember you," Roseanne said, not shaking the hand. "Wasn't that your husband, the guy who stole everything from everybody?"

Patricia lost all the healthy color from the gym.

"Would you excuse me?" Tony got out of the car. He pointed to his mother, and she followed him up the steps.

He slammed the front door. "That was unbelievably rude. Apologize."

"What's the matter with you?" She waved the idea aside. "I want grandchildren! I bet that woman *has* grandchildren!"

"*That* is irrelevant. You go back down there and shake Patricia's hand."

Which she did, with little warmth or interest.

"This was a mistake," he told Patricia calmly, putting the damn bottle of wine in the backseat and strapping on his seat belt.

"There are no mistakes," Patricia said, with a finality that chilled him.

WHEN HE GOT TO HIS DESK that morning, Sprague gave him a look. He raised an eyebrow. "Just watch out," Sprague said quietly.

The Lieutenant pointed at him, and Tony trudged into Greeley's office to find out what fresh new insult awaited him.

"Ballestrino: I just want to know. How stupid are you?"

Every day Ballestrino got a hair closer to bashing this man in the face.

Greeley placed a large black-and-white photo in front of him: Anthony Ballestrino kissing Patricia Greiff in front of a Glendale bakery.

"Patricia Greiff is under Federal surveillance until her husband comes home, or until the *cows* come home." Greeley smiled with malice. "So I just want to know. Forget Departmental policy: are you an idiot?"

Nice shot, actually—they looked really good together. Ballestrino wondered if he should make a copy of the photo and show it to her.

❖

Conchita was vacuuming upstairs, and Erica would be going to Costa Rica in a few days. The water was soft and the rooms were hot in this house, factors Mitch had to weigh in order to get a stable pH in the tank. Ideally, he'd also need a halfway house tank, to quarantine new fish to get them healthy before introducing them into the big tank. And which fish? He wanted the perfect balance and the most variety.

People who thought small always got caught. He would not cut corners with the Ecosystem. Even the second tank he'd set up had been too small. A larger tank made for a more stable environment, more room for everybody to spread out, leading to fewer aggressive encounters. In both tanks, he'd started with only a few live plants, and then algae took over. So more plants right away, to get a head start, and more carbon dioxide to get the plants growing.

On the other hand, more wasn't always better: with the first tank, he'd overfed the fish, and they died. When he'd bought new fish, he hadn't made enough hiding places; the tang was harassed by puffer fishes: his tail was chewed to rags, and he died. Conchita entered the living room and placed another slice of carrot cake on the sleek new coffee table Erica had finally ordered from the Living Cove after nearly five months of his complaints.

Life was good.

He was in an upswing again, after a low period. Network news had been the first to drop him. In the *Times*, his story had gone from the front page, with stories in Business and Metro, to page twenty-three of the front section, to page eight of the Metro section, and then nothing. Even the tabloids had moved on.

At first, he'd been outraged. How dared they drop his story? Each day he opened the papers and looked in vain. It was like he didn't exist anymore. His mood was not helped by the inundation of periodicals that came to the house. During the media frenzy, he'd ordered a subscription to everything, to minimize visits to newsstands. The sheer volume of this paper now mocked him.

He'd had a difficult time switching gears, but fortunately, he'd been able to redirect his focus. He would order what he could from the Web site of an aquarium store on Long Island he'd dealt with before. He'd made arrangements to have it all delivered and set up. Erica would insist that he hide upstairs, and she would take care of supervising the delivery guys, complaining about all the work she had to do. Now that he wasn't her boss, he didn't particularly care for her office hours.

"I need you to be here when my tank gets delivered," he told her that night over the delicious soup Conchita had made.

"No," she said, head in the crossword.

"But what about the recognition factor? Aren't you worried?"

She put the paper down. "We've been through this," she said impatiently, "and you continue to ignore me. If it's too great a risk, don't take it. But I will not facilitate your bad decisions. Sitting in Queens waiting for your fish is not my job."

He called Conchita; she worked somewhere else on Wednesdays and wouldn't rearrange for him. He'd have to handle it himself.

The equipment was delivered by two Mexicans who barely looked at him. They set up both tanks in the living room, with hoses running from the kitchen sink. He began filling the holding tank first, a process that could take several days, as the water was filtered drop by drop.

When Erica arrived the following night, he realized that he'd been thinking about her all day and he couldn't wait a moment longer. He grabbed her bag and tossed it on the sofa, rolled her coat off her shoulders and began kissing her neck, kneading her rear end and leading her to the stairs.

"Hey," she said, coming up for air, "I need a moment."

As he pushed her up the stairs, she sat down on each tread. He jumped behind her.

"Mitch, I just walked in."

He reached under her arms and began dragging her up the stairs.

"WHAT DO YOU WANT FROM ME?" she exploded.

"I think that's obvious."

"Could I sit down for one moment? Could I wash my subway hands?"

He didn't like the way things had changed. He was always begging her for something and she was always saying no.

She barely glanced at the tank, and the next time she was over, she walked out of the house without commenting on the new vegetation he'd introduced. And when, after another Chinese take-out dinner, he triumphantly launched the first fish into the smaller tank, she sat down to watch the news. After she left, he found three new references to his name on the Web, but these turned out to be old stories. He brought the carton of remaining beef with broccoli upstairs, and returned to Aquarium.net.

Tangs can control the algae problem, he read, but in the aquarium, sometimes the "search image" may change from the natural food to the captivity food.

He dropped the bowl, spilling wet brown food on the dirty white carpet. What else was he doing now, besides eating in captivity?

The interview at the Chicago branch of Kessel and Partners was in a mirrored-glass building off a gray highway near O'Hare Airport. It went fine. A taxi took her to a hotel off the same highway, where she spent an evening watching trashy television, eating room service and enjoying a moment's peace at someone else's expense. On the plane back, she felt a longing for the blue Toyota. It wasn't Mitch and his damp hands smelling of tank chemicals, but the shiny metallic vehicle that she was looking forward to coming home to.

Some nights she drove for hours, sailing up the Northern State Parkway in the right lane. She had achieved forty miles an hour, and the speed was frightening. Other nights she could barely make it to Queens Boulevard before she was shaking and sweating. Sometimes she took the Long Island Expressway to a major road, then a lesser road to a development road, and turned around in a cul-de-sac. Sometimes she took the big road to the small road, then the country road to the dirt road, stopped at the fence and looked at a horse. She'd mastered the highway; wherever she went next, she'd have to cross over a bridge or go through a tunnel.

The weekend after Chicago, she dared herself. While he fussed over his fish, she took the Toyota. Just getting through the toll proved complicated enough: she found herself in the EZ Pass lane, but she didn't have an EZ Pass. No one would let her switch lanes. Rain throbbed impatiently on the roof. How were you supposed to get into the correct lane—be born there? Would she stay there, trapped, until traffic thinned at midnight? After an eternity, a van paused to get into her lane, and let her pass into his.

In front of her was the Midtown Tunnel, the escape route that had mocked her wanderlust all of her life. She turned off the radio and traveled into its unknown mouth. She made it through to the other side, hot and breathless, but pleased with her progress.

She turned right on Third Avenue, and found the bridge approach without event. With thousands of others for whom it was a twice-daily nonevent, she took the Queensboro Bridge. Gripping the wheel, she drove slowly in the right lane, petrified by the expanse of navy blue water and splotchy lights flashing by. The other cars drove aggressively; her wheels careened over ruts; the noise was alarming. She arrived at the other side in one piece, and pulled over as soon as she could to catch her breath and gloat a little.

She'd made it to thirty-six without going anywhere, pretty much. In the last year she'd been to LA once, Costa Rica and St. Kitts twice, the Cayman Islands three times and up and down the length of Long Island repeatedly. Now she'd done the bridge and the tunnel. She was adept at handling the vicissitudes of travel, and wondered what Geri King had found so difficult.

Erica had to get a car of her own. She had to get a wig and a wardrobe for Debbie. She was running out of time.

❖

Ballestrino pulled up in front of Brian Greiff's building and noticed the unmarked car parked a regulation length down the street. Across the street, a trench coat lurked under a portico with a telephoto lens. Mistakes were instructive; Tony wouldn't let his guard down again. He went upstairs, helped Patricia bring her luggage down, loaded it in the trunk, blew a kiss to the camera and drove off, watching the trench coat sprint ahead to a second unmarked car.

"Why are you doing this?" he demanded. "Move in with me."

She gave him an address.

"Listen, I want you to know that you're under surveillance."

She grunted, as if to say nothing could surprise her anymore.

"The Feds are right behind us."

She turned to look. "That cab?"

"Blue car behind the cab. They're probably tapping your phone."

Now she would look out the window the entire ride. She was as beautiful as ever, and as inaccessible.

"I'll get my own place," he pleaded.

"You should get your own place," she said. "Not for us, but for you."

He looked at her profile. "I don't expect anything from you. You could just live there with me." He tried not to want this so much. "It would be great."

She didn't respond. Her friend lived in a nice brownstone in the West Village. How did people find these places? Patricia got out of the car and scanned the street. "You mean those guys?" She nodded at the car, which had stopped twenty feet behind them.

"Yeah, and there's another one. He'll drive past us and park up ahead," Ballestrino said, just as the trench coat and his partner drove past, looking right at them, and then ducking their heads. "I don't know why they don't just put 'FBI' in big red letters on their car."

He brought the luggage to a small but swanky one-bedroom, furnished entirely in red. Patricia hadn't mentioned if this friend was male or female, and the mail on the table addressed to "Lee Hamlin" didn't tell him much.

She went into the bedroom. He followed her, closing all the shades.

"I want you to be careful on your cell phone. Don't give out any information." He came up behind her as she bent over her suitcase. He wrapped his arms around her stomach and she squirmed out of them.

"Why do you always push me away?"

"Tony," she said, removing his hands, "I want you to leave."

"You told me yourself this is the most fun you've ever had. So why are you running away from me?"

She shook her head and began unpacking. "It's not fun anymore, and it's just not . . . *appropriate*."

"Oh, *fuck* appropriate." He sat on the bed. "Do you want your life to be wall-to-wall misery?"

"My life is not wall-to-wall misery, thank you."

"You're right. You're just homeless, unemployed, without friends or contacts." He pulled out some pillows and propped himself up against the headboard.

She stood up straight. "I'd like you to leave now."

"How can you say you'd rather be alone, sitting in a borrowed apartment, afraid to go outside, than with me? I am the best thing in your life. You'd be a fool to send me away."

"Tony, I don't have patience for you anymore."

"I don't see anyone else helping you, Patricia. You need me."

She fixed an intense look on him with her turquoise eyes. "If you don't leave right now, I am calling the cops."

"Oh, she has a sense of humor, this one."

"I am not just calling the cops, I am calling your Lieutenant, the one who told you to leave me alone. He called and gave me his direct line."

He sat up. "He called you?"

He grabbed her arm and she kneed him in the groin. "I have nothing further to say." She dialed the phone while he recovered on the bed. "I wish you well. Now get out of this apartment, and leave me alone. Hello, Lieutenant, this is Patricia Greiff."

He heard Greeley: "Mrs. Greiff: are you in trouble?"

"No, I'm fine, thank you," she said. "I just wanted to let you know that Detective Ballestrino is leaving now. He's promised not to call anymore."

TONY SLAMMED OUT OF THE BUILDING in complete frustration, tasting the veal Parmesan he'd be eating the rest of his life. He drove back to the Building in a rage, forgetting to give the Feds the finger.

❖

"Why did we do this?" Mitch asked. "Remind me."

They were eating in the car in front of the Pastrami King as the light faded; she had driven. The snow was too wet to stick. It was bleak and messy outside.

"You wanted to get out." Erica took the lid off a container of coleslaw. "You were bored with every element in your life and disgusted with every person in your life, from your wife to your kids to your partners."

"That's right." He nodded, hands on his lap, staring out.

She ate a forkful of coleslaw. "You didn't want the responsibilities."

"That's right."

"You said, 'If I walked out of my life today, I don't think anyone would care. It might inconvenience them, but it wouldn't bother them.' Remember?"

He sighed. "Yes."

"Having second thoughts?"

"No, I stand by what I did." He bit into his sandwich without energy. "Why can't we move to Chicago now?"

"Because I haven't been made an offer yet."

"Why do you need an offer? We have plenty of money."

"We've been through this."

The previous evening he'd seized her in glee: he would start his own Web site, where people could find the most up-to-date and thorough information about fish, coral and live rock. Nobody would know who was behind it; he was uniquely suited to the project. He did an exuberant dance on top of the couch, and bowed in mock homage to his tank.

Now he looked like someone had shot his dog.

She wasn't sure how she should handle these moods. It was clear he needed to find some kind of focus, but if he started a Web site, she knew who would be running it. She dropped some coleslaw on the steering wheel.

He exploded. "That's it! There will be no more eating in this car! It's turning into a pigsty. It has to stop!"

Erica decided to spend less time in Queens.

"May I help you?" asked an alert, attractive woman behind the counter of a new cosmetics store in Amagansett.

"I need a present for my former mother-in-law," Patricia began.

"What a conflict! What can I show you?"

Her mother-in-law and her sister-in-law were, in a real sense, what remained of her family. "Whatever I get her will be wrong. . . ."

"It's important to do the right thing." The woman nodded, and showed her a wall of smartly wrapped packages. Patricia began smelling soaps.

She'd fled New York City as if she were being chased. And in fact, Tony hadn't accepted her good-bye: he called three times a day. She changed her number. So he called her on the new number.

"Patricia," he began, and she felt chilled. "You're avoiding a *Detective*. What were you thinking?"

She was thinking that New York, New York, was a small town. She wanted to start all over in a new place, meeting new people. She hung up on him. The following day Patricia sold her car and took the train east to Amagansett. She walked from the station to the still-unsold summer house with her one remaining suitcase. She was trying to keep an open mind.

She'd been flattered by Tony, but she needed something simpler, less charged. She needed to be able to walk into a restaurant and not cause a commotion. Perhaps she didn't need a man at all, but she certainly didn't need an obsessive one who demanded so much attention, affection, supervision.

The woman began wrapping Lenore's present. Her hair was a stylish, if unnatural red, and her makeup was done meticulously. Patricia was suddenly in the mood to buy a lot of makeup, and have this careful woman apply it.

"Are you Patricia Greiff? Is that why you look familiar?" the woman suddenly asked.

"Yes, I am."

"I'm Mara. My ex-boyfriend did your deck."

Patricia smiled. "I love my deck. Bill was very easy to work with."

"I wish he'd been so easy with me. I hear your house is for sale."

"It is, and it's not selling. If you know of anybody who's interested in either renting or buying, let me know."

"You'd rent it out?"

"I have to find something cheaper. And then I have to get a job."

"Well, you could work here. I wanted someone for the season, but I could really use help now. Would this interest you?"

Patricia didn't even think about it. "When do I start?"

She rode Randy's old bike to her first day of work at Claire de Lune, leaving her cell phone at home. Mara showed her how to ring up a sale, asked her pointed questions about her skin care and hair color, showed her how to operate the vacuum, presented her with the cleaning supplies and asked her what she'd planned for lunch. Patricia showed her the salad she'd brought.

"Great! We can have lunch on the deck if it's nice." Mara spun out the door. She came back, ducking her head. "Oh, and we need to clean the bathroom," which Patricia took to mean, "You need to clean the bathroom."

Patricia cleaned the bathroom first. Mara returned an hour later, while Patricia was on the floor cleaning out the shelves. "Look at how fast you work!"

They sat on wire furniture on the back deck, taking in thin March sunshine in their coats and sunglasses. While avoiding why Patricia needed to work in a cosmetics store for an hourly wage, Mara nonetheless managed to grill her: Where did she get her hair done in the city? Had she met Jerry Fabrikant? Was he gay? Had she met Celestina? Where did Celestina get her hair done in the city? At some point Patricia stopped talking. Then Mara confided details about Joe, her current disappointment.

At six, Patricia closed up the shop and pushed off on her bike. She had forgotten how dark it got at that hour. She pedaled down the spooky, badly lit streets and arrived home feeling energetic, capable, fine. She was doing all right. She didn't need a police escort.

At the end of March, Patricia held a yard sale, in which thirty years of chipped, stained and broken pieces of family life lay out on the lawn for all to behold. That night Mara took her to the loud speakeasy on Main Street. They sat at the bar and toasted the end of one life and the beginning of another. Various local types came over to chat, and Mara gave her the lowdown on each in a loud whisper, sending away anyone who got too pushy. It was a reasonable amount of male attention. Patricia managed to have a fine time, and went to sleep in her empty house feeling light, yet in control.

The following day, she canceled her cell phone service. She met a contractor to see if a fresh layer of gravel in the driveway might help sell the house. The gravel contractor wore a baseball cap on his head, a pencil in his ear, reading glasses on a chain around his neck and the smile of a man who was aware that he'd peaked in high school. His name was Nick. Within minutes, she'd learned that he had a twenty-two-year-old son from an early failed marriage, knew everyone in town and had a lot of time on his hands, especially in the winter. He measured her driveway. The estimate was shockingly high.

"Okay, if I can't do your gravel, could I take you to lunch?"

She laughed. "You mean now?"

"Why not?"

He took her to his cousin's deli in the Springs, and they had sandwiches on his friend's deck overlooking Napeague Bay. They discussed the weather. Patricia was never so glad to make small talk in her life. It gave her hope.

Within a week he'd found a buyer for her house. Within ten days he'd found her a cheap sublet half a mile from his house. He was six years her junior (an old man of the world, compared to Tony), he'd dated most of the divorcées in town (excluding Mara), and many summer women. He caught his own fish, which he cooked for her on a pan in his kitchen. He had a broad, interpretive sense of humor, and measured things by the ton. She enjoyed his company.

For Patricia, Amagansett at this stage of her life was what Greenwich Village had been in the sixties: a land of chance encounters, favors and possibilities.

❖

"Tony, move on," said Sprague.

Patricia had cut him off completely. She'd left the red apartment and moved out of her house in Long Island, which was under contract for sale. She hadn't used her cell phone in weeks or been in contact with her friends in months, and she didn't have credit cards anymore. He wasn't sure whether she'd stayed on Long Island or had gone elsewhere. She'd vanished into the cash economy. He was worried.

"Maybe she is the most wonderful woman in the world, but if she's not interested, move on."

"But *why* isn't she interested?"

"We've been through this," Sprague said.

They had. Not everything ended happily ever after. He would find someone else. He didn't need Patricia, or any girlfriend. He could just move out of the house. Tony dialed Brian Greiff's office again.

Sprague hissed. When Tony looked up, the Lieutenant was pointing at him. He hung up and made his way to Greeley's hot seat.

"Ballestrino: what are you working on?"

"The chat-room securities fraud."

"Is Brian Greiff a material witness to the chat-room securities fraud?"

He exhaled. "No, sir."

"Is calling Patricia Greiff three times an hour helping you solve the case of the chat-room securities fraud?"

He didn't respond.

"Ballestrino: do you like your job?"

A fair question, one that he couldn't answer so easily. "Yes, sir."

"You are abusing the Department and cheating the taxpayers. I already warned you once. Next time I find you pursuing personal obsessions on Department time, your ass is back on patrol in Crown Heights."

Back in the squad room, everyone had their head down. He went to his desk and took out the chat-room securities fraud file.

He had never been this low.

"DETECTIVE, COME ON IN," Frank Defina said as he shook Ballestrino's hand and introduced him to a small circle of people around him. The women at this brunch party were well groomed and stuck-up-looking in sweater sets. Each held a baby and/or was supervising a child or two from a distance. The men dressed in turtlenecks, tweed trousers and butterscotch suede driving moccasins. It was hard to believe Ballestrino was in his own neighborhood.

He wouldn't be rude or defensive; he didn't begrudge Frank Defina material rewards. Out of nowhere, a day after Tony had identified the disgruntled employee who'd been tampering with Frank's payroll, Frank had offered him a job: Chief of Electronic Security at his investment bank, with real money, and all kinds of corporate perks. *Chief*, Frank had stressed, with a team beneath him. Ballestrino had asked for some time to consider the idea.

He'd thought about it that night in his room. If he took this job, he could get his own place, in Manhattan even. Patricia might move in with him.

He'd woken up at four the next morning drenched in sweat. He'd never supervised anyone in his life. How did he know he'd be any good at it? Did he want to be responsible for someone else's work? What made him think he would find administration rewarding? Would protecting the sanctity of an investment bank's systems be satisfying? Had Frank's disgruntled clerk been brought to justice? No, he was merely asked to leave the company, with a severance package. What was the point of identifying him?

Without discussing it with anyone, he turned down the offer. The Job was poorly paid, no question. But it was inherently interesting and frequently satisfying. There was something, too, about being one of the good guys fighting for the right cause.

That had been his thinking at the time. Since the Lieutenant had busted him the day before, he was wondering if he'd made the right decision.

"Beer's cold, Detective," Frank Defina invited.

"I'll take a soda." It came out stiff and judgmental. Tony added, "I'm on my way to work after this."

A short, squat female perked up. "What do you do?"

She had a ring. "I'm a cop." He picked up a tiny sandwich.

"Oh, wow," she squealed. "Do you carry a gun?"

"Yes."

"It's the off-duty cops with guns that always get into trouble, isn't it?"

He faced this pest. "Is it?"

"Play nice with my cop, Jenny," Frank warned.

My cop? *My* cop? Thank God he hadn't taken that job.

"You guys get in trouble *on* duty too," said a lazy voice. It belonged to a woman with a face like a shovel, who materialized out of nowhere, in a loose dress no doubt made from hemp.

I got 40,000 friends, he thought. You want to take me on, lady?

"I wish you'd take my offer and come to work for us," Frank said. "This man"—Frank draped an arm around his shoulder—"found the employee who'd been looting our payroll for months. In one day! Can you imagine? He gets paid nothing as a cop, nothing."

Ballestrino wasn't about to argue that one. "I like what I do." He moved slightly, and Frank's arm dropped. "It gives me satisfaction."

"I bet," said the ugly liberal, as if she'd caught him torturing someone. Even she was wearing a wedding ring.

"Can I see your gun?" asked the pudgy party guest. He pulled his jacket aside. "Oh, please, can I hold it?"

"This gun never leaves me. I have a shower cap for this gun."

Ballestrino set off his beeper, enjoying how it made the shrimp jump. He excused himself and walked through the front door, and stood on the stoop outside in the fresh wind. He called his partner. "What's up, buddy?"

He heard shrieks in the background. "I'm trapped in New Jersey," Sprague said darkly, "watching small children burst into flames."

"You need some help out there?"

"If you know what's good for you," Sprague said, "you'll stay the hell away from here. I've never seen such chaos in my life, and this is just the beginning: more kids are coming, they tell me, and a pony ride. Indoors."

Ballestrino hit 2 on speed dial. Bobby Setzer picked up right away.

"Hey, Tony!" Bobby said. It sounded like beer, couches and hockey on TV in the new house in Islip. "Hey, Ryan, say hello to Tony," Bobby called.

"Fuck Tony," Ryan said.

"That's nice," Bobby said, "Ryan said hello. So when you coming over?"

"Now. You need anything? Beer or anything?"

"Na, just come."

He went back inside. "I'm sorry. I've been called in on a case."

Fascination spread over the smooth, clean faces of the rich civilians.

"Did somebody die?" the little party guest asked him, thrilled.

"Let's get together soon, Tony," Defina said in a proprietary fashion.

He walked to his car. A futile day. A pack of investment bankers cycled by, outfitted for the Tour de France. Brooklyn was going to the dogs. He'd spoiled everything with Patricia. There were no single women.

He turned on the radio to a hard-rock station and drove to a white suburb of Long Island to be in the company of cops, cop wives, cop kids and cop food. He felt at home among cops, in a way that he didn't anywhere else, including his own home. The Job was the Old Neighborhood now.

CHAPTER ELEVEN

There was a lull in the volume of computer-generated crime, perhaps because the magnificent weather was sending felons out-of-doors to commit crimes without electronic assistance. This allowed the members of the CCS, Sprague and Ballestrino among them, to clear up some lingering cases.

One bright, cool day in early May, Sprague came across some random notes involving Erica King. He thought a moment, and called the personnel office of Friedman, Greiff and Slavin, now Friedman and Slavin. He received a fax immediately. The Lieutenant was out, so he sauntered into the Captain's office, as much to soak up the light from his windows as to talk to him.

The Captain faced Sprague. "Tell me something good, Dennis."

"I think we should revisit Erica King."

"Are you losing weight?" the Captain squinted at his midsection.

"I am, as a matter of fact," Sprague said proudly. He had lost eleven pounds. Cathy had lost fourteen. He was now playing basketball once a week among a small group of middle-aged men with knee problems; twice a week he hit the gym with Cathy for weight training. None of this came naturally, and he was well aware that the minute he slacked off, he'd be closing his one pair of valid pants with a safety pin again.

"Looks good." The Captain smiled.

"Erica King," Sprague prompted.

"You know I have CRS," said the Captain.

"Senior Account Manager, worked directly for Mitch Greiff, the fugitive celebrity accountant?"

"The one so boring she put us to sleep just hearing about her life?"

"That's the one."

"You think nobody could possibly be that boring?"

"Oh, no, she really is that boring." Sprague smiled. "I just think she might be boring and very wealthy all of a sudden."

He held up the fax from the personnel office, and told the Captain about the many sick days, personal days and vacation days Erica had already taken that year, after ten years of a near-spotless attendance record. The Captain agreed to let a team watch her for a shift or two.

"No need to get Greeley involved yet," the Captain said, and winked.

Sprague had the Greiff files brought out of storage, and began sifting.

Sometimes, lately, Sprague was so positive about life, he was bursting. He hit his desk in the morning with energy and thought, "What can I accomplish today?" Colors were brighter, healthy food tasted better, he and his partner were completely in tune, the District Attorney's office didn't always let him down. He loved the Job, he loved his wife, he loved life.

Other days he looked at the piles on his desk, his chair, the floor around him, and nearly collapsed with exhaustion. "What can I get away with today?" he would wonder, and get angry at himself for going to the gym during prime thinking hours. Fitting into pants was fine, but it wasn't everything.

He would backslide. How long could he keep this up? It was so time-consuming. He had to walk a good twelve blocks to get an acceptable salad for lunch. There were days he needed a nap so badly at three o'clock, he wanted to lie down on the floor. The total-body fatigue he was feeling didn't encourage extended periods in front of the computer. It could be that healthy living was interfering with the quality of his police work.

He called Flynn at Daley Consulting, and chatted for a few minutes about the Greiff case.

"Hey, come to a dinner we're having next month at the Waldorf," Flynn said. "It's our annual shindig, we invite all the clients. You and your partner might do some schmoozing. You never know what might come out of it: a hook within the Department, a parachute out of it?"

"That's a nice invitation, Bill. I'll talk to Tony."

When he hung up the phone, the Lieutenant called him in.

"Invitation," he said, staring at him.

"What invitation?"

"I heard you on the phone saying that's a nice invitation."

"That was an old partner of mine. He invited me and Tony to dinner."

"Would this be a corporate function?"

"Yes, sir."

"Well, you know, any invitation you get, you have to clear with me, and then I have to clear it with the Chief of Detectives."

"I didn't think this qualified, because—"

"Because you had worked a case with them," Greeley said. "In your capacity as a member of this Department. I'll talk to the Chief, though. Maybe he'll want you to go."

Sprague spotted an open box of cookies on Chang's desk. He quickly called up the Fordham Law library and inquired about the *Law Review* in the years Erica King attended. A librarian agreed to fax him some articles she'd written. He eagerly pounced on the articles when they came over the fax. They were as dense, dry and impenetrable as Ms. King herself.

AT HOME, CATHY WAS CHASING down a new canary. When he emerged from the shower, she was reading a fitness magazine on the sofa. Even in repose now, she had an active look about her. Pounds were melting off her. Things were getting more and more interesting between them since they had begun to get healthy—more interesting and more frequent.

"Where's the dog?" He took a cucumber slice from a plate.

"Wendy's at the clinic." She handed him his gin and diet tonic.

"Don't tell me she ate the plants again."

"I think we should talk about adoption."

"Why the formality? She lives here anyway, and hearty welcome. The birds are filthy, and the cats give me the creeps, but I like that dog. She's got spunk."

"Adopting a child."

This information hung in the air like dust clouds after a landslide.

"A child? I thought . . . " he said.

"I know, so did I. But you know, I think we'd be great parents."

He sipped the alcohol carefully. "Didn't we go through this? Didn't we have enough trouble, individually and collectively, on this issue?"

"Yes, yes we did."

He stood up to pace. "Didn't we agree that we were busy enough, that this household is busy enough?"

"This household doesn't have to be so busy." She looked impatient. Or was she angry? "I don't need to bring everyone home every night."

"Bring a kid in here, it'll be a hell of a lot busier than it already is."

Cathy sighed. His second wife used to do that. "Well, I wanted to bring this out in discussion," she said, and began misting the ferns. "We don't have to make this decision now. But I'd like you to think about it."

He went into his home office and turned on the computer. Mitch Greiff, with or without Erica King, had diverted $103 million. Why that amount? And why from so many sources? Wouldn't it have been easier, more efficient, to focus on the highest-net-worth individuals and steal more money from each one? Why was the theft spread around so democratically? Surely more transactions left the thief more vulnerable to detection.

He heard Cathy clattering around in the living room. Things were fitting together: the previous week, instead of her usual film noir double feature, Cathy had brought home *The Muppets Take Manhattan* and *Baby Boom*. Lately they'd been spending Saturday afternoons with Lily and Mark and their kids, instead of going out to dinner with Lily and Mark on Saturday night.

The Job was exhausting. Healthy living was time-consuming. And now a child. And from where? Small-town teenagers with bad luck. Chinese couples with extra girls. Bleak, terrifying orphanages in the evil, corrupt, disintegrating Balkans. Who knew what you were getting?

On the other hand, how could you know with a child of your own? His older brother had done time in prison and now drove an eighteen-wheeler in a rage. His younger brother was an architect, had won an award for a hospital design. On the third hand, he knew what his genes would have spawned: a fat kid with thin, colorless hair, bad teeth, weak knees and perfect vision, like everyone else in his family. Cathy's people were more diverse, although they all wore glasses.

Where would they put a child? In this very room, his office. When would they play with the child? At night, when they were both exhausted. He supposed he could work four to midnight, to be around during the day, to see the kid. Would she continue working? Would she bring the kid to the vet? This was unsanitary. Would she stay at home? That would cause a drastic drop in household income. Healthy food was more expensive, and they had both joined a pricey gym.

He peeked out his door. Cathy was in the bedroom. He sneaked into the kitchen. Anything worth eating had been removed in the purge. He was too tired to go out. He took the jar of organic peanut butter and the box of melba toast back into his lair.

Weren't they happy? Wasn't it enough?

JOE FAUSTO AND CECILE BIALKIN came in at ten A.M. with a report: Erica King had left her office on Wednesday night at six-thirty.

She took a 7 train to Jackson Heights, Queens, carrying something that looked like take-out food. She was greeted at the door of a two-family home by an elderly woman. At eleven, Fausto and Bialkin had packed it in: she might have left later; she might have spent the night. The woman's name was Maddie Olsen; she'd lived at that address for twelve years. Previously, she lived a block away from Erica's building.

Sprague asked that Erica King be put on twenty-four-hour surveillance for three more days. The Captain agreed, probably because nothing much else was going on.

❖

Mitch was sprinkling fish food into the tank. The phone rang, and he paused as the machine picked up. A mechanical voice congratulated him for being chosen to participate in a radio survey. He had a new relationship with the phone. It would never be for him unless there was a serious problem. But that threat kept him alert, and the shrill, demanding quality of the instrument persisted.

Back in his old life, he used to pick up the phone directly, like an idiot.

"Oh, Mitch, I'm so glad you're there," his mother began, three times a week, whining about how hard it was without his father. He hired a live-in companion. Then she called more often to complain about the companion.

His sister would call with an emergency voice, asking him to come over to talk about her situation (sluggish son, vindictive ex-husband suing over assets from their flower shop, no dates since a bad fix-up in the Clinton administration). If he pleaded too much work, she would whimper, "Oh, *please*?"

For years, Mitch believed he was being tested in order to make use of his gifts. If he was not wise, prosperous and kind, why would these people keep coming to him? But he realized that his sister had him on speed dial because, well, who *else* would pay her legal bills when she bleated? He was asked to deal with his father's estate because, well, who *else* would put in the time or energy?

He had a sudden rage against his sister, from the armchair in Queens. From the beginning, all the family's energy had been spent on Phyllis, a sickly child with endless needs. He had to waste his free time in doctors' waiting rooms, being quiet, for Phyllis. When she was a teenager, he was pressured to quit the baseball team, to spend time with Phyllis, who had no friends.

The phone rang in Queens, interrupting this resentful reverie, and he picked it up automatically, steeling himself for a new family annoyance.

"Mr. Spivak?"

"Who's calling?"

"I'd like to speak to Mr. Spivak."

"Unless you tell me who this is, that will be impossible."

"I'm calling from Dominant Technologies, sir; how are you today? Good. I'd like to discuss home security with you today. May I ask you, sir, do you have an alarm system in your home?"

No, actually, he didn't. "Why, do you plan to rob me?"

"No, sir, we are offering a free alarm system today."

"I have one, thanks."

"Are you satisfied with it today, Mr. Spivak?"

"Yes, I am, and I'm hanging up now."

Why didn't he have an alarm system? Another item Erica had forgotten. He began picking up algae from the tank with the sponge stick.

Mitch had done taxes for his parents, his aunts and uncles, his sister and (even after the divorce) his brother-in-law, as well as assorted cousins and friends. Several had enlivened the transaction by cracking jokes about the tedious nature of his profession. None of these people had paid him. And what had any of them ever done for him? Had his cousin the dentist offered to do his root canal for free? Had his sister ever sent him flowers to thank him for his many house calls?

Was it just money? Or was it the idea that their services or time were more important than his? Increasingly, he felt used.

He carefully measured strontium solution and poured it slowly into the tank. Patricia blamed him for Randy. Why? There was no lawbreaking in his family. How dare she point a finger at his side? On the other hand, here he was, on the lam. Not that he'd actually stolen anything: he'd delegated. Why was he wasting time thinking about this? He was free. Randy and Brian were adults. They'd had every advantage. At what point were they responsible for their own lives?

The phone rang again, and stopped ringing before the machine picked up. The idea that it couldn't possibly be for him—initially refreshing—was, finally, depressing. Erica barely called.

He needed new goals. He returned to the idea of an aquarium store, with the best equipment, the rarest fish and coral. Erica had tossed a tank of water on this idea. But was that even what he really wanted, now that he could do anything? To be in retail? He resumed reading the second volume of Churchill's memoirs. By now he should have been finished with the entire series, but he was frequently distracted. He was having trouble shifting gears.

He wasn't having the last laugh. It wasn't over yet.

❖

One morning, as Ballestrino spoke to some VIPs from the Mayor's office, the Captain came to greet him like a long-lost brother.

"Tony, I'm so glad you're here!" he interrupted. "I can't work the Xerox, could you just make me four copies of this? Last time I tried to figure out that machine, I almost lost an arm!"

That afternoon, Greeley accompanied him and Sprague to the DA's office, to shop the Greiff/King case with the new director of the Frauds department, Len Miles, a tall, thin, slow-talking African American male individual in a beautiful navy pin-striped suit. They were going through the case, and the phone was ringing constantly. Each time, Miles excused himself and answered it. Each time he returned, he pinched his creases and said, "Where were we?"

"Search warrants," Ballestrino said, too loud.

Greeley asked Miles where he grew up. Miles began a long, slow story about a small town in Michigan. Then the Lieutenant made pointed remarks about the FBI, and a secretary came in with something for Miles to sign. Miles picked up the phone and asked someone to come in.

This was taking forever. They had to close this case in his lifetime. Greeley cast an angry look at Ballestrino: his knee was bouncing.

A striking redheaded woman walked in. She wasn't as beautiful as Patricia. Miles introduced her as Liz Isaacson. So Ballestrino assumed she was Jewish.

"Liz will prosecute this case. Tell her everything you told me."

So they had to go back over the whole thing. Liz had freckles. Patricia was a redhead, but she had white-white skin, no freckles. When they got to Erica King, Liz said, "That name sounds familiar. Why would I know her?"

"She's a Senior Account Manager at Friedman, Greiff and Slavin," Sprague said. "She lives on East 32nd Street. She went to Fordham."

"Ah, Fordham. You have a picture?"

Sprague pulled out one of the shots Ballestrino had taken in the Citicorp atrium. "Fordham College eighty-five, and Fordham Law eighty-eight."

"I was Fordham Law ninety, so we did overlap," Liz said, studying the picture. "But I can't say I knew her. This looks like a wig."

"Yes, it does," said Miles, who was looking over her shoulder.

"I know about wigs," she said.

"You Orthodox?" Ballestrino asked.

"Certainly not!" She looked at him directly for the first time.

"So how come you know about wigs?"

"I'm sure that's my business."

He looked at her red hair, which seemed natural. Moreover, she looked Irish; maybe she'd married a Jew. How did she know about wigs, and why bring it up if she didn't want to talk about it?

Miles cleared his throat. He pointed out that there was nothing specific to tie Erica—or Mitch, for that matter—to the wire transfers, the computers or the phony voice mails. "There's not enough evidence for a search warrant," he said, "but I'd be glad to prosecute either one or both of them, once there is."

On the way back to the Building, the Lieutenant delivered a huffy lecture about appropriate behavior at the District Attorney's office, especially in the presence of members of minority groups. Since he was part of a military, or paramilitary, organization, Ballestrino said, "Yes, sir."

"And you're not going to that corporate dinner," Greeley said to Sprague. "Any invitations you get, come to me." He was pointing to his chest with two fingers, because clearly one wouldn't do the job. "Understood?"

"Yes, sir," Sprague said loudly.

"So where's the invitation?" asked Greeley.

"It was verbal. I'll have Flynn give you a call."

"Do that," Greeley said.

When Ballestrino was new on the Job, he couldn't believe the stories the Senior Detectives told. They had to be embellishing: people didn't cut each other off at the knees that way. These guys were bitter old men, trying to one-up each other in their misery. Now he knew better: every word of those stories was true.

They had a very late lunch at a health-food place in SoHo.

"Either they pay you well or they treat you well," Ballestrino told Sprague. "They can't pay you poorly *and* give you shit."

"Where'd you get that idea? They can and they do." Sprague called the waitress over and gave her his plate, with plenty of food remaining.

"Look at the discipline!" Ballestrino praised him, glad to be distracted from the original topic. "How much weight have you lost?"

"Not enough," Sprague said, "but thanks for noticing."

WELL-HEELED MANHATTAN TYPES poured into Tessio's, an upmarket Italian place on the East Side. Anthony Ballestrino sat alone at a table. He could imagine the old Patricia here. He looked at his watch. In rock-bottom despair, he'd given in to his mother and called Gloria

Florimonte. One minute more and she would be late. He was already annoyed at her. The prices were outrageous. He was too old for this. He'd been on too many dates in his life; he was beginning to feel like damaged goods. But he'd been all backed up since Patricia had gone, so he'd initiated this blind date, outraged by the direction his life was taking.

At the stroke of eight, a dark, attractive woman sailed past the maître d' and came to stand directly in front of him, smiling.

"I'm Gloria Florimonte. My aunt described you perfectly."

He stood up, stunned. Gloria Florimonte was a good-looking woman. Not a house on fire, but nice. Well dressed. Clean, regular features. Long black hair. He asked to see some identification.

"I heard you were a tough nut," she laughed, and joined him at the table.

"Who told you that, your aunt Shirley?"

"Your mother." She signaled the waiter and ordered a glass of red wine. Which was sort of aggressive; what if he wanted to order a bottle?

He wanted to get back on track. "So I hear that you're in school?"

"I'm getting a certificate in Physical Therapy. I already have my degree in Massage Therapy, but I'm looking to get on staff at a hospital."

"*Massage therapy*," he said. "Now, why didn't my mother mention that?" He would have called her much sooner.

"Probably because my aunt didn't tell her. In my family, they think it means I'm a hooker. Not that I studied Chinese medicine."

"I work near Chinatown." He leaned forward, shifting his beeper, gun, Palm Pilot and phones. "I'm often tempted to go to one of those places."

"I can recommend a brilliant acupuncturist. He completely fixed my shoulder. He's not in Manhattan, unfortunately, he's in Flushing."

"Why unfortunately?"

"Well, I live in Manhattan," Gloria said, "so it's more convenient."

How could she afford Manhattan, he wanted to know. Soon she would begin the assault on Brooklyn; it happened every time.

"I live in Carroll Gardens," he said, as her wine arrived.

"With your mother, I heard." She smiled.

"You find that amusing?"

"Aunt Shirley thinks you dropped off a Christmas tree."

"Yeah? Where do you live in Manhattan, and how do you afford it?"

"Well, I work on the trading floor at Merrill Lynch."

"I thought you said—"

"Giving massages to the traders."

"Really? On the trading floor?"

"We have little soundproof rooms just off the floor. You can't imagine how stressed these guys are."

So she knew all kinds of Wall Street guys. Guys who probably asked her out to nicer places than this, hoping for more attention to their lower backs. "Do the traders treat you respectfully?"

"Oh, yes," she said. "They have to sign up for their appointments, and they always show up on time. They take it very seriously."

Now he was a little ashamed for taking her to this place. Too swanky: like he had something to prove. Now she'd think he liked her. She'd probably play games, not return his calls. She'd expect chic Manhattan Italian food every time they went out. Not possible, on a Detective Third Grade's salary.

"You like Italian food?" he asked, indicating the menu. "There's a little place on Court Street I go to a lot. But I heard nice things about this place."

They ordered. She was wearing a red silk shirt and a black cardigan. The combination was loose enough that the volume of her chest was uncertain.

"And what do you do for entertainment, recreation?" he asked.

She had a nice sort of a widow's peak to her thick hair.

"You keep a car? Where? How much does the garage charge? And you get the resident's tax abatement, yes? Where do you drive? May I see your license?"

She raised an eyebrow. "You ask a lot of questions, Detective."

"You know, I could find out almost anything about you if I wanted." He sipped his wine. "With or without your cooperation."

She inhaled as if surprised.

"I could do a workup on you that you wouldn't believe," he said, as the waiter took his plate. "But I couldn't live with myself."

At this point, she excused herself to go to the ladies' room.

THEY WALKED OUT into the night air, which was fresh. Her lipstick had faded, and she hadn't redone it, either at the table (which he didn't allow) or in the ladies' room (which would have been fine). What did that mean? Perhaps she didn't like him. She hadn't shown him her license.

"I'd like to thank you for a lovely interrogation, Detective." She shook his hand in front of the restaurant. "I've never been so systematically examined. I wish you luck with all your cases."

"Wait: where are you going, Gloria Florimonte?"

"I live around the corner."

"I'll walk you home," he said, outraged.

At her door (a tenement—he'd been in hundreds, no, thousands of them; he knew the layout, the fixtures, the chipping maroon enamel paint on the doors and the dirty floral carpet on the stairs), she said, "I'll send you the address of my acupuncturist tomorrow if you e-mail me."

I'll e-mail you when and if I feel like it, he thought.

"Thanks again," she called. The door slammed behind her.

She hadn't given him her e-mail address. Perhaps that was the first test. A good Detective would find it.

If he was interested.

The following evening, Sprague and Ballestrino sat in the Lieutenant's office when Joe Fausto called in. Greeley put him on speakerphone.

"We lost her." Joe sounded humiliated. The din of the subway screamed behind his voice. At six-thirty, Joe reported, he and Cecile had followed Erica from her office to the 4 train, which she took to Brooklyn Heights. They watched her as she walked a good ten blocks, picked up some groceries, entered the station at Bergen Street, and disappeared into the Queens-bound G train.

"The train was packed, and she moved to the next car between stops. By the time we pushed our way through, the train had stopped at Hoyt, and she was lost in the crowds. We got off here, at Hoyt, but we didn't see her. She could have stayed on the train or left the station."

Sprague exchanged a look with Ballestrino. Why buy groceries in Brooklyn to take to Queens? Why the sudden inclination toward the outer boroughs?

Fausto was talking: "Do you want to alert Transit, or the Eight-Four Precinct?"

Greeley shook his head. This case had gone nowhere. Worse yet, it revisited their earlier failure, making them look bad all over again. "No," he spat into the speaker. "Just get over to her apartment. And sit on it until your relief comes. Fausto and Bialkin: I am very unhappy with you."

He slammed out of his office, leaving Sprague and Ballestrino looking at each other.

DENNIS SPRAGUE DROVE NORTH on the West Side Highway, trying to prepare himself for his wife. Not once during the four collective years of his first two marriages—nor in the sixteen collective years between his marriages—had a single serious thought about adoption passed through Sprague's mind. Now it occupied all his free time. There had been further discussion that morning: Cathy wanted him to know that she would continue working once the child arrived. The quality of their lives wouldn't be affected.

He left for the gym. It was now *the* child, not *a* child. Who would take care of *the* child while they were at work? No illegal-Caribbean-staffed day-care center was going to raise *his* child, even if Dennis Sprague Jr. *was* a little Chinese girl. He threw himself into the rowing machine with an energy that surprised him.

The Discussion was now what he came home to every night and

woke up to every morning, what he was avoiding if he turned on his laptop and what he was impeding when he refused to talk. All at once, he really missed the schnauzer.

When he got home, he asked after the dog. Cathy told him she'd been taken home by a nice family who had swapped her for their Australian collie, who had been nipping their baby's thighs and herding her into corners.

"You gave the dog away without telling me?"

"She's been gone over a month!" Cathy snapped. "You never paid attention to her: why should I ask your permission to send her to a loving home?"

The subtext was heavy, and he dropped the line of questioning. But as they ate steamed food in silence, Sprague considered the idea of bringing home a new puppy as a way of redirecting Cathy's attention. The Discussion was scaring him.

Once you adopted a child, you couldn't trade it in if you didn't like it.

THE FOLLOWING MORNING, Fausto and Bialkin had the update from their relief: Erica King had come home at one-thirty A.M., and had gone to work at ten-thirty A.M. The third surveillance group was currently sitting in front of her office building and had nothing to report.

"She's getting more interesting," the Captain noted with approval, taking something out of a brown paper bag.

"Remember the old lady she visited in Queens?" Sprague asked, ignoring the bagel the Captain was buttering. Fausto and Bialkin nodded. "Did anyone check to see if our suspect was hiding under the sink? Or sitting in the living room?"

No response.

"Give me the address," Sprague said.

AFTER WORK, instead of going to the gym, Sprague drove far out of his way to make a house call in Jackson Heights. He rang the bell of a two-family home.

An elderly woman took her time answering the door. Oh, yes, Erica

King had been bringing her medicine and groceries for years, said the woman, who wore an ancient gray housedress. She had seen Erica grow up. She had known Erica's mother from the Center, right next door to her old apartment in Manhattan.

"When did you see Ms. King last?"

"The other night."

"Did she come for dinner?"

"No, she left a few minutes after she'd arrived. Is Erica in trouble?"

"Oh, no," he said, as if the thought were ridiculous. "It's just a routine investigation of someone else. When do you expect her again?"

"Oh, next week, two weeks, I don't know. Sometimes she calls; sometimes she just comes over. Would you like some crumb cake?"

He smiled, declining with regret. He trotted down the stairs to his car and called Fausto. He and Bialkin were sitting in front of the Friedman and Slavin building, waiting for Erica to leave for the day.

"The old lady says that Erica left a few minutes after she arrived."

"Really?" said Fausto. "I don't see how we could have missed her. We were both awake and alert. There was plenty of light."

Sprague got out of the car and took a look: the driveway of the identical house behind Mrs. Olsen's made an easy route to the next block, 80th Street. The house obscured the back door. Even parked to catch the widest angle, they wouldn't have seen her leaving out the back. Fausto and Bialkin were getting soft.

Well, now he didn't feel like exercise *at all*. He rang Mrs. Olsen's bell again. "Did Ms. King go out the back when she left?"

"Yes, I think she did. Crumb cake?"

"No, thanks, I'm trying to reduce. Does Erica have friends in the neighborhood?"

"Oh, no. A pity she's so plain. Her mother, now, *there* was a looker."

"Oh, really?" He smiled.

"Yes, and so popular. Got her into a lot of trouble."

He put on his bland, interested, talk-to-me face. "What kind of trouble?"

"Sure you don't want some crumb cake?"

"Well, if you insist." He sat down at the kitchen table. Erica King herself might have bought this crumb cake.

"Geri King always had to have her man," Maddie Olsen said cattily. "The mother."

"Mmm. Erica never really came into her own. There was the trouble with the retarded boy." She moved slowly to the cake plate and cut him a nice-sized piece. "I felt so badly for Geri. Nobody knew what to say."

You never knew what you might find out over a piece of crumb cake.

"Tell me about it." Sprague felt his pants getting tighter, his heart beginning to accelerate. Oh, he loved his job.

❖

It was exactly one year earlier in an Italian restaurant in the East 80s that Cynthia Landau had leaned in toward Mitch with a look of concern.

"I hope that thing worked out," she began.

"What thing?"

She looked around theatrically to make sure they weren't being overheard. "That *therapist* thing," she whispered.

"What therapist thing?"

"Oh! Oh, nothing then."

Cynthia seemed to be seeking eye contact with Patricia, but his wife was mesmerized by something Howard the skin doctor was saying.

"Oh, Patricia had told me that you were having, um, issues, and I had talked to my old roommate from college who is—*can* you believe it; I couldn't, let me tell you—a sex therapist, very famous, well regarded, in San Francisco now. Patricia mentioned you would probably be more comfortable talking to a man, so I asked her for a male sex therapist in New York, preferably on the Upper East Side, or in Midtown East, and she gave me the name of somebody who's a specialist in just exactly your problem." She took a big gasp of breath. "There! That wasn't so difficult, now, was it?"

He took a sip of iced water, electrified. "For whom?"

She flushed red on her neck and her exposed cleavage. He noticed that his wife, across the table, next to Howard, had also flushed down to her exposed cleavage. What had *she* just said?

"So you didn't go, then." She sighed and—unbelievably—went on. "She was afraid you wouldn't, after the last two didn't work."

"Cynthia, is there anything that *isn't* your business?"

"Where your wife is concerned?" She laughed. "No."

Patricia looked up at the two of them and smiled innocently.

He dropped his napkin on the uneaten veal, and walked out of the restaurant without looking back. It was July, and the street was steamy.

"What's going on?" Patricia called, her sandals slapping on the sidewalk.

He kept walking.

"What is it?" She caught up with him. "Was it Cynthia?"

He rounded the corner, and started walking down Third Avenue.

If she would only stop pestering him and let him walk. But no, she had to poke and pry and try to prevent him from walking. She refused to notice how extreme his anger was, this woman with whom he had lived for twenty-eight years, who had absolutely no clue how to handle him, or the children, who had always been clueless, who had never respected his privacy, who had chatted about him with her friends, who had gone home to gossip with their husbands, men who had discussed the market and the Yankees with him as if they knew nothing. He swung out and struck her, fast, hard, on the face, hitting bone with bone, the back of his hand. She reeled back onto a parked car, stunned.

She roared in anger, but she wasn't hitting back.

He left her there. He had belted his wife, and she had deserved it. He hadn't hit anyone since he was fifteen, not counting the sock he'd given Randy when he'd caught him licking a library sticker off a book the day after he'd bailed him out of jail. He stalked downtown to see Erica, simmering in bile.

Marjorie's apartment was cool, calm and dry. When he saw Erica on the big sofa, he was flooded with relief.

When he considered how dependent he'd become on Erica, Mitch was more than slightly afraid. Erica transferred the money; Mitch assumed the guilt. Erica had access to the money; Mitch had to ask. What if something happened to her? What if they stopped getting along? Lately his mind was on escape. He'd become a fugitive without planning. He wanted to escape again, and do it right this time.

"Do you know anyone who forges papers?" he asked Conchita as she washed dishes one night. "Passports, driver's licenses, things like that?"

She looked frightened. "I'm not getting involved in that."

"Of course not. You'd just be introducing me."

"I don't know anybody like that."

"But you know people who know people like that."

She inhaled. "Yes."

"So you could find out a name? I'd pay for the privilege."

"How much?"

"I don't know—what does an introduction like this go for?"

She dried a bowl with a dish towel. "The child wants Rollerblades."

His heart turned over at the limits of her vision. "Rollerblades it is."

The following day, Conchita gave him a matchbook with a number.

He met his new contact at a White Castle on Queens Boulevard and 43rd Street. Corey, no last name, sat at a booth in the back with a small, white, cylindrical pump on a napkin next to the remains of his lunch. "Hihowyadoin. Sit down. Asthma," he said, inhaling on the pump. "What can I do for you?"

"I need papers."

"Uh-huh, uh-huh. What you need?"

"Passport, driver's license. I don't have any immediate plans, but I want to be able to leave town if I need to. How does this work?"

"It may take some time." He inhaled again. "Two weeks."

"All right." Mitch felt better, safer. How much did he have to fear from a short, pale, thin asthmatic in thick glasses? "Fee?"

"Well, to be frank, I know who you are, Donald. So that ups the price right there. Great job, by the way. Some friends and colleagues of mine are unbelievably impressed with your work."

His hands began to sweat. "I see. How much?"

"Why don't we say $5,000 each for the passport and the license."

"I see. Do you take credit cards?"

Corey laughed. "Are you kidding?"

"That's expensive. How do I know the papers will pass for real?"

"Ask Gustavo."

"Who's Gustavo?"

"Who's Gustavo? Gustavo's the guy referred you to me. Get your act together, Donald! Don't make my friends and colleagues lose respect."

Mitch had sought this contact in the spirit of insurance, of having emergency backup plans, independent of Erica. The only thing he'd accomplished was having to ask her for more money.

❖

Now and then, a flash of the old Mitch—effective, appreciative, confident, seductive—shone through, and Erica was able to remember how she had once felt about him. Mostly, though, she felt like she was taking care of an obstreperous monkey, and she wanted to slam him across the room in frustration. Then she felt guilty, so she redoubled her efforts with him, in the hope that he might respond in kind, and she could like him again.

It was in this spirit of taking the high road that Erica arrived at the house on a Saturday afternoon with a recipe she'd clipped for linguine with tomato sauce, and the ingredients to make it. Mitch was out. She started cooking.

When he arrived shortly afterward, laden with shopping bags bearing Manhattan logos, she completely lost her cool.

"What THE HELL are you doing?"

"It wasn't like I was on Madison Avenue. I was in *TriBeCa*—it's like a different city," he said, with such ebullience she felt like punishing him.

"Are you trying to get us arrested?"

"Sometimes I think I should just go," he said, pacing the kitchen.

"Go where?" She stirred her sauce.

"Seattle, LA, Phoenix!"

"Interesting idea. How would you get there?"

"Car."

"Paying for gas how?"

"Credit card."

"And where would the credit card bills be going?"

"Here, and you'd send them to me when I got a place, or a post office box. You'd do that for me, wouldn't you?"

She didn't respond. "And you would access your money how?"

"Don't I have access to my own money?"

"*You* are going to Costa Rica," she said, amused.

"Can't you just get on a plane again?" he said, as if they hadn't been over and over and over the timing of her trips.

She took the pot off the stove, burning her wrist in the process. She'd lost all patience for him. He could make his own damn sauce. She went to the living room, hot and annoyed. He followed.

She took her wig off and flung it at the sofa. Without registering the change, he said, "When do you think we can start my Web site?"

He didn't even see her anymore.

SHE TOOK THE 7 TRAIN TO GRAND CENTRAL, walked east a block and boarded a nearly empty M15, sitting on a vacant bank of seats. A middle-aged woman got on at the next stop, surveyed the empty bus and sat down right next to her. Erica slid over a seat, leaving a space between them. People were so creepy. She opened her book, noticing again the burn from the completely unnecessary and yet hopeful tomato sauce.

The woman next to her reached across the empty seat to touch the welt on Erica's wrist. "What's that?" she said, her face inches away.

Too outraged to speak, Erica rose, rang the bell, exited the bus and stalked up Third Avenue. Both the woman who had touched her and the pouting teenager in his underpants stretched out on the side of the bus watched as Erica made her way up the avenue, trying not to mind the crowds, the exhaust, the hot wind whipping dust into her eyes. The world was conspiring to get her off the M15 and into the blue Toyota.

A block from her office, the sky opened up and a heavy summer storm fell out, pelting the windows and drenching the sidewalk. She threw herself into the revolving door, signed in with the security guard and took the elevator upstairs. The phone was ringing when she opened her door. It was seven o'clock, Saturday night: who knew she was there? Mitch wouldn't dare call the office, would he?

It was Detective Sprague. "Where have you been?" he asked.

Why had she picked up the phone? "What do you mean?"

"You've been out of the office a lot lately."

Had she picked up the phone because she thought Mitch would apologize? "I had a lot of unused vacation days. I was told use them or lose them."

"How'd you use them?"

"To tell you the truth, I've been looking for a job."

"Where?"

"I'd rather not say." She had become too relaxed.

"Who is David Findlay?"

She sat down, shocked. "Why do you ask?"

"Answer the question."

"He was a neighbor. I haven't seen him in a long time. Why?"

"How would you characterize your relationship with him?"

"Historical. Anything else I can help you with?"

"Not right now, thank you."

She hung up slowly. The critical thing wasn't whether she wanted to be with Mitch. The critical thing was not getting distracted by nonsense and doing stupid things like answering the phone. She changed into a spare suit she kept at the office. She put Maria's wig on under a scarf, then took the elevator down, passing by the sleeping security guard without signing out. She ran through wet darkness, alert to the street. They might be following her. She skipped Lexington and walked against traffic on Third Avenue, so she couldn't be followed by car.

She walked quickly, resisting the temptation to run. At Maria's, she stripped off her wet clothes, wrapped herself in a dirty towel, opened up the filing cabinet and began to shred. By the time she was finished, the storm had softened into a heavy rain. She dumped the bags in the garbage cans of several town houses a block away, and walked quickly back to Erica's with her head down.

CHAPTER TWELVE

M itch had his passport picture taken at the Photo Finish on Merrick Road in Baldwin, and met Corey at the KFC next door.

"Just a few formalities," Corey said, pushing a small stiff document at him. "Use this name, and sign here."

"Phillip Pitkin?" Mitch said.

"I'm sorry, you wanted Cary Grant?"

Mitch signed on top of the greasy table.

"You got the cash?"

Mitch pushed a paper bag at him morosely.

"Great." Corey counted the wad under the table. When he was finished, he looked up. "Let's meet next week." He took a shot from his inhaler. "I'm sorry to tell you, but it's gonna be an extra five."

Mitch plucked a five-dollar bill from his wallet.

Corey convulsed in breathless laughter. "Five *thousand*! I'm sorry, what can I tell you?" he said, wheezing and shrugging and laughing simultaneously. "It's a business, and sometimes you don't even break even."

HE FOUND HIMSELF IN BED with Erica, feeling shaky, suffocated, terrified.

"Worrying is counterproductive." She squeezed his arm.

She put on a bathrobe and turned on the computer. He lay on his side, and the terror eased into a heavy, thwarted feeling. He'd had moments of connectedness with Erica that were weightless, effortless. Everything now seemed an enormous struggle, beyond his reach.

Erica's anger (when not directed at him) was a powerful, mesmerizing force. She could look at something he never noticed—the simultaneous decline of phone booths and the proliferation of televisions in the public space, for example—and make a serious conspiracy case. Patricia, who had lots of anger, was entrenched in squads of friends, shrinks and gurus. Everything Patricia was involved with had a logo, a newsletter, a celebrity mascot and an annual dinner at the Pierre. Erica he saw alone in bleak, uncharted environments, standing firm against nameless, colossal, unstoppable forces.

She came back into bed with a bowl of oatmeal and a spoon.

"I forgot to tell you," she said, brimming with aggravation. "The plan for Glenn's new office renovation was unveiled today. He's going to knock down the walls and put up glass partitions," she raged. "Not even frosted-glass panels, no! See-through glass! The transparent accounting firm, to show that we have nothing to hide. Of course, he and Slavin will get their real walls. Peons like me will get to work in a fish tank. Selfish, pretentious son of a bitch," she muttered.

Erica had tragedy written all over her. He knew it would have to end with her, but he didn't know how. He couldn't see himself with Erica in five years. But then again, he couldn't see *himself* in five years.

❖

Debbie Goldman passed the written exam and the driving test, and was issued a temporary New York State driver's license. The permanent license would be mailed to Maria's address in two weeks. The following morning, Erica King was offered a junior partnership in the Chicago office of Kessel and Partners. She handed in her resignation with two weeks' notice. The office was agog.

One by one, they knocked on her door and demanded details.

Heather arrived. "Do you *know* anyone out there?"

"Oh, I know half of Lake Shore Drive, Heather."

Charlie joined them. "Who's the lucky guy?"

"You are, Charlie, now that I won't be around anymore."

Angie peeked in. "How much are your movers charging?"

"I'm just finalizing that now."

"It couldn't be very much, right?" Heather said. "I mean, you don't have that much stuff, just you, a single person, alone."

"Would you care to do an inventory, Heather, to make sure I have as pathetic a collection of objects as you've imagined?"

Glenn Friedman pushed his red face in. "How much they paying you?"

"That's a rude question, Glenn."

"Well, excuse *me*! I live in the real world."

"And I live in a fantasyland, where professionals have walls and doors."

"You know, after all we've done for you here," Glenn said, "I am floored that you could just walk away. Especially now."

"I want you to know how grateful I've been for the opportunity to spend eleven years here, without the word *partnership* ever being mentioned."

"Partners bring in business," Glenn sneered. "Who could *you* ever bring in?"

There was a collective hush as Glenn pivoted on a heel.

"You gonna miss us?" asked Charlie.

The entire city lurched, swollen, moist and heat-stricken, through the heavy, humid days of late July and the flattening haze of early August. Flashy storms swept through in mid-August, spitting forceful rain, toppling the tables of accessory vendors, scattering street trash and momentarily clearing the air. But soon the smog, the soot and the scorched edges were back.

Since the crumb cake breakthrough in Jackson Heights, Sprague had bought doughnuts on two separate occasions, and had enjoyed both of them without an ounce of guilt. He'd stopped playing basketball because of his knee. He'd stopped lifting weights because of his schedule.

One night over a lean, unsatisfying dinner, Cathy told Dennis that she'd made an appointment with an agency. She said the word *agency* with a nasty vigor. "I don't need to tell you," she warned, "but when we go in there, we really need to be together on this."

Sprague said nothing. He went out for ice cream by himself. He honestly couldn't see what might happen between now and the appointment that would make him *together* with her on this. She needed to be distracted. He'd planned to surprise her with a new dog from a reputable breeder. But he hadn't had time to do the research.

When would he?

THE FOLLOWING MORNING WAS GORGEOUS—cool for August—and Sprague had an energetic, back-to-school feeling. On the way to the Midtown stakeout, he stopped to buy an assortment of doughnuts. He got back into the car and offered one to Ballestrino. Ballestrino stared at him. "What's going on?"

"What do you mean?"

Ballestrino switched lanes. "How much weight have you lost?"

"Enough."

"Don't you feel better?"

"Yes, I do."

"So what are you doing? You have a good thing going!"

Sprague held up a chocolate doughnut, enjoying the plump, dark look of it in the full, late-summer sunlight. "I really have no explanation." He took a bite. It was better than anything he'd experienced in months.

"What does Cathy say?"

"We're actually at a bit of an impasse."

Tony stopped at a light. "She's eating healthy; good for her."

"Yes, but that's not the issue." Sprague finished off the doughnut with a pang of regret. Ballestrino pulled into a space with a good view of Ms. King's office building. Sprague broke a cinnamon-sugar in half and dunked it into his coffee.

"Stop!" Ballestrino said, as he threw the car into park.

Sprague wished he could.

"You get crap on this car, you clean it up," Tony warned.

"As always. Cathy wants to adopt."

"Give me that," Ballestrino said, pulling a powdered sugar out of the box.

"Cathy wants a kid, are you listening to me?"

"I thought the kid thing was over with."

"So did I. I've never seen her like this. She's on a rampage."

"She's mad? Good-time Cathy?"

This conversation was cut short by Ms. Erica King, who emerged from her office and began walking east. They followed on foot. She wore her favorite outfit: the ratty blue blazer over the long, colorless dress, and the dingy tennis shoes from the late seventies with the white anklets and supermarket panty hose.

They followed her to her regular spot, and watched as she descended on the escalator, sat down at a table and took out a phone.

"You remember Ms. Erica King having a cell phone?"

"Can't say I do," Ballestrino said.

Her face closed as they approached. She dropped the phone in her purse.

"Ms. King," Sprague said formally, "mind if we ask you a few questions?"

"Here?" She gestured to the Citicorp atrium. "Now?"

"If that's okay with you," he said, while she looked around.

"Do I have a choice?"

"We could take you downtown."

"Or you could come back to my office."

"Would you prefer that?" Sprague asked, all accommodation.

"No, let's get this over with now," she said. "Mind if I eat?"

"Not at all," he said. "Mind if we sit?"

She made an indifferent gesture.

"Tell me everything you did yesterday."

She pulled out her bag lunch and put it on the table. "I had a doctor's appointment in the morning, so I got in late."

He nodded at her to continue.

"I worked on some bookkeeping for a corporate client."

"And?"

"I had lunch here."

"With?"

"Myself. Same table, different sandwich."

She took her sandwich out, unwrapped it and took a bite.

"And then?"

"After work I went to a movie."

"Which theater?"

"The new Loews."

"I've tried going to that theater, but it was always sold out."

"You can always get a ticket ahead of time on-line."

"You usually do that?"

"Often, but last night I took my chances."

"And?"

"No problem. No lines."

"And then after the movie? Did you eat dinner?"

"I ate at the movies."

"Popcorn for dinner?"

"I had a sandwich."

"Don't tell me you brought outside food into the Loews!"

"Arrest me."

"Where'd you get it?"

"The bagel place across the street."

"You said a sandwich."

"A sandwich on a bagel."

"Myself, I prefer rye, but that's me. Then what?"

"I went home."

"And home is—"

"325 East 32nd Street."

"See anybody in the building?"

"I don't think so."

"Doorman see you?"

"He must have."

"What then?"

"Sleep."

"Right away? Didn't you take a shower?"

"Explain how that's relevant."

"You have a ticket stub?"

"From the movies? I doubt it."

"How'd you get the ticket?"

"At the box office, I told you."

"Okay, now tell me everything you did yesterday—"

She exhaled, annoyed.

"In reverse."

"What?"

"Tell me everything you did yesterday, in reverse. You went to sleep."

She stared at him, debating how to handle this.

Ballestrino was enjoying this maneuver. "If you really did the things you said you did," Sprague said, "you won't have any trouble with this exercise."

"I went to sleep," she said spitefully. "I came home from the movies. I attended the movie and ate an illegal sandwich. I took the bus from the office."

"You didn't tell me you took the bus."

"From the office to the movies, I took the bus."

"Which bus?"

"The M15 Express."

"The Express doesn't stop on 32nd Street."

"I *walked* two blocks," she said. "I worked in the afternoon."

"You didn't swipe your ID card yesterday."

"Of course I did."

Sprague shook his head.

"I didn't? How is that possible?"

"You tell me."

"I must have come in with someone who had swiped—yes, that's right. I walked in with some people. They must have held the door."

"You didn't swipe in *or* out yesterday. Maybe you weren't there yesterday."

"I was there all day."

"We'll have to ask around, see if anyone saw you."

"People don't necessarily notice me, but I'm always there."

She said this with such a morose air of resignation that he almost felt sorry for her, this wallflower with the bad complexion. This made him mad.

"We hear you're moving to Chicago."

"Yes, I've been made an offer."

"You'll need to register your new address with us before you leave."

"Really," she said, with her poker face in place.

"Really. Once again, Ms. King, from the beginning: you had a doctor's appointment. Which doctor?"

Erica was careful to walk back to her office as if she were only slightly annoyed. Now they really *would* be following her. These cops infuriated her. They could ask anything, just anything, and she had to answer. They wore a sense of entitlement, along with the badge and the gun.

In the previous ten months she'd moved most of the cash out of the safe-deposit boxes and spread it between the Institute for Well-Being, Mitch's and Maria's. There was only a small amount left at Erica's, and by chance, she'd brought some of it to the office that morning. She'd hidden it in a closet behind boxes of copy paper in the Xerox room.

She put the cash in her big black carryall when she left that night, walked to Bloomingdale's and wandered around, wondering who was on her tail. On the third floor, Erica took some clothes to a dressing room. She called the saleswoman in, gave her the price tag to a bright green cotton jacket and paid with exact change when she returned with a receipt.

She stuffed the jacket into her tote bag. Upstairs in a stall in the ladies' room, she changed into the jacket and Marjorie's hair, took the elevator to the main floor and milled with the crowds among the cosmetics counters. She took the 6 train to Astor Place, a cab to Brooklyn and the G train to Queens.

She all but threw the cash at Mitch. He had ruined everything. He lurked there, like a big child needing constant supervision—like Davey Findlay!

"Put that cash away," she told him on her way back out. "Conchita is coming tomorrow." She hadn't told him about the offer from Kessel and he hadn't asked. She was damned if she was going to carry this man cross-country.

"Where are you going?"

"I have to go."

"Not until you eat something. A ham sandwich!"

"Mitch! What do you want from me? I have to go."

"You don't realize it, but I do have some culinary talents." He pretended to make a flourish with some mayonnaise on a piece of bread. The knife flew out of his hands and clattered to the floor.

"I don't have time for this."

"The banks are closed now."

"I have things to do now so that I can be at the bank tomorrow."

"Tomorrow is Election Day. The banks are closed. What about tomato and lettuce?" He stuck his head in the refrigerator.

"Tomorrow is not Election Day."

"You're right!" He laughed like an insane man.

She took the sandwich off the plate and put it in a baggie. She shoved the baggie into her tote bag.

"You're taking it *to go*?"

She shoved half the sandwich into her mouth and chewed rapidly.

"What about me?" he whined. "Don't *I* get a sandwich?"

What was wrong with this man?

❖

Mitch woke up with a feeling of peril pressing in on him from all sides. The noises from the street were sharp and menacing. The idea of being out in public was too exposed, too dangerous. He had a terrible awareness that his number was up. He wouldn't go out. He would stay right where he was.

The sea anemone waved its pink fingers at him seductively. The tang was hovering near the inlet of live rock, waiting, perhaps, for him to introduce her to her mate. He'd avoided the idea of mating; tangs laid 6,000 eggs at a time: who had room for a school?

Shortly after she arrived, Conchita asked to speak to him. He gestured to the kitchen table, and she sat down opposite him. "My boyfriend wants to set up a video shop."

The eel looked pale. "Why? There are so many already."

"Whatever," she said dismissively. "He needs financing."

"All banks have loan officers who provide financing—"

"He wants you to finance him."

"Me? What do you mean? I've never met the man." He moved toward the back door to look at his concrete. The Southeast Asian or South American woman was scrubbing her driveway. Why hadn't he hired *that* woman to clean?

Conchita followed him, accusing. "You remember you needed a contact?"

He spun around, shocked. "You told him who I was?"

"No, I didn't tell him who you were," she said, fast and nasty. "The *forger* told him who you were." She knocked her forehead with two fingers: *stupid.* "Now Gustavo needs a loan. A hundred thousand dollars."

This stopped him cold. "A hundred thousand dollars?"

"He has to buy inventory and fixtures."

"Is he buying them at Sotheby's?"

They were leaning against the kitchen counters facing each other. "He'll tell you the whole thing, in person or over the phone if you want."

His mouth was dry. "This is extortion."

"Don't talk to me about it," she said in a tough Latina singsong. "I told you I didn't want to get involved."

"And now your boyfriend is blackmailing me!"

"It's a *business* proposition. He'll pay you back. Look, this is his number." She gave him a card. "Call him up and talk to him directly. I'm not gonna be in the middle anymore. I don't like being in this position, Mitch," she said, with some drama. She picked up her keys and bag and walked out of the house, leaving dishes in the sink and the vacuum cleaner sprawled on the living room rug.

He left Gustavo's card by the phone, and didn't call. The bubble coral was looking especially voluptuous. Whatever else you could say about Erica, she had taken him off the treadmill to nowhere. Of course, she'd put him on another machine, perhaps more dangerous. He was seeing less and less of her. She had stopped talking about Chicago. He had no idea what, if anything, she was planning, and he hadn't asked. He was afraid to hear.

Mitch looked around the half-cleaned house, and decided he needed to take a positive outlook. He wasn't being blackmailed; he was helping a local businessman get on his feet. He wasn't hiding in fear; he was enjoying life on his own terms.

In tribute to the woman who had brought him back to life, who no doubt would resurrect him again, he ordered Chinese. And because he was feeling paranoid, he was very specific with the woman on the phone: "Tell me exactly what it will cost. I'll leave an envelope outside with the exact amount, plus a tip for the delivery boy. The delivery boy is to ring the bell, leave the food on the ledge outside the door, take the envelope and leave."

He drifted back to the tank, and noticed the eel was not under the shipwreck, where it usually was.

Twenty minutes later the doorbell rang.

"Thank you!" he called through the door.

He waited.

The doorbell rang again. "Chinese delivery!"

"Thank you!" he cried angrily.

"Chinese delivery!"

"THANK you! The money is in an envelope on the ledge there."

"YOU OPEN DOOR. PAY FOR FOOD."

Mitch clenched his teeth. "THE EXACT AMOUNT, PLUS A TWO-DOLLAR TIP, IS IN THE ENVELOPE, RIGHT IN FRONT OF YOU ON THAT LEDGE THERE. Do you see it? It says 'Chinese delivery.' "

He was so small-time. Why had he not hired a chef? He was being sunk by the narrow, myopic vision of Erica King.

"Chinese delivery!"

Did the Weather Underground have to deal with this? Did Bonnie and Clyde?

❖

Chuck Dzergazi licked his chubby index finger, and paged through the *Post*. It was midweek, midmorning, slow. The pumps needed cleaning, the fish needed feeding, what else was new? He should get everything done before the kids arrived after school to make noise and dirt and bug him.

He finished his second corn muffin of the morning. Aquarium supplies in Rockville Center was several steps up from bait and tackle in Babylon, his previous business. Of course, this line of work had its irritants. Sometimes guys came in every day, needing to talk. When anyone had a fish croak, they barreled in with the dead body in a Ziploc bag, hoping for a replacement, and you had to have a very time-consuming conversation, because they were either blaming themselves or, more often, blaming you. You had to work them around to the fact that life has a limit, by definition, and fish *died*—all the time—for no reason at all.

The chimes signaled a walk-in. This guy had been in a few times, loitering by the eels in a hat. Chuck had recognized him immediately, but hadn't said anything. The old customer used to come in and pontificate about his Ecosystem. He'd spent hours chatting up novices in the store and bragging about his bubble coral. Since then, Chuck had received no fewer than five visits from the cops: had he seen the guy, big reward: $25,000. The cops called him once a week now, checking.

The guy was now hovering around the big tank. Chuck waited patiently. Sooner or later his marine aquarist would ask about the new filter Chuck was hawking up front: he was an equipment snob, as much into gadgetry as fish.

When the fugitive sauntered up front to ask about the new filter, Chuck offered no-pressure sales advice. He let the customer come behind the counter to look at the fish food and impulse purchases on the wall behind the register.

Then Chuck asked, "How's the bubble coral?"

"Couldn't be healthier. How did you know I had bubble coral?"

"I used to hear about it all the time."

The "new" customer put on a face. "I've only been here once."

"Oh, really?"

"Well, actually I was in once, and then I bought some tubing from your Web site," he admitted, and then made to leave.

Chuck blocked his exit. "They're looking for you, Mitch."

He twitched like a cornered rabbit. "Don't be silly."

"The cops call me once a week. I could give them your new address."

"How would you know my address?"

"*Nobody* buys off my Web site."

Mitch Greiff became very still. "What do you want?"

"Well, let's see here." Chuck had to smile. He'd been considering that question for some time. "I read that you took off with $103 million. So what do you say to half a million, Mitch? Oh, hey, make it 600 thousand: I gave you a big discount on those hoses."

"You realize this is not in cash."

Chuck had to laugh. "Oh, it would have to be in cash!"

"That's not so easy."

"You're good at what you do." Chuck smiled encouragingly, and gave him a salute as he released him. "You'll figure out a way."

CHAPTER THIRTEEN

*F*uck, Mitch thought, and slammed the car into drive. He flew down the Meadowbrook Parkway in a blind fury. This was by no means a final negotiation. It started with six hundred thousand, and would end with a phone call to the police. He had a moment of searing clarity under a threatening sky on the Jones Beach Causeway: how were Chuck, Gustavo and Corey any different from his wife, his mother, his kids, his insurance company and all the other institutions he'd paid in order to live his previous life?

Never mind: Chuck was history. Chuck had to go.

From a pay phone at the mostly deserted, rainy-day, midweek beach pavilion, he called Corey, the asthmatic forger. Corey listened, Corey wheezed, Corey feigned concern, Corey gave him a number.

He met Gennadi and Spartak an hour later at a Wendy's on Queens Boulevard. They exuded a pale, unhealthy Eastern European air, wolf-ing down their lunches next to a trash can hopping with bees. For $10,000 they'd scare Chuck, and for $15,000 they'd get rid of him for good.

"How do I know you won't set me up afterward? Come after me for more, or tip off the police?"

"A deal's a deal," said Gennadi, holding food in one hand and a lit Camel in the other. Both hands had scrapes. "We give you our word."

Mitch looked at the chewing thugs, and wondered what their word was worth. But he couldn't do this himself. This was a job for professionals. He gave them the address of the store. Gennadi then asked a series of questions:

"What he looks like?"

"Fat, very fat, with longish red hair, and a red beard and mustache."

"What kind of building it is?"

"Part of a strip mall."

"What kind of car he drives?"

"I've seen him in a white van with the logo of the store."

"We check it out. What do you want to do to him?"

The cars creeping slowly along the access road reminded him of the creatures in his tank. "Let's just scare him badly."

"We are capable of having done permanent brain damage," said Spartak.

"But that would be extra," Gennadi pointed out with a smile. "Either way, we need half up front to start research."

Mitch excused himself to go to the bathroom. In a scarred stall, he counted out $5,000 in cash, and put it in a paper bag. Spartak kicked open the bathroom door as he emerged.

"I was just coming to give you this," Mitch said.

"Good." Spartak took the bag with one hand, and threw a fast punch at Mitch's nose with the other.

The noise was unbelievable. Mitch reeled against the stalls, his face in wet pain. The thug then grabbed his shirt and tossed him up against the urinal. His head hit the porcelain with a loud, cold crack, and he collapsed back into the damp base. He looked up in terror.

"We can scare anyone badly, you know," said the professional, massaging his hand. "We expect payment immediately upon having been finished the job." He exited the men's room with a flourish of leather coat.

Mitch propped himself up. He was sitting in a cold urinal, with the dirty metallic taste of blood in his mouth, soaked in other men's piss.

This was no business for an aging Jewish accountant, he thought, and suddenly missed talking to his mother with his feet up on his desk in his old office. He used to look out onto the drab façade of the building opposite, and have normal, boring days full of documents, numbers and other people's problems.

❖

There was no telling what Sprague knew. There was no time. Erica arrived at the house in Queens and threw her bags down. Mitch was at his tank; he didn't even say hello. Fine. There was no time. She took the stairs quickly, hoisted her laptop onto the desk and connected it. While it warmed up, she went around the house snapping the blinds closed. Back downstairs, she pulled out two chairs from the dining room table.

"Okay, come here. I need you," she said.

He turned around. In shock, she fell into one of the chairs. His face was bursting with livid bruises. "Oh, my God."

"It feels worse than it looks."

What ridiculous timing. "What happened?"

He just stared at her through his raw face.

"If you don't tell me what happened, how can I help you?"

"What kind of help? It's over. It happened, and now it's over."

He sat down delicately, as if other parts were injured.

There were a hundred questions, but there was no time.

She felt awful. There was no way out of it. "Okay, we have to talk."

He looked up at her through the blood in his eyes.

She spoke carefully, so as not to upset him. She told him she wished him well, and wanted him to be happy. She wouldn't be giving him an address. She didn't want to know his whereabouts, or what he'd be doing.

He sagged a little, and closed his eyes.

"I'm sorry to get practical so quickly, but we don't have time. Of all the banks we have money in, which one would you like to visit?"

He gravitated to the tank, hanging over it.

She didn't have time for this. "Of all—" she said, but he cut her off.

"Bermuda."

"Okay." She darted upstairs. She removed Maria's name from those authorized to make transactions on the Bermuda account.

She went downstairs. "Go change your passwords on the screen."

"Why?"

"We're separating our assets." She led him upstairs, ignoring his limping. "You get half, I get half. We'll change our passwords. Is that blood in your hair?"

He pulled away from her inspection. He had scrapes on his hands.

She wouldn't get distracted by this now. While he typed, she began pulling cash out of the hiding places, making a mound on the kitchen table.

He came downstairs while she was in the midst.

"Come here," she called. "Count out 250 thousand, and put it on this chair."

Ignoring her, he gravitated back to the fish.

She could not give in to this. She climbed the stairs and transferred money from the Cayman account to the Bermuda account.

She dragged the heavy bundles out of the coat closet, and was out the door. Everyone on the street was coming home from work; no one was paying attention. She dropped the carefully wrapped and mutilated entrails of Marjorie's laptop into the can on the crowded corner of 81st Street and 37th Avenue. On Roosevelt Avenue, she placed Maria's damaged laptop—swaddled in some ugly Maria sweaters—in one of the teeming cans in front of a busy burrito joint. Across the street, she tossed a variety of mangled floppy disks into a dumpster, barely breaking her stride.

She returned to the house and began counting money in the kitchen. She counted out another $250,000, and put it in a shopping bag for him. She reached across the table and felt a searing pain slicing through the meat of her palm. A huge knife had been sitting on the table, hidden by some bills.

"What the hell is that doing on the table?" She shrieked on her way to the sink. He was a fool, but was he trying to kill her? She ran water over the slice.

"What?" he said.

"A fucking kitchen knife that just carved through a tendon?" The blood, surprisingly red, ran through her fingers under the tap.

"I was opening a box of food for the crab," he said indifferently.

She was angry and nauseated, but she couldn't get sidetracked. She found the first-aid kit and made a bandage with her right hand. She resumed counting. He was useless. Delicately she wrapped bundles of cash in aluminum foil as blood seeped through the gauze. She slipped the foil packets into white plastic pouches, and tossed them into tote bags and heavy plastic shopping bags. Each pouch contained $50,000.

The blood was really coming. When she raised her hand it ran down her arm. She wrapped the hand tightly in a dish towel; blood appeared within seconds.

She had to switch gears.

"Drive me to the hospital," she said. He looked up at her as if she were insane. "Don't think about it, just do it. Come on, get up. That's right. Get the car keys. Come on! I'm losing blood here!"

She pushed him out of the house. She opened the driver's door with her right hand and pushed him in. He sat, as if unable to move.

"Start the car. NOW."

He started the car.

"Where are we going?" he said, as if drugged.

"Elmhurst is the closest. It's three blocks away. COME ON! I could have been there already had I walked! Do you not see this blood?"

He stared at her hand with abstract interest. She struggled out of the car and ran down 80th Street. He was useless, fucking useless.

She presented the Erica IDs, as Erica was the only one with health insurance, and she wanted to be seen right away. She waited twenty minutes in an area filled with screaming infants, depressed elderly people and ranting psychotic cases. She was taken to a big room of tables concealed partially by curtains on tracks. A short male doctor arrived, said very little, stitched the wound and gave her a two-day supply of bandages.

Clearly she couldn't afford to rush, especially now that she was late.

Back at the house, Mitch was watching local news on the television at a preposterous volume. She called a cab, changed into Debbie's wig and glasses and looked at the coral softly undulating in the tank. It was beautiful, she had to admit. He continued to ignore her, taking in images with his swollen eyes. His cash was still all over the kitchen, but she wasn't putting it away for him. Taking care of him was not her job anymore.

"I hired a team of thugs to break someone's leg," he said.

Nothing could surprise her anymore. "Mine?"

"No, not yours."

"And they beat you up instead?"

"Hopefully, in addition. The fish store guy recognized me," he added, not looking at her.

This wasn't her problem.

When the cab came, she kissed him good-bye on the forehead while he stared straight ahead and pretended that nothing was happening. Which was preferable, she supposed, to a big scene with raised voices.

At LaGuardia she got out of the cab at Departures, walked downstairs to Arrivals and took the bus to Avis. She presented Debbie Goldman's license and credit card with her right hand, and signed below the counter with her bandaged left hand. There was no trouble of any kind. She was exhausted, but exhilarated, too, as she crossed the Triboro Bridge and followed signs to New England. It was a mess, and she was leaving it behind. The world was just beginning to open.

❖

Mitch arrived early at the parking lot of Dunkin' Donuts on Merrick Road in Valley Stream. In his lap, he felt the weight of the gun Corey had sold him ($1,000, including instructions on how to load it, shoot it and wear it). Mitch got the gun from Corey, in spite of the ridiculous markup, in order to avoid having to deal with yet another extortionist.

Before he'd had a chance to position himself in a parking space with a commanding view, Gennadi and Spartak drove right at him in a hulking Range Rover, preventing him from moving his car in any direction.

Mitch let the window down an inch. "You stay right where you are," he called to them, before anyone jumped out to toss him onto the highway.

"Okay, Donald!" Gennadi laughed. Spartak sat beside him, expressionless.

"What happened?"

"We took care of it."

"What did he say?"

"Say? He don't say anything!" Gennadi laughed. "He scream in pain."

A doubt flashed through him: "You let him know who sent you?"

"Of course. We tell him his mother send us."

This caused much mirth in the car.

Spartak leaned forward to be seen. "Where's the money?"

"You don't have to beat me up! I have your money."

The gun slid between his thighs as he stuck his arm out and up. Gennadi leaned down to take the paper bag. Mitch was petrified the gun might go off accidentally. The safety catch was on. Still, people shot themselves by mistake all the time. How did he know they'd done what they'd said they'd do? It would be stupid to ask them now that he'd already given them the money.

Spartak jumped out of the passenger side and walked around the front of the Range Rover toward him. With a racing heart, Mitch stabbed the close-window button in a panic. Spartak leveled an ominous look at him through the closing window. Why hadn't Mitch just pulled out the gun?

"A souvenir from the fat man," Spartak said, slapping a yellow tang on the windshield. The fish was wet and twitching. Was this supposed to reassure him? Spartak opened his leather jacket to reveal a large gun. "You will not leave till we will have counted the money yet."

"I'm not going anywhere," Mitch shouted through the window. They wouldn't kill him after taking his money, would they? Or beat him up again, just for fun? *Move the jacket and show the gun!*

On the other hand, he didn't want to escalate the tension. He didn't want to put himself in a situation where he had to use the gun. He merely wanted them to know that he had it, and would use it if necessary.

There was an endless wait while Gennadi counted the money. Spartak was standing, one hand on the roof of Mitch's car. His muscled, tattooed stomach was at Mitch's eye level, visible behind the black mesh undershirt he wore under the leather jacket. Spartak bent down periodically to smile at him sadistically through the glass. He had terrible teeth.

"You have made a big hit in the world of international finance, Donald."

The metal of the gun had warmed up in his grasp.

"What are you doing in tacky house in Jackson Heights, hanging around with this old witch with bad skin and fat ass?" Spartak grinned.

Mitch put his finger on the trigger. "What are you talking about?"

"You should be in Monte Carlo, Miami Beach, Bahamas, with sexy girl. You need help to find sexy girl? I have plenty. You can afford them now."

"Okay, Donald," Gennadi called.

Spartak, bored with him now, turned on his booted heel and strutted back toward their car.

Get out of here, Mitch decided, and shoved the gun and the jacket onto the passenger seat in disgust. He threw the Toyota into reverse.

"Oh, Donald," Spartak called in a playground voice as Mitch shifted the car into drive, "where do you hide your brand-new gun?"

Get out of here, he thought, and shot out of the parking lot into traffic. The tang was still on his windshield. He glanced back and saw their enormous car driving in the opposite direction.

He got on a highway, and wondered where to go. Whatever structure or interaction he'd had was based on Erica's presence in his life. Now he had nothing. He had no address, and no destination for her. It was blank where she had been. It wasn't clear what he should be doing. He cursed himself for not demanding more information.

The Cross Island Parkway slowed to a standstill. He was in traffic on a road that led to a place he wasn't even going to. This irritated him, both that he had no destination, and that his arrival was being delayed. He got off the highway and pulled into a gas station to weep in bitter frustration.

Eventually he went home, picking up some take-out chicken, beer and an action video on the way: a bachelor's dinner.

❖

Somewhere west of Boston, Erica stopped for the night at a motel on a brightly lit road catering to cars and the people in them. After she'd checked in, she drove over to the adjacent diner and parked her rental car where she could watch it. She ordered a cup of coffee and a piece of cheesecake.

Three women in their thirties, dressed to slay, sat down at the next table. They were shiny with makeup and expectations. They wore see-through clothes. They bumped into people and apologized excessively. The men in the diner—all blue-collar types who hadn't washed their jeans—were intrigued with this display. The three tilted toward them. It was Saturday night, Erica realized: everyone was out on the town.

The wig was hot.

If not Mitch, then who? Who would let her take her hair off? Where would she meet him? While she waited for her cake, she removed from her key ring the keys to Maria's and Erica's apartments, the mailboxes and safe-deposit boxes, the key to the house in Queens and the key to the blue Toyota.

After her snack, she walked outside into the thick August night. She distributed the keys one by one among the garbage cans she encountered in the ladies' room, at the gas station next door, in front of the liquor shop, in front of the motel. The end of an era. She felt so light it almost scared her.

❖

Ballestrino walked into the office and waited for Sprague to get off the phone. He'd just spent an hour with a Caucasian female individual named Frieda Walsh, who had taught gym at Bradley when Geri King was the school Nurse.

"I found out, among other juicy bits of gossip, that Geri King, Erica's mother, changed her name."

The Lieutenant paused in front of them to listen.

"Her name was Elena Krupalski Carlson," he continued. "She was living in Chicago, married to a Caucasian individual named Hugh Carlson, who took a swan dive off the fourteenth floor when it became known that he'd embezzled from his Union."

Sprague gasped out loud. "I'm getting chills!"

Greeley snapped, "Why didn't we know that about her father?"

"We'd heard he died in a car accident."

"From whom did you hear this?"

He and Sprague looked at each other. "I guess from her," Sprague admitted. "It was in her personnel file."

"Laziness." Red blotches spotted Greeley's face.

"The gym teacher said Elena legally changed her name, and her three-year-old daughter Maria's name, in Chicago, and then they moved to Manhattan. She said this was the late sixties."

"Where's Ms. King now?"

"She hasn't been home since Bialkin and Fausto lost her again Friday morning," Tony said. "But she's on her way to that junior partnership in Chicago."

"Assuming she's even going to Chicago," Greeley said. "You

shouldn't take anything she says at face value. Haven't you learned that much yet?"

Ballestrino opened the front door, and the phone rang. His mother picked up, and he browsed through the mail. "It's your aunt Kate," she called over the static of the police scanner. "She wants me to make you come over there for dinner Friday, but I'm not so sure you don't already have plans."

He liked his aunt Kate's minestrone. "I don't have plans."

Roseanne pointed to the pad on the counter. The pad said, *Gloria Florimonte,* with a Manhattan phone number.

"Well? Aren't you gonna call her?"

Ballestrino thought of Bobby Setzer and Ryan Mahoney, and the invitation he could have taken—should have taken—ten years ago. At this point, he would take even a scuzzy group house in Benson-hurst over a driveway of his own, and all the lasagna he could eat—the only benefits he could see here. He closed his door, took off guns, phones, beeper, notebook, Palm Pilot, shoes, socks, shirt, undershirt and watch. He lay on the bed and picked up the phone to call Gloria.

A voice answered, a really familiar voice.

"Gloria?"

A pause. "Tony?"

A pause. "Janice?"

"Yeah. Tony?"

"That's so weird," he said. "I didn't mean to call you."

"Well, good, 'cause I don't want to talk to you."

"I must have dialed you out of habit."

"I hear she's a massage therapist," Janice taunted.

Carroll Gardens was just getting too small. Ballestrino said good-bye—delighted that there was nothing to say to her. Janice was so long ago.

He dialed Gloria's number, with full concentration now, wondering how large her apartment was. He smiled when she answered.

"Hey, Gloria, it's Tony Ballestrino. I got a message that you called."

A pause. "You did?"

"Why didn't you call me on my cell phone?" he chided her.

"Well, this is curious, because I didn't call you."

A pause. "You didn't?"

"No. Who told you that?"

He breathed in. "My mother."

"I see."

He imagined Gloria Florimonte laughing in her Manhattan apartment. He clenched his teeth. If he didn't ask her out now, it would be weird. On the other hand, if he did, it was like he was either controlled by his mother, or using her as an excuse to call. He wouldn't ask her out. He let a moment pass.

"Well, would you like to see a movie sometime?" he asked.

"I would, yes, Tony. But I'm completely swamped with work and school for the next few weeks. Could I call you when I come up for air?"

"Sure, sure."

Anthony Ballestrino hung up the phone and went into the kitchen, where his mother sat with the tabloids and her cigarettes, affecting nonchalance. The scanner was reporting an assault in progress in Cobble Hill. Roseanne continued to page through her paper, ignoring him.

"Gloria Florimonte," he said, "did not call me."

"Did I say that she had?"

He wasn't letting this one go. "Why did you give me a piece of paper with her name and her number, pretending that she'd called me?"

"Girls like that don't grow on trees." She turned down the volume on the scanner. "You can't sit around waiting for a *girl* to call *you*."

Living with this woman was like conducting an interrogation: both demanded rigid, bottomless self-control.

"Don't you give me the Look," she bullied. "That may intimidate your perps, but it doesn't work on your mother."

He slammed out of the house.

"Oh, there he goes, Al Pacino, with his head on fire!"

Pacino, Travolta, De Niro, Stallone. These were the models of Italian manhood in Hollywood. Volatility, vanity, street smarts, brute strength. Screaming and shooting and grinding the weak into the ground. Period, end of story. There was no intelligence, no ambition—no legal ambition, anyway—and no subtlety. It was all anger, paranoia and machine-gun fire, and he was beginning to see why.

He stunned his Sergeant by reporting back for duty sixty-five minutes after signing out for the day.

❖

The call came, as usual, after midnight, while Anita Clemente was trolling in the preteen chat rooms, waiting for some badguy to bite. It was Jacobs of the Special Frauds Squad, who worked down the hall. While investigating something else, he'd stumbled across a Corey Fleming, a.k.a. Clare Fleming, a.k.a. Carey Denton, a petty forger, who happened to be holding, in plain view, at the time of his arrest, items of child pornography printed off the Internet that had almost caused Jacobs to lose his dinner. He was being held at the Tombs. Would she care to speak to him?

Clemente strapped on her equipment, and got into her car.

Someone once said that you could only keep three systems in your head at once. A job was a system. A family was a system. If you were learning a language, or an instrument, that was a system. Whoever said this hadn't been a cop, a cop's wife or a cop's kid. In the cop world, there was room for just one system: the Job. She parked around the corner from the Tombs, went through security and signed in. She followed a guard through a gray maze of halls to a large fluorescent-lit room with dirty Plexiglas partitions. She sat and waited.

Clemente met plenty of men, but the Job was one continuous emergency, and she had little free time. Occasionally she would take a man up on an offer, always calculating the risks of involvement. She had only one rule: no cops.

But lawyers and architects didn't understand her, never mind hematologists and urban planners. Why she had to sit with her back to the wall, with a view of the restaurant. Why she kept returning to questions that had been diplomatically avoided. Why she had to cancel three out of four dates at the last minute. Why she couldn't make plans in advance, especially on holidays and weekends. Why she wouldn't reveal where she lived. Why every encounter had to take place in a different hotel, where they arrived and left separately, and why she wouldn't use the handcuffs, even just for fun.

A cop would understand. What he didn't understand, he would intuit.

The perp was disheveled and oily, wearing smeared glasses and a plaid cardigan with a zipper. He carried a dirty white asthma pump.

"Before you say anything, I have information on something big." He inhaled deeply on the pump.

"I'm listening," she said.

❖

Mitch went to the lesser fish store, in Baldwin. They had fine fish, good products, and nobody looked at him twice. He left feeling like anything was possible. Afterward, he drove into Manhattan, parked four blocks from his former office, stopped at Saks and bought a linen jacket and three polo shirts. Nobody he knew. Credit card accepted. No alarms triggered. He picked up a sandwich at his old take-out place without event. The chicken salad was life affirming. He drove over the Queensboro Bridge feeling serene.

At home, in the hovel, Mitch cut himself a slice of carrot cake and poured himself a cup of coffee. He was sick of house arrest: he needed to find a place where he could open up a bank account and walk around freely. He wanted to get out of this drab, depressing house. Corey the forger had come through with the Phillip Pitkin passport, and he could go to Bermuda anytime he liked. After that, he would do research to identify where he wanted to live.

He would put together the Web site, and hire someone to get it up on the Internet, if he had to. The Web site would be his job.

Final goal: he needed a woman in his life. He didn't want to have to spend a lot of time looking for someone compatible, but he did need *some* companionship. He couldn't spend all his time alone. He decided to tackle this last one first.

❖

Patricia got the call from Detective Sprague at Claire de Lune, as she opened up on a perfect beach day her last week on the job. She steeled herself for annoyance, although Tony hadn't called her in two months, and she assumed he'd gotten over her.

"Mrs. Greiff, we think we've found your husband."

Her husband? Patricia sat down. Although she'd spent almost a year waiting for Mitch, screaming obscenities at him in absentia, willing him to return if only to explain, she was somehow not prepared to hear that he'd reappeared.

"You what?"

"We need you to come and identify him."

She was speechless. The Detective told her that an off-duty NYPD cop from Nassau County was on his way to pick her up in an unmarked car. Shaking and sweating, she called Mara to tell her she had an emergency and had to leave.

Mara made a guttural sound. After months of discretion, Mara had finally let her curiosity get the better of her, and she followed Patricia around the store as if she were a hard-nosed journalist working on a hot story. How long had she been faithful to Mitch? How much had Mitch actually stolen? How much had her house originally cost? Patricia always changed the subject. One day, when the shop was empty, Mara started up: Did Nick pay for her every time they went out? Where did he take her? Was he attentive in bed?

Patricia ignored her.

Mara said, "I asked you a question."

"I think that's a very personal question."

"We're friends, aren't we?"

Patricia said nothing.

"I hear from my friend Jan, who briefly—*very* briefly—dated your friend Nick two years ago, that he's, like, really *little*." And she cackled.

This was hardly part of the job. "Mara, that is your last inappropriate question. I'm giving you two weeks' notice."

"Patricia, don't be ridiculous."

Once again she'd taken the first offer, without doing any research. Nick, too: the very first offer, because she was afraid there wouldn't be others.

PATRICIA COULDN'T HELP HERSELF: she put on makeup to go to the police station. Mara arrived at the store within minutes, and demanded to know the details of her emergency. There were two customers up front, carrying on about eye cream.

Patricia pulled Mara to the back of the store. "I'm sorry to put you out on such short notice, but I need to go into town. They found Mitch."

Mara screamed, and the customers looked over. "Where did they find him?" she stage-whispered. "Was he with a woman? What will you say to him?"

A dark sedan arrived in five minutes. A mustached cop from Central Casting barreled into Claire de Lune. The ladies gaped as Patricia followed him out of the store and into the car. Another customer walked in, and over the chimes, Patricia heard Mara shrieking, *"They caught her husband, the thief!"*

THE POLICE RADIO BLARED all the way to Queens. The pep talk she'd been giving herself these last few months about her wonderful, unexpected new life on the East End seemed ridiculous. She was not twenty-three years old. This was not a movie that would end happily. She was about to identify the man who had cast her and her children into instability and shame. Even now, she couldn't actually think or say the words *ruined my life*. But there was no reason to be optimistic.

The car pulled up to a quiet intersection on a redbrick street in Queens.

"Why are we stopping here?" she asked. Tony and his partner got out of a car across the street. She tried to open the door. It was locked.

"Stay where you are," commanded the cop in the driver's seat.

Tony opened her door, and she got out, expecting to go somewhere. But then he opened the back door of the car. She got in; he followed. His partner got into the seat she'd just vacated, next to the off-duty cop.

Tony kissed her cheek and held her hand, breathing her name.

She pulled back. He was too young, too intense, too annoying. Why hadn't she stayed in the front seat? Why had she mindlessly followed his lead? This had better not be a social call.

"What is going on?" she demanded.

"We think we've found your husband," Detective Sprague said. "We need you to make an identification, and then we'll arrest him."

"Here? You found him here?"

"We got a tip this morning that he's living in a house around the corner. We want to be careful, as he's apparently armed."

"*Mitch?* That's a laugh."

"We have reliable information that he bought a gun," Tony said, sulking.

"He couldn't hit the side of a barn with it, I promise you."

"He's twice as dangerous if he's not in control of the weapon," Detective Sprague said.

Both the Detectives' cell phones rang at once.

"He's on his way out," Sprague said. "Should we stop him, or see where he goes?"

"Let's see where he goes," Ballestrino said, looking at her.

She folded arms over her chest and crossed her legs away from him.

The man they thought was Mitch drove off slowly in a blue Toyota. Tony didn't take his eyes off her. If he was in charge of the investigation, it was no wonder they hadn't caught him in eleven months. They drove through the endless streets of Queens in a convoy: the blue Toyota, their car and another dark sedan that Tony and his partner had been sitting in when she'd arrived.

The man they thought was Mitch stopped short in front of a Starbucks, oblivious to his escort. A blue Toyota—not very Mitch, but then, what did she know? She'd only lived with him for twenty-eight years, after all. Maybe this wasn't even him, she thought, as the man hesitated for a few minutes in his car with flashers on. Was she slightly hoping this wasn't Mitch? Wouldn't it be easier if Mitch didn't show up? She wouldn't have to confront him, and go through another round of front-page scandal.

The man they were following emerged from his car, pulling on a jacket.

"Is that him?" Detective Sprague asked.

She looked hard at the receding figure. His hair was longer, and he was a good twenty-five pounds heavier than Mitch. But it could be him. "I'd need to get a better look at him," she said.

Tony nodded at her, and she got out of the car. He cupped her elbow as they crossed the street; she pulled her arm away and shot him a meaningful look.

The three of them entered the coffee bar. The man who might have been Mitch was standing on line. He wore a linen blazer the color of wheat, linen pants the color of cream and brown woven leather loafers—a costume not in Mitch's repertoire. He spoke to a woman in front of him on line, who didn't respond. As he turned slightly, Patricia saw an earring. This couldn't be her husband.

He paid out of a blue Velcro wallet that she didn't recognize. He went to the sugar and milk station and tried chatting up a woman standing there, but this woman was having none of it either. This wasn't Mitch behavior: women were always trying to chat *him* up. He walked to the front, sat down at a free table and pulled out a pad and a pen. Within a few moments, he was speaking to another woman, and he rose to join her at her table.

As he turned, she saw his full face: the equine jaw, the boxy chin, the chicken pox scar on his forehead, the sad, guarded, hooded black eyes.

It was Mitch.

Now her heart was pounding. Her husband, the mastermind fugitive embezzler, was all dressed up like the king of a coffee plantation to chat up a twenty-one-year-old with visible stomach tattoos at a coffee bar on a Tuesday morning in *Queens*?

She nodded to the two Detectives in shock. "That's him."

MITCH HAD PAUSED in front of the Starbucks, checking out the place. He'd identified it previously as a fertile cove, but who knew? He wasn't sure he wanted to stay that long, so why go through the trouble of finding a parking space? What if he wasn't up to it? So he put the flashers on and went inside quickly. If he didn't feel comfortable, no big deal, he was double-parked right out in front.

He began random talk with a fortyish woman on line in front of him: "Do you think they have half-and-half here?"

"Right there." She pointed to the milk station without looking at him.

"Thanks. I haff to haff my half-and-half," he joked.

"I'm lucky to get two percent instead of skim," she said, and walked away.

Perhaps, at fifty-nine years of age, he should just hang up this line of activity. He'd waited two weeks for his bruises to heal, and this morning he'd spent an hour and a half preparing for this, assembling the correct outfit, being careful with the razor, applying aftershave, doing his hair, which required time and skill now that it was so long. He'd practiced conversation. So much energy, anxiety, embarrassment and time: what was the point?

Perhaps a younger woman wouldn't be so tough. "Do you think they have real sugar here, or is it just saccharin and NutraSweet?" he asked the next young one who came to add to her coffee.

"It's right there," she said irritably.

Perhaps he should talk to these women *after* they'd had their coffee. Or perhaps he should try a discotheque or bar?

This idea terrified him, so he sat down at a table and began working on the introduction to his Web site. Erica had saved his life, and then ruined it. It seemed impossible that just over a year ago she'd *worked* for him. She would have done anything for him then. She'd become so impatient, scolding him whenever he told her anything. When she'd walked out the previous week, it was as if the bottom of his tank had crashed to the floor.

He burned his tongue on his coffee.

He needed to move on. A young thing with long, messy ribbons of reddish-brown hair was staring out the window, clearly under-employed, if not unemployed. He asked if he could sit with her. When she agreed, he began telling her about the tank. She made encouraging noises.

With some kind of primitive instinct and peripheral vision, he saw a traffic cop down the block, ticketing cars. He had forgotten about his double-parked car.

Mitch ran out, holding his coffee high to avoid spilling it, hopping around pedestrians. He pressed the unlock button on his key chain, and the car chirped in response. This alerted the cop, who moved with unnatural speed, arriving at the car just as Mitch was opening the door.

"Where do you think you're going?" asked the cop.

"Home," he said. He should have just let the parking ticket happen. Even if he'd been towed, it would have been easy to pick up the car. If he ran now, it would be an admission of guilt.

"Let me see your license and registration," the cop said.

"Officer, I was just getting coffee. You know how those lines are."

He was in no position to run. The sprint from the table to the car had caused a stitch in his side. If, instead of eating carrot cake and growing coral all this time, he'd been working out, he might have been in shape to run. Of course, a trainer would have been one more open palm draining his resources.

The traffic cop gave him a tough look through her mirrored glasses. "License and registration," she said firmly.

Hands and head sweating, he reached into Donald Spivak's wallet and plucked out his license. While she looked at it, Mitch got into the car and leaned over to get the registration from the glove compartment. The gun almost fell out. He had to pay attention.

———

"SUSPECT IS FLEEING THE SCENE!" Sprague shouted into his cell phone, and suddenly he was hustling out of Starbucks, onto the bright street.

"Stay here!" Ballestrino commanded, and Patricia stopped at the glass door and watched from the vestibule as her former husband, the fugitive mastermind, tried to get out of a parking ticket.

Tony's colleagues across the avenue approached the scene slowly with their guns outstretched. Tony and his partner did the same from the sidewalk. From the looks of it, all traffic had been stopped. With her entire body on alert, Patricia pushed through the glass door.

But why? Did she really want a confrontation?

She saw him look at her through the windshield. He recognized her, and rapidly turned his head away.

———

HE COULD SEE THEM COMING at him at a crouch, four cops in plainclothes, yelling at the traffic cop, who froze openmouthed with her pen poised above her ticket pad like a tableau of municipal bureaucracy. Why had he not tried to find a legal spot? There was nothing but parking in Queens! He spilled the coffee that had gotten him into this stupid mess, getting it all over his new white pants.

The guns were pointed at him. Why? He was an accountant—a *former* accountant! He felt a track of sweat running down his back. Someone who looked like Patricia was standing on the sidewalk by the plate-glass window. But what would Patricia be doing in Astoria? He couldn't look at her to verify it.

Suddenly Patricia stormed into the street and planted herself in front of his car. "Yes," she said, pointing at him, and announced loudly, as if performing in a courtroom drama, "I identify that man as my husband, Mitchell Alan Greiff."

"Mrs. Greiff," called one of the cops, "get back inside."

Everything was suddenly clarified: the street was completely still, except for Patricia, who was flapping around in a gauzy white smock. She shouted, "Get out of the car, you selfish son of a bitch!"

Were there TV cameras around?

"Get out of the car!" She continued grandstanding. He looked at his hands.

"He can't look at me, the coward!" Patricia turned around and laughed. That angry laugh had preceded every major blowout they'd had in twenty-eight goddamn years together. He hadn't missed her.

"GET. OUT. OF THE *CAR*!" She pounded on his front hood, and he jumped.

He watched her twisted face snarling at him in the blazing heat. He'd be damned if he got out of the car. They could drag his ass out of the car if it came to that. Guns or no guns. He wasn't going *anywhere*.

Suddenly the air was saturated with head-splitting sirens. Within seconds he was surrounded on all four sides by squad cars, motorcycle cops, dark vans. Traffic was stopped. It looked like a hostage situation in a TV cop drama. The noise was physically painful. The smell of spilled coffee in the car made Mitch gag. He sat with his heart beating in his mouth and his head throbbing along. He needed a bathroom badly.

All the energy drained out of him. He put his hands up. He wanted to talk to his mother.

CHAPTER FOURTEEN

Sprague looked through the one-way window. The linen-clad suspect was sweating, shaking and a hair away from bursting into tears. Perfect.

He entered the room smiling. "I'm Dennis Sprague," he said, holding his hand out. The suspect rose, hand out, hopeful.

"You like that Starbucks stuff?" Dennis said, friendly, opening the folder and sitting down. "It's like diesel fuel."

The suspect looked relieved. "You need some more half-and-half," he said.

"I like cream; my partner is strictly skim milk. You know what I tell him? I say, 'Tony? We're gonna be dead for a long time. With my luck? *Forever*. While we're alive, we might as well live.' Right?"

The suspect nodded. "Exactly."

"Meanwhile, I'm bursting out of the last pair of pants that fit. So I see you live in Jackson Heights. Where do you eat around there?"

"Oh, it's the worst. Sometimes we go to the Pastrami King."

"I love that place. You get the corned beef?"

"I only eat pastrami at the Pastrami King."

"Well, if you're ever in the mood for a change, try the corned beef, it's excellent." There was a knock on the door, and Ballestrino walked in.

Sprague said, "This is my partner, Detective Anthony Ballestrino."

Ballestrino didn't shake the man's hand. He stood behind Sprague, leaning against the windowsill, arms crossed over his chest.

"You take out, or eat there?" Sprague continued.

The suspect looked back and forth between them. "I'm not saying anything," he said.

"That's your right under the Fifth Amendment." Sprague pulled out the copy of the Constitution he kept in his breast pocket. "I take this very seriously."

Mitch Greiff sat still, watching both of them.

"You received your Miranda warnings in front of the Starbucks on Ditmars Boulevard, correct? You have the right to remain silent, as we've just established. Anything you *do* say can and will be used against you. Do you understand?"

He nodded.

"You have the right to an attorney. If you do not have an attorney, an attorney will be provided for you."

"I *am* an attorney," the suspect said.

"Really?" he said with neutral interest. "Where do you practice?"

"I only practiced briefly, in a big corporate firm. In the late sixties."

"So you understand the right to counsel."

"I do," he said, looking over at Ballestrino.

"I want to make sure that you understand all your rights. I want you to remember this," Sprague said. "You and I are going over your rights one by one."

"I'm not telling you anything in this room," the suspect said.

"Excuse me?"

"This room is *disgusting*," he said with a mild hysteria.

"I am talking to you," Sprague continued, "about your legal rights. And I am not finished yet."

"It smells like someone lost control in here."

This was the genius that had eluded him for eleven months? Sprague made a mental note to find Mitch Greiff a fragrant cellmate.

"You may not make demands on me. That is rule number one."

"I want a different room."

Sprague was still. "Demanding behavior," he said, "is not tolerated."

He saw the streak of recklessness freeze into fear. Everything depended on the rapport he established with the suspect. The right move would open up a vein of gold. The wrong move would shut everything down.

"We're here to get to the bottom of this situation," Sprague continued evenly. "This is the process: I ask the questions, you answer the questions. You do not make demands on me; I do not make demands on you."

"You're demanding that I sit in a sweltering box that smells like a toilet!"

"This is the room," Sprague said firmly. "Since it's been over thirty years since you practiced law, and you didn't practice criminal law, I want to go through your rights, one by one. When we're in court, I want you to remember that you and I went through your rights one by one."

"All right, already. You read me my rights. Now let me out of here."

"Please note that the suspect has been notified about his right to counsel, and has requested that we move on."

Ballestrino took notes.

"You have nothing to charge me with."

"Your wife, Patricia Greiff, identified you."

The suspect stared down at the tabletop in sullen disregard. "So what?"

"So you lied to me, for a start," Sprague said.

"How?"

"You were asked for identification, and you provided us with this." He held up Donald Spivak's driver's license.

"So what?"

"So anything you tell me now you must prove to me, because you've already lied to me once."

"Fine," he said. "I'm Mitch Greiff."

"You admit that your name is Mitch Greiff," Sprague said. "Were you a partner at Friedman, Greiff and Slavin, the accounting firm?"

"Yes."

"Good. I will not lie to you. Do not lie to me. Shall we shake on it?"

"Fine." Greiff took his hand in a damp grasp.

Sprague held up the driver's license. "Where did you get this?"

"At the DMV."

"This is your address?"

"Yes."

"How long have you lived there?"

"Since last September."

"Do you own this apartment or rent it? Apartment or house?"

"It's a rented house. It's unbelievably small. And dark."

"You rented it under the name of Donald Spivak."

"That's right."

"How did you find the house?"

"I didn't. A friend did."

"And who would that friend be?"

"I have the right not to tell you. You yourself told me that."

"That's correct, sir. You'll appreciate, however, being an attorney, that it's in your best interests to cooperate with me now. An enormous amount of money is missing, and you are the prime suspect."

"You have nothing to connect me with that."

"With what?"

"Missing money."

"How do you know that?"

"Because I had nothing to do with that," Greiff said self-righteously.

Ballestrino leaned over Greiff's shoulder. "You come in here with information and a pretty face, you're only leaving with one of them."

Sprague changed the subject while the suspect pretended not to be having trouble swallowing. "Where did you get this name? You make it up?"

"I don't want to talk about that."

Sprague went through the wallet. "You had to produce several other forms of ID to get this. Here you have a credit card, okay," he said, handing it to Ballestrino. "You have a Social Security number in this name?"

"Look, I'll tell you anything you want. But I need to get out of this room."

"Why?"

Greiff rose suddenly, his chair falling behind him; Ballestrino had his gun on the man's neck before the chair came to a rest on the floor. "You looking for a bedside arraignment, Mr. Greiff?"

"No." The former accountant was breathing hard; he looked like he might faint.

"No?" Ballestrino deposited the suspect back into his chair. The suspect looked down, terrified.

"Look. We always start nicely," Sprague said with a smile, as Mitch Greiff attempted to catch his breath. "We can get nasty. We can get *vile*, if you like. So I'm asking nicely. Who rented the apartment?"

The suspect closed his eyes, looking tired. "It wasn't my idea."

"No? Whose idea was it?"

Greiff looked sick. "You can't hold me here for no reason."

"No? How about false ID?" Sprague let a moment of silence sink in. "The penalty for violating the False Identification Control Act alone can be five years."

Sprague wouldn't mention possession of an unregistered and un-licensed firearm, or hiring a team of thugs to beat up an alleged extortionist—not until they'd had time to check out the forger's story.

"Talk, Mr. Greiff."

The suspect was doubled over, rocking slightly.

Once in a while, Sprague got it right. This feeling was the best part of the Job, and it was coming right up. He could feel it. Any minute now.

"She planned everything. She did everything."

"She who?"

Greiff took a swallow and croaked, "Erica."

He didn't look at Tony; Tony didn't look at him. But the acknowledgment was there. "Would that be Ms. Erica King, of Friedman, Greiff and Slavin?"

He nodded, close to tears. Yes, sir, thought Sprague: the very best part of the Job.

"She set up bank accounts. She got me that credit card."

"Why?"

"I've been asking myself all this time. I honestly don't know."

Greiff looked like he was ready to talk. "Where is she now?"

"She's . . . gone." The former pillar of the community burst into wet, messy, racking sobs.

Sprague gestured to Ballestrino, who went out and came back with a box of tissues. Mitch Greiff pressed a tissue to his face. The weeping continued. It seemed sincere. Of course, he could be crying and lying to save his designer-clad hide. He blew his nose five or six times.

When the gasping and sniveling had subsided, Sprague asked, "Am I correct to assume this was a romantic attachment?" Greiff nodded. "For how long?"

"It started"—he wiped his eyes—"in March of last year."

"She'd been working for you for a long time."

"I know! Almost ten years."

"And all that time—"

"Nothing! And then suddenly, in March, I don't know, something changed." His face broke into a weak smile.

Sprague nodded, and waited with an open face.

"She's amazing. She's completely underestimated."

Not for the first time, he was in awe of the information he was privy to as a Detective.

"I know what you're thinking. No doubt you've seen my wife."

Ballestrino's leg began bouncing.

"My wife and I hadn't been getting along for a while."

"Were you thinking about divorce?"

"Yes and no." He sighed. "I think we both thought that it might get better. But it got worse."

"But you didn't seek divorce."

"The apartment was big enough for us to live separate lives. When I started seeing Erica, I just stayed at one of her places."

"Places?"

"She had three apartments. Then she gave one up, so she had two."

Sprague kept his face neutral. "Why?"

"I don't know."

"Where were they?"

"I'll write it down," he said, and Ballestrino passed him his notebook.

"So you started seeing her in March," Sprague said. "Anyone notice?"

"We played it cool at the office. No one would have believed it anyway."

"And you say she got you that Visa card. When was that?"

"Last May? April? It was before we went to California, I know that."

"What happened in California? Where'd you go?"

"LA, Santa Monica. We used the credit card."

"So you traveled under a false name."

"Yes. So did she. She had other names."

"What other names?" Sprague asked.

"I'll write them down," he said, and the notebook went back and forth again. He drew arrows connecting names with addresses.

Tony looked at the pad. "Slotweiner's one of your clients, isn't she?"

"Yes."

"But Slotweiner wasn't one of the ones you hit," Sprague remembered.

"I didn't *hit* anybody."

"Says you!" Ballestrino smiled. "Where'd she get the name Collecelli?"

"I don't know," Greiff said, looking more like a clueless, aging pretty boy every minute. Either he was a fool or he was faking it brilliantly.

"You think she might be at any of these places?"

Greiff closed his eyes. "She wouldn't tell me where she was going."

"You know we're going to check these places out," Ballestrino warned. "If we find out that you've lied again, there'll be hell to pay."

"Why would I lie?"

"That's what I'm wondering." Ballestrino leaned in on him. "Why would you walk around with phony ID? You tell me."

He stared at the table, looking like he might burst into fresh tears.

"Who would she go to at a time like this?" Sprague asked.

"She doesn't have any family that I know of."

"Friends?"

Here a slight shake of the head. "Just me."

"What about before you? Friends, boyfriends?"

"I'm sure there were, but I have no names."

"When did you last see her?"

"Friday night. At the house." He gestured to the driver's license.

"Where's the money?"

"There's some cash at home. The rest is in banks. When she left, she consolidated my half into one bank. She made me change the passwords. I don't know what she did with the rest of it."

"Which bank?"

"It's in Bermuda. I don't remember the name, but I can get it."

"You don't know the name of your bank," Ballestrino said, deadpan.

"I have it. But I don't know it off the top of my head."

"So before Friday, you both had access to these accounts."

"Well, officially, but I didn't really know the passwords."

"Why didn't you, really?"

"Well, I didn't need to know them. We decided it would be easier for her to be the conduit. Then I could lie low, not risk being recognized."

Ballestrino leaned forward, alert. "You expect us to believe that you let her establish accounts for you that you had no access to?"

"She's very honest."

Sprague laughed. "Especially when she's stealing."

Greiff was silent.

"She stole the money and you took the rap," Tony said. "That's what you're telling us?"

"I guess so." He looked miserable.

Sprague cut in: "Did Erica learn how to drive?"

"She was trying. She was terrible. I took her out a few times."

"Did she get a license?"

"I don't know. I hadn't been paying attention for a while."

Ballestrino hissed impatiently.

"What? She might have; I don't know. Sometimes she went out driving."

"Without a license," Sprague said, "in a car that could be traced to Donald Spivak."

"Yes."

"Yet you say she was cautious."

"Very."

"So it was highly uncharacteristic of her to take that kind of chance."

He shrugged. "She was determined to drive. She loved that Toyota."

"What I want you to do now is write down everything you did, everything she did: the entire story." Sprague gave him a blank legal pad. "When we come back, I want to read the whole thing. All the details. Leave nothing out."

They rose to go. "We're going out now to check up on what you've told us."

"Are you going to my place?" he asked, and Sprague nodded. "Could you help me out? I didn't feed my fish today."

Ballestrino smiled and sat down in front of him. "Really?"

"I thought I'd go straight home after I went for coffee. But then all this happened. Would you feed them? I can tell you what they need."

"So you're giving us permission to go into your house," Tony said slowly.

"Obviously."

"Okay, what I'd like you to do is to write that down, and sign it."

"That I give you permission to enter and feed my fish? Sure. Could *I* get something to eat?"

"You realize that anything we find in open view we can use as evidence."

"Well, you'd get a search warrant anyway, right? So go ahead."

The two cops avoided eye contact, both looking at the suspect intently as he composed a sentence on the legal pad. "All I had was coffee this morning," he said, as he signed it. "I really need to eat something."

"You don't want to eat here," Sprague warned.

"Can we have something delivered? I'm going to pass out."

Sprague smiled, opened the door and leaned out. "Could we get this guy something to eat?" he asked the officer outside. "Thanks a lot."

Mitch Greiff dropped a key chain on the table in front of him. "This is the top. That one's the bottom. The crab likes fresh fish but today just give him the pellets. You mustn't give them too much. They're really small. If they eat too much, they'll die. So just a pinch. And if you wouldn't mind checking the pH balance. I'll write down what you should do."

He handed the instructions and the keys to Sprague.

"Where are the computers that were used to make the wire transfers?" Ballestrino asked.

"She destroyed them."

"How?"

"She bashed them with a hammer, and cut things up with scissors."

This information sliced through Sprague's heart. "Where are the remains?"

"She threw them out."

"When?"

"Oh, I don't know. A long time ago."

"Any computers left?"

"I have a computer at the house, and she has a laptop."

"What kind, where'd she get it?"

"I don't know. She took it with her."

"Did she have a favorite brand?" Ballestrino asked. "Did she have a favorite store?"

"No, she could use anything. She bought sometimes through catalogs, sometimes on-line."

"Name of catalogs. Name of Web sites."

"I don't know."

"How did she transfer your funds to Bermuda?"

"I don't know."

They called the guard, who came to unlock the room.

The precinct Captain was waiting in the observation room. Sprague asked him, "Got any toughs who could sit with him for a while, make him sweat?"

The Captain nodded. "You want a nasty cop, or a scary street kid?"

Sprague thought about it. "Scary street kid."

"Hey, Bobby," the Captain spoke into his radio. "Make Tiny come up here."

"Why is he not lawyering up?" Sprague wondered aloud.

"He stole from his lawyer," Ballestrino recalled. "About 700 large."

"He knows another lawyer, surely."

"Looks like he wants to talk," the Captain said astutely. "Looks like he wants to cry."

"Dennis, I owe you dinner. He picked the drip for the girlfriend," Ballestrino explained to the precinct Captain. "I said no fucking way."

"Well, you were right about the fish," Sprague said. "So I owe you dinner too. I'll run her new names through the DMV, and send his IDs to the lab."

"I'll put a want card out on her," Ballestrino said, "and subpoena travel records and credit cards, in all three of her names, and in his new name."

A cop tapped Sprague's shoulder and handed him the perp's jailhouse sandwich. Sprague went back into the room and handed it to Mitch Greiff.

His face fell. "This is disgusting," he said.

"Don't tell me I didn't warn you," Sprague said.

❖

When they reached the squat brick precinct house in Astoria, Patricia was passed on to a young policewoman who took her through a sweltering reception room and up some humid stairs. She had already identified Mitch; what else was there to do? Tony had said something about paperwork, but she had the feeling he just wanted to interrogate her and touch her surreptitiously. Surrounded by municipal busyness and ringing phones, she was angry, impatient and hot. All she could think about was the enormous iced coffee she'd left on the table when she ran out of Starbucks after her husband, the celebrity accountant mastermind, who was nabbed by a traffic cop while double-parking. In Queens.

She didn't know whether she felt relief or contempt now. She'd been so angry for so long. She'd screamed herself hoarse on the street, and Mitch had just stared at her. After a flash of shock, his face soured into a look of complete disgust that she could feel through the windshield.

They'd frisked and handcuffed him, shouted his rights at him. She'd been pacing the sidewalk, unable to take her eyes off this impossible, spiteful, selfish *thing*, her former husband. Current husband, she remembered.

She felt like throwing up. She tried to breathe her way through it, under the sweltering sun on Ditmars Boulevard. She was frustrated. He hadn't explained, hadn't apologized. He hadn't spoken to her at all. She hadn't really had her say. But what kind of dialogue was possible in such a situation?

They took him away in one of the squad cars.

An hour later the cop steered her through a maze of desks and halls, and opened a door into a dark room with a window onto an enclosed, tiled room. Patricia took a breath and looked through the glass.

There he was again. He looked stricken, bloated and dirty. He'd gained a lot of weight, all in the gut. She couldn't get over the idea that he'd pierced his ear, bought a gun, been hiding out in Queens. Across from Mitch was a hulking Latin tough with tattoos on his arms, neck and face. How was she connected to this total stranger, her husband of twenty-eight years?

The young policewoman typed up her statement and asked her to sign it.

Patricia went out into the hall. Tony appeared with a white paper cone of water. She drank it without looking at him, and he refilled it again. Before he could get personal, she asked if she could have a lift to the train station. He insisted she have a police escort home. He was a decent man, she thought.

He squeezed her upper arm, grazing her breast. She pulled away.

Too young, too needy, too touchy, too obsessive.

A flash of anger passed across his face. "Take care of yourself, Patricia."

He walked away. The policewoman led her to a different patrol car. There was heavy traffic, no air-conditioning and the sweating cop had the police radio on the highest volume. She should have taken the train. Too bossy, too controlling. She sat plastered to the sun-baked black vinyl seat, feeling punished.

The look of hatred Mitch had tossed at Patricia had shaken her. She had thought she'd been beyond shock for some time. Why hadn't they been happily married? What had turned awful, and when? Could it have been avoided? Was it her fault? Why had he done this?

SHE CALLED BRIAN when she got home.

"He was wearing an earring," she told him, feeling hot and outraged.

"Left or right ear?" Brian asked matter-of-factly.

"Does it matter?"

"Of course it matters."

Her tiny, dingy cottage in the Springs seemed like a narrow ledge on the far side of the world, hardly a home at all. She hadn't thought about Nick all day. She wondered what to do next. She was lacking a script. The drama was over. He was back and he was guilty. Now what?

She made herself a drink and put Carole King on the eight-track tape player she'd found in her pantry, remembering her husband's various snobberies, technology among them. She sat in an aluminum beach chair outside her back door and watched a large brown rabbit twitching on the edge between the lawn and the hedge. She thought about getting into bed with a bottle of gin for three days.

Or maybe she'd just go to work the following morning, and carry on as if nothing had happened. Meet Nick for dinner after work, go windsurfing on her day off. See her children from time to time, and try not to know too much about them. Claire de Lune wasn't the only place to work. Just the other day she'd heard that the Surf Club needed a new activities director. She could do that. Nick wasn't the only man in town, and she wasn't married to him. She could see other people. Life didn't end, after all.

❖

Ballestrino let out a growl: there was a fish tank the size of a Volkswagen in the living room. "I'm gonna *nail* the aquarium bastard who sold to him. Do you know how much time I wasted chatting up those guys? Every fucking week!"

Other than the tank, the place was average. Living room, dining room, kitchen downstairs, two tiny bedrooms upstairs. Dirty white carpet, books, TV, a stained couch and a broken recliner—hardly the chic, upholstered compound one retired to for the purpose of enjoying other people's riches.

On the other hand, he wondered how much rent Greiff paid.

Patricia had looked gorgeous. She'd been dismissive and vague when he asked about her life. What bothered him was not that she'd moved on, but that he hadn't. It had been a *long*, hot summer. He resented just about everyone.

Sprague whistled, and Ballestrino followed the noise into the kitchen, where a tsunami of cash had cascaded over every surface.

They examined the money—$50 and $100 bills—which looked real enough. Sprague looked around the room, doing a rough calculation. "Okay, fine, but this can't be half the missing millions."

Sprague pointed to a smear on a Duane Reade bag sitting on a chair in front of the kitchen table. There was another splotch on the table.

"Blood," Ballestrino agreed. "Think he offed her?"

Sprague thought a moment. "I doubt it, but he's here and she's not."

Upstairs was a bedroom, and an office with a computer.

"Computer on?" Sprague asked. This was a dangerous situation. Computers could be programmed to self-destruct at the touch of a key.

Ballestrino checked. "No," he called. He poked his head into the closet. Custom-made men's suits of gorgeous cloth took his breath away. Must have cost $1,500 each. There were at least twelve of them.

"I may cry from this closet."

Sprague was looking out the window. "I don't think this was his idea," he said. "*She* probably thought this was the last place we'd look."

"Well, she got that one right," Tony said.

THEY FED THE FISH, then drove back into Manhattan to check out the addresses that Mitch Greiff had given them. Afterward, they drove by Erica King's apartment and chatted up a doorman whom they'd chatted up before. Ms. King left before the weekend, he told them, with a bunch of small bags, in a cab.

They arrived at the Frauds Department of the DA's office in time to wait in the hallway for a meeting to break up. When staff began leaving, Len Miles waved them in. Liz Isaacson stayed seated, looking fetching and not particularly Jewish. Ballestrino felt sweaty, hot and disheveled.

They described the scene in the kitchen.

"He gave you permission, and his keys?" Miles asked incredulously.

Sprague presented Mitch Greiff's written permission, and Tony dangled the keys. Miles examined it through tiny gold reading glasses perched on the end of his nose. He folded his glasses slowly and handed back the piece of yellow paper.

"Greiff says he knows nothing about the money," Sprague said. "I'm inclined to believe him. To make this case, we need the wire transfers. She destroyed her laptops. But she may have made transfers from his computer."

"I'm afraid even the cash, and a written confession, assuming you're going to get one, isn't enough for a search warrant for the computer," Miles said.

"There's over a million dollars in that kitchen!" Ballestrino said.

Len Miles turned to him. "And?"

"Well, if *you're* not interested in it, the IRS surely will be," he shot back.

"There's a possibility that she's injured or dead," Sprague said. "We saw what looked like blood on a bag of money and the kitchen table."

"We also have some uncorroborated news about Greiff from an inmate in the Tombs," Sprague said, and explained how Corey Fleming had spilled his guts about the passport, the thugs for hire and the gun he'd provided to Mitch Greiff.

Liz Isaacson said, "Did you see a gun in plain view in the house?"

"No, just the fish and the cash."

"Talk to the guy he had beaten up; maybe he'll file charges," she suggested.

"What about warrants for Ms. King's apartments?" Ballestrino asked.

"You have nothing on her except the unsupported statements of a co-conspirator," Isaacson said.

"But we went there," he insisted. "The names and addresses check out."

"So what?" Miles said. "If he gave you *my* name and address, it would check out. If Greiff swears on his oath, maybe. Find a link between Ms. King and the laptops, or the phony voice mail, or the bank accounts."

Ballestrino felt stupid. "Nice guy," he said, as they took the elevator down.

"He's right," Sprague said. "We got nothing on her."

They stopped for refreshment in front of the courthouse.

"Still"—Ballestrino took a bite of chili dog, careful of his shirt and tie—"he doesn't have to be so nasty about it." He got ketchup on his pants.

"Street food!" Sprague said enthusiastically. "Makes me feel young again!"

BELLS RANG AS THEY ENTERED TROPICALIA, and Ballestrino saw the morbidly obese, red-bearded Caucasian male proprietor grabbing an aluminum baseball bat behind the counter. When he saw them, he relaxed, but only for a moment.

"Mr. Dzergazi, hello," Ballestrino said, noting the evidence of damage on his face. "Do you remember me?"

"Sure, sure."

"I was in here a few times, and we've been speaking once a week for the last eleven months, remember? I asked you to let me know when you heard from Mitch Greiff, marine aquarist at large. We spoke yesterday, remember?"

"Right." His bruises had yellowed, indicating a beating about a week earlier, which corroborated what the forger had told Sprague. "Haven't heard from him."

"That's not what I heard," Ballestrino said, hands on the counter, which was unpleasantly wet. "What I heard, you *did* hear from him, and you mentioned that he might want to offer you some compensation for not calling me, and then he sent some gentlemen to beat the living daylights out of you."

Dzergazi tried to smile. "I don't know where you got that information."

"You know, hiring somebody to beat up another individual is as much a crime as beating someone up yourself," Sprague offered.

"Oh, really." Dzergazi got busy unpacking a box.

"Can you identify who did this to you?"

"No, thanks." He slapped stickers on plastic bottles with a price gun.

"Why not?"

"Those guys were *deranged*," he said with feeling. "They got cousins and friends and brothers-in-arms who'd drive straight here and finish me off."

"We can protect you."

"Right," wheezed the fat man, continuing to hit the bottles with the gun.

BY THE TIME THEY GOT BACK to the Four-Six Precinct in Astoria, it was after four, and Ballestrino was roiling from the chili dog and seething with anger. The rich stealing from the richer. The accountant not keeping track of the money he stole. The gorgeous suits going to waste in a closet in Jackson Heights. The ketchup on his pants. The beautiful wife taking care of the fish while the husband porked the ugly accountant. The beautiful wife pushing him away for no good reason. The aquarium guy swearing up and down, "No, haven't seen him, Officer." The ugly accountant with three apartments in Manhattan.

Some people didn't even have *one* apartment in Manhattan. Some people didn't even have one apartment in *Brooklyn*. The whole thing pissed him off.

Upstairs, Mitch was sitting and staring at the door in the same room, with the same empty yellow pad in front of him. Why had Patricia married this clown?

"We saw the tank, Mitch," Ballestrino said with enthusiasm. "Nice coral!"

Mitch smiled.

"But you could have had ten tanks without *stealing*. Am I right?"

Greiff held his hands open.

"Where'd you get the fish, Mitch?"

For the first time Greiff looked like he was lying, or about to lie. They stared at him.

"Where's the rest of the money, Mitch?"

Ballestrino popped a mint into his mouth and offered one to Sprague. Mitch watched the exchange. "Could I have one?"

"Sure, here you go," Ballestrino said, and dropped the mint on the floor. "Oh, sorry. That was my last one."

The fugitive deflated.

A clerical worker gave Sprague some faxes from the DMV, with pictures of Marjorie Slotweiner and Maria Collecelli, which he showed to Greiff.

"This the way she looked as Marjorie and Maria?"

Greiff nodded.

"There was blood on the counters, Mitch," Ballestrino said. "Whose blood?"

"Erica's," he said. "She cut her hand."

"Must have cut it badly."

He shrugged. "She went to the hospital."

They exchanged a look; Ballestrino left the room and went to the map on the wall of the squad room. The closest emergency room to the house was at Elmhurst Hospital. He called. Yes, they'd treated an Erica King on Friday evening for a cut to the hand. He returned to the custodial interview.

"So tell us about the $50 million you have in Bermuda," Sprague was saying. "That's a handy chunk of change."

"I didn't do anything."

"So let me get this straight," Sprague proposed. "She stole the money, and you disappeared? What was the thinking behind that?"

"I was ready to make a change in my life, and she had this idea."

"You weren't worried that she was setting you up?"

"I was more worried that she wouldn't go and get the money. She was so cautious. She's not into clothes or good food. She doesn't need very much."

"And yet you say she paid rent on three apartments," Ballestrino said.

"Yes, but look what they were," the fugitive said. "Tiny, crappy, rent-controlled places in marginal neighborhoods."

An old grudge beckoned Ballestrino.

"And she was carrying those apartments back when all she had was her salary," the fugitive added, warming up now, chatting. "Believe me, if she spends $100 a week on food, I'd be shocked."

"Where do you suppose she's not eating and not spending now?" Tony asked.

"She hadn't really traveled anywhere before we started seeing each other."

"Where did you two go together?"

"Los Angeles. The Cayman Islands."

Ballestrino asked, "Did you open up bank accounts while you were there?"

Mitch shook his head. "She did. I didn't really pay attention."

"Which banks did she open up accounts in?"

"Oh, I don't know."

"You don't know." Was it possible for someone to be this oblivious?

"Are you willing to swear on your oath that you and Ms. Erica King conspired together to make illegal wire transfers from your clients' accounts, and that she used computers in these three separate apartments to do this?"

"Actually, I think she went someplace else with the laptops, but sure."

"That's not good enough," Sprague insisted. "We need to get into those apartments to prove your story."

"Did she ever use the computers in any of the apartments to move the money around?" Ballestrino asked.

"She was always on one of the computers."

"Did she have a separate laptop in each place?"

"I don't know."

"Who is Phillip Pitkin?" Sprague asked.

The suspect brought his head to his hand.

"Mr. Greiff? Phillip Pitkin?"

"I want a lawyer," he said. "Now."

"All right, that's enough for now," Sprague said.

The guard arrived to take the suspect to a cell in the Tombs.

"Whoa." The suspect became visibly agitated. "You haven't charged me with anything: you can't keep me here. You didn't let me speak to my lawyer."

Ballestrino picked up his yellow pad, and held out his hand. "Pen, please."

"Let me have it," Mitch Greiff begged.

"Give me back my pen, you thief."

"I need it! I have nothing!"

"Get used to it," Ballestrino said pleasantly.

CHAPTER FIFTEEN

Mrs. Marjorie Slotweiner, a dolled-up widow in her early seventies, greeted Sprague and Ballestrino in her black-lacquered living room on Fifth Avenue, and offered them a glass of sherry and tiny bowls of spicy nuts. An elderly butler in a white dinner jacket poured drinks and stood at attention by the door.

Mrs. Slotweiner seemed thrilled that someone had stolen her identity. She hadn't noticed bills for a new Visa card starting three years ago. She didn't pay her bills. She didn't even open them: the bills had always gone directly to Friedman, Greiff and Slavin. She hadn't switched firms after the scandal because Friedman and Slavin themselves assured her that she hadn't been affected.

"Morris had great faith in them," she said, "and he knew what he was doing. I certainly don't, so why would I change firms? More sherry?"

Another person rich enough not to care.

When Dennis got home, Cathy was talking to him about dressing nicely the next day. He kissed her, and opened up his file of the subpoenaed bills. He communed with the credit card statements for Maria Collecelli, Marjorie Slotweiner and Erica King for the last two years. This was some strange woman, he thought, noting all the one-day shopping sprees in Boston and Philadelphia, and all the furniture from the Living Cove catalog or Web site. In two years as three separate women, she hadn't bought a single thing in a New York store. Marjorie Slotweiner's bills confirmed Greiff's story about trips to LA and the Caymans. He supposed that Ms. King could have continued indefinitely with a victim as cooperative as Park Avenue Marjorie.

THE PHONE RANG at two in the morning. Cathy jumped out of bed, cursing.

"I figured out how we can get into his computer without a subpoena," Tony said. Sprague listened, hung up and went back to sleep smiling.

They were on to her now.

THEY HAD MITCH GREIFF CALLED UP from his cell in the Tombs the following morning. He looked awful, and sat down delicately.

"What's going to happen to me?" he said, near tears.

"We're here to figure that out," Sprague said. "Look what we brought you." He took out the Entenmann's box. "Let's talk about your computer."

"What about it?" Mitch Greiff scarfed down a doughnut.

"Corey the forger told us he provided you with a variety of services. He was caught with some child porn that defies description. You into that?"

"Of course not!"

"So you say," Ballestrino said, leaning over him.

"Oh, please, don't be ridiculous. That's disgusting. You went to my house. Did you see anything like that?"

"Well, he was caught with stuff on his computer. We didn't look in yours."

"There is no pornography of any kind on my computer, I promise you. Search my computer! Go ahead: search it!"

"Okay," Sprague said, smiling.

They divided and conquered: Ballestrino went to pick up the computer, and Sprague returned to the office to call the Social Security

Administration. Although it was probably pointless, he tried to find out anything at all about Donald Spivak, including whether his Social Security number was correct.

He was told that such information was not available.

"Isn't it interesting," Sprague wondered aloud, "how the CIA doesn't have secrets anymore, but the Social Security Administration does?"

"I wish I could help you," said the Social Security investigator, with a lassitude that was almost sarcastic.

"Don't hang up! Could you just tell me if there's an investigation on his number? Could you just do that for me?"

"Yes," said the bureaucrat. "I can tell you that there is no investigation under way on that number. Should there be?"

"I wish I could help you," Sprague said, and hung up.

Sprague went to the main branch of the public library, and looked up Donald Spivak in the *New York Times* database. The name popped up in an obituary for a Muriel Spivak, survived by son, Donald. Donations instead of flowers to the Autism Society. Sprague hurried back to the Building, composed a request for information about Donald Spivak and faxed it to the NYC Social Services Department.

Ballestrino was back at his desk exploring a copy of Mitch Greiff's hard drive. "He's right," he called. "There's no pornography on this computer."

"Fuck pornography: what about wire transfers?"

"Not as far as I can tell. There are no bank sites bookmarked, and he hasn't checked out his money in Bermuda yet, at least not on this computer."

"What has he checked out?"

"Fish Web sites and the Living Cove."

"That would be Erica." Sprague nodded. "She likes their stylish interiors."

THEY SPENT THE AFTERNOON looking through the subpoenaed records. The subpoenas to the Airline Reporting Corp. for all travel records in the last two weeks under all of Erica's names had come up empty. But when Sprague sifted through the cell phone records, he noticed that as recently as four days ago, a call had been placed on Maria's phone from the Hartford, Connecticut, area, to Continental Airlines reservations. He called Continental: a Maria Collecelli was booked on a flight to Chicago, leaving from Newark at six twenty-five. It was now four forty-one.

Sprague clapped his hands to get his partner's attention. "She's flying out of Newark!"

"I'll get the car." Tony hustled into his jacket.

Sprague called the Detective office of the Port Authority Police at Newark. He asked the Detective on duty to watch for a female Caucasian, thirty-six, five-foot-eight, with either medium-length, medium-brown hair, thick eyebrows and oval tortoiseshell glasses; medium-length dark red hair with aviator glasses; or short blond hair, thin eyebrows, no glasses. Wanted for questioning only.

"How tight a surveillance?" asked the detective on duty.

"A team at curbside, to catch who drops her off, a team at check-in and a team at the gate. Thank you, Detective."

"Call me Howard. We can get you a room for questioning."

"Terrific. What's your fax number? I'll send you photos now."

It was Friday evening. It was late August. They put the siren on and fought inch by inch through the mobs of angry people in cars trying to start their weekend. Howard called to say that almost every Caucasian woman at Newark fit her descriptions. They drove up the Departures ramp at five fifty-nine, and hustled directly to the gate, where an unsympathetic airline employee was announcing further delays to a sweating mass of previously annoyed passengers.

They waited. They sifted through the crowd with their eyes. Sprague had a bad feeling. Nothing continued to happen. The plane took off without her, an hour late. Six Port Authority officers were still in place. Howard called. Did Sprague want to set up surveillance at the other airlines? At LaGuardia or JFK?

The adrenaline had sizzled out, and they were left standing in the evening sun, strangely unable to shift gears.

"Okay, let's get dinner," Sprague said, finally, extending the invitation to the six Port Authority officers and Howard. Four took him up on the offer; of these, two had been in the Navy, one in the Marines. Plenty to talk about.

CATHY WAS HOPPING MAD when he got home at eleven-fifteen, slightly soggy from the airport beer. He went to the couch and automatically shooed away the current cat, and noticed that there was no cat.

Cathy paced in front of him. She'd gone through the interview at the agency alone, she told him. The woman in control of the limited supply of babies was disappointed and unimpressed that her husband couldn't be there. In the waiting room, she saw a classmate from high school, who was there with her husband, a pharmacist, who had managed to take an hour off from *his* work. No doubt *they* would get the next available child. She paused at the window and turned to face him.

"The waiting list is *long*, Dennis. It could take *years*."

He wanted to be sorry, but he felt strangely guilt-free. "This is what I do, Cathy. Emergencies are part of the job. You knew that when you signed up."

She made a noise, shooed him off the couch and turned the VCR back on. She was watching *Mary Poppins*.

In the bedroom he saw the one nice black suit she kept free of pet hair on the floor. She'd wanted to make an impression at the agency. But the classmate from high school with the present husband would get the child instead.

He was in the midst of composing a partial apology to her when something occurred to him; he went directly to his briefcase in the office to find notes from the crumb cake session. Name of retarded boyfriend from high school? David Findlay.

He hadn't heard back from Social Services about Donald Spivak, nor, come to think of it, on his first routine request about David Findlay, from a month ago. Goddamn civil servants. On City of New York letterhead, he printed out another terse query reiterating his need for information on both Donald Spivak and David Findlay, and faxed it, no doubt into the void.

By the time he arrived in the bedroom, she was asleep, or pretending to be. Which was fine, really, because he was too exhausted for anything else.

THE FOLLOWING MORNING she was gone when he woke up. He made himself coffee and took a bowl of cereal to the table. There was a strange stillness to the apartment. The cat and dog cages were empty and cleaned. The birdcages had been removed completely. There were no animals in the house.

He closed his pants with a safety pin and drove to the gym. He found her there, pounding on the treadmill. She stared straight ahead at the TV.

He stood for a while, waiting for her to look at him, watching her for signs of anger. "Are you not talking to me?" he asked finally, as she turned off the machine and dismounted.

"I don't know what I am," she said puffing. She drank some water, and he saw, as if a shade had been lifted, that she was a good four sizes smaller than she used to be.

"Do your own thing and leave me alone," she said bitterly. "Which you would do anyway. I'll call you when I'm ready to talk to you."

And she disappeared into the ladies' locker room, leaving him feeling truly frightened for the first time in years. Anything could happen.

❖

Sprague signed in at eight the next morning and was shocked to find a fax on his desk with current addresses for Donald Spivak and David Findlay. He went directly to Independence House, a newly renovated facility in a tenement on Tompkins Square Park. An attentive Hispanic female social worker led him to a reception area painted a sassy, bubblegum pink. It was really too early for this color.

Five minutes later, she came back holding David Findlay's hand. Erica's high school boyfriend was forty years old, unshaven, unkempt and uncoordinated. He had a closed, absorbed look to his face. Sprague didn't try to shake his hand. Although David Findlay was facing away from him, he held up his badge, and said slowly, "I'm Detective Dennis Sprague." No response.

"I'm looking for a woman you may know. Her name is Erica King."

"Bad Erica," David Findlay muttered.

"Why is Erica bad?"

David Findlay slammed out of the room.

The social worker sprang after him through a swinging door.

Sprague waited for a moment, listening. There was a high-pitched shriek. He darted through the door, remembering not to pull his gun. The social worker was struggling with David on the pink linoleum floor. Sprague tried to separate them. David kicked himself free and landed near the wall.

Just avoid the lawsuit, Sprague told himself, and turned to the social worker, who was sprawled on the floor, holding her side.

David began to rock by himself in a ball facing the corner.

"Are you all right?" Sprague asked.

Breathlessly she said, "Let's just all sit down now, okay, Davey?"

The social worker pulled herself up into a cross-legged position, and Sprague did the same. Everyone caught his or her breath on the pink floor.

"Everything is calm now," she said, and Sprague found himself nodding his head in time with David's rocking.

It was a good long time before anyone spoke.

She cooed, "Much better, Davey," and nodded to Sprague.

"Much better, Davey," Sprague cooed.

"Asking questions, Davey," she said.

"Asking questions, Davey," Davey repeated, still facing the wall.

"Davey, when you saw Erica," Sprague said, "where did you go?"

"Nothing."

"Did Erica take you somewhere?"

"Nothing!"

The social worker said, "Erica came to visit a few times, isn't that right? She took you out for lunch, didn't she?"

Davey suddenly exploded in speech: "Wait on line! Wait on line! Bad Erica!" He put his head back on his knees and rocked.

"Davey, did Erica take you to the Social Security office?"

"Social Secuuurity, Social Secuuuurity, Social Secuuuurity . . ."

This could go on for quite some time, Sprague decided. He rose, thanked Davey and shook the hand of the patient young social worker. He drove quickly through the stricken, Saturday streets of late August.

BALLESTRINO HAILED HIM with enthusiasm. His queries to Customs had yielded tropical fruit: Maria Collecelli had been to Costa Rica and St. Kitts once, and the Cayman Islands twice. Marjorie Slotweiner had been to St. Kitts and Bermuda twice.

"There must be hundreds of programs for retarded adults. How would she choose," Sprague asked rhetorically.

"She wouldn't start with a list from Catholic Charities, right?" Ballestrino said. "She'd find a convenient place."

"But not her own neighborhood, she's known there."

"Apparently not," Ballestrino said. "She was strolling in and out of three separate apartment buildings in a variety of wigs and nobody noticed."

"It's Saturday. Let's focus on programs that have housing," Sprague said. "Somebody'll be there to answer the phone. I'll take Manhattan."

Ballestrino sighed. "Why do I always get the outer boroughs?"

They began calling assisted-living programs to ask about volunteers or visitors named Erica King, Marjorie Slotweiner or Maria Collecelli. There was no guarantee that these institutions kept track. But you had to start somewhere. Sprague spoke to people of varying reliability, and to machines. After an hour he received a call back from the Rainbow, an assisted-living facility in the East Village. They'd had a Marjorie Slotweiner the previous November.

"What were the names of the adult female members of the community at that time, could you tell me?"

The social worker gave him eight names, and he thanked her.

He alerted Ballestrino, who cut short his call. "Shall we continue?"

"No, call the widow Slotweiner of Park Avenue, and ask her did she volunteer at the Rainbow last November."

Ballestrino reached Mrs. Slotweiner at her summer home in Greenwich. No, she didn't volunteer for the autistic. She gave money to the ballet, and for research into colon cancer, her husband's disease. Would the detective like to give a talk about identity theft to her bridge ladies in Greenwich?

SPRAGUE CALLED UP THE DMV and ran the names of the eight female residents of the Rainbow through the system, finding matches on four of them. Calling up full records with pictures, he found that three of these belonged to women who were plainly not Ms. King. The fourth name produced a flurry: there were six Deborah Goldmans issued licenses since November of 1999. He found one Deborah Goldman who miraculously seemed to share an apartment with Maria Collecelli on East 26th Street. He scrolled down for the picture. This 26th Street Debbie looked like Erica, but with short dark hair and black glasses.

He traced car registrations in the name of Deborah Goldman and came up with nothing in the last six months. He typed in *Marjorie Slotweiner* and *Maria Collecelli* for the hell of it. Nothing.

Ballestrino subpoenaed the Airline Reporting Corp. for all travel information on a Deborah Goldman since the previous Friday, from all three area airports. Sprague called up the major car rental companies and searched for Deborah Goldman; he came up with twelve Deborah Goldmans in the last two weeks. At length, he discovered that a New York State license holder, Deborah Goldman, of East 26th Street, had rented a car at LaGuardia, and returned it to Logan airport a week later—two days previously.

He called his wife. "Cathy! We picked up her trail."

"I am ready to have a discussion with you."

"As soon as I have twenty minutes free," he promised.

"What about dinner tonight? I rented *Oliver*."

Ay ay ay. "I can't tonight, hon. I'm so sorry."

She hung up. He had to deal with this, and soon.

❖

When Ballestrino came home from work at eleven-thirty, there was a message on the pad next to the scanner. *Gloria Florimonte called,* said the message.

He stalked into his mother's room and woke her up.

He waved the message. "This has to stop."

She struggled up from sleep, groggy and bleary. She looked awful.

"She called at six forty-five. I swear on my mother's life."

"*What* is your problem?" he asked angrily.

"You don't believe me? Fine. I don't care. Let me sleep."

She was never going to marry again. She would live to a ripe old age. He would never get out of this house.

MITCH GREIFF HAD ACQUIRED a state-appointed lawyer, who was requesting a "Queen for a Day." This was an ironclad agreement between the DA's office and the suspect that he would talk, and whatever he talked about would not be used in the direct case against him, but could be used to develop leads on other people, or other charges against him or anyone else.

"He's hardly benefited from the crime," said the Legal Aid attorney.

"Guilty but in need?" said Miles, unconvinced.

"Did you see his house in Queens?" Mitch's attorney asked Sprague and Ballestrino. "Would you say he benefited from the crime?"

Mitch Greiff looked out the window; he seemed to be fading in and out.

"Are you suggesting we shouldn't prosecute him because he has bad taste in furniture?" Isaacson asked.

"So he pleads to some crime," the lawyer continued. "Say, falsifying business records. Or conspiracy. Or criminal facilitation. And you use what he has against her. *She's* the mastermind, here."

"So we shouldn't prosecute him because *she* has bad taste in furniture?" Isaacson asked.

"Over one hundred million dollars is missing," Miles said, raising his voice and speaking directly to Mitch Greiff. "*Somebody* is going to jail."

❖

Sprague searched for Marjorie Slotweiner, Maria Collecelli, Erica King or Debbie Goldman in the Boston area, and found four Debbie Goldmans. He called the RMV in Boston and asked to speak with a supervisor.

"Can you cross-reference a license with a car registration?"

"Certainly," the supervisor said, and began entering data.

"What kind of cars do these Debbies drive?"

"Let's see. Debbie in Braintree drives a green Toyota."

"Yes! That's our girl."

"Hang on. Debbie in Cambridge also drives a green Toyota, and it's a new registry, just last week."

"What do they look like?"

"Well, Braintree Debbie Goldman is African American. . . ."

"Really?"

"Forty-three, five-foot-two . . ."

"Okay, what about Cambridge Debbie Goldman?"

"Caucasian, short brown hair, thirty-four, five-foot-eight, little glasses . . ."

"That's the one. Could you give me her address?"

BALLESTRINO'S SUBPOENAS to seven popular Internet providers for a user at 39 Ellery Street, apartment 2R, came back with an AOL account paid for with a Visa card. They both put her on their "buddies list," so that they'd be alerted each time she logged on. They subpoenaed phone, electricity and credit card statements for Cambridge Debbie. They drew up a search warrant to send a Trojan Horse.

Cathy called. "Are you coming home for dinner tonight?"

"Hon! We just found out where she lives!" he shouted, wanting to tell her.

"Thrilling." She hung up the phone.

Cathy had always been fascinated with his work. She wasn't a cop groupie, enthralled by the gun, the handcuffs, the power; she wasn't a professional cop wife, the kind who knew enough rules and regulations to be a PBA representative. Cathy was a voyeur at heart, excited on some level by the drama, the gravity and the unpredictability of crime. She genuinely enjoyed hearing about the minutiae of Detective work, the weird details and the psychotic behavior. Or she used to.

❖

Ballestrino called on Mrs. Maddie Olsen in Jackson Heights. In the course of the conversation, over a piece of sticky peach pie that wasn't very good, she referred several times to "the Center."

"The Center," he said.

"The Grief Center. Shelly's place. It was, oh, was it on 31st Street? Or 32nd? That's where I met Erica's mother," she said in a narrative fashion. "She was so beautiful then. You never saw such hair, the color. Like pale corn."

He took a sip of coffee.

"Of course, it wasn't *natural*." She cackled, breaking wind.

WHEN HE RETURNED to his office, there was a pink message slip on his desk: *Gloria Florimonte called*. He dialed his mother.

"Roseanne Ballestrino, did you call my office and leave a message?"

"Why would I do that? I have your cell phone number."

"Did you call my office," he pressed, "and leave a message that Gloria Florimonte called?"

"I just told you I didn't. Are you calling your own mother a liar?"

"Answer the question."

"Don't you beat me up with Detective language," she shot back. "If she called you, you'd better call her back. I didn't raise you to be rude, I don't care cop or no cop."

BALLESTRINO FOUND THE INSTITUTE FOR WELL-BEING after an hour and a half of walking up and down 31st Street, asking for the Grief Center.

The head of the Institute was a spry if elderly gent named Sheldon Linzer, with a shock of white chest hair leaping out of an unbuttoned green silk shirt. Of course he knew Erica! He and Erica's mother had been close friends, *close* friends, and he'd seen Erica grow up. She would soon be moving her office into the top floor. Why was the Detective looking for her?

"Oh, just a routine investigation of someone else," Tony said, looking up. "This is one gorgeous house. How long you live here?"

"Only all my life. Come take a tour of my headquarters, Detective."

Sheldon Linzer led him around the building, describing the mission, the services, the metamorphosis from the Center to the Institute.

"So Ms. King's putting an office up on the fourth floor?"

"She'll have her work cut out for her: there's sixty years of junk up there."

He followed Sheldon Linzer up the stairs. "So when did you last see Erica?"

"Oh, when she came back. I hadn't seen her in years. We talked about her renting the space."

"When was that?"

"Sometime last summer."

"Have you seen her since then?"

"I saw her from afar once or twice, moving things in. We didn't talk or anything. She used her key," he said, and paused to catch his breath. "That's it there," he pointed. "The first door on the left. She hasn't done much of anything up here."

The landing was a disaster area, leading to two rooms. The first door was slightly ajar, revealing a roomful of crap spilling out into the narrow hallway. A worried female voice floated up the stairs. "Shelly?"

The old swinger spun around with an infusion of energy. "Would you excuse me, Detective? I'm needed. Maureen will see you out."

On the way down the stairs, he spotted a Duane Reade shopping bag wedged between old paintings on the landing. He leaned in closer: something that looked like blood was smeared on the outside of the bag.

❖

The unflappable Len Miles raised an eyebrow at Ballestrino across the table. "She the only one who shops at Duane Reade?"

"On three separate occasions, when we were doing surveillance and interviews, she carried a Duane Reade bag to Citicorp," Tony insisted.

"Are you suggesting it's the same bag from her lunch last year?"

"This one had what looked like blood on it." Ballestrino got up to pace. "Just like the one in Greiff's kitchen in Queens."

"So she has a matching set." Miles smiled. "Chic."

"Blood on the bag in Greiff's house," Ballestrino insisted, "blood on the bag at the Institute. I bet there's blood on the money inside the bag."

"Every other day," Miles said patiently, "Duane Reade opens up another store and hands out shopping bags."

"She's gallivanting around, enjoying her freedom!" said Ballestrino.

"Here's the sworn statement from Mitch Greiff," Isaacson said, showing him the confession she'd supervised. Miles read it.

"Okay. Let's run it by a judge, see what kind of reaction we get."

THE JUDGE READ MITCH GREIFF'S sworn statement and the search warrant request. She saw fit to execute the search warrant for the fourth-floor landing of the Institute, where Ballestrino had seen the bag. But only the fourth-floor landing, not the room that Erica King would be using as her office.

That afternoon they rang the bell at the Institute, cruised past a flock of elderly Caucasian females in sweat suits and white sneakers and marched upstairs with their rubber gloves on.

On the fourth-floor landing, they found $7 million in a variety of bags, many of them smudged with blood.

"This enough to arrest her?" Ballestrino asked across Len Miles's table.

"This Mr. Linzer says it's not his money?"

"He says not."

Miles tipped back on his chair. "You got her fingerprints on the bag?"

"We got one full fingerprint and several partials on the bag in his house in Queens, in blood. We got two partial fingerprints on the bag and two full ones on the money at the Institute for Well-Being, in blood."

"On the money!" Miles clapped. "In her own blood?"

"We assume it's hers: Greiff says she cut her hand, the ER in Elmhurst confirms she was given stitches on her hand, the prints are hers."

"How'd you get her prints?"

Sprague smiled. "She was a summer intern in the Manhattan DA's office."

"Oh, my!" Miles burst out in laughter. "This is getting too interesting."

"I wish I remembered her," Isaacson said wistfully.

Len Miles breathed in. "But money by itself—even covered in blood and fingerprints, even this amount of it—isn't a crime."

"Are you insane?" Tony demanded.

Miles smiled at him.

"Reasonable people," Tony shouted, "do not keep $7 million in cash on a landing in someone else's home!"

"It's unusual, I grant you that."

"Is it enough to send her a Trojan Horse?" Sprague asked.

"A what?"

"We send her an e-mail with a key capture program embedded in it," Ballestrino said. "When she's on-line, we'll be able to see every move she makes, as she's making it. She won't know what hit her."

"It'll also let us search through her hard drive," Sprague added. "Surreptitiously, from a distance."

"You'd need a separate search warrant for that," Isaacson said.

"Naturally," Sprague said. "We thought you'd help us write it."

A search warrant was written, submitted and granted.

Sprague and Ballestrino wrote a code and sent the Trojan Horse to Deborah Goldman's e-mail in Cambridge, advertising 40 percent off at the Living Cove.

CHAPTER SIXTEEN

A week passed. Debbie Goldman wasn't logging on to her e-mail. They knew this because one or another computer was turned on all day and night, and neither Sprague nor Ballestrino had been alerted that their "buddy" was on-line.

Ballestrino continued his seven-to-ten schedule, avoiding his mother. She left a pan of something on the stove every night. He left it there every night, untouched. The fourth night there was nothing on the stove. On his way into the office one morning, instead of going to Duane Reade, he stopped by the old-fashioned drugstore on Henry Street as an act of solidarity with the little guys. He asked for a bottle of ibuprofen.

"Anthony Ballestrino," said the old coot behind the counter. "How come you didn't call that lovely niece of my friend Shirley Florimonte?"

"I'm sure that's my business, Sal."

"She's a gorgeous girl, Tone. You're not one of those fruits, are you?"

So much for the little guys.

When he got to work, the Captain and the Lieutenant called them in for a progress report.

"You don't even know this is her," Greeley accused.

"It's her," Sprague said.

"*How* do you know? You didn't see her. You have nothing."

"We have her new Massachusetts driver's license photo," Sprague said, "which is clearly her."

"Wasn't she moving to Chicago?"

"We checked it out," Sprague said. "She never showed up at the new job."

"The computers were destroyed," Ballestrino told the Captain. "She's skipped town, leaving apartments that we can't get into. She's rented a place in Cambridge under the name of Deborah Goldman. She hasn't logged on to her computer yet. Perhaps she has another name now, another computer."

"This the boring one?" The Captain turned to Sprague. "Eating her egg salad every day at the same time in the Citicorp building?"

"Yes, Captain," Sprague said. "Not so boring anymore, I'm afraid."

"She finds a retarded woman around her own age, brings her to Social Security to get a number. She sets up a new identity in the name of the disabled individual, and eventually gets a bank account, driver's license and credit card. Yes?"

So he did read their reports. "Yes."

The Captain thought a minute. "This takes time. Right?"

"Yes, sir," Tony said. "Time is on our side right now, unless she's been working ahead, and has new names across the country already set up."

"If I recall, she didn't have a driver's license originally, right?"

"That's right. She's only been driving since April."

"And she's only missing for two weeks?"

"Two and a half."

"And you've placed her in Boston for one of them."

"Cambridge, yes."

"So the trail's still fresh, boys," the Captain said, and everyone stood up.

"Call when you get there and check in every hour," Greeley said by rote.

❖

On the three P.M. shuttle to Logan, Sprague reviewed his notes on Ms. Erica King and wondered what an interview with her would be like now. She was guilty of false personation, at the very least, but they had no hard evidence of anything else. It was Greiff's word against hers, and he'd disappeared for the better part of a year, while she'd been showing up to work every day on time. They'd need to scare her pretty badly to get anything out of her—he couldn't see tears and spilled guts, like Greiff. He wondered which was stranger: Greiff's attraction to King, or King's attraction to Greiff.

They rented a car and Ballestrino drove.

At a modest house in Cambridge they rang a bell. No response. A gray-headed Caucasian male lumbered up the steps on his way from the trash area. Thick, wooly gray eyebrows gave him an unstable look.

"Yeah," he responded. "I'm the super *and* the landlord."

They showed him their NYPD shields and told him they were looking for Debbie Goldman in apartment 2R.

"Why? What did she do?"

"What makes you think she did something?"

"You're the police," he sneered. "You're looking for her, you tell me."

"Routine inquiry, in connection with an investigation of someone else."

"It's so routine, what are you doing here, ha?" He raised an eyebrow. "This is out of your jurisdiction."

"Does Deborah Goldman live in apartment 2R?"

"I don't talk to pigs," he said.

"Of course not," Sprague said soothingly, ignoring both the content and the tone. "Did Deborah Goldman sign a lease?"

"For a year. She paid six months in advance."

"Have you seen her since she signed the lease?"

"No."

"You think she's out of town? Has mail been piling up?"

"She just moved in last week. What kind of mail do you expect?"

"Light bill, phone bill?"

"Her rent covers utilities. She had a cell phone."

"She told you that, or you saw it?"

"She told me she didn't need a phone line," he said.

"Not even for a computer?"

"She didn't say anything about a computer."

"What about cable—she install that?"

"Nah, none of that." He made a wrapping-up gesture, foot on the staircase. "Okay, we done here?"

"What moving company did she use?"

"She didn't. The apartment is furnished. She came with a couple of suitcases the day after she signed the lease."

"So you did see her after she signed the lease?"

"Yeah, that one time, moving in."

"How did she pay?"

"Cash."

"You didn't think that was odd? All that cash at once?"

"I *appreciated* all that cash at once. Cash is still legal, you know."

"Would you describe her for us?"

"You guys are unbelievable. There's nobody left to lock up in New York, so you're coming up here now, ha? To hunt down people that you don't even know what they look like?"

"We'd like you to take a look at a group of photos," Ballestrino said, and began pulling the photo array out of his bag.

"You want to arrest me, go ahead," he said, thumping his chest. "I'm not saying one more word to you pigs." He climbed the steps, opened the door and slammed it shut. They heard a series of locks clacking into place.

"No computer, not our girl," Ballestrino said.

"You think she's moved on? Shall we start calling around to area homes for retarded adults?"

"That could take forever." Tony sighed. "Let's think this through first."

Sprague called Cathy to tell her he wouldn't be home for dinner.

She was in tears, sitting with a Scottie who would surely be put to sleep the following morning, she told him, if he made it through the night. "He's suffering so, but he's such a gentleman, even now," she whispered miserably.

"Ah, sweetheart. I'm so sorry. We'll be taking the last shuttle—should I pick you up on the way home?"

"Yes, come as soon as you can, although I'll probably stay here with him tonight."

Sprague hung up the phone, optimistic for some reason.

As they began their descent into LaGuardia, he realized that he preferred Cathy at the hospital with a pet—even a dying one—to Cathy at home watching *Oliver*, fixated on the absence of a child. They needed a full-time puppy, and fast.

Two weeks had passed since they'd sent Deborah Goldman the Trojan Horse. Sprague and Ballestrino sat with Miles and Isaacson at Miles's table.

"The Trojan Horse with the key capture program only works if she picks up her e-mail," Sprague explained. "She may have abandoned the account, the apartment, the whole identity. She may be on to a new name."

"So how can we get the Trojan Horse to her," Miles asked, "if we don't know her e-mail?"

"We find her new e-mail," Ballestrino said, looking at the ceiling.

"How?"

There was a silence.

"With a cookie," Ballestrino said.

There was a pause. Isaacson spoke up: "Does she like cookies?"

"Oh, he's brilliant," Sprague smiled.

"I'm sure you're right," Miles said dryly. "Tell me why?"

"A cookie is an authentication device," Ballestrino explained. "It's a text file that facilitates entry into, or movement within, a Web site.

You'll notice if you go to a Web site more than once, everything is faster the second time—both getting there, and moving around within the site. That's because a cookie has been attached to your computer, supplying your information. The Web site recognizes the cookie, and it lets you through."

Isaacson stopped doodling. "Sounds like EZ Pass."

"Kind of," Ballestrino nodded. "Say you're shopping on-line. The Web site asks you questions. Name, address, credit card, method of shipping. The Web site doesn't want to store all that information on its own computer, so it stores it on *your* computer. So the next time you come back, it doesn't have to ask you all that stuff again. It's on the cookie that it attached to you."

Miles nodded. "Go on."

"The cookie doesn't have any information about you other than what you've provided." He smiled. "Except . . ."

They all leaned in.

"It recognizes your computer's ID, which is the original name that you give your computer when you start it up the first time. You can also figure out from a cookie where the computer is physically located: what country and city it's in."

Isaacson whistled. "Nice."

"So how would this work?" Miles asked. "How do you send it, and to whom?"

"We don't send it to her. She comes to us. It has to be done from the inside, at one of the places we know she'll come back to."

"The Living Cove!" said Isaacson.

"I was thinking about her bank," Tony said. "One of her banks, anyway."

They all thought about this for a moment.

"What if, as you say, she's using a different name?" Isaacson asked.

"Doesn't matter, if she's using the same computer."

"So you're saying, even if you go back to the Web site using a different name," she repeated, "you still have the same cookie."

"Exactly."

"Nice!" Isaacson said.

"This assumes she's using the same computer," Miles said.

"Yes."

"What if she's using a different one?"

He and Ballestrino looked at each other. "Then we're out of luck."

"You're going to need another search warrant for this," Miles warned.

"Actually, when you enter a public Web site like a bank, you forfeit any right to privacy," Sprague said. "What we may need is a subpoena for the bank's Web records. They may not want us fishing in there."

"If she's as sophisticated as you say, wouldn't she know about cookies?" asked Isaacson.

"There's a way of setting your machine to not accept cookies and a way to clean up existing cookies, but it's impossible to block all cookies," Ballestrino said authoritatively: he'd tried it. "It's like trying to prevent junk mail."

"So all you need is her bank account number?" Miles asked.

"Actually, all we need is the bank," Sprague said.

"You have the bank?"

"No." Ballestrino sighed.

There was silence.

"She paid rent for the Cambridge apartment in cash," Sprague said.

"But if she went to all the trouble to register her car," said Miles, "and rent an apartment—to set up the identity, in other words—she was going to set up a bank account, right?"

They all nodded.

"So how many banks could there be in Cambridge?"

THE ANSWER WAS NINE. They wrote up subpoenas for every single one of them, requesting information about a Deborah Goldman. There were three hits on the name. They narrowed it down with the birth date on her driver's license. A Deborah Goldman had opened an account at First Cambridge Marine with an initial wire transfer from a bank in St. Kitts.

Ballestrino called up First Cambridge Marine.

"NYPD? *Wow!*" shouted the IT manager. "How can we help you?"

Ballestrino discussed the situation, and the IT manager put the Web statistician on the phone. "NYPD? *Cool!* What do you need?"

Ballestrino asked him to search his records for the date on which Deborah Goldman's account was opened. The Web statistician found the wire transfer.

"Okay, now look at the Internet protocol address to find out where she was calling in from at the time."

"This is a Boston-area number," the Web statistician said. "She's using Microsoft Network. Hold on, I'll find out about the phone number."

Ballestrino toyed with a loose thread on his jacket button. He hadn't been to the dry cleaner in weeks. In a moment, the Web statistician came back on.

"I called a friend of mine at the phone company," he said. "The jack she was using was located at the Boylston branch of the Boston Public Library."

Ballestrino went to work with First Marine to capture her new information when she logged on to the bank site.

❖

Deborah Goldman's account page at First Cambridge Marine lay dormant for over a week. Labor Day weekend was looming like Judgment Day, but all they could do was wait. Sprague was perusing snapshots on an animal shelter Web site when Tony waved at him frantically. Dennis ran over to his desk.

"It's First Marine Bank of Cambridge," Tony said. "Jack? You're on speakerphone. Tell Dennis what you told me."

"The eagle has landed," the Web statistician whispered with glee. "Someone just wired $22,000 from Deborah Goldman's account into

an account at a San Francisco bank account under the name of Beth Lipschitz."

"She's brilliant, I tell you!" Sprague cried. "Who would change their name to Beth Lipschitz?"

"She's almost brilliant," Ballestrino said. "Her computer's original ID?"

"Erica?" Sprague guessed.

Ballestrino shook his head. "Maria."

"Maria," Sprague sang, and wrote up a subpoena for the San Francisco bank.

They sent a Trojan Horse to Beth Lipschitz's e-mail address in another "Save 40 percent" offer from the Living Cove.

BETH LIPSCHITZ MUST HAVE NEEDED FURNITURE, because she clicked on the offer almost immediately, opening the door for the Trojan Horse.

Sprague broke out a box of doughnuts, and every member of the squad gathered around as Ballestrino directed his computer to the Living Cove Web site. They watched, entranced, as Erica King browsed among sofas and end tables, checked her bank account in the Cayman Islands, ordered groceries on-line and sent an e-mail to a Mail Boxes Etc. in Cambridge, closing down her mailbox. Within an hour of searching through her hard drive, they had a map of her money, which was earning interest in five separate countries.

LATE THAT AFTERNOON they arrived breathlessly at the DA's office and presented their evidence to Miles and Isaacson.

"Well, what are you waiting for?" Miles smiled. "Bring her in, gentlemen."

The Lieutenant seemed to be levitating when they showed him the arrest warrant. It was so rare to see him crack a genuine smile.

"Get her back here in one piece," Greeley demanded. "Don't forget to sign your vouchers. And summarize the case while it's fresh in your mind."

It was clear, windy and freezing cold when they arrived in San Francisco. They took a cab from the airport and drove up and down impossibly beautiful streets lined with exotic trees and smart houses with beautiful architectural details. There was a snap to the air and a sense of optimism. They gazed out their windows, entranced.

What a gorgeous place I could find if I lived here, Ballestrino thought, although real estate prices here were second only to Manhattan.

How healthy I would be if I lived here, Sprague thought, although there were pastries here, too, just like everywhere else.

They met their counterparts, Jack Nyad and Neil Waring, in the spacious, newly renovated offices of the San Francisco Police Department's Computer Investigations Unit. The unit had new equipment and magnificent views of the city. The floors were freshly carpeted, garbage was deposited in clean new receptacles lined with plastic bags, and fruit flies didn't dare loiter.

How wonderful it would be to work here, they both thought.

They briefed Nyad and Waring about the case, and established that the crimes Ms. Erica King had committed in the State of New York were also crimes under the laws of the State of California. They established that the evidence that they'd developed against her was both gathered in a legal way and reasonable proof of her guilt. Nyad and Waring agreed to arrest Beth Lipschitz, arrange a room for her interrogation and assist them in getting an extradition warrant to bring her back to New York City.

All four cops piled into Waring's car. Nyad said that her address on Broadway was in a quiet, swanky neighborhood. They drove and double-parked a block away. Her house was a three-story stucco dwelling that had been a large single-family home at one point, but had been cut into three apartments. She'd come up in the world from the dingy rent-controlled boxes on Second Avenue. On the other hand, her used green Toyota was parked three spaces from her door.

Broadway dead-ended at the Presidio, which was originally a

Spanish garrison, then a U.S. Army base, and was now a national park, according to Nyad. Waring took a left before the dead end, drove up the hill to Pacific Street and parked. They walked down the staircase next to the Presidio, all four of them checking out the situation.

Waring returned to the car, drove it around the block and double-parked with a good view of the house. As Ballestrino positioned himself in the alley to the right of the house, and Nyad stood on the sidewalk with a view of the front windows, Sprague trotted up the front steps to ring the bell.

There was no response.

"UPS," Nyad called, and Sprague rang the bell again.

A curtain flashed at the window. A moment later they heard smashing glass.

Ballestrino saw something fly out of the second-floor side window, and he rushed toward it. It was a laptop. It clipped him on the side of the head, but he managed to catch it. He set it on the ground behind him.

Sprague and Nyad meanwhile knocked down the front door; Sprague saw a long-haired woman climbing out the window onto a trellis. It appeared she'd been doing bills at the dining room table.

Ballestrino's right ear was ringing from the laptop blow. He saw a woman in jeans emerging from the second-floor side window, using the trellis as a ladder. She got about four rungs down before the wood snapped under her weight; she grabbed at the air and fell about ten feet onto garbage cans below with a thunderous sound. She landed and rolled, facing a wall, tangled in broken trellis, plants and garbage. Ballestrino approached her. She appeared to be in pain, catching her breath, holding her ankle. She looked up and he stopped smiling.

She was looking very California now, with long dark hair, bangs in her eyes, ethnic jewelry, jeans and a green sweater. In spite of the ivy and the garbage, it was clear she'd cleaned up her act. She wore lipstick. In fact, Ballestrino might have mistaken her for Janice, from afar. He didn't want to think about it. He stared at the transformation, uncomfortable.

She didn't seem surprised to see him. But she hadn't said a word.

She struggled to get up from the mess on the ground, and he held a hand out to her. She took his hand and rose to stand. There were so many questions he wanted to ask. She hurled her entire body weight at him, knocking the wind out of him before he landed on his tailbone on the cement. She seized the laptop, darted out of the alley and began racing to the end of Broadway, trailing garbage, splintered trellis and vines.

Ballestrino scrambled upright, infuriated. Nobody knocked him down, never mind a woman, never mind an unattractive, out-of-shape accountant with bad skin and a repellent personality. Why had he given her a hand? He gained on her easily, reached out to grab her shoulder, and caught her hair, which slipped off her head.

She ran free, bald and fast. He stopped, appalled, holding the hair.

He threw down the wig in revulsion, then resumed the chase. She turned the corner and took off down a narrow flight of steps that went on as long as he could see.

Meanwhile, Waring had slammed the car into reverse and was driving back down Broadway. Sprague and Nyad waited for backup to secure the apartment as a crime scene. When the squad car showed up, they scrambled out of the building and onto the street. Sprague picked up the wig in the gutter and followed on foot.

Ballestrino was ten yards away from the suspect, who had just knocked down a middle-aged Asian female individual walking a German shepherd.

"She's running north down Lyon next to the Presidio," Nyad shouted into his radio.

Ballestrino got entangled in the barking dog's leash; Nyad hopped around the sprawl. Sprague brought up the rear, feeling adrenaline rushing through his veins, overriding the limitations of his joints.

"Description of suspect," someone on the radio demanded.

"Suspect is a bald Caucasian female individual wearing a green sweater carrying a laptop computer," Nyad continued, panting as he ran. "She's running downstairs with three Detectives in pursuit. Suspect does not seem to be armed."

The stone steps were endless. Sprague wished he'd spent more time at the gym, but that was his only regret. If ever there was a perfect chase, this was it. He could see everything from the top of the hill: the sky was intensely blue, the park on the left seemed thick and deep, a neatly clipped green hedge ran to the right and left of the stairs in a geometric pattern, framing the fleeing suspect, with her shining white head. She ran quickly, jumping over a Caucasian male teenage individual doing abdominal exercises on a stone landing.

Where would she go? The park on the left had a fence at least eleven feet high. The solid, glamorous houses on the right were well fenced, lushly landscaped and fronted by snazzy automobiles; barriers to entry seemed inevitable. Ballestrino was right behind her, and Nyad was right behind him. Sprague clutched her wig as he took the steps: it might be evidence.

Waring pulled up on the street below, jumped out of his car and trotted up the steps toward her. Erica King stopped short, leaped over the low hedge to the left and began scrambling in the brush in front of the high wall to the park.

Ballestrino had nearly caught up with her when she hurled the laptop over the wall.

All four computer cops held their breath, watching the evidence in flight.

But the machine lodged in bushy evergreen foliage, just above the wall.

Erica King struggled to climb the wall, but she hadn't been to the gym lately, either. Ballestrino picked her off easily, grabbing her green sweater and pulling her to the ground. Erica King was down in the greenery, lashing out with her legs and arms, growling low like an animal. Ballestrino twisted one arm behind her and put his knee on her back. Sprague and Nyad arrived panting.

"Go ahead," Ballestrino said, and Nyad hopped over the hedge.

"Erica King," Nyad began, and Sprague felt an electric excitement racing through his veins like carbonated coffee. "You are under arrest for embezzlement, identity fraud, wire fraud, mail fraud, Social Security fraud and false personation."

As Nyad recited her Miranda rights one by one, and Erica King responded to each with a grunt, Sprague stood hunched over on the steps, hands on his wretched knees, catching his breath, smiling in the sun.

He could see Ballestrino staring at her in disgust and fascination. Why had she shaved her head? The sight was unusual enough that passing masochists in Lycra on their way up the stairs at a trot had to stop and watch.

Ballestrino pulled her upright by the handcuffs, and Waring called for a ladder to get the flying laptop out of the tree.

Nyad sat down on one of the endless steps and laughed. "I can't believe she tried to escape into the Presidio!"

Ballestrino felt a satisfaction bordering on glee. Relief and pride mingled in his stomach as he dialed the squad and got the Lieutenant.

"Ms. Erica King was apprehended and Mirandized one minute ago in San Francisco while fleeing the scene on the longest staircase ever built," he began. No job at a private bank could ever give him this high, and no amount of money would compensate for the lack of it.

"Don't wait to write up the Unusual Case Reports the way you did last time," Greeley said tersely. "I want them on my desk immediately when you get back. And don't forget your vouchers."

On the other hand, no job in the private sector could ever make him feel as small as he felt as a Detective, Third Grade.

EPILOGUE

The morning after Erica King was arraigned, Sprague and Ballestrino were summoned upstairs to the Police Commissioner's Office with the Captain and the Lieutenant, in the Police Commissioner's private elevator. It was a first for both Sprague and Ballestrino.

The Chief of Detectives, who had yet to turn on anything more complicated than a light switch, introduced them to the Police Commissioner by saying, "Here come the geeks! They left their propeller hats downstairs."

The Police Commissioner was a more thoughtful man. He congratulated them on their arrest, and then said, "Tell me what you need to make your jobs easier."

The Captain answered immediately: "More training, more manpower, more equipment and more cars."

"Cars!" exclaimed the PC, who had made his name in Patrol. "Why do you need cars?"

"For when we go out on investigations."

"You guys do *investigations*?" the PC said, astonished.

❖

Ballestrino couldn't create a fair deal—never mind fanfare—in an uncaring bureaucracy. He couldn't do anything about the soot, the dust, the fruit flies by the windowsill, the roaches in the coffee closet or the fermenting sludge at the bottom of the garbage cans. But he could clean off his desk and organize his files when he solved a case, giving himself a pause to prepare his mind for the next problem. Which was what he was doing when he heard the Captain shouting.

Everyone ran into the Captain's office and watched the Captain's TV. The FBI was holding a press conference taking credit for the apprehension of the masterminds behind the celebrity cyberfraud at Friedman, Greiff and Slavin. The Lieutenant stalked down the hall, his face a dangerous red.

The Captain merely smiled. "You gotta love this job, don'tcha?"

Sprague gave the usual shrug on his way to the coffee closet in search of sugar and starch. Ballestrino took the rest of the day off.

He went directly to the offices of a Silicon Alley headhunter who had, at one time, called him regularly with offers. The office had been a hive of activity when he'd visited four years ago. Now the headhunter spoke on the phone in an empty room and a thirty-year-old Asian female individual—the only other person in the office—supervised the removal of her office equipment.

"I have to be honest with you," the headhunter said, looking over his résumé. "This is not such a great time to be looking for a job."

Ballestrino ran through his major talents.

"Okay, right away," the headhunter interrupted, "deemphasize anything to do with police work. And don't go in there like a cop, either."

"You mean, swinging my nightstick and barking orders?"

"Exactly."

"What do you think I am?" he asked the weasel. "I have a master's degree. I don't beat people up."

"Of course not," the headhunter took a swig of designer water.

FROM THE STREET, Ballestrino called Frank Defina and made an appointment for the following day. Over a healthy lunch in the Grandview Group's executive dining room, surrounded by a panoramic vista of the harbor, the ferry terminals and the Statue of Liberty, Detective Ballestrino and Frank Defina discussed the job of Chief of Electronic Security.

Ballestrino's only item of negotiation was a fully paid corporate apartment.

"Actually, we have apartments in this building," Defina said. "Would that interest you?"

After lunch, Defina took Tony on a tour, introduced him around like a big shot and ended with a visit to a handsomely furnished apartment that could be his. Ballestrino signed a contract and drove home to Carroll Gardens, light-headed. The apartment had never looked so small and poky. He told his mother.

"Well, about time," she said.

The scanner was silent for once.

"It's so I can be there in a minute if there's trouble," he explained gently.

"Sounds great, Tony." She helped herself to more garlic bread.

He felt a little guilty. "I hope you'll visit me," he said.

"Of course." She nodded. "And you know you're always welcome here. I'll make you dinner anytime you want, right?"

Wait: she *wanted* him out of the house?

❖

The morning Ballestrino handed in his resignation, the Captain assembled everyone in the squad room for an announcement. Because of their solid work as a unit, the Police Commissioner and the Chief of Detectives had given the Computer Crimes Squad the go-ahead to buy a quarter of a million dollars of new equipment.

There was a moment of stunned silence. Then they all began to cheer.

"Also!" the Captain shouted. "Our personnel will increase from seven to twenty-five detectives!"

A riot of applause.

"You see, they need eighteen people to replace me," Ballestrino said, and was completely ignored in the revelry.

He wanted to rejoice, but it was too late. He was no longer a member of the squad. Was it his imagination, or did his colleagues close ranks, giving him their backs? He left them celebrating. On his desk he found the pink message slip with Gloria Florimonte's number and he dialed the number, for whatever reason, and without much thought.

"What took you so long to return my call?" she said right away.

Interesting. "I was out of town, arresting a fugitive. Speak to me."

"My exams are over."

"Your hands must be tired," he tried.

She said nothing.

"Just joking. Would you like to go out and celebrate? How about tonight?" he said, thinking, How about now?

"Busy tonight. What about Thursday night?"

"Thursday looks good."

They hung up. He wheeled his chair over to Sprague's desk, where Dennis was staring at a doughnut on a napkin, as if it might speak to him.

When he'd told him about the job, over dinner to celebrate Erica King's apprehension, Sprague had given him the sad smile he seemed to give everything lately. He hadn't tried to talk Tony out of it. "We'll miss you," he'd said. But he hadn't said, "*I'll* miss you."

Now Ballestrino said, "Gloria Florimonte really did call me."

"That's nice, Tony."

"We're having dinner Thursday night."

"I'm glad."

Ballestrino raised a shoulder and sighed. "Eh."

"What's the matter with you?" Sprague turned away from his doughnut and asked as if he really wanted to know. "You weren't going to call her because you weren't sure if she liked you. Now she calls you so you know she likes you. So what's the problem?"

"Everybody knows about her. It's like a public thing. That moron at the drugstore hassled me about her. I haven't even had a first date with her."

"I thought you took her out for Italian."

"That was the blind date. I had to do that. The first date is when I know who she is, and then I ask her out."

"So Thursday night's the first date."

"No, because she called me. The clock doesn't start running until *I* call *her*."

"I'm beginning to understand why you've got such bad phone karma," Sprague said.

❖

After work on Friday, Dennis met Cathy at the shelter. When he pushed open the glass door he was hit with the aroma of puppies and all their fluids. He simultaneously groaned and smiled. This was what his life was going to smell like from now on. He looked at his wife, who was chatting up a man in mint-green scrubs. Cathy was in her element. If she had a tail, it would be wagging.

She steered him back to the cages, where animals romped and panted on top of mounds of shredded paper.

"We will not fall for the first animal we see," he warned her.

"Certainly not," she said. "We'll be selective."

In the first cage, a tiny greyhound lay on her back, legs splayed, while a hyperactive terrier pounced on her stomach and bit her face and tail.

"Gruesome," he said. She nodded, and they moved on.

Two black-and-white shih tzus slept fitfully in the next cage.

"Inattentive," she said, and they moved on.

When they paused in front of the next cage, a black chow turned his head away from them to look up and off to the side.

"Arrogant," they both said at once, and moved on.

The spaniels in the next cage were fighting wildly over a red plastic bone, although there were several other plastic toys in the cage.

"Demanding," she said.

"Exhausting," he agreed, and they moved on.

In the next cage, a dainty beagle with a face full of intelligence and hope sat as if waiting for her ship to come in.

Cathy put her hand on her chest and gave him the same look the dog was giving him. How could he turn down such a creature?

He reached down and pulled the dog out of the cage and held her up. The dog licked his nose, and he put her on the floor. The dog jumped around.

"You like this one?" he asked.

The dog was gazing up at him seductively, batting him affectionately with her tail.

"Yes, but this is not for me. This is for *us*," she said, bending down to let the dog smell and lick her hands.

"That's right." He bent down to pat the dog.

"And we will share equally in the daily tasks of raising this dog?"

"That's right," he agreed. "And in this way, we will see if we're ready to take on larger responsibilities."

The dog sat still, looking back and forth between them, as if aware she was in the midst of delicate negotiations.

"I am willing to be part of this experiment," she said, "but I'd like to make sure it has an end date, when we revisit this question of taking on the responsibilities of someone larger."

"I think that's fair," he said. "You pick the date."

"Three months?"

Three months was way too soon.

"One year." He squatted down to play with the dog's ears.

"Six months," she bargained, squatting down to pat the dog's rear end.

"You're on."

"Oh, this is thrilling," she said, kissing him above the dog. The dog butted in to lick their faces.

"Okay, little beagle, you're our first child," he said, and picked up the new pet.

The dog responded by giving him a grateful look and urinating on his pants, the only pants that fit.

Prison was a continuous nightmare of humiliation, degradation and frustration. It was disgusting. It was horrifying. It was worse than anything Erica could have imagined. She checked her wig with her other outside clothes and walked around bald all the time now. She wasn't the only one.

ONE MORNING the Deputy Warden asked her into his office.

"I understand you have computer skills." He gestured to the guard to take his hand off Erica's arm and let her stand on her own.

"Yes, I do," Erica said.

The Deputy showed her his computer, which had frozen in the midst of an application. "What's wrong with the damn thing?" he asked, massaging his right hand.

"May I?" she asked, and he nodded. She sat down in front of the ancient, wheezing PC, and the Deputy Warden stood over her to watch. A box of accounting software sat on the desk on top of an old-fashioned green budget ledger. The chair was nicer than anything she'd experienced in weeks.

"Were you trying to add new software?" she asked.

"Yes! It's so frustrating," he pleaded with her.

"What's wrong with the damn thing is that it was made"—she looked back at him—"in 1995?" He shrugged. "And this software came out last year. They don't speak the same language. You need a set of drivers to help the two communicate."

He looked at her fearfully.

"Shall I write it down for you?" She gave him a brand name to ask for, and suggested an 800 number to call. She rose from his chair.

He stood up and nodded. "How do I get out of this in the meantime?"

She sat down again, turned off the computer and started it up again.

"I understand the nature of the crime you committed to get in here," he said, while they waited for the machine to reboot. "But you need a job here, and we have nobody with office skills."

"I'd be glad to help out," she said honestly.

"If I'm satisfied that you are truly sorry for the crimes that you committed, and will use this time as an honest and productive member of our community"—he looked at her over his pipe—"I'll switch you from the garbage detail to this office. I hope you appreciate how unusual that is."

"Yes, I do," Erica said slowly, looking the Deputy Warden in the eye, and choosing her words with care. "I am truly sorry for what I did. I'm here to do whatever job you think is appropriate for me. If I can be of use to you and our community, I hope you'll take advantage of my skills."

Erica began her job in the Deputy Warden's office the following day.

It was immediately clear that Erica's first task was to help the Deputy Warden convince the Warden that the equipment needed to be updated. Apparently the Warden was of the abacus school of office management.

She coached the Deputy, helping him make a concise, convincing case. She suggested that he practice the presentation repeatedly to get it right.

"I promise you, you'll be so much more effective without notes," she said, taking away his index cards. He memorized the speech she'd written.

Erica waited in his office with a security guard the following day while the Deputy made his case to the Warden. The Deputy returned triumphantly twenty minutes later. He had changed the Warden's mind.

"Do you know what we need?" he asked her.

"In general," she said, sitting up straight in the Deputy Warden's visitor's chair. "But give me an idea of how you use the equipment you have, and then tell me, in an ideal world, what you'd really like to be able to do."

———

WHEN THE NEW EQUIPMENT ARRIVED, Erica began setting up the system. She explained to the Deputy Warden the amount of clerical work involved in creating a database, and asked if several other prisoners could help with the data entry.

"No, I think you should do it," he said.

"That's fine; I just want you to be aware it will take more time."

In this way, Erica was given permission to work late, avoiding the humiliation of lineup and the despair of lockdown. The first night of this, she returned to her cell block an hour after lockdown to catcalls and obscene screaming. Her cellmate kicked her in the stomach for no apparent reason. The second night she came back late, her cellmate beat her up, hitting her in the face with a metal-loaded sock. The following day, the Deputy Warden looked over her bruises and had her transferred to a cell of her own, closer to his office.

Once the prison structure and all the inmates were in the computer, Erica began creating a new system to streamline the purchasing, keep track of the prisoners and organize personnel schedules. She saved him money. She saved him time. Every Monday she gave him a list of items to discuss with the Warden, and coached him on his presentation.

With some research, she found him a huge discount on a new car at a nearby dealer. He gave her permission to take her lunches with him in his office so that she didn't have to interrupt her work. She offered to teach him how to navigate the Internet, but it was clear he didn't want to touch the mouse.

"Is there something wrong with your hand?" she asked.

"Just constant, relentless pain," he said.

"It could be a repetitive-task injury, like carpal tunnel syndrome," she suggested. "Have you seen a doctor?"

"Yeah. He said it was nerves, and that I should squeeze on a ball."

"You should get a second opinion," she said, and made an appointment with a hand specialist covered on the prison staff health plan.

After this, the Deputy Warden gave Erica permission to eat dinner in his office by herself after he'd gone for the day.

Within four months, Erica King was doing the bookkeeping for the penitentiary, cutting checks for vendors, suppliers and payroll and making appointments for the Deputy Warden's haircuts and physical therapy sessions.

One frigid afternoon in February, she helped the Deputy Warden do his taxes.

ACKNOWLEDGMENTS

This book could not have been written without the professional expertise of the following people:

For helping me understand how criminal investigations are conducted and how the New York City Police Department works, I would like to thank Detective Walter Burns, director of the NYPD Public Information Office; Captain George Duke, Detective John F. O'Boyle and Detective John M. Ryan of the Major Case Squad; Lieutenant Robert Groth, Detective Daniel Heinz and Detective Caroline Shebunia of the Special Frauds Squad; Detective Sergeant Paul Helbock of the NYPD–FBI Joint Task Force on Terrorism; Sergeant James Boyle of the Computer Investigations and Technology Unit, and Don Calahan, formerly a detective in the Computer Investigations and Technology Unit; Detective Thomas McHale Jr. of the Port Authority Police–FBI Joint Terrorism Task Force and Detective Investigator John P. Heintz of TARU. I am indebted to Sergeant Richard DelGaudio of the New York City Police Department Police Academy, for allowing me to audit sessions of the Criminal Investigation Course, Specialized Training Unit.

For giving me an inside look at how white-collar criminal cases are prosecuted, I'd like to thank Barbara Thompson of the Public Information Office of the Manhattan District Attorney's office, and LeRoy

Frazier, director of the Manhattan District Attorney's Office of Special Prosecutions.

I'd like to single out two police officers who were extraordinarily receptive to the project: Detective Michael Fabozzi of the Computer Investigations and Technology Unit, whose detailed instructions on the art and craft of computer forensics proved invaluable; and Detective Thomas Nerney of the Major Case Squad, a thirty-six-year veteran of the department whose generosity of spirit and enthusiasm for the project were truly remarkable. These detectives went out of their way to help me understand both detectives and criminals, patiently answering questions, correcting misconceptions and inaccuracies along the way. If any mistakes in police procedure remain in this book, they are my own.

I relied on several excellent books for background on police work, computer crime and identity theft: *Turnaround,* by William Bratton with Peter Knobler; *Target Blue,* by Robert Daley; *Missing Persons,* by Fay Faron; *Armed and Dangerous,* by Gina Gallo; the novels of former NYPD detective Dan Mahoney; *My Father's Gun,* by Brian McDonald; *Bulletproof Privacy,* by Boston T. Party and Kenneth W. Royce and *23rd Precinct: The Job,* by Arlene Schulman.

For their professional expertise and patient advice about the world of accounting and bookkeeping, I'd like to thank Fred Slomovic, senior account manager at Hecht and Company, P.C., and Ed Riall, partner at Deloitte & Touche LLP. For their introduction into the world of marine life and aquariums, I thank Pal and Joanna Czech.

I am indebted to Mrs. Drue Heinz, DBE, and the trustees of the International Retreat for Writers at Hawthornden Castle, Lasswade, Midlothian, for generously granting me a monthlong fellowship in the Scottish countryside in order to begin work on this book. I would like to thank Adam Czerniowski, administrator, for all his help and patience during my stay at the castle.

I thank my brilliant and delightful editor, Nancy Miller, for her hard work on my behalf. I thank Gina Centrello of Ballantine Books for her vote of confidence in my work.

I thank my literary agent, Gail Hochman, for her wisdom and energy. I thank Marianne Merola of Brandt and Hochman for her enthusiasm and good humor.

Barbara Block, James Block, Karen Dukess, Lydia Heller, Sally Higginson, Abby Knopp, Mameve Medwed, Lisa Miller, Alexis Romay and Pamela Schneider read early drafts of this book. I thank them for their diplomacy and constructive criticism.

I'd like to thank my family for being so supportive of my writing.

Most especially, I'd like to thank my husband, Alexis Romay, who is my first and best reader and the source of much inspiration.

ABOUT THE AUTHOR

© Jamie Watts

VALERIE BLOCK is the author of the novel *Was It Something I Said?*
She lives and works near New York City. Visit the author online at
www.valerieblock.com.